Reviews for *Before & During*

'One of the most fascinating books in post-Soviet literature…
even twenty years after its publication and translated into English, Sharov's *Before & During* reads as if it were completed
yesterday.'   Mark Lipovetsky, *The Russian Review*

'If Russian history is indeed a commentary to the Bible, then
Before and During is an audacious attempt to shine a mystical
light on (Russian history), an unusual take on the 20th
century's apocalypse that leaves the reader to look for their
own explications.'   Anna Aslanyan, *The Independent*

'A Menippean satire in which historical reality, in all its
irreversible awfulness, is for a moment scrambled, eroticized…
and illuminated by hilarious monologues of the dead.'
                    Caryl Emerson, *The Times Literary Supplement*

'Translation should not strive for perfection, but for excellence.
Perfection is impossible, whereas excellence is only nearly
impossible. And excellence is what Oliver Ready achieves in
his rendering of *Before and During* by Vladimir Sharov. He
captures the clear voice and confused mentality of the narrator
who is able to love both Christ and Lenin, who prays for the
sinner Ivan the Terrible and who tries to unravel the legacy of
the Bolsheviks.'   Jury of the 2015 Read Russia Prize

Dedalus Europe
General Editor: Timothy Lane

The Rehearsals

Vladimir Sharov

THE
REHEARSALS

Translated by Oliver Ready

Dedalus

Published with the support of the Institute for Literary Translation (Russia).

AD VERBUM

Published in the UK by Dedalus Limited
24-26, St Judith's Lane, Sawtry, Cambs, PE28 5XE
email: info@dedalusbooks.com

www.dedalusbooks.com

ISBN printed book 978 1 910213 14 8
ISBN ebook 978 1 910213 61 2

Dedalus is distributed in the USA & Canada by SCB Distributors
15608 South New Century Drive, Gardena, CA 90248
email: info@scbdistributors.com   web: www.scbdistributors.com

Dedalus is distributed in Australia by Peribo Pty Ltd
58, Beaumont Road, Mount Kuring-gai, N.S.W. 2080
email: info@peribo.com.au

First published by Dedalus in 2018
The Rehearsals copyright © Vladimir Sharov 2018

Printed and bound in Great Britain by Clays Ltd, St Ives plc
Typeset by Marie Lane

The Author

A historian of late-medieval Russia by training, Vladimir Sharov (born 1952) turned to fiction in the early 1980s. One of Russia's most distinguished living writers, he is the author of eight novels. *The Rehearsals*, which was written in the mid to late 1980s, is the second of his books to be published by Dedalus, following *Before and During* in 2014. He is the recipient of several awards, most recently the Russian Booker Prize in 2014.

Disputing the characterisation of his fiction as 'alternative history', Sharov has said: 'God judges us not only for our actions, but also for our intentions. I write the entirely real history of thoughts, inventions and beliefs. This is the country that existed. This is our own madness, our own absurd.'

He lives in Moscow.

The Translator

Oliver Ready teaches Russian at Oxford and is a Research Fellow of St Antony's College. His translations include Dostoevsky's *Crime and Punishment* (Penguin, 2014) and from contemporary fiction, works by Yuri Buida and Vladimir Sharov for Dedalus. In 2015, he received the Read Russia Prize for Sharov's *Before and During*, and in 2005 the Rossica Translation Prize for Buida's short-story cycle, *The Prussian Bride*. His book, *Persisting in Folly: Russian Writers in Search of Wisdom, 1963-2013*, was published in 2017.

Translator's Foreword

More than thirty years after he abandoned historical research for literature – and occasional poems about nature for wildly imaginative prose about people and peoples – Vladimir Sharov is now finally established in Russia as one of the essential novelists of his time. The flurry of awards that have come his way in recent years has forced his name out of the pocket of 'highbrow', 'provocative' literature to which he had been consigned for too long. As so often, these honours express overdue acknowledgement within the literary fraternity of an author's fundamental originality and influence, and Sharov has certainly left lasting traces on the work of younger contemporaries, from Dmitry Bykov and Mikhail Shishkin to Evgeny Vodolazkin, the literary phenomenon of the past five years. This belated recognition may also be due to the irony that the theme of Russian messianism, which is explored so persistently by Sharov in the key of tragedy, finds its unironic echoes in dominant strains of Russian ideology today. Indeed, Sharov's novels of the 1980s and 1990s are arguably more 'relevant' in 2017 than when they were first written.

It is through these earlier works that Anglophone readers can now begin to acquaint themselves with Sharov's oeuvre. As the author himself has said, all his novels 'supplement' the ones that came before – just as they supplement the established historical record, and just as, within those same novels, children supplement, and mourn, the prematurely aborted or frustrated lives of their parents, relatives and ancestors. Much of Sharov's extended family perished in Soviet prison camps, and the young Sharov heard the stories of Gulag returnees at first hand in his parents' flat (his father Aleksandr, born Sher Izrailevich Nyurenberg, was also a writer, whose books for children are still widely read). As Alexander Etkind, among others, has recognised, Sharov's novels are an ongoing work of bereavement – and attempted understanding.[1]

Before and During, the first of Sharov's novels to be published in English (Dedalus, 2014), is one of several candidates for the title of 'last novel of the Soviet era' (it was completed just as the August putsch of 1991 got underway). Grandiose in conception and canvas, it transmutes the well-worn parallel between the French and Russian revolutionary eras into a fantasy whose extravagant plot belies its seriousness. In Madame de Staël's second life, she becomes the lover of Nikolai Fyodorov (1829-1903), a philosopher passionately opposed to both social inequality and reproduction, which can serve only to extend the path of sin. In her third (and last) life, she becomes Stalin's mother – and lover. In all de Staël's encounters, the forces of vitality, creativity and fertility are pitted in a losing battle against the forces of death, asceticism and dogmatism, against the Revolution that arrived too late and too old. These are all mere stories, of course, mere fables or parables, but they are parables passed on to the reader by a kind-hearted journalist in a dementia ward in late-Soviet Moscow who is desperate, somehow, to redeem the past.

Directly before that novel, Sharov wrote an apparently quieter, yet no less disturbing work, *The Rehearsals*, which takes us further back in his 'search for the seeds of history',

---

1 In his valuable book *Warped Mourning: Stories of the Undead in the Land of the Unburied*, which includes a discussion of *The Rehearsals* (pp. 229-32), Etkind assimilates Sharov to a genre of recent Russian writing that he labels 'magical historicism'.

as Rachel Polonsky has put it, back to pre-Petrine Rus and to archaic, still resonant dichotomies: Christians and Jews, Russians and outsiders, Old Believers and the officially Orthodox. Of all Sharov's eight novels, it is the one most often referred to in Russia as a modern classic.

The Rehearsals is an uncompromisingly dark fantasy that develops, as if organically, from the people and ideals that have shaped Russian history, and equally from the Russian land itself, from the plains and bogs traversed by Sharov's itinerant characters. Most of Sharov's other novels, including *Before and During*, take the Russian Revolution as their centre of gravity. By contrast, the main story of *The Rehearsals*, when it eventually gets underway after a series of seemingly unconnected digressions, begins in the mid-seventeenth century, in the years leading up to the Schism within Russian Orthodoxy whose consequences for Russian history up to the Revolution and on to the present have, in Sharov's view, been drastically understated.

If the Schism does still register in the general global consciousness, then it is mainly thanks to the dissenters – to the Old Believers, still with us today, and in particular to the extraordinary memoir written in a dugout in the Arctic Circle by their most charismatic leader, the exiled Archpriest Avvakum.[2] In *Rehearsals*, by contrast, the main historical character is the Patriarch Nikon, who became the *bête noire* of both Avvakum and the clerical establishment, which deposed and exiled Nikon while approving many of his reforms to the sacred books and to modes of worship: the sign of the cross should be made with three fingers rather than two; believers should process around the church *against* the direction of the

---

2 *Archpriest Avvakum, the Life Written by Himself*, trans. Kenneth N. Brostrom (Ann Arbor, 1979).

sun. Nikon's reforms were aimed at bringing worship in line with the Greek Orthodox Church and thereby increasing the Russian Church's international influence, but many saw them as a catastrophic rupture of national tradition and, as 1666 approached, a sign of imminent apocalypse. Crucially for *The Rehearsals*, this conflict was a personal drama that only then unfolded into national catastrophe. Nikon and Avvakum were born in the same part of Russia, they had been friends in their youth, and they had belonged to the same reforming movement as 'Zealots of Piety'. Still more important to the novel than their relationship, however, is that between Patriarch Nikon and Tsar Alexei, the two 'great sovereigns' of the country – equal rulers, for a time, of their respective domains.

Much of this context emerges coherently from the novel itself, though readers wishing for a fuller picture may turn to the scholars, or indeed to the primary sources which, at certain moments, Sharov follows very closely, treating them almost as a common cultural patrimony.[3] They may also visit the Monastery of New Jerusalem outside Moscow around which both the novel itself and the circumstances of its writing pivot. What we cannot do, alas, is physically transport ourselves into the vanished world of the book's composition, the garrulous and bibulous world of unofficial late-Soviet culture, with

---

3 See, for example, Nickolas Lupinin, *Religious Revolt in the XVIIth Century: The Schism of the Russian Church* (The Kingston Press, 1984). For shorter accounts, see the relevant pages in James H. Billington's classic work of cultural history, *The Icon and the Axe* (Vintage, 1970) and Nadieszda Kizenko's article in *A Companion to Russian History*, ed. Abbott Gleason (Blackwell, 2009). For an account of Nikon's life by his own confidant, see *From Peasant to Patriarch: Account of the Birth, Upbringing, and Life of His Holiness Nikon, Patriarch of Moscow and All Russia Written by His Cleric Ioann Shusherin*, translated and edited by Kevin M. Kain and Katia Levintova (Lexington Books, 2007).

its friendships and squabbles, public absurdities and private griefs, and eclectic intellectual and spiritual quests. An essay Sharov wrote just two years ago does, however, give a tantalising glimpse into the atmosphere, personal and social, from which *The Rehearsals* emerged – and is included here as an afterword.

Though decades old and deeply rooted in the Russian classics, *Before and During* and *The Rehearsals* are likely to strike many readers as utterly singular. Sharov's compositional method and, more intangibly, mood have no obvious analogue in world literature. The great theorist Yury Lotman ended his last essay, dictated shortly before his death in 1993, by accurately diagnosing the crisis of post-Soviet Russian literature: 'should it preserve its age-old national tradition (namely: 'the transformation of life') or turn into mere entertainment?'[4] Sharov has chosen neither 'mere' entertainment nor the transformative didacticism of his beloved Leo Tolstoy. Rather, he asks the reader to share with him, and his narrator, in his labour of understanding, to join him down rabbit-holes that eventually prove to be a highway to the past – and to the Siberian prisons that haunt his fiction. In return for this effort, he offers the fundamental experience many readers seek: the sensation of gradually being drawn into something without immediately grasping how or why, of being charmed by ordinary words conferred on ordinary lives in extraordinary situations.

St Antony's College, 2017

---

4 Jurij Lotman, 'The Truth as Lie', in *Gøgøl: Exploring Absence*, ed. Sven Spieker (Slavica, 1999), pp. 35-53.

Note on the Text and Acknowledgements

This translation is based on the authoritative and most recent edition of the novel (*Repetitsii*) as published by Arsis Books in Moscow in 2009. Some minor inconsistencies or errors have been amended in consultation with the author, and other small changes made. The Biblical translation used is the New King James Version. Footnotes have been kept to a minimum.

I would like to express my sincere gratitude to Vladimir Sharov and to his wife, Olga Dunaevskaya, for patient and illuminating replies to several hundred questions about the novel, and to the author for accompanying me on a visit to New Jerusalem Monastery. The explanations and memories supplied in the course of these precious exchanges have improved the translation greatly. My thanks are also due to Evgeny Reznichenko and the Institute for Translation in Moscow for supporting the translation, and for organising lively biennial conferences among fellow translators from Russian. A workshop convened by Andrei Rogatchevski in the appropriately atmospheric setting of Tromsø in mid-December, 2016, offered further opportunities for dialogue. For sharing their thoughts and interest I also thank Philip Bullock, Lijana Dejak, Boris Dralyuk, Ilya Kalinin, Ania Ready and Michael Rozenman. Lastly, I would like to acknowledge a debt to Paul Lequesne, whose translation into French appeared in 1998 (Actes Sud). I borrow from him the idea of setting the first paragraph of the novel as a separate page, and am envious that only his title, *Les Répétitions*, can fully capture the novel's twinned themes of rehearsal in art and recurrence in history.

Peter the Apostle told the Jews: 'Repent therefore and be converted, that your sins may be blotted out, so that times of refreshing may come from the presence of the Lord, and that He may send Jesus Christ, who was preached to you before, whom heaven must receive until the times of restoration of all things, which God has spoken by the mouth of all His holy prophets since the world began' (Acts 3). The Church interprets these words to mean one thing only: the conversion of all Jews to Christ must precede the Second Coming of the Saviour and the victory of the righteous.

In 1939 Isaiah Trifonovich Kobylin ceased to be a Jew, and the Jewish nation, of which he was the last, ended with him. For two thousand years Kobylin's 'stiff-necked' people, as the Lord had called them, did not want to repent and turn to the true faith, for two thousand years, indulging the impious, they obstructed the Second Coming of the Saviour for whom all believers were praying and waiting, and now, when the life of Jews on earth had ended, the time was at hand. Time for Him to appear in His glory.

I learnt the story of the Jews' extinction from Kobylin himself in Tomsk in 1965, but I'll begin seven years earlier and on a different topic. In 1958 I began my studies at the University of Kuibyshev (Samara), in the Faculty of History and Literature. That same autumn I got to know a man who was trying to understand God. His name was Sergei Nikolayevich Ilyin. We met every evening all winter and spring, taking strolls in the little park by Freedom Street. He preached to me, then disappeared from my life when he saw that I had understood his teachings. Ilyin was seven years older than me, and at the time of our acquaintance he was working as a guide at the Alexander Radishchev House Museum.[1]

I myself was baptised when I was three months old, with

1 Alexander Radishchev (1749-1802), author of *Journey from St Petersburg to Moscow* (1790), an indictment of Russian serfdom and autocracy for which Radishchev was exiled to Siberia.

my parents' tacit consent, though ostensibly without their knowledge. The ceremony was carried out by my nanny in the church of her native village, Trinity, six miles south of Kuibyshev on the banks of the Volga. She was dismissed soon after: she turned out to have a rather unpleasant skin condition – probably psoriasis – and my religious education went no further.

Ilyin was half-Russian, half-Jewish. His mother, who hailed from an old rabbinic family, was a baptised Jew, while his paternal ancestors were no less illustrious: they were merchants who helped found the famous Old Believer settlements on the Irgiz River. The nation to which a promise had been made and the Son of Man had been sent, but which had not accepted Him and had not followed Him, was combined in Ilyin with the nation to which nothing had been granted or promised, but which had believed in Christ and would be saved. Their bloods had not mixed well, and Ilyin's face was asymmetrical. He was fond of saying that in medieval times he would have been burned at the stake as a succubus or incubus who had been branded with the devil's seal. Now, casting my mind back to Ilyin, I realise with some astonishment that during our strolls I always walked to his left, and it is only his left, Jewish side – dark and sad – that I remember clearly.

There was a particular rhythm to Ilyin's speech and even to his train of thought. Just as, during a tour of the museum, he would single out the crucial, stress-bearing words, deeds and objects in Radishchev's life and skim over everything in between, merely sketching the general outline of events with his rapid stride, so too with Christ: as he tried to elucidate what it was that had come with Him into the world, that had been proclaimed by Him to the Jews and other nations, Ilyin consciously avoided dividing the temple of his understanding into side chapels and altars, and merely laid the cornerstones of his faith; he built the frame but not the walls or the roof, keeping everything as it might be in the desert – open to the four winds.

That November, the trees on the path were bare and heavy, like pillars, and our progress between them seemed less like a stroll than a set itinerary; we had a topic, a purpose, and a pace to match. As he selected the stone he needed, found a spot for it and placed it, Ilyin would slow right down, almost emphatically dragging his feet, but once he had completed this part of the task he would effortlessly make up for lost time, as if with a single brushstroke. The evenly planted trees set off the unevenness of his own progress, but he took no notice: for him the trees were just a scale by which to visualise the size and proportions of his own construction.

He would say to me: 'Seryozha, put your trust in God, love Him, remember Him; do not hide from Him, tell Him everything, let neither joy nor grief bring you shame; believe, ask, pray. He is there for you; His face is turned towards you. He will understand and He will help.' Prayers reach God, Ilyin would say; prayers work and prayers matter, not least to Him; they are a connection between Him and us, a connection that binds us together and makes us His – God's – creatures, without which we would be nothing to Him and He to us, and we would know nothing about Him and would not believe in Him.

In the Bible, Ilyin would say, God creates and God rests, He suffers and grieves, feels sadness and remorse, He walks, sees, speaks, looks, hears, remembers, smells, He loves and envies, rejoices and rages, punishes and forgives; He has eyes and ears and strong hands in which He holds the sceptre and the enemy-slaying sword. These human things are said about

God in the Torah not because there were no other words to choose from, or because human beings were in their infancy and would have understood nothing without them; no, God really is like that and really does feel all these things, for our rage and joy, our remorse and sadness, our attitude towards the true and the false are also created in the image and likeness of His rage and joy, His sorrow and love.

Ilyin would say: nobody knows and nobody can know the Lord in his entirety, but we can and must understand the part of Him that is turned towards us, the human part. The Lord wants us to understand Him, wants more from us than faith, good deeds, repentance, and observance of the Law. He needs us human beings to understand Him, to be children, yes, but children who can reason. Were this not the case, He would not be able to teach or explain anything at all, and we would be complete strangers to one another.

Christ, Ilyin would say, is not only the true God and the Son of God – He is the Godman, and His two natures, divine and human, cannot be separated and cannot be fused. They make a whole precisely because they both come from the Lord and are both created in His image and likeness, resembling each other so much that they are inseparable in Christ. Christ the Godman, moreover, is a metaphor for the relationship between God and human beings, for what that relationship will look like when people repent and follow the path of righteousness; then, not only will we be granted the Sacrament of the Eucharist, and not only will we receive Holy Communion – the blood and flesh of Christ – several times a year, but we shall all be united forever in Christ, and in Him and with Him we shall be united with the Lord.

Ilyin would say: the Lord could not do evil, and in fact there was no evil in the world before man. There was knowledge of evil, but not evil itself. The world was like an alphabet, which had been given to us for our good, but which could be turned to evil. The Lord made man, and man was the first to be given the opportunity and the freedom to do both good and evil. The Lord believed that man, knowing what evil was and knowing that he could do it, would himself choose good and do good, so the world which the Lord had brought into being *was* good.

Heaven was the time of man's childhood. Playing, he gave names to the animals and the fish, the birds and the trees, to everything that the Lord filled His world with and that would live with mankind. Heaven was where man came to know good and evil, and came to know them too soon, while he was still a child and his soul was still raw. His first act of evil was to break the Lord's interdiction, then run and hide; this was merely the sin of a foolish child and yet, having once appeared in the world, evil began to beget evil, it multiplied and grew, and man, whose soul was ill-trained to distinguish good from evil, merely helped it along in his ignorance. We fight evil and think that since it is against us and since we are fighting it we must be good, but that's not true. The other man also thinks that he is good and that by fighting us he is fighting evil, and in this fight two evils come together and a new one comes into being. We do not understand, or we forget, that good is something entirely different, that good is what everyone will see, from wherever they happen to be looking.

Evil, Ilyin would say, is a retreat from God, a wall between Him and us: we can see the Lord neither over it nor through it, and we remain all alone in a world where there is no God, where there is only us, and then, bewitched by the fact that we are alone for the very first time, that there is no one above us and we are free to do evil, we do it again and again. The wall between us and the Lord grows higher and higher, our faith weakens, and around us there is nothing but evil, the evil in which we are drowning and choking, but even then He will hear us, even then He will save us, if there is just one person amongst us who will repent and turn to Him.

Ilyin would say: many claim that the Jews of the Old Testament do not act as God's chosen people ought to act. They kill the innocent, they renounce and betray the Lord, and it's hard to understand what's so special about them. These same people say that the Song of Songs and Ecclesiastes are not divinely inspired and that it is far from clear how and why they entered the canon. They fail to understand that the books of the Old Testament are a conversation between God and human beings, the most important of all the conversations that man will ever hold; everything they contain – the treacheries, the betrayals, the renunciations – actually took place. This is the path man walked, the story of his return to God, and there is nothing more important than that story or a single one of its parts, each of which is a part of the path towards knowledge of the Lord: good or bad, every step of this path must be preserved in its entirety and must be accurately and fully conveyed, whoever it was that walked it.

Ilyin would say: the life that Christ the Son of God lived on earth was a time without precedent – for God, for man, and for everything there has ever been between God and man. All the previous times known to us when God dwelt on earth, including the seven days of creation, are as nothing compared to the thirty-three years that Christ spent in the world. To be closer to man, the Son of God even accepted the human flow of time. The experience which both God and man drew from thirty-three years of the most intimate contact – and I am speaking not just of those who followed Him, but above all of God and Man within Christ Himself: that is where it all began, and it was only after He spent almost thirty years getting to know man within a single body, as if inside Himself, where there can be no separation, no view from the outside, that He went off to preach to the chosen people – well, this experience was the foundation of the next two thousand years of human history. Without it we will understand nothing either about the events of the New Testament or about what followed.

Ilyin would say: from the moment the Jews appeared on earth, the basis of everything that tied them to God throughout the ages was faith, daily prayer and sacrifice. There was also something else: the fact that He had chosen them, that their fate and history had meant more to Him than those of any other people; after all, at the very beginning of their existence the Lord Himself had come down into the world, spoken to them and exhorted them, even if later this happened more rarely. When the Jews multiplied, they remained bound to God, as before, through prayer and sacrifice, but He also gave Moses a Law for his people, and this nation even built a kind of dwelling place for the Lord – the Temple. When the nation sinned and forgot God, which happened often enough, the Lord sent prophets to exhort the people in their faith and righteousness, to lead them, as if they were blind, onto the path of truth. So it continued for more than a thousand years, and it seemed that a lack of faith was the one and only cause of every woe, but on the cusp of the era, when Rome already controlled the entire Mediterranean and even Judea, a great deal changed. Never before had there been so few idolaters in the country, and never before had the rituals been performed so irreproachably in the Temple; hundreds upon hundreds of the most learned Levites continued to analyse and apply the laws given to Moses, and there was only one thing driving them: the fear of committing sin before the Lord. These interpreters and teachers of the Law were more respected than anyone else within the nation, because the guiding aim of all the Jews was the avoidance of sin. At that time the majority of those living in the Promised Land was prepared to accept exile and death if it was the only way of keeping the Temple pure. And during the Jewish War, just a few decades later, the Sicarii, Zealots, Pharisees and many Sadducees would indeed go into exile and perish, losing their land but remaining faithful to God. This loyalty would endure through two thousand years of persecution and execution, and only those who stayed faithful would be Jews, while the others would not; they would spread, scatter and dissolve among other nations, and no memory, no trace would remain of them.

Ilyin would say: even so, the Jews, for all the devotion they showed Him, are still guilty before God; even in God's Promised Land, evil multiplied year after year, filling His Land to bursting, and neither the Lord nor their faith could contain it. The Lord saw and knew all this, saw that His people were devoted to Him – exactly how devoted is, of course, not for me to say, but more so than ever – and that they were ready for what lay ahead. But His world was greater than the Promised Land, and it was not only Jews who lived in it.

So the Jewish nation was scattered over many different lands, it settled and mixed with many different peoples, who learned from the Jews about the Almighty, the one whom, in the time of Noah, they had once worshipped themselves but had managed to forget long ago, living ever since like foolish children who knew no sin. Another story of good and evil. Learning about God once more, they learned that they had, as it were, become strangers to Him, and also that they were not children and had not been children for a very long time, and they immediately felt so much sin upon them, felt so worthless and so lonely, that they were sure they could never be saved. The Jews had no desire to help them, and they only had themselves to blame. So when news of God reached the nations, they were further away from Him than ever and no longer cared how much evil was upon them. They, too, were His children, however prodigal and sinful, but they had moved away from Him and had not yet taken a single step back towards Him, nor did they wish to, because they thought they were strangers to Him and He would not accept them. And anyway, the path towards Him was so hard that there was no point beginning. So then the Lord came to them Himself, and came, as they learned, through His people.

Ilyin would say: the Lord decided to live the life of an ordinary man, to live it far away from the Temple, in a place, Galilee, where there were more pagans than anywhere else and where faith was weaker, to live a full life – childhood, youth, maturity – and live it piously and honestly, in full observance of the Law. When that life was over, He would know what to do next. We should emphasise, by the way, that the Law is not questioned by the Son of God here or anywhere else, even in part. He says: 'Therefore whatever they tell you to observe, that observe and do' (Matthew 23). 'Do not think that I came to destroy the Law or the Prophets. I did not come to destroy but to fulfil. For assuredly, I say to you, till heaven and earth pass away, one jot or one tittle will by no means pass from the law till all is fulfilled. Whoever therefore breaks one of the least of these commandments, and teaches men so, shall be called least in the kingdom of heaven...' (Matthew 5). And perhaps most importantly, both for us and for an understanding of the entire fate of the Jews, just think how loyal they were to the Covenant if, despite all the thousands of miracles worked by Christ, they judged whether He was truly the Messiah solely by His devotion to the Law.

Ilyin would say: was Christ a real person? I don't think so. Yes, He was conceived by a mortal woman, who carried Him in her womb and gave birth to Him, but His conception was, and had to be, immaculate, and Christ was free of original sin, the burden which we have borne, bear and will continue to bear until the end of time. All the same, the Lord, having assumed the image of Christ and having united in Him with human nature, found Himself closer to man than He had ever been, and His experience of life on earth, among ordinary people, His experience of sharing human, mortal and, for Him, infinitely deficient nature was the most important event in human history since Abraham went out from Ur of the Chaldeans.

Ilyin would say: Christ is different from man. He is pure and without sin, feels that He is right and has every right, knows that both this world and that world are His, that He can always leave the earth to which He has descended, that He will leave it and will ascend. And there is something else: the world has been created by Him and can be changed, remade, reformed by His will; in other words, He, Christ, is its master, and try as the Lord might to relinquish His omniscience and omnipotence, Christ will not manage to absorb man's view of the world entirely until the very last hours and minutes of His life, just before He is led to Golgotha, and then on the cross itself.

Ilyin would say: uniting with man in Christ, the Lord wants to recall and renew His own knowledge that such a union with the human race is possible, that it is organic, essential, inevitable. It is, as I have already said, a prefiguration of what awaits us all. The Lord's expectations become reality: the Son of God and the Virgin Mary is born on earth, but in some peculiar way, even before the infant Christ begins to walk, His birth ceases to be a secret and changes the world. Everything changes: the structure of life, the commensurability and correlation of its parts, the very edifice of life, and even notions of right and wrong; yes, right is still right, and sin is still sin, but in the gap between them something has been disturbed, displaced, distorted. Many people lose their way, confused by the lodestar that guides the Wise Men to Christ, and the aim these people have always set themselves, knowing that their own strength is limited, suddenly disintegrates and can no longer be true, at least not while Jesus Christ still walks the earth. I am reluctant to say this, but it would seem that when Christ appeared on earth, only one path remained to the righteous in the country where He lived, in Israel: the revolutionary, lightning path walked by the Son of God and His disciples.

Ilyin would say: the Wise Men and the shepherds, who lived beneath the stars, were the first to notice this disturbance in the natural order of life and to see how powerful it was: God had come down into a world where man was meant to look after himself, and it had proved too cramped for Him. This disturbance of the normal way of doing things, this overwhelming advent of God on earth (remember that nothing similar had ever happened before, or has ever happened since) inevitably altered the fate of His chosen people – the Massacre of the Innocents in Bethlehem was just the beginning.

On earth, the Son of God took the road which the Jews had been walking for two thousand years. Retracing their flight from hunger, He flees to Egypt and hides there, escaping persecution, and when people in Palestine have forgotten all about Him, He goes back and lives there, unobtrusively and unnoticed, for almost three decades. He is waiting for His time to come to pave the path for His nation, the path which the nation should walk and will walk, just as Christ Himself did, in its entirety, from Nazareth to Golgotha. And so, the first part of the life of Jesus Christ is the life of a man of His people; it ends when He turns thirty and a second life begins – the life of a prophet and Messiah who foretells the destiny of the Jews. Even so, He does not begin it right away.

Ilyin would say: John the Baptist, just like the Wise Men, knew who Jesus was, knew He was the Son of God, and could not fail to know this, which is why he said to Him: 'I need to be baptised by You, and are You coming to me?' But at that point nothing had been decided yet and another forty days separated the lives of Jesus the man and Jesus the Messiah: His baptism by John, the descent of the Holy Spirit, and the long fast in the desert, during which the devil tempted Christ three times, tempted the man in Christ, and only when the man had resisted and endured did Christ become the Lord's Anointed. One can feel, in the conversation between Christ and John the Baptist, a certain tentativeness on Christ's part. Perhaps this was because the time of His mission had not yet come, perhaps because His trial had not yet ended, but it seems – though nothing is actually said about this – that initially the Son of God was only meant to be incarnated as a man; after all, it was the fault of man and no one else that the world had become as it was.

Ilyin would say: the fact that the Lord sent another, greater prophet while John the Baptist was still alive, that He sent His own Son, should not be taken as proof of John's inadequacy (as was assumed in the disputes between John's disciples and Christ's); no, the appearance of Jesus Christ and His teachings signified something else: they signified that before He, the Son of God and the Saviour, had come between God and humanity, man had lacked the ability and the strength to overcome sin.

This in itself was a kind of exoneration of man – something exceptionally important and unexpected for God – and Christ, by choosing for His disciples people who were living the same ordinary life in the world as He, reinforced this verdict.

Ilyin would say: Jesus spent three years walking and preaching in Israel, and what has remained from these years is not only what He told His disciples and what has come down to us through Scripture – that part of His teaching has enjoyed the most straightforward, natural fate – but also what He told the Jews who did not follow Him, who rejected Him, and what He Himself understood during that time. Christ's arguments with the Pharisees were crucial for the Jewish nation, as they were for Christ and for God. The entire subsequent history of the Christian world, as well as the Jews, is wrapped up in them.

What conclusions can be drawn from these arguments? First: linear development, formal logic and the primacy of the merely external lead faith to a legalistic dead end. But this, too, is clear: the Pharisees live for God alone; He is their every thought and desire, and all their rigour derives from their devotion to the faith of their fathers. I have already said that Christ never questions the truth or rectitude of the Law given to Moses; the Law bears no blame for the failure of God and the nation to understand each other. Jesus even amplifies the significance of the Law and takes it further, albeit in a different, more human direction from that taken by the Pharisees. And this is easy to explain: He has the right to interpret it – He is God – while they have the right only to take the law to its logical conclusions. Even so, what matters most here is not Christ's interpretation of the Law, and it is not the fate of the faithful and the righteous that most occupies Him, for it is not to them that He has been sent: 'Those who are well have no need of a physician, but those who are sick' (Matthew 9). Far more important is a different knowledge gained by Christ on earth: that only miracles can help mankind. The Lord does not console the crippled and the sick; He has no words for them. Nor does he exhort them to accept their lot: He heals them – and that is the whole point. The fate of the crippled, the maimed, the possessed is so awful that words without salvation are nothing. The sheer number and variety of miracles performed by Christ on earth show how essential, how salutary miracles are; there is no getting by without them. Miracles are worked by the Lord in the conviction that the world is terrible and He, Christ, has been sent to save it.

Ilyin would say: all the disputes between Christ and the Pharisees come together in the parable of the labourers in the vineyard, where one path to God competes with another: a landowner hires some labourers for a denarius (eternal salvation); when midday passes, he hires some more; and an hour before the end of the working day he hires a third group. He pays them all the same wage (one denarius), and when those who have worked since the morning object, he says to one of their number: 'Friend, I am doing you no wrong. Did you not agree with me for a denarius? Take what is yours and go your way. I wish to give to this last man the same as to you. Is it not lawful for me to do what I wish with my own things? Or is your eye evil because I am good? So the last will be first, and the first last. For many are called, but few chosen' (Matthew 20). (Here we see that miracles and goodness are greater than justice, greater than long, slow, heavy labour – greater than anything.)

Ilyin would say: good is at the core of everything that Jesus Christ, filled with the Holy Spirit, does on earth. Having lived for so many years among men, having seen so much evil, He, ceasing to be a man and becoming the Messiah, becoming God once more, cannot help doing good, as much good as he possibly can, good for the weakest and the maimed, and for sinners too. Essentially, He violates the way of doing things that He himself established: not the slow path of man's repentance and reform, not the slow path of salvation from sin, with eternal bliss as its reward, but simply mountains and mountains of good, whole sackfuls of good, and the unhappier, the weaker and the more sinful you are, the more goodness and mercy you deserve. To bring more good into the world, He sends His disciples off in all directions, telling them: 'Heal the sick, cleanse the lepers, raise the dead, cast out demons,' and then: 'Freely you have received, freely give' (Matthew 10), lest they pause to ask themselves whether or not to do good, whether or not the man beseeching them is deserving of mercy.

Ilyin would say: Christ is the great joy of the God who is able to do good and can finally do it, who no longer has to wait for man to be reformed and to observe all the endless woes and sorrow of human life, who loves man as His child, for what is man if not His child, His continuation made in His image and likeness, and in His suffering too? God no longer has the strength to watch man's misery, to see evil spawning evil, more and more of it each day. Is this really how God's world should be? And does He not remember how and when evil first entered the world? It entered when man was a child, when he could scarcely answer for his actions, and anyway, can the evil done by that child really be compared to what followed? So the Son of God, filled with love and the desire to forgive, the desire for evil to end and equality to reign – why should some have everything, even righteousness, while others have nothing? Don't all people stem from a single root, from

Adam? – gives to those who have nothing, to those who have least (the poor, the sick, the maimed, the dead) the miracle of forgiveness and deliverance.

But in that case, Ilyin would say, the purpose for which God created man, to whom it is given to do good and evil and who, God believes, will reject evil one day and freely choose good, thereby proving the truth and goodness of God's world, will remain unfulfilled, and all that came after the birth of man, all that evil, will have been pointless, merely evil spawning evil. And the deeds of the righteous will also have been pointless, and God is all on His own, and above all good is no better than evil, for men have not chosen it. Either they didn't want it, or they ran out of time. So Christ stops.

Ilyin would say: miracles are the work of God, and it is only in the love and pity that inhere equally in man and in God that we can even guess at His humanity; but the closer to the end, to Golgotha and death, the more we see the man. Golgotha, in fact, will divide them. The fate of one, as He knows all too well, is to die; the fate of the other, as He also knows, is to be resurrected. I am not dividing them – they are one – but still, God cannot die; He can suffer, but not die. A world without God is unthinkable, and for Him that instant does not exist. The closer to Golgotha, the more human Christ becomes.

Ilyin would say: in Jerusalem and on Golgotha Christ is already a man, but a man who still has the knowledge of God. He knows that Judas will betray Him, knows that Peter will deny Him three times, knows that He will be crucified, but he continues along the path sketched out for Him long before, and not by Him, and He is not free to turn off it. He says to the Lord, beseeching Him: 'O My Father, if it is possible, let this cup pass from Me; nevertheless, not as I will, but as You will'; and then: 'O My Father, if this cup cannot pass away from Me unless I drink it, Your will be done' (Matthew 26). But the cup does not pass away from Him. He will be crucified on the cross, and such is the solitude of man in this world, so forgotten and abandoned is he by God, that even Christ, who was closer to the Lord than anyone has ever been, who was united with Him inseparably and lived with Him inseparably from His conception onwards, even Christ will cry: *Eloi, Eloi, lama sabachthani?* which means, 'My God, My God, why have You forsaken Me?' (Mark 15).

Ilyin would say: the main thing that divided Christ and the Jews was the case of Barabbas. Judas was Christ's disciple, he followed Him, walked the entire path with Him and, like His other disciples, would have left the Jewish faith. Judas listened to Him, stood side by side with Him, did good deeds through His power, rejected the path of the Jews completely and, having betrayed Christ, did not return to it; he was paid – nothing more. He wanted to return and give the money back to the Temple, but it was not accepted, which meant that he too would never be accepted, and Judas, left quite alone, as alone as any man can be, hanged himself. Christ's opposite is not Judas but Barrabas; it is because of him that the people say, 'Christ's blood be on us and on our children,' him they choose to save when the choice arises.

Matthew describes Barabbas as a criminal who made a rebellion in the city, but all four Evangelists set him apart from the villains punished together with Christ, for whom, in any case, the people make no appeal. Barabbas, it would seem, was among those who tried to incite an uprising against Rome. I am not interested here in the choice other nations would have made in such cases; that isn't the point. Christ and the Jews were separated by a matter of mercy – and that is astonishing. Let's set aside for the moment the fact that the opposition

Christ-Barabbas is a simplified one, that Barabbas is declared a criminal and a murderer, and put the question as follows: who should have been saved – God, who in three days would be raised to life, or man? Here, saving one meant condemning the other, and in this situation the Jews, I think, were right. The weakest had to be saved, the one who could not defend himself and who did not have God the Father to protect him. If the question is who to save, man or God, the answer is always man. To defend Christ, the Jews would have had to kill a man. That was the price.

I studied at Kuibyshev University for almost three years, and just four months or so before our move to Tomsk, where my father had been offered the position of chief regional radiologist, I was suddenly registered on a special course, 'Gogol and Comparative Literary Criticism'. The dean's office had given neither me nor my five fellow students any choice in the matter (there hadn't been a single volunteer) and I managed to attend precisely half the course before our departure – five lectures all told. These were delivered by a decrepit octogenarian philosophy professor from Kiev known to the entire university as 'The Idealist'. Professor Kuchmy more than lived up to his sobriquet.

Vladimir Ivanovich Kuchmy managed to make a name for himself even before the Revolution; then, after Soviet power had been definitively established in Ukraine, he made an honest attempt to adjust to the new regime and even wrote a two-volume work called, if I'm not mistaken, *The History of Philosophy in the Light of Historical Materialism*. But he must have adjusted too slowly or too freely (his study was subjected to vicious, even humiliating criticism), or perhaps he simply stuck out like a sore thumb in pre-war Ukraine – one way or the other, he was imprisoned in 1940, charged with spreading idealistic philosophy and, at one and the same time, with being a Ukrainian nationalist. Kuchmy spent fifteen years in the camps, but when he was released in '55 Ukraine had not forgotten his supposed nationalism and refused to take him back. Moscow, after brief deliberation, offered him a part-time position in Kuibyshev, not in the philosophy faculty, needless to say, but in the sleepy faculty of Russian literature. We were his final audience: he retired that same year.

Ostensibly, Kuchmy's special course was devoted, as I have said, to Gogol, but he only got on to him at the end of his third lecture. In fact, it wasn't really Gogol that interested him but a fanciful blend of literary criticism, sociology and gibberish. In a cool, methodical manner, he explained to us why the people who had lived on this earth, entire tribes and nations, were essentially not people at all, or at any rate no more than phantoms and mirages wandering over deserted spaces, as he put it himself. Starting from this premise, he expanded at great length on the senselessness and aimlessness of earthly existence and on the resemblance between humans and plants: equality in life, equality in death, and both leave only one thing behind – a seed. The lives of those who leave nothing behind, he would say, are an illusion. Seriously: where are those lives? We think they suffered, but that's only by analogy with ourselves, with our own suffering. Those who were once here left long ago, and now it's no longer even possible to say why they were born, why they lived, and whether they even existed at all.

After posing this question, Kuchmy said nothing for a long time before telling us, in the same cool and methodical way, that he had gone too far, that he had a habit of going too far and that this had cost him dearly in the past; his duty now was to renounce his own words. He had been warned more than once by the department of pedagogical methodology that by calling human beings phantoms and mirages, whether or not those people were still alive, he was distorting the truth and undervaluing the achievements of other disciplines, notably archaeology, which had definitively established that every human being leaves at least something behind. Even if that something is only bones, Kuchmy would still be wrong, because neither mirages nor phantoms have any bones. He agreed with this critique and assured us that he would permit himself no further comments of this kind, but he had also told the department, and was telling us now, that he had a tendency to fly off the handle during scholarly argument, that he was a passionate person in general and that this flaw, alas, had to be taken into account. In the dispute between him and archaeology, he would tell us, there could be only one winner: encampments and interments are the work of human hands, and this has been proven beyond reasonable doubt. Archaeology is indeed the queen of the sciences: it literally resurrects the dead. Give it a bit more time and we'll know the deceased as well as we know ourselves, if not better. Only recently, he continued, three miles from the city, archaeologists had discovered in rapid succession two of our countrymen's – or perhaps even ancestors' – encampments, and now we know that one of the encampments represents Linear Pottery Culture and the other Comb Ceramic Culture, which, by the way, fits neatly with Comrade Lenin's famous statement about the presence of two cultures within the frame of a single national culture.

He evidently felt that with these peculiar comments he had paid Caesar his due, because he went on to declare that the most accurate term for all these people who had once walked the earth would be 'unfinished product' – only halfway towards what might properly be called *homo vivus*. As Kuchmy would have it, all that has survived of the past, whether ancient or very recent, are matted heaps of human prototypes – a result of the imperfections both of human nature itself and of the means of reproduction. Humans, he would say, are blurred around the edges, amorphous, plastic, waxlike. As a consequence of time and their own weight, they quickly lose their shape, tangle and curdle, turning into a homogeneous, well-scrambled mass, which historians like to call a 'people' or 'nation'. Not a single personality or human being has come down to us from the past, and not a single feature has survived even of those whose names we know from inscriptions on the earliest monuments.

Our current method of producing children, Kuchmy would say, is the oldest and the most primitive on earth, founded as it is on the copulation of two sexes. The possibility of autonomous, independent reproduction is virtually excluded. Accordingly, a child is, at best, the fruit of a compromise; more often, he or she is the result of the crude, mechanical mixing of two individuals. There is nothing organic about this process, and no continuity. Any given child is a metis, a mongrel, with all the deficiencies inherent in the different breeds from which it derives. It is precisely this endless mixing of all with all – and what else, when you get down to it, is history about? – that we have to thank for the senselessness and talentlessness of the human race...

'But I cherish the hope,' the professor went on, 'that the time will come when lust, which dissolves human beings in their likenesses and leaves nothing behind, which dissolves what little there is in us that deserves the name personality (and nothing expresses the hatred we have for our own personality, our difference from other people, better than the ecstasy we experience in those moments), becomes a mere vestige of the past and gradually dies out.'

Apropos of this, he recalled his fellow Ukrainian, Trofim Lysenko, and declared that the philosophical basis of Lysenko's view of nature had been widely undervalued.[2] A person who, like all living creatures, is produced by the vulgar mixing together of two sets of inherited characteristics, each of which is itself a mixture and so on to the beginning of life, *is* capable in the rarest of circumstances, with a particular combination of education and self-development, of becoming a personality, removing all superfluity from his genes and turning into a relatively harmonious being. But just imagine if someone comes along and tells him that his children will begin from scratch, that he is unable, biologically, to pass on anything that he has accumulated?

'Or to put it another way,' Kuchmy continued, 'are we really supposed to accept that the children of two convinced Marxists can be born as devoid of political and ideological substance as the children of any other parents? And is it really possible to claim that consciousness is matter in its highest form if it surrenders so readily to matter, time and again, on this most crucial question?'

Kuchmy's second lecture was devoted partly to a deeply peculiar branch of literary scholarship, and partly to the character and physiological idiosyncrasies of various authors. Writers, Kuchmy believed, represent that distinct and as yet very meagre offshoot of the human race that has propagated itself through the loftiest, perhaps even perfect method. If Kuchmy, as I have said, considered real people to be unfinished

---

2 Trofim Lysenko (1898-1976), the agrobiologist who acquired notorious influence under Stalin (and beyond). Lysenko rejected modern genetics, maintaining instead that characteristics acquired within the lifetime of an organism can be immediately inherited.

products, a mere collection of attributes, then writers produce people who are complete and therefore authentic and true. Some writers reproduce by parthenogenesis, others are herma-phroditic, but both give birth to higher beings whose lives last for entire generations, or even millennia, and never actually cease; at worst they merely fade. Here he quoted Lermontov – 'Not for me the cold sleep of the grave... / Give me instead eternal rest, / Life's strength a-slumber in my heart, / A gentle heaving in my chest' – and some medieval mystic who claimed that manuscripts don't burn, just the paper, while the letters themselves fly back to God. There was only one role that Kuchmy conceded to normal human beings: the role of catalyst. It's not ordinary people we know, remember, imitate and emulate, but characters in books – like Pushkin's Tatyana – and the past we remember is theirs.

'Actually,' Kuchmy said, 'most of these literary ruminations do not belong to me, but to an investigator by the name of Chelnokov. I must give Chelnokov his due: in all the eighty years of my life I have never come across a more profound or subtle mind, and I am grateful to fate, despite all the hardships, for bringing us together. When I was arrested in 1940, the two investigators who were initially given my case demanded that I confess that I was working towards the separation of Ukraine from Russia and that I was the head of a clandestine armed group whose raison d'être was bombing and sabotage (and whose list of members was duly presented to me). I considered myself innocent and put my signature to nothing bar an old failing – my allegiance to the camp of idealist philosophers. This was hardly enough, of course, for a show trial. So I was put on the so-called 'conveyor belt'. For nearly a month I was interrogated and beaten, beaten and interrogated, and I had long been ready to sign whatever was put in front of me, anything to put an end to this hell, were it not for the terror I felt at the thought of slandering people who, in most cases, I'd never met. Then it all came to an abrupt end, and I was given a breather. A whole week passed before my next interrogation. By this time my case had been passed to another investigator – Chelnokov. He apologised for the behaviour of his colleagues, assured me they would be properly punished, and continued as follows:

"'It's people like you that we, the secret police, want to save, and save you we will. It's our duty. Writers have been summoned to play the leading role in our revolution, and the only people who will live in their books will be those who know exactly what needs to be done to ensure its victory. The enemies of the revolution will be relegated to the background, while the others – those who only think about their own interests, who want to wait it out on the sidelines – will have to be stamped out, along with every memory that remains of them. They will have to disappear for ever, for all time, disappear in such a way that neither their children nor their grandchildren will know the first thing about them, not even that they existed. They must vanish as the illiterate Polovtsian and Pecheneg nomads once vanished, dissolving among other nations. Such is the sentence that has been passed, Vladimir Ivanovich, and literature will carry it out. But we, the NKVD men, are saving these condemned souls. All those who pass through our hands will be saved. We will even resurrect many of those who have already died. A year ago I got some new folders for new cases. They bear the words, 'Keep forever.' These folders terrify suspects like the flames of hell. Thanks to this inscription they are convinced that we will shoot them every day for all eternity. What rubbish! They are doomed anyway, and this inscription will preserve them, save them from disappearing.

"'Picture the scene. A suspect is brought into my office. I write down the number of the case, his surname, open the file and begin the interrogation. I already have a scenario for him in mind. But if I see it doesn't fit the accused, I'm quick to scrap it. We talk every day, and every day I understand him better, every day it gets easier to pick out connections, contacts, accomplices, and eventually to settle on a crime. He believes no one, understands nothing, fears everything. He tries to tell me that he doesn't know the first thing about revolutions or counter-revolutions, that all he ever wanted was to save himself, hide, wait it out, as that's all he's ever done, and where's the crime in that?

"'I listen to his voice, the very tempo of his speech, observe his eyes and his hands, and he starts to become transparent to me, familiar and even dear to me, and the hardest things to find – the details – suddenly become obvious. Here, every trifle matters: the place, the setting, the weather, the time of day. People can act one way in the morning, quite another in the evening. It's the details that make a painting more than the sum of its parts, that make it live. If the details are authentic, the painting will begin to speak to you. And then the moment arrives when the accused realises that I am right, that that is who he is, that I, like a father, have begotten and created him, and he confesses. This is the crucial stage, to which everything else has been leading. There's a sudden verve and brilliance in the stories this ordinary man begins to tell me about himself. All the fear has gone. He talks and talks, breathlessly, unstoppably, tells me astonishing things that I, the very person who brought him into the world, never even suspected. Every writer knows that the best parts of a book are never the ones he makes up and writes down later, but the ones that feel entirely new to him while he's writing them, when his characters have already come alive and are thinking and living for themselves. It's like that with us. Don't you see? There's no need for a court. It's just you and I."

'At this point, Chelnokov paused and gazed at me for a long time, as if trying to remember something, then looked away and left his desk. He rested his forehead against the wall, and his arms went limp. He was clearly exhausted. Then, with his back still turned, he said he would arrange for me to be moved from the cell I was sharing with ordinary criminals to solitary confinement, where, he believed, I would feel better and calmer.

'"No one will touch you for five days, so do whatever you like. Sleep round the clock, if that's what you want. I only ask one thing: that you give some serious thought to what I've been saying. Who if not you, a philosopher, can understand me?"

'Five days were enough for me to see that he was right, and when I was brought in again for questioning I told Chelnokov that he and his comrades were engaged in a sacred task – saving human beings – and that I was ready to help them and sign whatever they wanted me to sign. On one condition: that what he had said must precede my own confession in his final report, so that not only would members of my own organisation live forever, but so would his words, those words by which all of us can be explained and justified.'

Then Kuchmy returned to the topic of the sexual life of the literati. He was convinced, he said, that demographic policy all over the world would soon be based on the propagation of pure lines, as represented by writers. Writers, after all, are not only organic, undivided beings, they are also unusually fertile. According to even the most cautious estimates, some of the Russian greats have spawned more than a thousand direct descendants in their own works, although, if we judge by Dickens and Balzac, that's hardly the limit. He concluded the first hour of his lecture with the remark that all writers should be granted the title of Mother Heroine, and with it the full range of benefits and privileges accruing to this particular category of women. The mood was upbeat, the bell had rung and we had already got up from our seats, when he said, in a suddenly lifeless voice, that writers lack the maternal instinct: they are self-sufficient, which is why they always kill their favourite children. They are criminals and murderers.

The second hour was devoted to sociology. Kuchmy declared that a full and rigorous investigation of literary protagonists was long overdue. Comparison with data collected in conventional surveys would permit us to understand, *inter alia*, the correspondences between so-called art and so-called life in the most precise possible terms. It isn't just the quantity of characters that needs to be thoroughly analysed, he said, but age, social background, the number of marriages and children, educational history, professional status, housing conditions, which vary from era to era, and hundreds upon hundreds of other parameters, as well as personality types and happiness levels in childhood, maturity and old age, and what these depend upon, aside from age; not to mention the type of weather encountered in novels, food, colours, smells, illnesses, tastes, times of the day and of the year, moods, and, particularly in the case of Russia, the landscape, trees and flowers – an entire ecology, no less, which will lead to the reappraisal of some of our traditional notions regarding, for example, the duration of an evening in the nineteenth century: not two or three hours, as is usually thought, but about eighteen.

In his third lecture Kuchmy finally turned to the topic

of his series, although Nikolai Gogol, you couldn't help thinking, was not among his favourite writers. He took a couple of passing swipes at Gogol's excessive enthusiasm for Ukrainian exotica and second-hand plots before making a few unsuccessful jokes about his nose, after which, without our even noticing, he moved onto the story bearing that very name, 'The Nose'. We thought he would develop the parallel further – the entire lecture seemed to have been leading up to it – but no, he changed tack once more. Citing the scholar V.V. Vinogradov, Kuchmy said that the plot of the story is far from unique: the nose is the hero of many jokes, and a joke is precisely what Gogol intended with his first version of the tale, where everything that happened to Major Kovalyov turned out to be a dream. But then Gogol rewrote the story: the action began unfolding in reality and immediately seemed to hang in the air, turning into the purest, most ethereal fantasy. The story only gained from this transformation, becoming even stranger than it already was. But for Gogol, Kuchmy said, there was always more to the story of Kovalyov than its jokey, abstract conclusion, something much more terrifying, and this something is encoded in the dates of the action, which endow the entire tale with a quite different explanation and meaning.

Although the events presented in the second version are no longer Major Kovalyov's dream, the time in which they unfold is nevertheless tainted and distorted, a time never seen on earth; in other words, these events don't really occur at all. If this period of time is real, then it comes from the world of the devil, not God.

The nose vanishes from the Major's face on March 25, the most important day for all humanity – the Annunciation – when the fate of mankind was decided and changed, and when the path to salvation began. Ever since Adam, mankind's

46

sin and suffering had multiplied and grown; on the day of the Annunciation, the nations learned that they would be saved. Catholics celebrate this date on March 25, the Orthodox – on April 7, the day Kovalyov gets his nose back, and since the entire calendar and history of humankind begins with the Annunciation and the birth of Christ (that is to say, the new birth of man) and since there can be no history outside Christ, this interval of time is imaginary, non-existent, a time when the good news of Christ's birth had and had not been given to man, when humankind did and did not know that it would be saved and that Christ, the Son of God, would soon be sent into the world at long last, to redeem the sins of man with His blood. In essence, this discrepancy in dates and calendars, projected back two thousand years, is the main difference between the Orthodox and Catholic faiths, and this divergence, widening with every century, engenders a strange, truly demonic time, a time that doesn't exist and that increases all the while.

Gogol, Kuchmy would say, inherited from his mad mother a vision of hell that was so extraordinarily vivid and real that it could be neither denied nor forgotten. Hell, with its torments, sufferings and sinners, was always at his side; it began where Gogol ended and, perhaps, even took possession of him, at least in part, and lived within him. He spent his entire life explaining, processing and amplifying this constant proximity, from his earliest years of conscious existence, to eternal torments that could not be borne for even an instant (the ailments and aches that never left him were their antechamber, just as his abrupt, apparently puzzling decisions to change address or run away, his almost ecstatic, faith-filled passion for the road, betrayed his hope of hiding and finding salvation). Following the Pythagoreans and the Cabbalists, he used his date and place of birth, his own fate, to piece together an understanding of who exactly he was and of the role that had been ordained for him in the destinies of Russia and the world.

Gogol was born in a place where two religions, Catholicism and Orthodoxy, had intertwined and intermingled for centuries, where brothers in blood (Poles, Russians, Ukrainians) and brothers in faith were locked in the most intense, vicious and long-lasting of enmities, where Christians killed Christians – a place that could truly be described as demonic. Ukraine, the borderland (*ukraina*) of both Poland and Russia, was born of their mixing and their hatred. That frenzy of the unclean spirit which we find in Gogol came from his belief that the country was cursed, that in no other place on earth could this spirit flourish more than it did there. But this same belief also gave rise to the bombastic pathos of prophet and reconciler, unifier and mediator, teacher of life and herald of peace, brotherhood, union and tolerance between the Catholic and the Orthodox, not to mention Gogol's entire missionary activity, so badly misunderstood by his contemporaries, and his life after Ukraine, first in the Orthodox capitals of St Petersburg and Moscow, then in the Catholic capital of Rome, and the dream he eventually fulfilled: his journey to Jerusalem, to the home of primordial, undivided Christianity.

April 1 – Gogol's birthday according to the Gregorian Calendar – falls precisely midway between the Catholic and Orthodox Feasts of the Annunciation, in the belly of a dead, troubled time, when unclean forces are on the loose, but it is also the date when a compromise should have been reached, if it were ever to be reached, between the two Churches, when they could have come together, stood as one and destroyed this unclean time. Behind such mysticism lay Gogol's belief that he, like a messiah, was preordained to unite the Catholic and the Orthodox with his own person, perhaps even in his own person; this was the foundation of everything he did and wanted, his whole reason for living. But behind it there also lay madness, and reality, and terror, and the impossibility of fleeing and hiding from all the demonic forces that tempted and surrounded him, just as they had once tempted Christ in the desert. In his books, too, he only ever wanted to write what was radiant and beautiful, to be a teacher, a creator of all that was ideal, pure, harmonious and true, but he succeeded only in his caricatures, those incarnations of the unclean spirit rendered with almost demonically lifelike precision, succeeded only in depicting evil and farce, and when he burned the second part of *Dead Souls* before his death, it was his way of acknowledging that he was only capable of describing humanity's impurity and iniquity.

Our family moved to Tomsk, as I have already said, at the very end of 1963. I didn't want to go. Kuibyshev is my home town, I love this city, the Volga, the steppe, the warmth; I was leaving my friends and the girl I'd been in love with since school and very nearly married the day before our departure. But we had nowhere to live and nothing to live on, so we decided to be sensible and hold off till summer. That summer, though, I went on a field trip and never made it back to Kuibyshev. We stopped writing to each other, then she got married and I got married, both making terrible choices and both getting divorced soon after. Now we've started writing to each other again, meeting up once a year and wondering whether to come full circle and do what we promised to do. She's called Natasha, she has a little boy from her first marriage – young Kostya – and perhaps the only thing stopping me is the thought of how Kostya will take to me.

Although neither I nor my mother wanted to move, it was

clearly the right thing to do. My father's career in Kuibyshev never took off. His exceptional professionalism, energy, industriousness, conscientiousness – the list of positive qualities could easily be extended – had got him nowhere, and he felt increasingly depressed and cheated by life. The invitation from Tomsk was his last chance, as we realised all too well.

In Tomsk, I struck lucky on one count, at least: as I soon came to appreciate, its university was on the up (Kuibyshev's paled in comparison). Halfway through the third year, we began a course on the history of Siberia. It was taught by one Valentin Nikolayevich Suvorin, great-nephew of the publisher of Chekhov and others, and he certainly stood out among the usual run of professors in those years. I opted to complete my degree in Suvorin's department, and became his student a year later. Suvorin's fate repeated that of Kuchmy, albeit in far milder form, and although as personalities they were chalk and cheese, knowing Kuchmy made it easier for me to get along with Suvorin.

Suvorin had been living in Tomsk since '33, when he was exiled here from Moscow, having been sentenced, along with many other historians and archive specialists, for supposed White-Russian sympathies and connections. He'd been the favourite and, it seems, final student of Sergei Platonov, who was exiled to my home town in '31; my parents knew and remembered him well.[3] All this emerged in the course of our very first conversation; Suvorin and I, it turned out, had many memories in common – almost a common past.

Suvorin got off lightly in 1933 and his luck held out afterwards as well: Siberian exile protected him from any further punishments. If he'd stayed in the capital in the

---

3 S.F. Platonov (1860-1933), author of historical studies of sixteenth- and seventeenth-century Russia.

1930s and come out with the kind of comments he had made in Tomsk, he would have found himself in the camps soon enough. Certainly, I'd never seen anything like it, even though my social circle in Kuibyshev was unusually free-spirited and even free-thinking. What was more, Suvorin was a celebrity at the university, which meant he was a celebrity in the town as well, since there was nothing else in the town except the university (Tomsk was probably the only real university town we had at that time, apart from Tartu in Estonia). Regional party chiefs came and went, but each took good care of Suvorin.

They weren't the only ones to protect him. Suvorin chaired the leading department within the Faculty of History and Literature, which happened to be the faculty favoured by the town elite. Of the eight regional secret police bosses who worked here in the Stalin years, according to Suvorin himself, seven had children who studied under Suvorin – an additional safeguard. Suvorin's was the best Department of Siberian History in all Siberia and supplied almost half the faculty's published output, nearly all of which, remarkably enough, was written by Suvorin himself. This was due not to a fear of rivals, but to his pathological sex drive.

Suvorin arrived in Siberia from Moscow with a wife and one-year-old son in tow; a daughter was born in Tomsk a few years later, in '38. His wife, everyone said, was a sweet and unusually attractive woman who seemed untroubled by his endless philandering, but after one particularly scandalous episode she decided that enough was enough and they separated just before the war. In '53, immediately after Stalin's death, she moved back to Moscow with the children, and Suvorin settled into the life of a bachelor. He was past sixty by the time I arrived, but he loved women just as much as ever, and just as indiscriminately; in his tastes, at least, he was a true egalitarian.

Among his lovers I met students, seventy-year-olds, genuine beauties (he himself had an impressive, imposing presence) and grubby fieldwork cooks never seen sober who didn't look much like women at all.

The composition of Suvorin's department was determined exclusively by his love life: a female student who managed to hold on to him for any length of time – no easy task – would be taken on for graduate study by way of a commission, and if Suvorin was still seeing her three years later then he would write her dissertation before arranging her promotion within the faculty. This system ran so smoothly and suited everybody so well that not once during his life in Tomsk did Suvorin have a single graduate of the male sex. Until now. His decision to take me, his first and only such student, was motivated not by any loss of virility but by a desire shared, as far as I can tell, by all major scholars: the desire to leave behind disciples, a school. So I was lucky – very lucky.

Aside from his traditional course on the history of Siberia from the Palaeolithic to Stolypin's reforms in the early years of the twentieth century, Suvorin also had a side interest in the Schism, which he had been researching from all sides since before the Second World War. The history of Siberia, after all, is also the history of the Schism. The Old Believers who were exiled here from Russia in the seventeenth century, or fled here of their own accord, were the first to colonize and cultivate these lands. They were needed here, so the authorities didn't interfere with their faith, turning a blind eye to the fact that they crossed themselves with two fingers, not three, and processed around the church 'sunwise'. They lived for centuries in the remotest backwoods of Siberia, such as may still be found to this day, thinking, praying and praising God, and nobody so much as suspected their existence, just as they did not suspect anyone else's.

While researching the Schism, Suvorin amassed an enormous collection of Old Believer books and manuscripts, and every year he set off on field trips of his own, taking with him two or three students, and in later years only one – me. Following a strict plan, we went from district to district, village to village. Suvorin had a written-off but superbly restored 'Gazik' jeep, the only car that could more or less cope with Siberian roads. When even the Gazik could go no further, we would hire a horse in the nearest village or, more often, walk. The jeep was a recent acquisition; previously Suvorin had walked everywhere, but now, aged sixty, he was no longer up to it. We found our richest pickings in deserted villages that had either been abandoned over time or had been emptied during collectivisation, which hit Western Siberia especially hard. He learned their location from his students, many of whom had grown up in the sticks and knew the territory; in the summer, these same students, or their relatives, became our guides.

From my very first trip, I was struck by the ritual Suvorin would unfailingly observe in these empty, dead villages with their meadows long overgrown with bushes and with their log huts sunk in nettles and weeds almost up to their roofs. Before setting foot in a house, he would spend about a minute stroking the wood as if it were a dog, caressing and taming it, and he would only go in when he felt that he had been accepted, that nobody feared him. Once inside, however, he ransacked the hut in the blink of an eye, with the zeal and swagger of a burglar on a lucky streak, and never allowed me or anyone else to help him; then he gave us instructions as to how and where to pack the findings, if findings there were, and went onto the next dwelling. There, the same process was repeated. What astonished me most was the fact that he remembered every single village, whereas for me, whether it was a village that might have been abandoned in the last century if not earlier, or one that had stood empty only since the 1930s, or a recent post-war settlement, they all resembled old rural cemeteries, with their grass growing thick on the rich earth, their dampness, coolness and abundance of birds. And cemeteries, essentially, is what they were.

Aside from the books he quarried during his annual fieldwork, Suvorin purchased manuscripts from his own specialist suppliers in Tomsk. In or around May, just before he got himself ready for his next trip, he would give most of the manuscripts he'd acquired, read and catalogued over the previous year to the university library, keeping only a few for himself: those he found most interesting or still needed for his research. These gratuitous donations of manuscripts that in many cases had been paid for out of his own pocket were probably the main reason why both the city and the university authorities took such a sympathetic view of his passion for collecting and even went out of their way to help him. My trips with Suvorin – everything he showed me and told me, how he worked with his sources – represent ninety-nine per cent of my education, and even though by joining him I ended up losing Natasha, I was, perhaps, not wrong to do so.

I heard about Suvorin's field trips some six weeks after our move to Tomsk and immediately decided that I would do all I could to get him to take me. I knew nothing about Siberia – neither its nature, nor its people – but I was going to be living there a good long while. With Suvorin I would have the chance to see the deepest hinterland, those places worthy of the very name Siberia; few prospects could have been more appealing, but I had also discovered just how hard it was to get in with him. Every third student on the course was desperate to join him on his trips, they were a very capable group, and several had the advantage of knowing two or three languages as well as Siberia itself; everything around was theirs, while it would take me years to make this land my own, and even if Suvorin were to choose me I could hardly be as useful to him as the local lads. I understood all this, but that didn't stop me tagging along with the other candidates to his home in the middle of April.

Exactly how many people Suvorin would take with him each year remained a secret until the very last day. The selection process was fully democratic: like everyone else, I was asked why I wanted to go, who I was and where I came from. I told him and we spoke for quite some time about the Kuibyshev region, which had also been a periphery once upon a time and which, just like Siberia, was still densely populated with Old Believers and other sectarians. I kept the conversation going ably enough, but I could see I wasn't making much of an impression. It was only later, over tea, when Suvorin asked me some more casual questions about Kuibyshev and I mentioned Ilyin and a few other things that he became interested and wanted more details; then, as if starting over, we chatted on until midnight. When I was finally getting ready to leave, Suvorin suddenly asked if I wouldn't mind summarising Ilyin's teachings for him there and then. I said I was happy to do so, though I couldn't vouch for completeness or accuracy. He gave me several sheets of paper and went to another room to make some phone calls, so as not to distract me. My memories of Ilyin and all he had told me were still fresh, and it was easy enough to single out what I considered to be the most important bits of his teaching and reduce them to a dozen theses. When I finished just half an hour later, Suvorin was still on the phone, probably to a woman. I didn't disturb him, left the sheets on the table and went home.

There was no follow-up. Convinced I had no chance of being chosen, I planned to spend the summer in Kuibyshev with Natasha – in fact, I'd already written to her about it – but in May Suvorin unexpectedly called me at home and said that if I hadn't changed my mind and still wanted to go, he would take me; what was more, it would just be the two of us. Refusing was out of the question – and it would have been stupid, too. I wrote Natasha a short and shameless letter which made it perfectly clear that I was choosing the field trip over her (I'd always demanded complete honesty from her, and my letter was written in that spirit). Suvorin and I spent almost two months travelling across Siberia together, and in that time we became friends. Out on the road, he proved to be an easygoing, open sort of man, not remotely superior or offhand, and when we got back I found myself elected, as it were, to the vacant post of disciple and heir.

Aside from the specific history of the Schism, Suvorin was fascinated by how ideas evolve, by the very mechanics of change, whether from external influences or – his particular interest – internal causes. The path which the Old Believers travelled in the space of a hundred and fifty years, from staunch defence of every last feature of the Old Belief to an array of the most radical sects, demanded explanation. The Old Belief contained hundreds of branches, and even neighbouring villages often went about their faith in very different ways. Such variability is astounding, especially when you consider that it all grew from a single, undisputed root and in many cases was subject only to internal processes in virtually sterile, laboratory conditions: villages amid the Siberian bogs and taiga. What's more, this mushrooming of beliefs and tendencies, with mutations as rampant as in any geneticist's fruit fly, occurred even though nobody actually wanted to change anything – just the opposite: the aim was always to preserve the faith in its original holiness and purity. And least of all were these changes, these abrupt breaks with the past, visible to those who were themselves changing with such monstrous speed. Siberia, of course, was uniquely rich in material for observations of this kind, and the patterns of succession and evolution traced by Suvorin among the branches of the Old Belief were no less meticulous than those reconstructed in historical studies of the old Russian chronicles.

Beginning in April (though not every year), Suvorin would host seminars every Tuesday on the history of the Russian Church for those preparing to join him on his field trips. He would give a lecture of no more than an hour and then, over cups of tea, each of us would comment on what we had heard. We would talk deep into the night, rarely reaching a consensus, but Suvorin wasn't interested in making our views converge, and he limited his own role to providing information and, if we really insisted, his expert opinion based strictly on facts. For a long time I thought – and he made no secret of it – that he simply enjoyed listening to us chat: it was all so different from the usual university routine and so similar to what he had known in his youth. Later, I learned that he had also learned a lot of useful things for himself.

During our debates, we would come out with striking and sometimes magnificently paradoxical ideas. The combination of our excitement and his detachment created a free, uninhibited mood, and it was easy for him to isolate these flashes of inspiration which, however accidental and feebly substantiated, often found their way into his own research. Unfortunately, the unusual format of the Tuesday seminars meant that none of us, as far as I know, kept any records or summaries. It had been this way since the 1930s. Suvorin's lectures were so far removed from the conventional view of things that, for all his many patrons, such records would have cost him his life if they had fallen into the wrong hands.

He never prepared for his lectures, which were pure improvisation; we knew this, felt this, and readily followed his example. Here, too, there was a sense of freedom, a lack of completion and polish, an openness to error, and it was Suvorin who set the tone. It was only shortly before his death – not that Suvorin himself was in any hurry to take stock: neither he nor anyone else had any inkling of his approaching end, and he was still so full of life and energy – that he finally decided to go over what he'd told us at the seminars and tie it all together. He told me he'd made a start, but the only thing we found while sorting through his papers was a fragment of the first, introductory lecture.

The history of Russia and those Eastern Slavs who called themselves Russians interested him only from the time when Russia started to hive itself off from a single, common Christian culture and differentiate itself from other countries; in fact, such differences – whether in personality or culture – were the only thing that interested him.

Suvorin considered the Russian state to have been deliberately built from the very beginning not on the slow and ponderous growth of economic ties, on the reality of day-to-day life, but on ideas, on its understanding of its place and territory in the world of ideas, its understanding of its destiny, its mission, of what set it apart from the destiny of everyone else, brought and bound together those who lived here, and made of them a nation. Without this sense of otherness, there would be no Russia. It seems to have been born from a very feeble source – ever-deepening solitude. Either there was no one else around or there were only strangers: pagans, Muslims. The Russians had been abandoned and forgotten by their brothers in faith, they were surrounded by enemies, and thought they were the last ones standing. This sense of being alone and being the last quickly became the centre of the Russian way of thinking and was quickly recognised by both the authorities and the people as the chief support and foundation of the state.

Suvorin had a rather peculiar notion of the development of the human race. He thought that people have two genomes: a biological one, like all living organisms, and a second one – the 'genome of the soul' – which starts to be formed after the child is born. No sooner did man appear on earth, Suvorin would say, than he realised that his life here is but a negligible fraction of all life, and earth a negligible fraction of the world created for him by God. Among the thousands and thousands of tribes who have walked the earth since the creation of humankind, not one has ever thought otherwise. Every man, by learning to live in the big world of God where even death is the start of new life (and what is faith, if not a way of learning about that world?) by learning to penetrate and comprehend its construction, its rules and laws, its aims and meaning, has always thought of it as one whole and adapted to it accordingly. The worlds of man have always been incomparably broader, larger and more complex than the world inhabited by animals and birds ignorant of God. There have been a great many such worlds, and the various nations that have inhabited them have had only their earthly, smallest part in common, which is why it's so hard, even impossible, to understand other nations, other cultures, and why, if an enemy has occupied your country, he has occupied only your land, and you will manage not only to survive but even to recoup your losses if you keep your faith.

Drawing a parallel between the history of the human race and the history of Russia, Suvorin said that it was precisely the big world which had played the leading role in the formation of the Russian state, that it was for the big world that it was built and fitted; few of those who had made this state had thought about the land itself, which could differ to a staggering degree from one part of Russia to another. That was still the time of childhood, still the time of infancy and nursing, but the child was not loved, it was despised and shamed; its only schooling was the stick, and the nation that grew from it was like the ugly duckling convinced it would turn into a swan, waiting and living only for this. Both then and later, this discrepancy gave rise to serious problems and complexes, and to a very uneven development: in the big world the nation left everyone, or almost everyone, in its wake, while on earth its development was retarded and deficient.

The history of the Russian state began in the fifteenth century, under Vasily the Dark, Grand Prince of Moscow. Despite twenty-five years of internal strife and despite Vasily's own imprisonment and blinding, the state grew and grew, and did so again during the reign of his son, Ivan III. But it was under Vasily, as the state began to take shape and came together on the map, that the need arose to understand where this was all leading, what it was all for. At this point, the event took place that 'made' Russian history. In 1439, at the Council of Florence, the Catholic and Orthodox churches sealed a union after four centuries of schism; the Turks were laying siege to Constantinople, preparing to storm it any day, and the Orthodox Patriarch, counting on the pope's assistance and trusting that he would be able to summon a new crusade and save Byzantium, accepted the union and acknowledged the primacy of Rome. But the popes were not what they used to be, few took up the cross, and the Byzantine Empire fell fourteen years later.

Russia and the Russian Church were represented in Florence by Isidore, the Greek Metropolitan of Kiev, who was in favour of the union and supported it at the Council. On his return to Moscow he was deposed and thrown into prison, and Russia became the only one of the Orthodox churches present at the Council to reject the union. This was Russia's first independent act and its first demonstration of what it understood that independence to mean. The Orthodoxy which the Russians had been constructing since the arrival of the Tatars, outside any contact with Byzantium, and the attitude towards faith which had been worked out over generations, with encirclement and isolation at its heart, were brought to completion in Florence. It was after Florence that Russia perceived itself as the sole, last guardian of the true faith. In its eyes, the fall of Constantinople was confirmation of the punishment meted out to the Greek Church for its treachery and betrayal: the Lord would have saved it, just as He has always saved the righteous, but they, the patriarchs, went and ruined everything. And when, shortly after the empire had fallen, the Greeks also severed the union, it was clear to all in Russia that they were merely following in the footsteps of the Russian Church, which alone had remained steadfast and faithful to God. And so, in the words of Jesus Christ, the last had come first. Now and forever.

Over tea one of us asked Suvorin about Patriarch Nikon and his New Jerusalem Monastery of the Resurrection.[4] How could a replica of Jerusalem's Church of the Holy Sepulchre,

---

4 Nikon (born Nikita Minin, 1605-1681): Patriarch of the Russian Orthodox Church between 1652 and 1658, when he unofficially resigned from his position and moved to New Jerusalem, outside Moscow.

known to the Orthodox as the Church of the Resurrection, have even been considered, never mind built? How could the principle of sacred space have been jettisoned? And why had this happened specifically in Russia? At first there was a slowness and vagueness about Suvorin's reply that took us by surprise, as if he were dithering and hadn't even made up his own mind. This was strange and out of character, not least because there was nothing very complicated about what he was saying, nothing that could warrant so much caution and uncertainty. Or perhaps this had nothing to do with a lack of confidence, perhaps he just wanted to turn off the path onto which we were trying so hard to coax him and by which he felt constrained. Clearly, we wanted more precise answers than the questions permitted and he, with his love of precision and completeness, was dodging the issue. We expected answers in the same language we used to put the questions, but he was already moving onto a different level, into a different lexicon; he was more interested in Nikon's character and personality – that was something warm, something alive – than in what Nikon had built and whether or not he was in tune with his country. But Russia also fascinated Suvorin, and he considered our questions perfectly legitimate. He had long begun to outgrow what he had taught us, but our opinions still counted; after all, we'd learnt everything from him.

'It's beautiful on the Istra River,' he said, as if this explained everything, 'and there could be no better place for the monastic life. After his removal from Moscow, Nikon settled in New Jerusalem and did not leave until he was exiled to the far north, to the Monastery of St Ferapont. He dreamed of going back to New Jerusalem, or at least being buried there, and eventually Tsar Fyodor allowed him to return, but Nikon never saw his monastery again: he died on the way. He was, however, buried in the Church of the Resurrection – the very place he had prepared for himself before his exile.

'All in all,' Suvorin said, 'Nikon founded three monasteries: the Iversky Monastery, the Monastery of the Cross, and the New Jerusalem Monastery of the Resurrection. The last, the youngest, was his favourite; the others led up to it. In 1653, in the Novgorod lands on the shores of Valdai Lake, which he renamed Holy Lake, Nikon began building a monastery in honour of the miracle-working icon of the Mother of God of Iversk and of the newly canonised Metropolitan Philip, whose relics he had transferred from Solovetsky Monastery. The Iversky Monastery was to be built, as New Jerusalem would be, "according to the image and likeness", replicating as far as possible the contours of the Iviron Monastery on Mount Athos. During its construction, Nikon travelled frequently between Moscow and Valdai and almost always broke his journey in Resurrection Village (*Voskresenskoe*), which was thirty miles from Moscow and belonged to the provincial governor Roman Boborykin. It stood on a high bank of the twisting, fast-flowing Istra, and if they arrived while it was still light Nikon would ask his entourage to prepare his lodgings while he went for a stroll, always alone. He liked it here, and occasionally he would live in Resurrection Village for two or three days at a time before moving on.

'Nikon began the construction of New Jerusalem Monastery in 1656, just as soon as he received the consent of Tsar Alexei. It was founded next to a village on a patch of land surrounded on three sides by a bend of the Istra. In the middle of this patch was a thickly forested hill which sloped gently down to the south and to the west, while to the north, over the river, it ended abruptly in a steep, almost vertical bank; it was on this hill that the monastery was to be built. During the first year the forest was cleared and a long, deep channel, or perhaps it was just a ditch, was dug around two sides of the hill, and the earth was carried up on carts, raising the southern side.

'The work proceeded apace and by the following year, 1657, the skeleton of a wooden citadel with eight towers was in place, a fraternity had been assembled, and the Church of the Life-Bearing Resurrection of Christ, to whose consecration Nikon invited Alexei and his entire entourage, had been completed. Nikon consecrated the new cathedral himself. Then he took the Tsar to see the places he loved most – along the river, around the monastery – told him what he wanted to build and where, and on the way back, when they had already climbed the hill which is now known as the Mount of Olives and were standing side by side, gazing at the monastery under construction, at the river and the range of hills beyond it, the Tsar said: "Truly did the Lord bless this place from the very beginning, that there might be a monastery upon it, for it is beautiful like Jerusalem."

'One might think it was Nikon who put this idea in the Tsar's mind, telling him as they were walking, about the Holy Land and Jerusalem – its gardens, hills, springs, groves – and constantly hinting at parallels with the new monastery. The parallels remained beneath the surface: not once did Nikon name Jerusalem and his monastery in the same breath, but there was no need to because they saw before them the Istra, its hills and copses, but they spoke of the Jordan, Jerusalem and the Church of the Holy Sepulchre. He was right to restrain himself and avoid any direct comparison: it gave Alexei the feeling that he had come up with the idea himself, as well as the joy of telling Nikon about the resemblance between his monastery and Jerusalem and of seeing Nikon's delight at hearing this, seeing that he had either guessed, or suggested, the very thing that Nikon so desired. Still rejoicing that he had managed to please Nikon – the Tsar always wanted those around him to be happy – and that the visit itself had gone so well, Alexei wrote a letter to Nikon a few days later from another monastery, the Savvino-Storozhevsky Monastery in Zvenigorod, in which the name "New Jerusalem" appeared for the first time and in which he granted his permission, consent and support for Nikon's labour – the labour of his life.'

Just telling this story put Suvorin himself in fine spirits. He was visibly delighted that Alexei had shown himself to be such a warm and intelligent man, that the Tsar and Nikon had got on so well, and that everything had been resolved to everyone's satisfaction and with so little trouble. Looking at his smiling face at that moment, I – and, I'm sure, not only I – thought how good life can be, especially when you don't know what tomorrow will bring. Then Suvorin also remembered what happened next between the Tsar and Nikon, and continued in a very different voice, one that was dull, even bitter:

'There's plenty of evidence to suggest that Nikon was expecting the beginning of the end of the world either in 1666 – the more likely date – or after a further thirty-three years (the span of the Saviour's life on earth). He was no exception. It's well known that in both the Western and Eastern Churches the dates for Easter had been fixed no further than 1666 and, despite the vogue for rationalism, expectation of the end was all but universal.

'If the Old Believers saw in the Schism within the Russian Church that stemmed from Nikon the main corroboration of the fact that the last days were upon them, then Nikon himself, in amending the holy books and sacred rites, was preparing the Orthodox Church not for the continuation of life, but for those same last days, which could not arrive for as long as Moscow, the "Third Rome", persisted in worshipping God incorrectly. Nikon knew that all Orthodox believers had to be united, above all the Russians, Greeks and Ukrainians, and that there should be no difference whatsoever in how they praised God, or else, when the hour struck, they would not acknowledge one another as brothers and the Lord would not acknowledge them. And secondly: so that Christ might come down to earth once more and save mankind, he, Nikon, should build in Rus a church just like the Church of the Resurrection in Jerusalem and thereby complete the centuries-long relocation of the Holy Places – their names, realia and sacred history – to Russian soil, and with them the transformation of Rus into the Holy Land.

'Here,' Suvorin said, 'we must remember the fate of Nikon and his main adversaries: Avvakum, Ivan Neronov, Pavel Kolomensky. All of them, both Nikon and the leaders of the Schism, were either Mordvins themselves or from Mordvin lands, either recent converts or from the land of converts; faith for them, or for those around them, was still new and fresh, not yet a ritual, and they had all the passion and devotion of proselytes. To them everything was alive and raw, everything touched them personally; through their piety and devotion they had to catch up with those whose faith went back many generations, and they quivered at the thought of what would have happened if they had not been baptised in time for the Last Judgement. It seemed to them that they were the last to have managed to do so. For the most part, they were bookish types who valued the written word, who had learned their faith from Scripture and the Church Fathers. Indifferent, ritualised faith was alien to them all, regardless of character or temperament, and they fought it and resisted it as best they could. Since their own faith, in many cases, had not been handed down to them from their fathers and grandfathers, it became a matter of the most rigorous observance, and they stopped at nothing in their search for the truth. Recent conversion obliged them, in their devotion, their righteousness and their deeds, to redeem the sins of their ancestors, whose cult they still honoured and perhaps even practised.

'And yet, their faith was divided. They knew the Christianity of tradition, the Christianity that surrounded them: the main thing in it was the cross, and the sign of the cross – no more was needed. Crosses scared off unclean forces and saved people; they were everywhere, and they were bare: without Christ. The similarity of the sounds – cross and Christ, *krest, Khristos* – allowed people to combine them and eventually squeeze out Christ. Christ was nowhere, neither on the bell-tower nor on the believer's chest; there was only the cross – so similar to the sword: blade, crossguard, hilt – with which they pierced the enemy and nailed him to the spot, as if Christ really had come to bring not peace, but the sword. And another thing: the icon painters were able to depict Christ's humanity, but his divinity was beyond them, or at any rate it came out weaker, less complete than his human nature, and so the cross – an instrument of torture, but also the symbol of the crucifixion, of the suffering endured by God for man – became for the Orthodox the symbol of Christ's divine nature, obscuring and eclipsing His humanity, of which Scripture says so much.

'In their youth Nikon and his fellow Mordvins reread the New Testament (and in some cases the Old Testament, too) with fresh eyes, and what astonished them was the virtual absence in Holy Scripture of anyone except Jews. In the New Testament there are the Jews who crucified Christ and there are the Jews who acknowledged Him and followed Him, and that's about it, or at any rate Christ doesn't know, and doesn't want to know, about anyone else, and He makes this perfectly clear. Only in the letters of the Apostles do other nations appear, but their faith, too, has been learnt from the Jews. The narrowness of this world, its insularity, was impossible for them to ignore. It wasn't even clear how the Jews could be judged when there was no one to judge them, no one to find them guilty. And above all: there was no Holy Rus in the Gospels, no new chosen people, no keeper of the true faith, no saviour of mankind. Many Old Testament prophets had foretold the coming of the Messiah, but no one had foretold the new chosen people, and Christ did not even seem to have suspected its existence.

'The only way of reconciling Holy Rus and Holy Scripture was through a symbolic reading purged of history, of everything that actually happened. The notion of sacred space had played an enormous role in Christianity since its earliest days, the sacredness of anything and everything that was related to Christ, that had either come into contact with Him or had at least been close to Him and had received and preserved a part of His holiness. This was important for the Russian Church, too, but in Russia an attempt was made to understand the New Testament in a purely verbal, figurative fashion, to rip the events of the Gospels from their Palestinian setting, from the reality of Palestinian life, and even from time; to transfer even the names, buildings and actions to a different place, while preserving untouched their holiness and power. This attempt succeeded and permitted everything to be created afresh in Russia: the holy people, the Holy Land, and Jerusalem – the holy city. The sacredness of place was destroyed, leaving only the sacredness of the name. The single most important component of Christianity was lost and vanquished: its historicism, everything that made the life and fate of Jesus Christ unique, that made it linear not circular, irrevocable and unrepeatable.'

Suvorin died in October '65, when I was in my third year of postgraduate study and I'd just typed up a draft of my dissertation to give him to read. He couldn't have chosen a more appropriate place to meet his fate: he had only two passions in life, work and women, and didn't squander his energies on anything else. It was the second passion, which was really his first, that did for him.

He died while still in the prime of life: he was sixty-five, but barely looked fifty. He died in the flat of one of his postgraduates, Nadya Polozova, and if evil tongues were to be believed, not just in her flat but in her bed, right on top of her. These stories stayed around for a long while. Nadya was systematically hounded and then, to draw a line under the whole episode, kicked out of university.

Nadya was widely disliked and considered stupid, if not insane. She managed to annoy everyone by insisting on being met off the tram, whatever the occasion, and being accompanied back again to the stop at the end of the evening. She couldn't go on her own, she said, because she was afraid of dogs. We thought this was just her way of flirting and, when duty beckoned, we cursed her soundly. But actually, she was telling the truth. A month before Suvorin's death she and I were crossing a courtyard when she noticed a little mutt in the distance and immediately grabbed my arm, squeezed it and shoved me forward as hard as she could, so that I was standing between her and the dog and, as it were, protecting her. When I looked round I could see she was clenching her teeth and doing her best not to scream; her whole face was quivering – eyes, cheekbones and especially lips. When the dog went off, Nadya burst into tears.

It all seemed very exaggerated and ridiculous, and I asked her sarcastically where she had acquired her canine phobia. She stroked my arm and explained, tearfully and penitently, that she hadn't been scared of dogs at all until she was two, in fact she'd quite liked them, but then her mother had had to go off somewhere and she'd been left for a long time with just her dad, who was terrified of them, far more than she was now. A sheepdog had bitten him when he was a child and almost killed him, and he couldn't see a dog without screaming. In the past she'd been the same, but she'd coached herself out of it. She fell silent and I realised that she was waiting for me to praise her and show my approval. Not knowing what to say, I kissed her hand. She calmed down a bit, let go of my arm and walked alongside me, still moaning about her bad luck: whenever someone accompanied her, there was never a dog in sight – today was an exception – but if she was alone, they'd be right there waiting for her.

The persecution of Nadya was seen as a sign of love and reverence towards Suvorin, whom, according to the general consensus, she'd literally fucked to death. Everyone agreed that Nadya was not his type and put the longevity of their relationship – it had gone on for more than five years, ever since her second year of study – down to her immoderate sexual appetite and endless pestering. But that's all lies. Nadya wasn't just thrown out of the university; soon afterwards, she was forced out of the town as well. Some five years later I happened to see her at a pedagogical conference in Kemerovo and she'd aged terribly, even though she wasn't yet thirty. We were standing in the same queue in the canteen and she must have recognised me straight away, but I only worked out who she was when I saw a woman doing everything she could to avoid me noticing her. I ignored these ploys, went up to Nadya, tried to look overjoyed at seeing her and asked her how she was doing. She hadn't got her PhD – although I remembered that Suvorin had managed to write her dissertation before he died – was working in a school teaching history from antiquity to the present, hadn't married and had no regrets. We chatted until the next session.

If truth be told, I feel sorry for Nadya. Suvorin seduced her coolly enough – stylishly, even – before my very own eyes and in my own home, and when they withdrew to my father's study I would have happily swapped places with him. He hadn't had a lover like her for years: she provided him with drink, food, clothes, and did so unobtrusively, without pressure. In fact, I met some people who not only thought but said out loud, that now he might finally settle down. Who could have known how it would all pan out? She was unlucky, of course. This whole story of his death, regardless of where exactly it happened – on her or beside her – broke Nadya, and it's hard to imagine her recovering, just as it's easy to envy him.

After Suvorin's death the main question on everyone's mind was the fate of his collection, and in particular his manuscripts. The university library, which had long got used to receiving a dozen or more manuscripts from him every year, didn't move a muscle, convinced that it was the collection's rightful owner. After the mandatory six months, it would send a researcher to fetch the entire collection and start processing it: nice work for someone – a first-class dissertation on a plate – and plenty were interested. But things turned out differently. Suvorin had never written a will, and that was no surprise: he had never spoken about death and never even seemed to think about it. The library was delighted, only for it to transpire that Suvorin had direct heirs. Everyone had forgotten all about them, but they existed, and in the end the courts – at both regional and republic level – found in their favour. The university's position, it must be said, was fairly strong: firstly, it was Suvorin himself who had always handed over the manuscripts gratis while he was alive; then there was the somewhat dubious legality of the field trips; and thirdly and most importantly, the library had promised to preserve the manuscripts as a single collection by which to remember him and perpetuate his name. The last was a powerful argument, but the court still came down on the side of the heirs.

Of Surovin's closest relatives – his wife, whom he had never officially divorced, his son, who was thirty-four, and his daughter – only the son came for the funeral, saying that his mother and sister couldn't afford the tickets. He was a strange lad: a hulk of a man with blue eyes, almost albino hair and a simple peasant's face (as everyone noted with pleasure) who arrived carrying a small suitcase in one hand and a wicker basket in the other containing three charming kittens. He took the kittens with him to the funeral, explaining, with a sweet smile, that they were scared of being left alone in a town they didn't know and he couldn't bear to traumatise them. He spent precisely two days in Tomsk. Suvorin had left no money, only debts, albeit small ones, and it was money that his son Alexander so desperately needed. He didn't seem to have enough even for the return flight, and he offered the manuscripts to the library for just two thousand roubles – an exceptionally good deal. But the library was still convinced that it would get the collection for nothing, and refused point-blank. So then he turned to me.

I was run off my feet with the funeral arrangements and had no time for the manuscripts. So he had to negotiate with the university on his own and showed up for an appointment in the rector's office with kittens still in tow; all that came of it was an embarrassing, completely pointless row. Before his departure, he set about trying to persuade me once more that the university was digging its heels in for nothing: the court would undoubtedly side with the family, and he repeated his offer to sell the manuscripts for two thousand. In Moscow, no doubt, he could have got far more for them, but the memory of his father was dear to him and he wanted the documents to remain in Tomsk. A lawyer we knew also thought his family would easily win in court, if it came to that. As he was leaving, Alexander asked if I could lend him a hundred roubles. I did so and we were already at the airport when he suddenly suggested that I should get the money together over the next six months and buy the manuscripts myself, otherwise my research would grind to a halt. Would it really be so hard for me to find a couple of thousand roubles, either on my own or with the help of some of Suvorin's other pupils? It wasn't a bad idea; in fact, he always seemed to display a strange combination of common sense and idiocy.

My grandfather had died two months before this conversation, leaving my father fifteen hundred roubles in his will. At a family meeting it was decided that this money should be given to me in the form of a new car, a Moskvitch, as belated compensation for my agreeing to leave Kuibyshev. My father had had a bad conscience about this for some time, especially after it became clear that Natasha and I had split up as a result of the move, and he had been looking for a way to make it up to me. A Moskvitch would have been a treat, but I had already given some thought to what Suvorin's offspring had told me and decided he had a point: the money would be better spent on the manuscripts – without them, I really would be stuck. I had a word with my mother, then my father, and both were surprisingly quick to agree: the money, my dad told me, was mine to use as I saw fit. Two months later, when the issue of the inheritance was finally resolved, I wrote to Alexander in Moscow, offering all the money I had – 1800 roubles. A week later I got a telegram: fine, send the paperwork.

There was one other thing I had to take care of without delay. I didn't want anyone in the university thinking I'd somehow walked off with Suvorin's library, especially now that it had lost two hundred roubles in value. That would have been catastrophic for my career and everything else. In fact, I would probably have met the same fate as Nadya Polozova. Having prepared my lines in advance, I went to see the rector and gave a detailed account of the entire story and of every conversation I'd had with Suvorin's son. Eventually, I got what I was after: he said I'd done the right thing and declared me a true friend of Tomsk, a man who had spent his last kopecks rescuing manuscripts for the university. We agreed I would hand over all Suvorin's books to the university without delay but there was no rush with the manuscripts: we would wait until the library had scraped together enough money to buy them off me for the price I'd paid. Then the whole affair was forgotten and nobody, needless to say, came up with the cash, but by allowing all and sundry to use Suvorin's collection, I have managed to hold onto a reputation for decency and even altruism.

Half a year later, when the archive had already been moved into my flat, a man by the name of Kobylin turned up and told me that he had sold manuscripts to Suvorin for many years, naming some of the most interesting items in the collection. He was willing to start supplying new ones to me, if I wanted them. Needless to say, I did. Kobylin's manuscripts and the little he told me about himself are the basis for the work that follows here. In fact, they were all I had to go on, for Kobylin met all my attempts to persuade him to take me to his source with categorical refusal.

The first items he offered for purchase were not Old Believer manuscripts, but books, diaries and other papers that had belonged to a French theatre director, Jacques de Sertan, who had owned an itinerant troupe of actors – that was as much as I could decipher on my own. They were written in Breton, and three years passed before I managed to find somebody in Siberia who knew the language and agreed to translate for me. I found him right under my nose, in the next house along, just when I was on the verge of giving up and travelling to Moscow to flog my wares to the first taker. But that was the last thing I wanted to do, or else why would I have held onto the diary for so long, month after month, coming up with one excuse after another? Now all that waiting had paid off.

The translator's name was Misha Berlin. He was a gloomy, deeply unhappy man. His father, Paul Berlin, a French Jew, ended up in Moscow on Comintern business in the early 1930s and stayed on in the French section until the winter of 1939. After France capitulated, he was arrested and died in a camp in the northern Urals when the war was all but over. Misha's mother was Russian, and after her husband's imprisonment she and Misha were exiled from Moscow to Irkutsk. Just like my father, she was a doctor, a urologist; later, in the sixties, she and Misha moved to Tomsk, where her sister was living.

Though he had no memory of his father – he was arrested when his son was not yet two – Misha idolised him and was even obsessed by him; in fact, the entire home was a shrine to Paul Berlin and to everything French. Misha had a superb knowledge of French history and literature, especially medieval verse, which he had always enjoyed translating for his own pleasure. His father was from Brest, he had spoken

Breton since childhood, and Misha could read and speak it, too.

Jacques de Sertan's biography coincided with that of Paul Berlin to an extraordinary degree. Both came from Brittany, both, having arrived in Russia, spent exactly eleven years there, and both were exiled to Siberia; Sertan died en route, in the village of Dry Ravine (*Sukhoi Log*), having already crossed the Urals, while Berlin, who had another five years ahead of him, spent them in a camp a few hundred miles to the north, near Krasnoturinsk, and died there in April '45. Berlin and Sertan arrived in Moscow on one and the same day, January 14; both were exiled to Siberia on July 17; the convoys to which they were attached both passed through Dry Ravine; and both men died at the age of forty-four. This was all very peculiar, and as we were translating the diary day after day, page after page, I noticed, with some surprise, that Misha was more and more inclined to think that Sertan and his father were somehow connected; it was a mad idea, but from time to time I also felt something similar. In any case, the endless parallels between the lives of Sertan and Paul Berlin, which Misha immediately identified and expounded in detail, could not fail to astonish us both. The resemblance affected Misha far more powerfully than it affected me, needless to say, and from the very first day of our work on the translation he, lacking any personal memories of his father, started supplementing what he had heard from his mother with bits from the diary, as if he considered Sertan's life to be up for grabs and wanted to take it for himself.

Sertan as such was of no real interest to Misha, whereas for me it was the other way round. Though I had no strong feelings about either man, Sertan was closer and more alive to me than Paul Berlin. Stupidly – and I remember this well – I went out of my way to protect Sertan from Misha, often without being too civil about it, which led to one argument after another. The playing field was far from level. For Misha, nothing could matter more, while here was I advocating some abstract notion of fairness.

It took a while for us to really get going on the translation. Initially, that wasn't even the plan. All I wanted was some idea, however general, of what the diary contained. For me, the life story of a French theatre director in Russia was more a welcome distraction, a curiosity, than an object of research in its own right. No doubt, it would have been very interesting to know why it was that a group of exiles took a notebook written in a language none of them knew all the way to Sibera and then – or else how had it survived? – looked after it tenderly for three whole centuries. This might have shed some light on the history of that sect, or that branch of the Old Belief, whose manuscripts Kobylin had brought me together with the diary, but I was far from imagining that the diary itself was the key to everything, that that was exactly where I had to begin.

I found Misha Berlin in May 1969, soon after Victory Day. We met up every day until the summer, always at my place. On Misha's first visit I learned that the notebook written in Breton was a diary, I learned who had kept it and when, and I learned bits and pieces – unreliable bits and pieces, as it later turned out – about the fate of the author. My initial curiosity was sated, but we continued to meet up.

Misha probably interested me no less than Sertan. I had always been fascinated by anyone with a direct link to the Revolution, anyone who had been close to it and those who made it. There was no one of that ilk in our family. As a rule, we kept as far away from politics as possible, no one more so than my parents. We never got involved if we could help it; we just observed. Misha, on the other hand, was both insider and spectator; after all, it was his father, not he, who had taken part in it, and even his father had a very different perspective from those who had lived their whole lives in Russia. Paul Berlin, you might say, had tried on the clothes he found here, but never really got to wear them himself. True, he died in Russia, and died just like those who did wear them, but that changed little. There was more to his fate than the special bond you find in our country between victims and executioners, or the way they often switch places; though he believed as we did, he came to this faith by a different route, and the form in which his faith had been preserved in Misha was something else again. It seemed important to me to know what that form was: to know how Misha saw his father and how far he had moved away from him.

Every new coincidence we found between the fates of Sertan and Paul Berlin would almost inevitably give rise to yet another conversation about Misha's father, putting all further progress on ice. I think it was during our third meeting, once we had already got to know each other a bit and had set out our stalls for a long friendship where we could talk about anything without beating around the bush or biting our tongues, that, having barely sat down to translate, we stumbled across another parallel and I suggested having a break and a drink. I came up with a personal anniversary as a pretext and told Misha, after the very first shot, that I loved him, called him my best friend, and thanked Sertan for bringing us together – but now it was time to talk about something else. Then, after we had gone to the shop for a second bottle, I lost the plot. I was always forcing things, and seemed incapable of keeping my friendships on an even keel. I needed change, movement. I've met very few people who share this feeling, so most of my friendships have petered out quite quickly.

On this occasion, I suddenly took offence at God knows what – I suppose it was the fact that it looked like I didn't love my father as much as he loved his; actually I'd forgotten his father had died and mine hadn't, and then I remembered, but even that didn't stop me asking: did Misha really not understand that if his father had won the victory which he had dreamed of and fought for, then France and Brittany would have ended up like Russia or even worse; after all, pupils often outdo their teachers. I told him that of course I felt sorry for his father – you wouldn't wish a death like that on your own worst enemy – and yes, I was sure Paul was a good, kind man, but that wasn't enough. Maybe he had never wanted to kill anyone personally, but what about everyone else: they hadn't wanted to either, so much so that it took a third of the country to die before their frenzy abated. In fact, we should probably be grateful for the fact that at a certain point they forgot about other people and started butchering one another, getting so carried away with it that they were still doing it now. No doubt, I probably said all this rather more gently, and I didn't insult him directly: it all came out more like a question, though not one I was entitled to ask. And a question was how he understood it, because he'd been saying the same sort of thing to his mother for many years. Not once had she given him an answer. To me he gave the following reply, word for word: 'You can't equate the murdered with the murderers.'

We both knew that there was more to it than that in those years, so I said, 'But Misha, they often switched places.'

'No,' he replied, 'the murdered never became murderers.'

'Of course they didn't,' I said, 'but many of the murdered had murdered themselves. Just think how many secret policemen were shot – they didn't even spare each other.'

'Not all the murdered were murderers.'

'Not all,' I agreed, 'and it was never anyone's intention to become such. As children, they were just like any other children, and even later the only thing they really cared about was universal happiness, but they were told that this was what they had to do, that there was no other way – and, sad to say, there were few who hesitated. Some, of course, did it with great gusto, others from a sense of duty, but refusing was the exception, not the rule. And why?' I asked him. 'Why was it the exception?'

He realised I was asking about his father.

'Seryozha,' he said, 'my father was innocent of the crime for which he was charged and killed; you know this yourself and I think you agree with me. Now for your own accusation. My father never killed anyone, and in my view it's wrong to judge a man for crimes he hasn't committed, just as it's wrong to judge anyone by the example of others. Now let's take the ideas which my father professed and which, you are convinced, had to make him a murderer – and if he didn't become one, it was only because he ran out of time. In my view these are the very same ideas of equality, goodness, justice and happiness that have always existed and will always exist. It's not about the ideas, it's about the people who absorb them and the means by which they spread them. We all know that these ideas have never once been put into practice in ordinary life. But if we were to abandon them – that would be the end, the end of everything.

'It seems to me,' Misha would say, 'that the only place man can attain goodness, equality, happiness and justice is within himself and only he can know how much progress he's made. If he wants to attain them fully, without compromise, such as only saints ever manage to achieve, he should probably begin by leaving everyone and living on his own. In the past, people used to go off to the desert to do this, and later the monastery, and that made perfect sense. There used to be a rule, observed by some if not all, that when a man abandoned "the world" for the monastery he was supposed to obtain the consent of his family, because to choose a sinless life by causing pain and grief to your loved ones is itself a sin – good should not be the cause of evil. Times changed and fewer people chose the monastic life, but trying to begin afresh while staying in the same place turned everything into a lie; so it had always been, and so it would remain. To avoid this lie, people who stayed in the world had only one option: to make a clean break with the past, strike it out of their life, erase it for its imperfection. A man leaving for the monastery can leave his own past at the same time, not so the man who remains, yet neither have the right to touch the past, if the past is not theirs alone.

'A man holds no power over another person's past,' Misha said, 'or rather, even if he does have this power, he cannot and must not use it. It's wrong to destroy a past shared with other people, wrong to clear a space for a new truth. And another thing: God has arranged things in such a way that the good you wish to bring to all will not redeem the evil you bring to those nearest to you. Good depends very much on distance. The good directed at those you love is always greater than the good distributed among all. If you cause pain to your loved ones for the sake of everyone else, the evil will outweigh the good; it's as simple as that.

'Of course, it's not easy to accept that you have to leave, that everything you've understood has meaning only for you, that even those closest to you, those you've spent your entire life with, those you've loved, who've borne your children, are unwilling and unable to share this with you, that they shove it back down your throat, stop up their ears, anything so as not to hear, not to know what seems to you most pure, most beautiful, most bountiful, what you dream of giving to all while leaving nothing in reserve, knowing that your gift will never run dry, that these are the loaves which, however much you break off, will never diminish – but your loved ones shove piece after piece back down your throat and refuse to understand. So then the practical realisation of the idea begins. Why do they reject something so beautiful, why don't they want to accept it, why won't they exchange evil for good, or are they just foolish children and isn't it your duty – as father, as teacher – to take them by the hand and lead them onto the right path?

'There's nothing more dangerous than teaching,' Misha would say. 'A father doesn't answer for his son, nor a son for his father, but a teacher answers for his pupils and disciples. You must renounce teaching. People say that it's a sin to know something good and not to teach it, not to pass it on, but that isn't true. If you're a teacher, you need power. Power increases the efficacy of your lessons many times over, and you will want to have more and more of it, you'll want to exploit it, enjoy it.

'Such a terrible thing – to reject your past, to write off all, or almost all, your life. Everything that was in it is declared evil and false, torn out by the roots, and no one can emerge from this process with their health intact. Yes, the thrill of a newly discovered truth may suppress the past, may allow it to be forgotten, but behind you everything is empty and dead. And there's something else: being born from an idea rather than a mother's womb makes everything artificial and unnatural, and the world created within and around themselves by those who've rewritten their life, who've managed to purify themselves and be reborn, is just as artificial. That world, of course, can be easily adjusted, taken apart, put together, moved about, but other people, people incapable of simply dismissing their previous lives, can't fit in and can't keep up.'

I interrupted him.

'But didn't you just say that we mustn't judge people for what they haven't done, mustn't judge them by the example of others? Now you're the one comparing and judging all and sundry. Anyone could be made to fit your accusations, so how come your father is innocent?'

'My father's guilty,' said Misha, 'but his guilt is that of a different generation. One generation was on its way out, another was on its way in, and they were strangers to each other. Those who were there at the beginning, at the source, would never have acknowledged those who were there at the end as their brothers.'

This was less than convincing, but I could see that Misha had been finding this conversation burdensome for some time, and I didn't try to pursue it further. Some kind of line had been drawn, and we returned to Sertan. Meanwhile, I decided in my own mind that I'd been wrong to raise this subject and wouldn't do so again. But a month or so later, Misha suddenly revived it himself, and we picked up the conversation at exactly the point we'd left it.

'The division between these generations was an ethical one,' he said. 'It was an understanding of what was permitted and what wasn't, of the limits which they themselves imposed on their power. Stalin, for example, had no such understanding, and thought everything was permitted, towards everyone. He was the last link in the chain. Idealism was being washed away, generation by generation, and it was being replaced by power. Idealism is stuffed full of taboos, it's fixed on the ultimate aim, not on today, which is why it never survives in the real world. Power, on the other hand, is flexible and pragmatic.

A politician who takes his cue from idealism can only gain power when power is at its weakest, when it has just been born or is just about to die. Power rids itself of idealists the moment it takes root. By 1932, the power of the idealists was history, and all that remained was to destroy them physically.'

'Why '32 in particular, and not '29, when Trotsky was exiled?' I asked.

'Trotsky's exile mattered, of course, but it was by no means crucial. Far more symptomatic was the persecution of the avant-garde and the disbanding of RAPP, whose purpose, after all, had been the creation of proletarian art, of an entirely new art for an entirely new life.[5] Don't get me wrong, Seryozha, I'm no admirer of that organisation – RAPP was repellent and stupid, but its stupidity was born solely from an idea. You could even call it the purest, most naïve conclusion drawn from the idea for whose sake the Revolution was carried out. The destruction of RAPP signified the end of that idea. And the end of the generation which held power before Stalin. That generation also tended to think that everything was permitted, towards everyone, but it excluded from that "everyone" its own comrades-in-arms; amongst themselves, the observation of moral norms was considered desirable. True, they were the ones who introduced the thesis, "Whoever is not with us is against us", but in practice they distinguished between the two categories. And as for their precursors, they were convinced that only enemies and only those who were personally guilty should be punished; the innocent should not suffer.'

Neither of us spoke and both seemed to be relieved that the conversation was over. Nevertheless, I still asked him how

---

5 The Russian Association of Proletarian Writers, established in 1925 and disbanded, along with other literary and artistic unions, in 1932, when the Soviet Writers' Union was founded.

power moved up that ladder, from rung to rung; what was the mechanism behind it? And I asked him about Stalin: idealism may have been on the decline for some time, but he was the one who finished it off. That was something new, a kind of peak.

'Fair enough,' I said. 'I agree with you that Stalin had such a lust for power that he put paid to anyone who might become a threat to him without a second thought; for him, the mere preservation of power was sufficient justification for terror. But tens of millions followed him. For the most part, of course, that was thanks to excellent propaganda, but still, that propaganda must have been based on something, it must have had something to put in the place of the ideas that came before, in place of proletarian art movements and all the other naïve brainchilds of the Revolution.'

'The revolutionaries who seized power in October 1917,' said Misha, 'were themselves not short of pragmatism, otherwise they'd never have succeeded with so few resources. Their skill was noted by everyone. When the Civil War started, between half and two thirds of the Russian officer class defected to the Bolsheviks. These officers betrayed their oath and defected because they couldn't stand weakness or sissies; in their eyes, only the Bolsheviks were strong enough to preserve the empire. During the Civil War they shot their own men – as Stalin did later. In that respect, he was their pupil. The officers who went over to the Bolsheviks defeated the officers who fought the Bolsheviks and defeated them on the most crucial point for both sets of men: they had defended the fatherland, saved Russia, preserved the empire. By betraying, they had shown Russia their loyalty. Nobody would call them a traitor now. If you ask me,' Misha said, 'it was precisely those Russian officers who made Stalin understand that for the sake of Russia's greatness you can shoot your own men. He was following their example. And history vindicated him, too.'

Until March 1970 we translated sporadically at best, but in spring Misha took some time off so as to dedicate himself fully to Sertan, and things moved quicker. It was hard work. Although Breton, like any dead or almost-dead language, had not changed much, Misha, who'd learnt it from books three centuries later, struggled to make sense of the text. Sertan's handwriting was even harder to understand. Here, funnily enough, I was able to help him: I didn't know a word of Breton, and wasn't any the wiser by the end of our labours, but I had the knack of reading manuscripts. I quickly mastered the shape of the letters and sailed through the passages in which Misha got hopelessly bogged down. So we ended up working in parallel: I would copy, or rather draw the letters – just as the scribes of the Russian chronicles and liturgical books had done for centuries: not many of them were literate – and he would translate.

In 1645, by the will of fate – or more prosaically, in search of work – the theatre troupe owned by Jacques de Sertan washed up in Poland, where it toured extensively and successfully until the Cossack-Polish War, which had begun in 1648, brought them to ruin. For another five years Sertan dragged his thinning company across Belorussia and Lithuania; the Polish-Lithuanian Commonwealth was sliding into poverty, aristocrats invited them into their castles ever more rarely, and they usually found themselves performing in towns during fairs. They still had plenty of work, but everything had become so expensive that it was difficult to make ends meet. The actors started drifting apart. Some took up soldiering, which was not only more profitable but safer: all around there was looting and killing, but if you were a soldier you had weapons, comrades, a wage and, if you got lucky, spoils. Others joined the Cossacks: then you would also be armed, but without needing to answer to anyone – and, unfortunately, without any pay. Little by little the company was dying, and by the time the Russians entered Vilnius in 1654 and added Sertan to their trophies, his entire troupe had been reduced to a single man: the artist, Martin.

Sertan had picked him up six years earlier in the town of Kielce, where Martin was living the life of some holy fool, drinking heavily and long out of work. His paintings had exceptional power. He was particularly good at the Last Judgement and the torments of hell – all thanks, no doubt, to the devils he saw at the end of his drinking bouts. Not even Bosch could compare with Martin in the vividness of his depictions of hell or in the strength of his conviction that he, the artist, had been there himself.

Now that Sertan had lost everything, he no longer cared what happened to him. His money soon ran out. Vilnius was going hungry and all the people who might have helped him had long since fled the town. The owner of the coaching inn where he was staying hadn't thrown him out yet, but Sertan knew that this, too, was only a matter of time. He would roam the town all day long, sometimes going round and round the same little streets until evening, sometimes, as if settling scores with Vilnius, walking straight across it, north to south then east to west, making the shape of a cross.

One day Sertan wandered by chance into a courtyard where all the scenery from his theatre had been dumped. It had been a wet summer, and the canvases were soaked through and beginning to rot. The Streltsy guarding all the stuff in the courtyard were quartered in a house nearby, and Sertan asked their leader to let him take care of the scenery and save it from ruin.[6] Permission was granted. Sertan and Martin dragged it all into a shed, began slowly restoring it, and ended up staying there. The soldiers fed them, and they were happy enough.

Some two months later, when the war moved further west and the Streltsy moved with it, two large wagons turned into the courtyard just as it was getting light; the driver, who was in a tearing hurry, shouted for Sertan and, as soon as he appeared, ordered him to load everything in the shed onto the wagons. When that was done, he and Martin were told that they were going too. Only once they were beyond the city gates did the coachman tell Sertan that they were bound for Moscow.

The journey proved extremely lengthy; the carts inched along, the highway, crammed with soldiers, was all muddy from the autumn rains, and it was October before they reached Smolensk. Martin went missing somewhere along the way, and Sertan was on his own. After Smolensk the pace picked up, but even so it wasn't until the winter of 1665 that he finally got to Moscow.

On arriving in the capital, he was immediately brought to some chancellery or other where he was thoroughly interrogated, first in Polish and then, when they realised where he was from, in French, and Sertan couldn't help noticing how well the clerk who was questioning him knew the language. Following somebody's advice, Sertan identified himself in the course of the interrogation as Protestant rather than Catholic, and in fact he did come from a Protestant family, but he had converted to Catholicism in Italy many years before. This went down well and after three days locked up in a wooden hut close by, Sertan was released.

He was taken to the diplomatic chancellery and told that

---

6 The Streltsy, armed with arquebus and sabre, were Russia's first standing army, established by Ivan the Terrible.

from that day forward he would enter employment as the court dramatist, for which he would receive a salary, albeit a modest one for now. There, he was also informed that one of the Tsar's daughters wanted to know which plays he could put on and what he needed in order to do so. With the help of one of the clerks, Sertan drew up a list of ten plays, adding a detailed account of their contents. This was passed onto the head of the diplomatic chancellery, Ordin-Nashchokin, who, according to chancellery officials, declared himself satisfied and gave it to the Tsarevna – after which everything ground to a halt.

Sertan kept a low profile until spring, then things started moving again and he paid a few visits to the Tsar's father-in-law, Miloslavsky, who, along with Streshnev, a boyar, would act as his patron for some time to come. Miloslavsky was very courteous to Sertan, always put on a wonderful spread for him, and always told him that everything was just about to be decided in his favour: the Tsar had long wanted to see the same plays as his brother – the King of France. Once Sertan was even brought into the treasury, shown his own scenery and asked whether it would be suitable for the plays he had included in his list, or whether he needed something different. Sertan said it would do perfectly well and nothing else was needed – he could start staging the plays right away if they gave him some actors. The chancellery secretary accompanying him said the Tsar had some actors among his captives, and three of them, if he wasn't mistaken, were French. Sertan was sure that two of these three were his own men, because he'd seen one of them at the market back in the winter. This conversation took place in the middle of summer, and the secretary told him that the play should be ready within half a year, for Shrovetide. Then everything stopped again.

Sertan paid many visits to the chancellery, and several to

Miloslavsky, warning that if these delays carried on much longer he would never be ready in time, but all to no avail. The officials were friendly enough and often gave him useful tips, although by this point Sertan had already worked out for himself how things were done in Muscovy. He'd heard that a large number of boyars, and even the Tsar himself, were keen for the court to have a theatre every bit as good as those in foreign lands, but powerful voices were opposed to it. Chief among these was Nikon, the Patriarch. Nikon – and not only Nikon – held that the theatre was a satanic spectacle and that anyone who watched it imperilled his soul. This had long been the way in Russia: novelties were not welcome, unless of course they were cannons or the like; they might harm the faith – especially if they came from the West, from Latin lands.

Sertan knew that if he did get his way and became the Tsar's dramatist, he would soon recover everything he had lost in Poland, but nothing was moving and nor, by the looks of things, would it ever. He continued hoping for another couple of years, but after the Russians made peace with Poland and began exchanging prisoners of war, he asked if he, too, could leave. He was refused once, then twice, but in winter, 1661, permission was finally granted.

He got himself ready, found some travelling companions, and was all set to leave in just a couple of weeks when a monk walked into the log hut where he was renting a room, introduced himself as Grigory from the hostelry of the New Jerusalem Monastery of the Resurrection, and said he had been sent to him by Nikon, Patriarch of All Russia, who insisted that Sertan should visit him before his departure: he had something important to discuss with him.

All this was said in a cold and disapproving tone; Grigory was clearly disgusted by his assignment and disgusted by the sinful business of having to talk to a 'player'. For Sertan, this was nothing new, and he realised this was the way it had to be: actors were little loved in Rus, wandering entertainers and jesters were punished with death, and the same fate would have awaited Sertan but for the Tsar's protection. Counting on this protection, he could even have declined the Patriarch's request and said he was too busy with the preparations for his departure, especially since he knew that the Tsar and the Patriarch had, by all accounts, fallen out very badly; the Patriarch even appeared to have been deprived of his title and was living in semi-confinement in Resurrection Monastery. But only recently Nikon had been the second man in the land, and Sertan had heard that many of the boyars were still on his side, still thought he was in the right; everything could change in the wink of an eye, even before he managed to leave Russia, so there was no sense at all in angering Nikon by declining his request.

Still, he did make enquiries through his allies to see whether Alexei might be against this idea, might think that Sertan was siding with the disgraced Patriarch. It took a week before he received assurances – founded, as he had requested, on the words of the Tsar himself – that no, he was free to go, and in fact ought to go. That same evening he sent a boy in his service to the hostelry of the Monastery of the Resurrection and at dawn the next day, at the head of three carts heavily loaded with supplies, there appeared the familiar figure of Grigory to take him to New Jerusalem, to Nikon.

They travelled almost without a break, but it was already past midnight when they reached a large village belonging to the monastery. Here they ate, fed and watered the horses, had two hours' sleep, and pressed on while it was still dark. They had spent the previous day travelling through well-cultivated, densely populated land, but no sooner did they leave the village than they heard the howling of wolves very close to the road. The wolves accompanied them until daybreak, but didn't dare assault them; according to the coachman, they rarely attacked people until the snow lay thick on the ground.

The next diary entry is dated six days later. Here, Sertan writes that he has already been living in New Jerusalem for a week, walking around, observing the construction of the monastery, exploring its surroundings; nobody was stopping him from do-ing anything or bothering him in any way, but he was none the wiser as to why Nikon needed him. After this, Sertan suddenly jumps back a week and describes his arrival at the monastery.

'From a distance, the monastery that the Russians call Jerusalem looks very much like a fortress. It has ten towers and yet another, a wooden one, rises up over the gates, with beautiful decorative carving in the Russian style. By the gates there are five cannons, as well as the Streltsy whom the Tsar recently dispatched to the Patriarch for his protection. There is a large square in front of the monastery, and before reaching the gates you pass a house where Nikon receives lay visitors. Here you will also find the smithy, the bell foundry, brickworks, stables, icon stalls, stone quarries, and quarters for the workers.

'When we entered the yard, Grigory took me over to a round-faced, bright-eyed man whom he introduced as Dionisy Ivanovich. Later I learned that he was from Riga and that, like me, he had been taken captive in Lithuania, after which he was rebaptised by the Patriarch and made his personal secretary one year ago.

'Dionisy Ivanovich welcomed me and almost immediately we were joined by Nikon himself. I bared my head and bowed down to the ground. Near us was a large grey stone; the

Patriarch sat on it and started talking. He spoke courteously, even cheerfully, and told me that I shouldn't bear him any ill will; hadn't the Lord commanded us to forgive those who do us wrong? At this point,' Sertan writes, 'I began crying and kissing his hands. Then the Patriarch said that what I do is a terrible sin and that I am poisoning my soul, which is why he, Nikon, had always had it in for me. We are created in the image and likeness of God, and only pagans may alter their faces or wear masks.'

This entry is directly followed by a character sketch of Nikon, entirely different in tone: 'A clumsy, ill-mannered man. Wears an angry expression, powerfully built, quite tall, red in the face, bad skin. Sixty-four years of age. Very fond of sweet Spanish wine. Keeps saying, appositely or otherwise: "These good deeds of ours." Nikon, people say, is rarely sick, and complains of aches and pains only when the weather turns, but just as soon as it begins to rain or snow he feels better again. Ever since he left Moscow four years ago, a comb has never touched his head…'

Such were Sertan's first impressions of Nikon. In general, his diary contains a great variety of entries about the Patriarch, most of them detailed and substantial. Nevertheless, for all the diary's merits and for all the similarities between Sertan's and Suvorin's views, it would be unwise to trust Sertan every time he writes about Nikon. The fact of the matter is that only for the first of the six years they spent living in the same place could one call their relationship normal. For all their apparent authenticity and precision, the entries recorded during subsequent years are highly questionable and should be taken with a pinch of salt.

Sertan often calls Nikon a child and, no less often, a hounded, persecuted child. Moreover: 'All that was bad about him came from his childhood. He was unpredictable: petty and jealous one moment, generous the next. Temperamental and impatient. He liked to complain, to be pitied, and he was always quick to argue, to start criticising and threatening, but then he would take fright, repent and want to make it up straight away.'

It's astonishing how quickly, to judge from the diary, Nikon became attached to Sertan. Misha and I noticed this from the very first New Jerusalem entries we translated. He had clearly singled Sertan out from the people who surrounded him. But Sertan did not notice, or did not want to notice; he was as wary of Nikon as he had ever been and resisted all overtures. He had good grounds to do so.

It was Nikon who had persecuted him all his years in Moscow, Nikon who had almost destroyed him. Thanks to him, Sertan could not leave Russia even now: Nikon was keeping him under duress, and that was no way to earn a man's loyalty. All the stories Nikon told him about his own life irritated Sertan and struck him as either maudlin eccentricities or cunning ploys. But Nikon, noticing nothing, felt more and more drawn towards Sertan. The latter's attitude towards him was clearly irrelevant to him. Misha's explanation for this was that Nikon was innately incapable of any kind of dialogue, of making any kind of adjustment; he was born to change the world around him, not to adapt himself to it. He had chosen Sertan for the role of confidant, and that was all he needed from him. A year later Sertan would be relieved of this role, but that had nothing to do with his attitude towards Nikon.

Nikon was the type of man whose fate and whose mission was to persecute or be persecuted, who knew that if he was neither persecuting nor persecuted he was failing to serve God as he should. He could live no other way (the Archpriest

Avvakum and Ivan Neronov were of the same ilk) and he did everything he could to make this happen.

Nikon had had no childhood, or not much of one, and like any person deprived of an entire phase of his life, he turned back at the first opportunity, so as to join his past to his present. He would turn back and then stop: once again a gap would open up in front of him, and once again he had no way of getting over it.

More often than not, the stories Nikon told Sertan were about who had tried to kill him, when and where, and how God had saved him. They were stories which were also questions: why did God save him? This pattern of persecution and miraculous salvation constituted a unique path that only he, Nikon, could walk, and only because God was leading him along it. He had been walking this path for many years but only recently, and with no small thanks, it seemed, to Sertan, had he begun to understand where exactly God was leading him and what He was preparing him for. There were three particular episodes from his childhood that Nikon would mention or refer to in almost every conversation. All three were easy to understand, good and evil were clearly visible in them, and so too – most importantly– were miracles.

'When Nikon, born Nikita, was six years old (his mother Miriamna had died soon after giving birth to him and his father had got remarried to a woman who already had children of her own and tried to wipe her new stepson from the face of the earth by not feeding him and beating him till he bled) he was left alone in the log hut and, hungry as ever, went hunting for food in the cellar. His stepmother spotted him as he came up and hit him on the head. He fell back down and was badly hurt. But somehow he survived.'

Judging by the diary, Sertan heard this story for the first time on May 12. On May 13, Sertan recorded: 'Today he told me once again, in every detail, about how he tumbled into the cellar.' On May 16, the cellar again. May 18: 'Today he told me how the Lord saved him on another occasion. This is what happened.

'In winter, during a severe frost, Nikita climbed into the stove to warm up and fell asleep there. His stepmother found him there the next morning and decided to burn him. She stuffed the stove with firewood and set light to it. Nikita woke from the heat and the smoke and began screaming in terror, begging her to spare him. Fortunately, a neighbour, Ksenia, was walking past and heard his screams. She cleared out the burning wood and saved Nikita.

'Why, when remembering his childhood, does he always talk about himself in the third person?' Sertan wrote in the margins of the diary. 'It's almost as if he splits himself in two and no longer understands that he and Nikita are the same person. Perhaps he is right to speak like this: these are stories about God, not him. He is not important here, he is nobody.

'May 25. Now, every single day, he tells me both stories one after the other. I cannot bear it. To think how many people he has already destroyed and how many more will be destroyed on his account, and yet he is convinced that he is the victim. He believes he is still that same little boy his stepmother and other evil people wanted to wipe from the face of the earth.

'May 30. Saved by another miracle. This one seems to be his favourite: he cries as he tells it. Such is his sorrow for Nikita that I forget he and Nikita are the same person. He would make a good storyteller – that much you can tell from the way he begins, but self-pity gets in the way. He speaks very slowly and softly. He wants you to listen hard. This is what he told me today.

'Nikita's father, Mina, was often away on various business.

He loved his son and when he would return home to find Nikita beaten black and blue, he would punish his wife. This did not temper her anger, it merely inflamed it more than ever. She thought long and hard about how to end Nikita's life, and eventually decided to poison him. She ground some arsenic and set about trying to show Nikita a mother's love: she spoke tenderly to him, set piles of tasty food before him, and told him to eat his fill. No sooner had the starving Nikita taken his first bite than he felt a powerful burning in his throat (that was God protecting him), stopped eating, drank as much water as he could all night long, and saved his own life with God's help. Thus did the Lord thrice show Nikita that He was with him, that He had not forgotten him and was watching over him. Then, a few years later, his stepmother and all her children died; though Nikita himself had long forgiven her, the Lord avenged him sevenfold and seven times sevenfold.'

Nikon spent the other part of his childhood – those years when he already knew that the Lord would forever be at his side, whatever might happen – in the home of a village priest, Father Ivan, who was gentle and affectionate towards him and knew Scripture well. Until his dying day Nikon would remember him with tenderness and love.

In those years, the Nizhny Novgorod region was densely populated. It had emerged almost unscathed from the death and devastation unleashed by the Time of Troubles;[7] in fact, its population had grown, as people fled there to escape starvation. Besides the town of Nizhny Novgorod there were many old and wealthy villages in the region. Three neighbouring ones are mentioned particularly frequently in Nikon's stories, and

7 The Time of Troubles (*Smutnoe vremya*): the name given to the interregnum (1598-1613) between the Rurik and Romanov dynasties, a period marked by famine, unrest and foreign occupation.

Sertan lists them in his diary: Vildemanovo, where Nikon was born; Grigorovo, where the priest was one Father Pyotr, who was also of Mordvin stock, like Nikon, and had a son, later to become famous as the Archpriest Avvakum, of the same age as Nikon; and Kolychevo, where Nikon grew up in Father Ivan's house with Ivan's son, later to become famous as Bishop Pavel Kolomensky, a leader of the Schism and follower of Avvakum.

All three knew each other from an early age. At first they walked side by side, later their paths would keep forking and merging, but eventually their different forms of worship made enemies of them: Nikon and Avvakum separated once and for all and fought over the true faith as few had ever fought, even in the times of the apostles; each held his ground and the result was that they divided the chosen people between them and led them off in different directions.

The source of the conflict was the eternal struggle between the establishment (Pavel and Avvakum were born into the priesthood) and the parvenus. Nikon was the parvenu. But he, Nikon, knew what the others did not: that God was on his side, that the Lord was leading him. And he found the words in Holy Scripture to confirm his view that he, not they, was in the right: 'And the last shall be first.' Nikon's faith was the faith of the last who shall be first.

Both then and subsequently the three men would always gravitate towards each other, and the life they lived was merely the continuation and development of the relationships they had formed as children. However far apart fate might pull them, they would still come back to each other. In essence, they managed to preserve everything they had shared in childhood; and to preserve themselves in that childhood. They held on to the same points of view, the same convictions, merely broadening their struggle by every means possible, drawing new people into it, recruiting ever more followers and converts. And it didn't matter how close they were, geographically speaking, at any given moment, nor even whether or not each knew where the others were or what they were doing. What mattered was that they were always turned towards each other, wherever they were, and this was the only thing they kept in mind. The past and future of each were meaningful only within the context of their relationships, as part of the endless struggle for victory that they were waging. And whatever they did was filled with such childish faith in their own rightness, such childish conviction, honesty and refusal to compromise that all of their many followers remained loyal to the end.

Later, Sertan would write: 'They are not separate people, but parts of a single whole. Parts which, having broken their ties, having freed themselves from each other's constraints, from the need to answer to one another, from the need to undertake common, mutually agreed actions, are beginning to grow uncontrollably. Their growth is equal to their freedom.'

Absorbed in the struggle, Nikon, Avvakum and Pavel never became adults; all remained children. Life never managed to enter their game, to reform them, push them towards compromise, smooth or soften them. They turned out to be stronger than life, precisely because they were able to convince everyone that life was ending.

The times were in their favour. In those years thousands upon thousands were expecting the Last Judgment, the Second Coming of the Messiah, and the end of the world. The faith of Nikon and Avvakum was firm, and the Orthodox accepted it; they realised that now was the time, just as when Christ came into the world, to decide whose side you were on: with Him or against Him; the time to separate the wheat from the chaff, the faithful from the sinful. What started then must end now. The beginning and end of all things.

Their followers also became children; they abandoned everything they had and left day-to-day life, where whatever is better than anything else is 'good'; left it for the ideal, for truth, where whatever is not the truth is equally bad, equally false. They abandoned their fields and ceased tilling and sowing, because there was nothing left to come. They gathered, prayed, fasted, confessed their sins to one another, lay down alive in their coffins and waited for the trumpet to sound, while their northern brothers burnt themselves up in their log cabins, hoping to escape omnipresent evil through a baptism of fire.

In all the years granted to Nikon by the Lord there was, nevertheless, one long period of 'ordinary' life. When he was about twenty, he married Nastasya, daughter of Father Ivan, the priest who had long taken the place of Nikon's father and who yielded his parish to his son-in-law soon after the wedding.

On becoming a priest, Nikon lived an almost monastic existence, did all he could for his flock and, it seems, did not deviate an inch from the path prepared for him by God. It was the same in Moscow, where Nikon decided to move several years later at the invitation of merchants who had heard about his sobriety and good knowledge of Holy Scripture. There, too, he was respected by his parishioners; he did not fawn on them, and he was strict but fair in his faith.

Many would have been content with this life, but time passed and the routine of a parish priest, the need to be among people at all times, became ever more burdensome to Nikon. It was his own children who made an adult of him during these years in Moscow. They explained a great deal to him, showed him things that he, a grown man, did not know. He was especially grateful to them for teaching him how to make things, to enjoy that kind of game. He loved watching them build castles, fortresses, weirs, but he would always exhort them to build something heavenly, so as to please God and aid their souls. He would bring them icons showing Jerusalem or famous churches and monasteries, and as he watched them trying to replicate these images with clay, sand and pebbles he thought that if the Lord would only grant him the strength he would cover all holy Rus with foreign shrines and adorn her as no other country had ever been adorned. But his children were hindering him; having made an adult of Nikon, they had taken his place, forced him out of his own childhood and, for as long as they were near him, for as long as they were alive, he could not be a child.

Then they all died in the space of a year. The Lord cleared the space around him, chopped down the underwood, and now nothing impeded his path. He persuaded his wife to take the veil and, following her example, entered a monastery. In order to retrace his steps and find his own path again, in order to forget his recent life in Moscow and erase it once and for all (by taking back his children, God had given him the clearest possible instructions: he was a good priest, but that was not what the Lord needed from him) Nikon had to go away from Moscow – the further, the better. The Lord had arranged things in this way because the path before him could be walked only in solitude, and now it was time for him to find a remote cloister where he could learn once again how to be alone.

In 1635 Nikon was tonsured in Solovetsky Monastery, on the White Sea, and settled in the hermit community on Anzer Island, famous then and subsequently for its strict regime. The island lay almost fifteen miles from the monastery, and only monks had ever lived there.

It was a small brethren of a dozen or so monks, and they

lived not in cells but in log cabins they had built themselves and which were scattered all over the island. They only gathered on Saturdays, in church; the psalms would be read in full throughout the evening and the night, and when morning broke the liturgy would begin. Then the monks would go their separate ways, and the rest of the week would be devoted to prayer, silence and heavy labour. Nikon told Sertan that he brought books with him to the monastery and read a great deal, as much as he did as a child. When the weather was calm, he enjoyed taking a small boat out to sea to catch fish.

Nikon spent more than six years on Anzer Island. He was in his element; he had always loved praying for long periods at a time, had always loved silence, solitude and books. Hard work was also nothing new to him, and for all these years he felt like a prodigal son who had returned at last to his father's house. He was calm and at peace. Then, once again, people began to persecute him, once again, as in childhood, he was almost killed, and once again the Lord saved him.

In 1641, the Father Superior of the hermitage, Eleazar, took him with him on a nine-month journey by boat and on foot from Archangel to Moscow. They were collecting money for a new church and stopped at every town and village they passed. The journey was a success. They collected enough to build the church and returned without incident. Once they were back on Anzer, however, Nikon began to suspect – and, it seems, with good reason – that Eleazar was intending to steal the money, so he set about persuading the brethren to take it off him. When Nikon eventually succeeded, Eleazar decided to get his own back. He told the brethren that Nikon had broken the vow of obedience, so Eleazar was taking upon himself the sin of killing the wilful brother in their midst. In this all-male monastery where all the monks, except Nikon, were Pomors or peasants from around Novgorod, such things were not unusual. Eleazar even told the brethren that he knew how Nikon would die: every night he would dream of Nikon, and every time a black snake would wind itself around Nikon's neck and strangle him.

Nikon was scared of dying and prayed to God to ask Him what he should do. His own desire was to flee, but he asked the Lord to counsel Eleazar and make peace between them. But God decided Nikon should go. A few months later, in August, Nikon, a Pomor pilgrim visiting the island and one other monk secretly fitted out a small boat in a secluded cove, loaded it with provisions and books, and set sail on the eve of the Feast of the Dormition.

The smallness of the boat, the cliffs and the August storms made such an attempt nothing short of desperate. They had chosen the longest possible route: to throw off their pursuers, they decided to sail almost due south over the Onega Bay. Lapland, to the west, was much closer, but entirely deserted, while the mouths of other rivers – the Kem, Vyg, Suma – were dotted with underwater ridges and too dangerous to even consider. Powerful winds carried them across the bay for several days, not allowing them to put in anywhere, but when the boat began to leak and, despite all the fugitives' efforts, was already half-full of water, they were finally cast ashore on a tiny island ten miles from the mouth of the Onega River. The date was September 3. They gave thanks to the Lord, and the very next day Nikon knocked together a large cross from driftwood and erected it on the edge of a high promontory, in memory of the miracle. Then they sailed across to the mainland and went their separate ways.

From this point onwards, Nikon's path, in his own words, lay straight and true. He told Sertan that he had served the Lord faithfully, and the Lord was raising him higher and higher. The Lord wanted him to correct the liturgical books and restore the ancient rites in Holy Rus, and he did this. He had no lack of powerful enemies, but with the Lord's help he overcame them. He had been hated, hounded and persecuted, not only in Novgorod, where he had been bishop, but also in Moscow, where evil people had driven a wedge between the Tsar and him, before driving him away from the patriarchal throne; but he knew that this was not the end, only the beginning. He feared nothing, for the Lord was with him.

This entry is followed by an entirely unexpected change of topic: Annette – an actress in the troupe who died in Ukraine – suddenly appears in Sertan's diary for the first time since his arrival in Russia. He writes about having dreamt of her the previous night. From this day forward, Sertan writes about Annette almost as much as he did in Poland. It's almost as if, during this second month of his life in New Jerusalem, he turns back to the past: the diary entries alternate ever more frequently with episodes from his life in Germany, France, Italy; there is an abundance of new events, names, details, all of which, strangely enough, are much more vivid and colourful than anything he has to say about Nikon. It's obvious that he wants to go back there, to the past, that he wants out of Russia. Perhaps this fierce, sudden onset of nostalgia is linked to the fact that several Dutch merchants had just stopped by at the monastery on their way to Riga. Their stay in New Jerusalem is described by Sertan in some detail.

The Dutchmen, Sertan writes, were given a lavish reception; Nikon himself took them to see the church under construction, and when the guests had finished admiring and praising both the Church of the Holy Sepulchre and its location, he brought them to the refectory. Sertan was also invited, and his diary includes a sketch of this meal.

The food was served on silver plates; drinks were poured from alabaster jugs. There were ten dishes, all fish, but no dairy products as it was a day of fasting, a Wednesday; there was plenty of good beer, though, which was drunk to the Patriarch's health.

According to Sertan's report, Nikon's mood kept changing over lunch; he was excited one moment, gloomy the next. He began by asking the Dutchmen what kind of send-off their envoy had been given by the Tsar, and on hearing that it had not been a good one, said: 'This is what happens now that I am no longer in Moscow and nobody asks for my blessing. The Tsar and his court are quarrelling with all and sundry... When I was in Moscow, I was blamed for every misfortune! And now?!'

Next he began grumbling that he was too scared to hang his own portrait in the monastery lest he was accused of wishing to be considered a saint in his own lifetime, that barely a day went by when he wasn't slandered about this or that – for example, of not praying for the Tsar – and then, without hiding his joy, he suddenly added: 'Yes, there are bad things in store for the Tsar now that he is deprived of my blessing...'

That same evening the Dutchmen visited Sertan, and he talked to them until the early hours. They offered to take him with them, promising to get him out of Russia, but he merely gave them a letter to take, one he had written for no obvious reason. It was addressed to his mother, who, as he firmly believed, had died long ago.

The Dutchmen left the next morning and the old routine resumed. Sertan, as before, spent day after day strolling in complete solitude around the monastery; he even visited the neighbouring villages. Everything was still bare: the trees, the earth – black and moist after the snow – the riverbank. During one of these strolls he was crossing the makeshift bridge over the Istra (the Jordan, as it was now called) when he met Nikon, who invited him to take a look at the old books and icons in his library. Sertan was bored without books and he was only too pleased to accept.

It was a big library, but the books, to his dismay, were all in Russian or Church Slavonic; the Patriarch knew no other languages. Nikon had just received a letter from Jerusalem containing inscriptions copied from the churches there, and he wanted to replicate them in Russian in his own monastery. One of these inscriptions was in Latin, and the Patriarch asked Sertan if he could translate it. Sertan did so, and that was when Nikon finally told him why he needed him.

He began in the pompous and sententious manner he usually assumed with foreigners, as if they were in public, not alone in a cell: 'The Almighty, in His divine love for man, has granted two great gifts to humankind: priests and rulers. The first group,' he said, stressing every word, 'serves the affairs of God, the second controls the affairs of man and takes care of them. Both come from the same root. Nothing brings as much good fortune to the Tsar as the veneration of prelates. Every prayer that ascends to heaven must concern both authorities. If there is harmony between them, blessings descend on human life. But harmony has long been lacking,' he suddenly said with sadness, 'as has the veneration of prelates. And blessings, too.' All his grandiloquence disappeared as he began plaintively recalling his quarrel with the Tsar; Sertan even feared he was about to burst into tears.

Then Nikon seemed to digress and began telling Sertan that he wanted to move all Palestine's sacred places over here, onto Russian soil, not only those made by human hands, but also mountains, hills, rivers, springs, groves; he wanted the monastery to be surrounded by the same towns and settlements, fields and roads through which and along which Jesus Christ had passed with his disciples on his way to Jerusalem. 'This is essential for the Orthodox faith,' he said. 'The land of Israel has been defiled by the Hagarenes; there is no end to their sacrilege. Its holiness has given way beneath the infidel's yoke; it is sick and weak. Pilgrims to Jerusalem attest as one that in the Holy Land they fear for their life every hour of the day, but this is not the worst of it. From the moral point of view, to see the sites of Christ's redemptive suffering in such neglect does not purify the human soul; if anything, it harms it. Whereas in Russia,' said Nikon, 'the land which, despite all calamities and temptations, has preserved the true faith whole and pure, these holy places – if God will only give me the strength to transfer them – will be resurrected and reborn, filled anew, to the very brim, with their former sanctity.'

If he, Nikon, succeeded in carrying out his plan it would be like a second christening for the Russian people, whose knowledge of Scripture was still poor but who were devoted to Christ like no other nation on earth. On the opposite page Sertan caustically noted that to Nikon, who had christened and rebaptised so many foreigners and non-Russians in the course of his life, the idea of a second christening must be very dear, especially in New Jerusalem. Moreover, Nikon continued, he wished not only to replicate the names of the holy places and their buildings, but also to populate them. And when the Church of the Holy Sepulchre would be completed here, on this new Holy Land, the events of the Gospel story, from Christ's birth to His passion and resurrection, would unfold exactly as they had in Palestine 1662 years before.

He asked Sertan whether he had ever been involved in staging the mystery plays which, he had heard, were so popular in France and Germany. Sertan replied that he had staged only two such plays, a long time ago, but that he had seen a great many others, including the most famous in Arles and Munich, after which he fell silent, unsure whether he should say any more about them. Nikon also kept silent, but then, taking Sertan by surprise, he said in a dark, hostile tone: 'Listen, you heretic: you have to do everything just as it was done then. This cannot be theatre. Everything must be exactly as it once was.'

Then he softened again and told Sertan with disarming frankness why he needed him: 'The Tsar loves the divine, but he also likes worldly pleasures, especially theatre. Let him think this is theatre – he will be unable to resist such an unusual spectacle and will be sure to come. All this will take many days. He and I will be alone, the Lord will make him see reason, and he will drive away all those who set him against me. The Lord must reconcile us. For as long as there is no harmony between us, all blessings will cease.' He said these last words softly, as if to himself, then he brought the conversation to an end by holding out his hand; Sertan kissed it and left.

This conversation was resumed soon enough. Nikon asked about the most minor details of the mystery plays, and Sertan omitted nothing in his replies: how the stage was arranged, how paradise, purgatory and hell, Christ's life on earth and His ascension were represented, who acted in these plays (professionals or amateurs) and where: in churches or on public squares. Nikon was especially interested in how the miracles were staged: the lodestar guiding the Wise Men, the five loaves of bread with which Christ fed the thousands,

Christ walking on water. If the weather was inclement, they talked in Nikon's cell, otherwise they went for strolls around the monastery. Nikon would show Sertan where this or that church, outbuilding or workshop was to be built; it was barely more than an outline for now, but things were moving along quickly, without interruption.

Nikon pitched in with everyone else, as if he were just an ordinary monk. This spurred the workers on and helped matters greatly. But for all this zeal, it was still hard to imagine that the building work could be completed by 1666, in however rough and ready a form, especially given the lack of organisation and competence among the workers. Sertan wrote in his diary that the Russians build infinitely better in wood than they do in stone; the bricks were lousy – Nikon complained about that himself – and it wasn't unusual for whole sections of wall to collapse during construction. In winter, whatever was left unfinished would be covered in snow, soaked through and rot, and in spring part of the work would have to be undone and begun again. And yet, not only Nikon but everyone Sertan spoke to believed that, with God's help, the monastery would be erected in time.

A whole medley of nationalities was involved in building the monastery. Foreigners were a rarity in Russia in those years, not as rare as under the previous Tsars, perhaps, but still very conspicuous, like patches cut from a different cloth; in New Jerusalem, however, there were dozens of them. There were Jews, whom Sertan had never seen before in Russia (he had heard that they weren't even allowed into the country), and Poles and Germans and Greeks, all of whom Nikon had either christened, like the Jews, or rebaptised, like the Poles and Germans, but even though they were now Orthodox they still looked no more like each other, or like Russians, than they had before, and the monastery, surrounded as it was by monotonous, monoethnic Russia, resembled the Tower of Babylon more than it did a Christian cloister.

Some three weeks after their first conversation, Nikon, while receiving Sertan in his nearby hermitage by the Jordan, told Sertan once more that he wanted him to repeat, day by day, the events of the Gospels here in New Jerusalem, to repeat, in so far as was possible, every single one – from the birth of Christ to His crucifixion and ascension, to repeat the miracles, the healings, the shared meals, the arguments with the Pharisees. To this end, Nikon would give Sertan as many people as he needed. But among them there should be not one professional actor, and above all nobody from Sertan's troupe; he could use only those who had never been on stage before. He, Nikon, understood that this would be an exceptionally difficult task, that Sertan had never seen or staged a mystery play like it, that he didn't know how to work without professional actors and had no experience of doing so, and this would make things even harder. If he agreed, he would have to live for many years not just in a foreign land but in a monastery, and didn't Sertan want to leave Russia? And lastly: if he did decide to stay, he would find it much easier if he converted to Orthodoxy, but he, Nikon, would not insist on this – that was Sertan's private matter.

Sertan immediately replied to this with a categorical no, and Nikon repeated that he was not insisting that he convert. As for compensation, he would be paid a hundred roubles a year for all the work and the considerable inconveniences. By the standards of the time this was an enormous salary; even the Tsar, were Sertan to be his court dramatist, would not have paid half that amount. Yet Sertan decided there and then that he would turn it down, or at any rate make another attempt to turn it down. He told Nikon that he had to think it over and needed to return to Moscow for a few days.

In Moscow, he immediately tried to find out how the court would react were he to accept Nikon's proposal. Tsar and Patriarch were, to all appearances, drifting ever further apart, and Sertan hoped that this time he would be advised, however diplomatically, to turn it down. But, contrary to his expectations, the outcome was just the reverse, exactly as it had been two months before, when he had asked if he should travel to see Nikon. Now Sertan had driven himself into a corner and could no longer refuse. The Tsar's complicity in Nikon's actions, his silent approval, would continue to remain a mystery to Sertan, but it was clearly present. Later, once he had already been living in New Jerusalem for two or three years and his position was more secure, he asked Nikon about this, and the Patriarch, showing no surprise at the question, said that the Tsar recognised the full significance of the construction of the New Jerusalem shrines, had long been seeking reconciliation with the out-of-favour Patriarch and, therefore, had not prevented Sertan from visiting him.

Nikon took Sertan's return from Moscow to mean his assent, and they never returned to the subject again. Nikon merely told Sertan that he could begin at any time: how and in what order was entirely up to him. He, Nikon, would not intervene in any way, but whatever assistance Sertan might need – and he would need plenty, of all kinds – would be provided by him without delay. He, Nikon, was deliberately emphasising this in order that Sertan could see how much significance he attached to his work and would not be too scared to ask. Next – the schedule: the play should be completely ready by the time the building works were finished, namely January 7, 1666. There could be no talk of delays or postponements; the year, month and day when the mystery play would begin were already fixed and would remain in force come what may. But there was still plenty of time, he added gently, and it was all at his, Sertan's, disposal. This conversation took place in September 1662.

It's clear from the diary that for the first year he and Nikon met almost every day. Usually they went on long walks together, and although Sertan was as fascinated by the Patriarch as before, the frequency of their meetings, and above all the intimacy they created, became more and more of a burden to him.

They would walk for hours around the environs of the monastery, usually in the evening. Sometimes they would go quite far out, working out and marking down what would be acted where, identifying trees that would need to be cut down to clear a space, and levelling, or even reshaping, the contours of hills and villages on their map. It was quite a task, and the names which the monastery villages later acquired – Bethlehem, Nazareth, Hebron, and so on – were the result of their discussions about where and how, according to Sertan's scenario, Christ and His disciples should pass.

A month after these walks began, Sertan started to become scared of Nikon. He was becoming more and more frightened by the speed with which Nikon picked up all the subtleties of the theatre, the facility with which he entered into them. Their education, the life they had lived, their faith – it was all so different that Nikon, or so Sertan believed, should not have been able to understand it at all, or at least not so easily, however clever he might be; and when it turned out that he did understand, that the wall which was meant to divide them barely existed, if it existed at all, and that he was unprotected on all sides, Sertan started to become scared. This continued for a long time. He suspected Nikon of anything and everything, could not forget for one moment that he would have to go walking with him the very next day, be near him for several hours, and drove himself almost insane just thinking about it. Strange as it may seem, the actual encounters with Nikon brought some respite. Sertan learned how to arrange things so that either they walked in silence or Nikon did all the talking, and for as long as Nikon was plunged in his own thoughts, Sertan felt safe.

It was only in the middle of August, when it began raining day in day out, that Sertan was finally given a break from this routine. Plagued by rheumatism, Nikon did not set foot outside his hermitage. But even when he was no longer seeing Nikon, Sertan was unable to stop thinking about him and everything Nikon had told him until one evening, having already said his prayers and got ready for bed, he suddenly realised that he was beginning to understand Nikon and, more importantly, understand why Nikon understood him, Sertan. From this day forward they slowly began to draw level in their knowledge of one another. Sertan became calmer, and his fear gradually abated.

It was the story of how he had become Patriarch that opened Nikon up to Sertan. This was one of Nikon's favourite stories, and he returned to it almost as often as he repeated episodes from his childhood. Nikon would tell him how, in his frequent conversations with the Tsar a good year before his consecration, he kept trying to persuade him – kept demanding, threatening, imploring – to have the relics of Philip, the Metropolitan of Moscow killed by Ivan the Terrible, moved to the Kremlin's Uspensky Cathedral.

'God Himself,' he would shout at Alexei, 'has conferred sainthood on this martyr, but the powers that be have still not repented!'

So it went on for several months, until at last the Tsar, on Nikon's instructions and, as it were, at his dictation, wrote a missive in his own hand to St Philip, begging the metropolitan to absolve his murderer, Tsar Ivan, of his sins and to return to Moscow. He asked Philip to make peace with Ivan the Terrible and assured him that the latter had repented of his actions long ago and had long been appealing for forgiveness. He wrote to Philip that the evil time that had divided the kingdom had come to an end, that the Lord had once again bestowed His blessings on Philip's flock, and that this flock was waiting for Philip one and all, begging him to return in peace and ready to greet him in that spirit.

Philip had been buried in Solovetsky Monastery, and Nikon himself took the Tsar's epistle to the islands of Solovki, accompanied by a vast retinue of boyars and bishops. Then the aged Patriarch Joseph died, and it was clear to all that Nikon would succeed him.

He was elected to the role and immediately renounced it, because, just as Ivan the Terrible had once ruled Russia according to his own will, so Nikon wished to rule the Church 'with a free hand'. He got his way. He arranged things in such a way that the Tsar and the boyars, gathered around the relics of St Philip in the Uspensky Cathedral, the relics Nikon himself had brought, prostrated themselves on the ground, pledged their loyalty to him and begged him not to renounce the patriarchal throne. Then he, Nikon, stood up, turned to the crowd and asked: 'Will I be honoured as archpastor and father, and will I be allowed to put the Church in order?!' Everyone wept, and swore that he would.

Recalling this story now, and rehearsing it twice in his own mind, Sertan suddenly realised, calmly and coldly, that Nikon knew the rules of the game Sertan had been playing all his life no worse than Sertan; in fact, he knew them a great deal better. He knew them better than Sertan, but they were still the same rules. He had clearly never studied theatre, nor could he have done, and yet, without even being aware of it, he had a consummate, exhaustive knowledge of the laws of drama, knew exactly what it is that carries a play from the first line to the last, how the play dissolves among those watching it, pulling them into its drift, making them a part of what is happening on the stage, forcing them to believe in it. Forcing even the actors to believe their own act.

Nikon did this intuitively, as we would now say; he himself believed in it all unreservedly and, unlike Sertan, had no doubt that the performance was genuine, that he was not acting at all, and that acting, 'playing', was an abomination and a mortal sin. That was his strength. He had ready access to the total immersion which Sertan, try as he might, had never been able to achieve, even though, in the very first days of his collaboration with Annette, there had been moments when he, too, had believed in the truth and reality of the life on the stage, or, at any rate, had believed that what was happening there was more genuine and more real than life. But only for a few moments. Nikon, on the other hand, never once left the state of faith, and here, it would seem, he was helped by the fact that he remained the child he had always been, and by his gift of persuasion, a gift rare both in its magnitude and in the confidence he placed in it. What was more, he had the knack of enriching and intensifying the plays he staged and transformed. The reason for this was that whatever he and the others involved in the play might be saying, and however plain those words might be, there lay behind them the will and the words of God, which the 'actors' were delineating and, unbeknownst to themselves, articulating. And only those who could see them understood what it was that they were articulating, understood that these were not their words but the words of God, the God who was always there on the stage beside them and spoke through their mouths.

It was this obligatory presence of the main and, essentially, sole real character – inaccessible and invisible, whose actions and words could only be sensed, though everyone knew that only He was speaking, that only He existed, while all the rest was a fiction, a mirage – this divine drama, this blatant, unmistakable presence of the Lord, a presence created by the words and movements of the other characters who drew Him and His will, that Nikon introduced to the theatre, and it was something entirely, staggeringly new. The actions, soliloquies and rejoinders in Nikon's stagings, while remaining perfectly natural, acquired at the same time their original, intrinsic purpose and meaning, like all that carries within itself a part of God's grace. In essence, Nikon's stories of his childhood were also descriptions of episodes in the lengthy drama that had begun in childhood and dragged on for a whole lifetime, that included a multitude of people, personages and characters; the relationships between them were complicated, entangled and fickle, yet above them all there soared and stretched – unmissably and unmistakeably for all and sundry – one single thread: the thread of the relationship between God and man, the thread of man's service to God.

The way in which Nikon succeeded in following this thread through the chequered turmoil of human words, intentions and actions, without once twisting it, losing it or weakening it, astonished Sertan, and there can be no doubt that he took much of his New Jerusalem staging from Nikon's own drama, and to this very considerable extent became Nikon's disciple.

On virtually every other page of his diary Sertan reproaches himself for having put himself in a situation in which he can no longer leave Russia and for having ended up in New Jerusalem with Nikon, and we, who know that eight years later he would be marched to Siberia and after crossing the ridge of the Urals (or the Stone Belt, as it was then called) would die on the way, should perhaps be inclined to agree with him; yet such entries do not dominate the diary. Sertan was clearly fascinated by what was happening at the monastery, by his own role in it all, and every year this fascination grew and grew. He plunged ever deeper into the work; it surrounded, engulfed, entranced him. This was because he loved the theatre, loved it deeply, and also because he understood that neither he nor anyone else had ever staged anything like this play and probably never would again – he certainly would not. His work in New Jerusalem was something entirely new to him; all his previous experience in theatre was of little use to him here, and not only because the actors were not professionals.

The reason did not lie in them, nor even in the astonishing, extraordinary idea behind it all, nor in the fact that he was still feeling his way and discovering daily much that was new to him and, he realised, not only to him – after a while he understood something else, something even more important: his rehearsals were clearly and unquestionably at the very heart of everything that was happening in New Jerusalem.

It turned out, remarkably enough, that Sertan's selection of actors, his sketches and *mises-en-scène* excited Nikon even more than the construction of the Church of the Resurrection. The latter was only a fraction of the enormous task conceived by Nikon and led by Sertan. Nikon and the monks, and with them hundreds upon hundreds of hired labourers and volunteers, were, it seemed, merely erecting the scenery for the spectacle that Sertan was directing. It wasn't until the end of his third year in New Jerusalem, or even the beginning of the fourth, that he finally realised this, once he had already started working with the actors; until then he had done his level best to delay the start of the rehearsals for as long as possible, telling both Nikon and himself that the *mises-en-scène* needed to be completed first, although in his own mind he was quite sure that trying to work with the peasants Nikon had forced on him was pointless, that telling people who had never seen a theatre or a play how to act was impossible, and that once Nikon and the monks also realised this he would be in serious trouble.

At the end of his third year in New Jerusalem he did, nevertheless, start matching the performers to the roles, or rather, Nikon forced him to do so, before which Sertan made one final attempt to demand that the main parts, or at least those of Christ and His closest disciples, the apostles, be played either by professional actors – he knew Nikon would never agree to this, but it might help him drive a bargain – or by educated monks well-versed in Scripture. And surely Nikon would be able to use his persuasiveness or sheer authority to force Jews he had recently baptised to take part in the play; without the spirit, colour, speech, texture particular to their nation the whole idea of trying to stage the events of the Gospels struck him as completely absurd. But Nikon refused these requests, emphatically so in the case of the last – to force the converts to take part; such abruptness was unusual since Nikon, who was becoming more bad-tempered, irritable and cruel with each passing year, clearly made an exception for Sertan: with him he was usually affectionate, meek and gentle.

At this point, Sertan thought that fate was giving him one more chance to have done with this mad business of Russian peasants acting the parts of apostles or members of the Sanhedrin, especially since the most recent attempt at reconciliation between Patriarch and Tsar had failed, and the gulf between them after this latest disappointment was wider than ever.

The reason Sertan cited for his departure is not known – the diary says nothing about it – but having reached Moscow, he visited the diplomatic chancellery once more and submitted an urgent request to leave Russia, offering the clerks bribes worth nearly a hundred roubles. At first, he was promised that it would all be plain sailing and he would be released in the nearest future; Nikon had lost all influence, so he had nothing to fear. Sertan could see that the chancellery officials were on his side, that they disliked Nikon, understood why he was running away from him and were ready to help. But later on, when he was already due to receive his authorisation to leave, they suddenly stopped taking money from him, the whole process slowed right down and, as if hesitating – at this point, he had still not given up hope – swiftly turned back on itself; Sertan was arrested and sent back to Nikon under escort.

While he was being taken to New Jerusalem, Sertan was convinced that either he would be executed or he would be incarcerated in the monastery prison, and in his mind he was already saying his goodbyes, praying for his sins and preparing himself for death, but Nikon offered him a bafflingly warm welcome, as if nothing had happened, and a month later, having recovered from the shock and afraid no longer, Sertan added this episode to his old conviction that in New Jerusalem he was more or less the main man.

Later, after he had immersed himself once more in his work with the actors and it was all going surprisingly well, in fact almost too well – a miracle was the only thing you could call it, but more about that further below – and he had already got used to spending all his time with the actors, talking to all the twelve apostles day in day out, explaining Holy Scripture to them, guiding and correcting them when guidance was called for, after he had got used to their unquestioning obedience, to the fact that this was how it had to be, that to them he was untouchable, not only because he was in charge of them, but above all because he was teaching them, because he knew precisely what had to be done next, he suddenly realised that a teacher was exactly what he was to them, after all they knew neither the course nor sequence of the Gospel scenes without him, only he could tell them who should say what and when, and when they were shaken by the words of Christ or by their own words, the words with which they taught the people and answered Christ – and it was their own words that astonished them most: after all, you always know what you are capable of, but never what somebody else might say or do, and it was nothing less than a miracle when, repeating after Sertan, they said things that they would understand only later, after they had slowly turned them over in their minds – what remained in them each time was the fact that they had learnt and said all this by copying him, and they were still following his cue now. And they didn't merely know all these things, they also knew that these things were right and they knew how to teach them to others.

Once they had all immersed themselves in their own roles, once they had understood and got used to who they were, they began to speculate about Sertan as well, about who he was, this man who had chosen them and was leading them, showing them what to do and how. And in their minds there was only one man who could do all this: the man who stood above them, the apostles.

They began thinking the most extraordinary things about

Sertan very early on, well before he did. It was the same all over again: he knew perfectly well who he was and they did not, yet in the end even he was infected, at least in part, by what they saw in him, as was Nikon, as were the monks. That was when Sertan became persuaded of the fact that everything here in New Jerusalem – the entire monastery, even the Church of the Resurrection – was merely the scenery for the mystery play that he was directing, for a play such as had only ever been staged once, more than sixteen hundred years before, but as to why and for what possible purpose it had been decided to repeat all this now, that was something he would not understand for a long time to come.

Before he started to believe that something might come of this whole idea, if only with the help of a miracle, he had one more clash with Nikon. At this point Sertan was already trying to rehearse with the peasants, and he was astonished when, for no obvious reason, Nikon forbade him to look for someone to play Christ. Sertan simply could not conceive rehearsing the play without Christ. He told Nikon that, as he knew very well, there wasn't a single scene without Christ in the Gospels that could be taken even as a starting point, that the Gospels were about Christ and nobody else, that not even a professional would be able to act without a partner and make do simply with being told that there's someone standing here and someone else standing there, so please tell him this or that and he'll reply like so or like so. Not even in Europe would you find such actors, or only two or three at most; he had certainly never seen any or had any dealings with them.

To this Nikon replied that it was not for him, Sertan – a Protestant or, for all he knew, a Catholic (this gave Sertan a fright, because if his Catholicism were to become known in Russia, he could face the most unpleasant consequences:

jail, Siberia, anything) – to find Christ on earth, to find and reveal Him to the world; that was simply inconceivable. Christ knows everything and, when the time comes, He will reveal Himself – that is His business, not Sertan's. Nikon went on about Christ for a good while longer, but all in the same key, adding nothing, as if he were trying to clarify in his own mind what would happen; it was clear that he was blindly feeling his way, that he knew nothing definite, nothing certain. It occurred to Sertan later that all of them – Nikon, Sertan himself, the peasants – were always speaking and acting as if they were being led by someone else, and only afterwards would they slowly begin to understand what they had done and why.

Here it should be pointed out that despite Nikon's refusal, despite his hint at Sertan's Catholicism and at the fact that he, Sertan, also had a clearly delineated role here which he must keep to and that someone else, certainly not Sertan, a Protestant or a Catholic, had a role infinitely more important than his – this happened just when Sertan was starting to think that he was the main man in New Jerusalem – Nikon was as gentle as before, as gentle he had always been in his recent conversations with Sertan, and Sertan quickly realised that he was in no danger, even if Nikon really did know he was a Catholic, that this had been said for no other reason than to put him in his place, when in fact Nikon was thinking about something else entirely, trying to understand what it was that he, Nikon, had started, what it was that he was doing, preparing. And even more importantly: was he actually the one doing all this, because he had understood something, knew something and thought something needed to be done, or was he being led like a child and, by virtue of being a child, was simply following the given path. Probably it was one thing and the other, all mixed up together; at first, Nikon would strike out confidently on his own, then he would forget or become scared and continue on his path, without remembering what it was that he wanted, only gradually, retrospectively understanding, from what he had already done, what it was that he was doing, whom he was doing it for and why.

Now, as Nikon spoke to Sertan, it wasn't Sertan he was worrying about, of course, but Christ: would He really appear, and when would He appear? Was Nikon acting according to His will, in which case everything was going just as it should and nothing was forbidden: he was just a performer, and a zealous one at that (what more could he wish for?), or had he thought up all this devilry himself, first and foremost Sertan, some Catholic who had turned up out of the blue (Nikon knew he was a Catholic)? Yes, the evil one was behind it all, behind this entire play of his, behind the New Jerusalem which he had dreamt up and coaxed the Tsar into associating himself with – it was all theatre, that truly demonic art. The very thought: some Catholic puts on a play, and the Patriarch and Tsar of Holy Russia bend over backwards to arrange the scenery for him, sparing no effort or expense. Or perhaps he, Nikon – who without Christ was repeating in Rus what had already happened in Palestine and thereby reminding Him that He was needed here on earth, that people remembered Him, were waiting for Him, almost as if to say that He, Christ, had long wanted to come Himself and end human suffering, and why was He not coming, people couldn't take it any more, they had run out of strength – was right after all? Or perhaps he was demanding and hastening something that must never be hastened, violating what had already been spoken and repeated far and wide: man does not know and cannot know when the last days will begin, and to think that you know, to believe that you know, is a sin, a terrible blasphemy? Or perhaps this really was nothing more than theatre, and he, by saying that Sertan should not look for someone to play Christ, was, as it were, calling Christ Himself to play His own role, calling Him to the theatre, otherwise the play would die? He kept going round in circles. Christ cannot act, cannot 'play', yet who if not Christ can play the role of the Saviour?

As for the fact that the actors would have to rehearse without Christ, Nikon told Sertan not to worry, everything would be fine, just as if Christ were right there amongst them as they acted; all Sertan had to do was tell him, Nikon, when he was ready to begin rehearsing. Sertan knew that everything would be far from fine, but he himself did not want this whole story to come to a sudden, catastrophic conclusion right there and then, and it seems that, although it was not in his interests to postpone the rehearsals for ever, he was also against the idea of definitively abandoning them now by forcing matters. He cut short the conversation, while taking note of the fact that, by sharing this concern with Nikon and warning him, he had one more trump card in his possession.

Four or five days after this conversation he, continuing all the while to recruit actors, began to audition and distribute the parts. Then it was time to learn the roles. This was the hardest period of all for Sertan; he worked with the actors round the clock and barely slept. The peasants could not read, and they learnt the parts by copying Sertan. No one else could do this job for him, neither a monk nor any other literate soul. The problem was not so much getting them to remember the words – although they found even this hard enough: their memory was weak and untrained, and although retelling the text came quite easily to them, learning it cost them enormous effort – as the fact that the words, concepts and attitudes were completely new and alien to them, and even when they did understand the words the sense often escaped them, and this, too, was something he had to notice or guess at before explaining it all to them; so in the end, this shared labour of reading and remembering was simultaneously a rehearsal and an explanation and many other things besides, but the one thing it wasn't was mere learning by rote. His efforts were not in vain; working with the actors day in day out, he saw how the word – slowly, gradually – was working inside them, saw how the word changes man.

When the actors repeated Sertan's words, trying to feel what it was that he was saying, he sensed the maternal instinct waking inside him, as in a bird whose offspring have just hatched; it was as if they were eating out of his mouth, and he would often forget that the words were not his, although, in our view, this was quite understandable. And so, while he was reading them the Gospels, all their strength was spent on remembering, simply remembering the words, and the intonation, and the speed with which they were spoken, and the actors would puff and pant, sweat and tire far more than when they were ploughing the fields. There was no question at this point of their having understood anything much at all; only when they felt that the main job of remembering had been done and they had earned a rest did the word begin to live inside them.

If Sertan struck lucky at the first time of asking and chose the right performer for the role, then that actor would quickly be consumed by his part, he would merge with it and cease fearing Sertan, cease thinking that if he had remembered all his words, if he had coped with that unbearably difficult labour then he could immediately down tools; instead, he would begin to understand that these were his own words, which he was not only entitled, but obliged to utter as he saw fit, and not as

Sertan showed him. It should be noted that this 'as he saw fit' referred only to the intonation, to what Sertan himself brought to the words, but the words themselves, every single one, were genuine and never altered by any of them, which meant that everything in the Gospels was also right; in fact, that was the subtext to all the words which the actors uttered after Sertan, and this, in turn, made Sertan feel good.

The auditions, the searching and the realisation that you had hit the mark gave Sertan inexpressible pleasure (he often thought that Christ Himself must have experienced almost the same delight when He found His disciples, when He saw one, two, three men following behind Him). Then he, Sertan, began to feed them, to feed with words, and the words did their work; the peasants he had picked out began to change in front of his very eyes, in every way, and it wasn't only Sertan who saw this, but everyone who lived in the monastery, and it was as if he, Sertan, were baptising them all over again, as if he were Andrew the Apostle, sent to baptise Rus.

Sertan realised that the job of recruiting actors would not run so smoothly for long; while he was filling the good roles everything would be fine, but when the time came to audition the peasants for the parts of those who did not follow Christ, who spurned Him and, above all, judged and punished Him, nobody was going to agree of their own free will and it was doubtful whether even Nikon would be able to help. But he was proven wrong: true, nobody wanted to take these roles and the peasants would have been only too happy if they had been allotted to the Jews recently baptised by Nikon (a fair solution, however one looked at it); Sertan himself, as I have already said, had held out for this, without success; and yet, those whom he ended up selecting as Christ's enemies were quick to accept their roles, to understand that it was just like life, where there are those who draw the long straw and those who draw the short straw, and there is nothing you can do about it. It was obvious to every one of them that this was how it must have been one thousand six hundred years before; if everyone had recognised Christ for who He was and followed Him, life on earth would long since have become like life in heaven, without hunger, sickness or death. After all, they knew in their own minds that they were sinners and that saving them would not be easy; it was simply impossible that they could all be converted at once, accept Christ and repent – impossible then and impossible now.

Later, Sertan often wondered: why did they agree so readily? There were three answers. Sheer fatalism – what must be, must be: after all they were no strangers to disaster and misfortune – was the first answer that came to mind; oppression and servility, an innate terror before their masters that outweighed even the fear of depriving themselves of eternal bliss – life contained so little hope, so little light that both faith and hope had vanished – was the second, and it merged seamlessly with the impression Sertan had carried with him for some time: that the Russians were not really a very religious people, or if they were, then only on the outside, on the surface, in fact they probably didn't even believe in eternal salvation, seeing in it little more than a comforting fairy tale, and only later did he begin to think, or start tending towards the thought, that there was something else going on here: they believed that the whole world and all it contained must end soon, as soon as possible, whatever that might demand of them; here was selflessness of the purest kind, but selflessness softened by the conviction that every person on earth has their own sharply delineated mission, and this was not fatalism, but an understanding that the world could be arranged no other way, that only the Lord was capable of defining and reckoning the paths and strivings of human beings, otherwise there would be chaos and turmoil, whereas like this they were part of an ordered world, however imperfect, and any order is better than turmoil – that was something they had learned the hard way.

Already during the first round of recruitment, when neither he nor anyone else had any doubt that the Jews would be played by converts, Sertan had gone to Nikon to ask about relieving his actors of their monastery duties. This was more than reasonable given that the main participants – first and foremost the apostles, but others too – were rehearsing all day long and had not a minute left for chores; in fact, not only should they be relieved of their labour, they should be given both grain and money. Nikon readily agreed and said he was prepared to let them all off, but the cellarer, Feoktist, who was present during this conversation, vigorously objected to Sertan's request. He agreed only to reduce the apostles' duties, but as for giving them, never mind the others, anything at all, that, he told Nikon, was out of the question: the Tsar had sent them very little money over the past two years, and the monastery didn't even have enough for the building works; they were behind with payment for bricks, iron and cartage, and the brethren, which wasn't getting nearly enough to eat, was exhausted and had been grumbling for some time. But Nikon was in no mood to listen to him and confirmed that he would carry out Sertan's wishes; he even gave Feoktist a very public dressing-down. The cellarer had never cared for Sertan, knew him to be a Catholic and a papist, and had opposed his invitation to the monastery every way he knew how. After this episode, he became Sertan's outright enemy.

Confident that the Jews would be played by recent converts, Sertan told Nikon that it would only be fair if all those who had agreed to these terrifying, soul-imperilling roles – who could tell where they would lead? – were properly remunerated, so that, for the time being, they could live at least a little more comfortably than the others. To this Nikon replied: 'Or perhaps it should be the other way around: shouldn't they act with a feeling of guilt and remorse, conscious that they are committing a sin, a terrible, irrevocable sin, and already incurring their retribution? They are already worse off than others, but this is only the beginning, only a drop in the sea of suffering and tribulation they will bring upon themselves later.'

Sertan objected that this was not how it was in the Gospels: there, the Jews who do not follow Christ, especially the Pharisees, are convinced they are doing the right thing, and the same goes for those who condemn Christ to death; all are convinced that even if Christ is innocent, they have no choice: everything else is worse. And that's the whole point: all those who have not followed Christ, who have not been tempted by His miracles, who have held firm and continue to bear the burden of the law of Moses on their shoulders are glad, content and self-confident – they have resisted temptation. They are like Christ, who did not give in to the devil's temptations in the wilderness. In the Gospels, their every word expresses their sense of rightness; if they had repented there and then, they would have become as Paul became later on. Like him, they would have converted and joined Christ, and there would have been no Golgotha, no Resurrection – nothing.

'And the most difficult task before me now,' said Sertan, 'is to inculcate in them a sense of their own rightness; if they act without it, if there is an air of doom in all they do, a sense of guilt about their every word, as if to say that they are not really like this, that they are just playing a role and God forbid that anyone should think they are actually against Christ, not with Him, then nothing will come of it all. Only the disciples doubt Christ in the Gospels, only they renounce Him, while those who are against Christ are convinced of their own rightness, proud of it, and have every reason to be proud, because they have not been tempted by miracles and have kept the faith of their fathers.'

As a sop to Nikon, he added: 'They were just like your Old Believers are in Russia: they clung to the faith of their fathers so tightly that they failed even to recognise the Saviour.'

This conversation also took place in Feoktist's presence, and once again Nikon ordered the cellarer to carry out Sertan's wish. But Feoktist loathed the converts. From the moment that Nikon had solemnly baptised the very first Jew to turn up at the monastery, the cellarer had openly doubted whether this was a godly thing to do. A long time ago, in the days of the apostles, when the faith was just spreading, this might have been necessary, but not now. People had lost count of the times that the Jews had rejected, abused and jeered at Christ, and by now they were so deep in sin that their repentance and conversion could only be false. You couldn't believe a word they said; they were two-faced, cunning and stubborn. It was their fear that had made them Christians, not faith. If it were left to him, Feoktist told Nikon, he would have all their faces branded with the crucified Christ, he would have them wear special clothes, and the same for their children, and their children's children, and so on till the end of the world, just like lepers, because what were they if not lepers? Then everyone who saw a man walking in these clothes would know that he was from the nation that crucified the Son of God, would know – and never let them forget – that they had been born to experience not joy, but torment, born to suffer and repent.

Feoktist could not accept that the Jews could be right about anything, could not accept that they could even believe themselves to be right, but what he found particularly blasphemous was the thought that these Jews would be baptised in his own monastery and that they would indeed be right, even if, in the play, they failed Christ once more. The Yids, it turned out, were either in cahoots with Sertan or they had tricked both him and Nikon, and this mystery play was just another Jewish plot to return to the old faith, and not just to return surreptitiously, under cover, in the constant awareness that if anyone were to give them away they would be put to death, but to return in full view of everyone, and in full view of everyone to crucify Jesus Christ once more. Meanwhile, the brethren and anyone else from the Russian Orthodox faith who saw fit to attend would stand to one side and watch the Saviour being crucified, watch them jeering at the Son of God, tormenting Him and running amok, and not one person would intervene.

And Feoktist, in his hatred for the Jews, thought up a way of preventing the converts from Judaism from ever believing themselves to be right again, from ever thinking that they were those same Jews who had once believed they were right not to follow Christ, a way of making them realise that they were Judases to a man – first following Christ, then betraying Him. He determined that they should receive exactly thirty silver coins more than the others as their annual wage, and before Sertan had even caught wind of the plan he ordered the money to be distributed and everyone to be told. Just as he had anticipated, the converts mutinied as soon as they heard about the thirty pieces of silver and none of them took the money, even though the cunning cellarer brought it to them in person. This angered the Jews even more; no sooner did they catch sight of Feoktist than they began hurling abuse and expletives in his direction and flinging the purses he gave them back in his face, but the cellarer bore it all meekly, said nothing in reply, picked up the coins and, as he was leaving, gently remarked that he had given no cause for offence; the money was not his idea but Sertan's, for the very good reason that the Jews were being asked to play especially difficult and frightening roles – who would want to crucify Christ all over again?

For Sertan, these handouts ruined a whole year's work. After this not one of the converts from the Jewish faith would agree to take part in the play, and although Nikon, who had baptised the Jews himself, kept trying to convince them, and even wept as he begged them to forgive the cellarer and resume the rehearsals, they refused. When Sertan heard what Feoktist had been doing, he was ready to kill him. Nikon was also furious, but the cellarer simply said that he had acted with the best intentions, according to his understanding of the situation.

Now Sertan had to start his search for actors to play the Jews all over again. Some two or three years later, Feoktist would tell him that he regretted the fact that the converts had pulled out; hating them as he did, he also believed that Jews, and only Jews, should play these parts, and the money was only meant to show the Jews *how* to play them. Finding new 'Jews' proved difficult: those who had been taken on earlier knew that these were 'their' parts, and after the episode with the thirty pieces of silver they rejoiced that God had spared them; all the rest knew that these parts were 'not for them', and refused.

Sertan was at a loss, so Nikon suggested that to avoid some families thinking that God had rewarded them by giving them apostles, while other families had nothing, Sertan should act according to the words of Christ Himself in Matthew: 'I did not come to bring peace but a sword; because of me brother will rise against brother, son against father', and take the Jews, His enemies and persecutors, from the same peasant families from which he had picked Christ's apostles and pupils. In this way, equality would be maintained, and family would not be set against family; rather, inside the family, as inside a man, sin would struggle with righteousness.

Sertan followed his advice and by August 1664 it had been decided – this time, definitively – who would play whom, and the rehearsals resumed. Shortly before this Sertan, taking Matthew as his basis, had divided the events of the Gospels into a sequence of scenes and dialogues, sketched out every road and path, and marked what should go where. He had done so not only in his notebooks but also out in the open air, using multi-coloured stakes and flags around the monastery precincts; there was even a person charged with looking after them all, if they needed mending or if cattle knocked them over. In short, the map of Jesus Christ's movements across Palestine had been drawn and repeated with maximal precision.

It was a complex task which called for a good land surveyor (not easily found in Russia) who could work out the correct scale and make everything correspond to the landscapes described in the Gospels – for Nikon, at least, this was almost more important than getting the dates and distances right; but despite the general similarity between the territory of the New Jerusalem Monastery and the Palestine of the New Testament, the match was far from perfect, and considerable ingenuity was required to achieve an indisputable likeness. New hills had to be raised, trees had to be chopped down or planted, ponds as big as lakes had to be dug (for the main one, the Sea of Galilee, they built a tall weir and flooded part of the Istra-Jordan Valley). The labour was very intensive but, to the cellarer's satisfaction, soon paid off: several mills and machines were erected on the dam for breaking and scutching flax, fulling cloth and making paper, all of which brought the brethren a healthy income.

Once the dam had been built, the cellarer's attitude towards Sertan improved markedly; now that the rehearsals were in full swing and Feoktist could see that progress was being made, that Sertan was not twiddling his thumbs, not robbing the monastery, not sponging his food, now that Feoktist himself, just like Nikon, had got used to walking past the stakes that marked the Saviour's path amongst us, now that he had seen how and where another land was emerging from the monastery's land, had got used to the fact that gradually, little by little, the land managed by him, the cellarer, was giving birth to the Holy Land, that the Holy Land was being born from the most ordinary, most simple Russian land, that a genuine miracle of creation was unfolding before his very eyes, and even better that he himself was a part of it, assisting or just observing this gestation every single day – from this time onwards he, too, became filled with a sense of the importance and uniqueness of what was happening in New Jerusalem, and gradually became Sertan's defender and helper.

To judge by the sketches in his diary, Sertan drew inspiration for his *mises-en-scène* from Italian art (which he knew well, having lived in Rome and Milan for several years), especially Bellini. The arrangement of the actors, their poses and, perhaps most important of all, their characters, as well as the composition as a whole – all these, unless they contradicted Matthew, came from the paintings. There were other sources, too: Sertan used the Lives of the Saints, as well the oral tradition that existed in Russia, and the apocrypha, but the paintings came first; he even followed Bellini's physical portraits, especially those of secondary characters about whom nothing else was known, and this sped everything up enormously – otherwise the task would have become simply boundless.

But for all the importance of these models, and of the actors' previous occupations (a third of the apostles were fishermen, as in the Gospels, and there was even a tax collector), something else mattered much more to Sertan. In his diary he left a short description of the auditions.

Sertan would begin with a fairly large group of candidates and, sensing when one of them was unwell or unhappy, tired or in distress, he would read him words of love and kindness from the Gospels, and say, 'Be comforted, for Christ has come...'; and if he saw the man's soul filling with joy and tenderness, if he saw that Christ's words had struck home, that they were lifting a weight of sorrow from his shoulders, that this peasant would follow Christ, should He appear, without a second thought, then he would take him and could say with a clear conscience that Christ would have taken him too.

I wrote just now that the cellarer, too, had soon begun to see how the Holy Land was being born, how it was pushing through the Russian earth like grass in spring when the snow begins to melt, but nevertheless, on account of his previous loathing for Sertan, he was one of the last to do so; the others had seen this long before and had already learned to perceive and sense the entire area as the Promised Land, as Israel. For the peasants engaged in the play, the split that had run through their life until just recently – when they had had to live in two worlds at once, and act and exist differently in each of them: their role in one life didn't coincide in any way with their role in the other, and their previous experience was inapplicable, it just got in the way – well, that split gradually ceased to exist.

By this point, the monastery was providing those in the leading roles with everything they needed, and all they had to think about was the play. For them, let me repeat, these were not roles at all – they were their life, their mission, their destiny. As for the actors engaged in the minor episodes, they continued to plough the fields, but they had no trouble separating their first and second lives; their ordinary earthly existence was entirely subordinated to the play, it was a makeweight and a temporary one at that, as temporary as their mortal shell, while the life turned to Christ, to God, was eternal and, in reality, only that life existed, only that would endure. It was according to the laws of that eternal life that Nazareth, Bethlehem, Jericho, Jerusalem and all their environs were emerging and growing right here, in Russia, while the past quickly began to be crowded out and forgotten, along with any sense of who these people were before, of their history and the history of their land. Their vision underwent a drastic change, and even where Sertan's plans were still only an embryo, they saw them as if they were already fulfilled; they remembered his words the moment they left his mouth, developed them in their minds, and, it seems, could see only one purpose in the ongoing corrections to the landscape: to help the others, those left out of the rehearsals, those who, like little children, needed to touch with their fingers in order to believe. In other words, we see in New Jerusalem the attempt to build another, higher world on earth, a world where spirit is breathed into the earth itself, where the earth is raised by the soul, for the soul, and this happens almost at the very beginning, in only the third year of Nikon and Sertan's work together.

As soon as Sertan finished adapting the Italian paintings for the stage, having drawn hundreds upon hundreds of outlines, sketches and other illustrations connecting the pictures, he decided that it was time to start the rehearsals themselves, otherwise the actors he had selected might burn themselves out, might become used to the words, which would begin to weaken and die inside them.

But a few days later, once the rehearsals were under way, he caught himself thinking that now, on the contrary, he was scared that the actors might begin to think of themselves as professionals and behave accordingly, they might find out somehow that this was role-play, that it was all just ordinary theatre; he himself had already begun to forget that it was theatre, to forget that there were such things as plays and actors on this earth.

But there was little danger of this: no one in New Jerusalem knew what theatre was, and no one in the monastery would have guessed that Sertan was teaching the peasants something along the lines of the performances put on in Rus by entertainers wandering from village to village; that was how different the two things seemed. He had nothing to fear. As we can see here, neither professionals nor amateurs suited Sertan, and it was only because his play was not theatre that he could carry on at all.

His old fear that he would not be able to get by without professional actors still persisted, but it was receding. The sense that everything might somehow work out had kindled within him, and it derived from the general conviction that it could be no other way, from the fact that there had already been several successes, and although this confidence could hardly put paid to his previous apprehensions – they were chalk and cheese – it somehow pushed his fear further and further into the background with each passing day, to the point that he no longer even thought about it.

By the spring of 1665, Sertan had been in Russia seven

years. In this time he had gained a reasonable knowledge of the language, met hundreds of different people and even become quite close to a number of them, but for all this he still felt mystified both by Russia and by what was happening in New Jerusalem. To judge by his diary, he actually had a fairly accurate notion of much of it, but this notion was so strange that he could not believe it himself. He kept asking himself, over and over again, why he had not been allowed to return to France, why he had been forced to work for a patriarch who had fallen out of favour and to stage this peculiar play. He came up with a thousand answers, each more bizarre than the last, and every single one of them – whatever he may have had in mind at the time – expanded so quickly that it immediately began to embrace Russia as a whole. The country he ended up with was so inconceivable, so impossible that there had to be some mistake. Presumably, Sertan did not understand Russia, did not understand where it was headed, what fate it was preparing itself for, and for a long time, almost up to his final days, he also failed to understand what he himself was doing here, thanks to his warped, incomplete relationships with the people with whom fate had thrown him together.

These relationships were nearly always one-sided. Questions kept being asked of him, detailed answers and explications demanded, but no one ever explained much to him. Yes, he had seen many fragments of their lives, but he was rarely able to piece them together. This was true both in Moscow, where he had had long conversations with the boyars and the chancellery officials, and in New Jerusalem (his relationship with Nikon was the sole exception, and his conjectures about Russia were based mainly on what he had heard from him) where the monks, the peasants and anyone who was involved in the play in any shape or form would listen to him and remember his every word, but never tell him anything about themselves in return.

Just a year after his arrival in New Jerusalem, he became aware of the astonishing, but apparently widespread belief that only his words mattered, only that which flowed from him to them, and never the other way round. Being curious by nature, he resisted this for a long time, but his resistance floundered in the face of their conviction that they had nothing important to tell him, in their inability to understand that he might want to listen to *them*. He was surrounded by his own voice, words and actions to such an extent that he began to forget what he had learned about Russia in Moscow, and even what he had been told right here by Nikon. It was only in the final months of his life, on the march to Siberia, when he had been freed of his responsibilities, that he seems to have fully understood that Russia really was waiting for the end to come.

They had been waiting for years, since the first decade of the century, waiting in the monasteries, in Moscow, on the Don, in Siberia. Waiting, and here and there even naming the antichrist, herald of the last days, who had already come to rule on earth. Some said it was Nikon, others that it was Avvakum; almost all were convinced that it was one of the two, though there were other candidates as well. Among the peasants at the monastery there were many followers of Avvakum – no less, perhaps, than of Nikon, and that was hardly surprising: the Patriarch's building project was draining all their strength, especially now that they no longer benefited from the Tsar's largesse. The monastery authorities were meaner and crueller than ever, and this only reinforced their sense that the end was at hand.

Almost from the very first day that Sertan began choosing actors for the parts, he and his work became the only extraneous and, crucially, neutral authority for both the Nikonians and the Old Believers in their disputes about the end of time (after all, the doctrine of the end of the world, of judgment and reward, was the main feature of Sertan's faith, too, so there was common ground here), and he himself, though it took him a long time to realise it, was at the centre of everything: of every relationship, conflict and argument, many of which were shaped by the interpretation of his own words and the course of the rehearsals. The following must also be noted: amidst this collective expectation of the end, amidst the hourly accusations that one man or the other was the antichrist, Sertan's rehearsals were the first real events that, for every person close to them and touched by them, undeniably testified that the last days had already begun, and that judgement was at hand. It was always like that with foreigners: while the Russians bickered amongst themselves about who was to blame and who was the antichrist, the foreigners would ignore these lofty questions and quietly go about their business. The position that Sertan occupied, and the respect he commanded, was without precedent, for various reasons: there was the particular affection shown to him and no one else by Nikon, and there was the fact that Sertan never interfered in anything, stood outside everything, every hierarchy, every relationship, and yet without him nothing ever got going, nothing moved, as if the entire monastery revolved around him.

There was something else, too: to ensure that they would do exactly what Sertan wanted from them the actors had to spend long periods praying with Nikon, and these prayers were meant to prepare them for their rehearsals without Christ and make up for Christ's absence (Sertan, as I have already said, was not allowed to let anyone play Christ). These hours spent standing before the Lord with the Patriarch, an experience quite unlike anything any of them had known before, were no more than a preliminary stage before the main event, Sertan's rehearsals, which, as rehearsals go, were perfectly unexceptional. The combination of prayers and rehearsals itself reinforced and supplemented the strange subordination of Nikon to Sertan, a subordination that was unthinkable, yet real; no one could fail to see it, but everyone was afraid of trying to understand it, sensing that this, too, was a sign of the end. Of the time when the last would be first.

Among the peasants who belonged to the New Jerusalem Monastery there were Nikonians, Old Believers, and heretics who, as followers of Monk Kapiton, believed that now, before the end, the Son of God had come to dwell in each and every one of them, and each and every one of them had become like Christ. All these large groups argued desperately about who was serving the antichrist and who was serving Christ, although there were many other people too, people who, in all that was happening, understood one thing only: the last days were nigh, and when they came many would follow the antichrist, because it would be difficult, even impossible to distinguish him from Christ. 'Many will be led astray by him' – and they did not trust themselves, did not believe that they would be able to tell them apart, after all even now they did not know who was right, Nikon or Avvakum, just like back then, but that did not matter; what mattered was that the antichrist and Christ were bound to each other by fate, first one, then the other, and there had to be some who would be led astray – there was no way round it – and in fact these would be in the majority. So the antichrist would reign – there was no way round his temporary triumph, either – and only then would Christ come, only then would He save everyone. Hence the necessity and inevitability of the antichrist, of his temptations, hence too his fusing with Christ, their peculiar resemblance, after all they were like two hypostases, two faces of a single being, and in the end only they could tell who was who and who would triumph.

It was well known that only a few would recognise them, which meant that everyone else had been cast as spectators or extras, present merely to set in sharper contrast the final victory of good over evil, of Jesus Christ over His enemy. Just as later, when, at Sertan's say-so, they followed the Christ who was not there, forming, almost miming, His distinct and precise outline with their movements, so now the antichrist had to outline Christ, and the fact that many would be tempted by him spoke not only of the reign of evil and the world's depravity, but also of the fact that evil is mysterious and incomprehensible, and how could one even begin to fight it if even the righteous would believe the antichrist and follow him? Human beings, with their slow life, their slow labour, their service to God, their merely partial and feeble righteousness were fading into the background, and the struggle of the universal elements, the struggle of good and evil, was beginning – of this there was no doubt. After all, it had long been known how it would all unfold and how it would end; the only thing that nobody knew was when. Through this final struggle and the final victory of good, all that had been on earth until then, all that man had done and wanted to do, whether righteous or otherwise, was coming to an end, and although the Last Judgement would follow, as was only fair, in order to give everyone his due and draw a line, even if it was only a line under the life of each individual person (which of course was also fair: everyone must answer for their own sins), the question of why man had been created, for what possible purpose, was left hanging.

In May 1665 Sertan gradually completed the preparatory

stage of his work – drumming the text of the Gospels into the actors and explaining it to them – and moved onto general rehearsal. As agreed, he went to see Nikon on the eve of the first rehearsal to tell him he was about to start. Together they carefully looked over Sertan's brief descriptions of the performers one last time (Sertan needed them so as to remember all the actors and not mix them up). Nikon pronounced himself satisfied and was particularly pleased that all the apostles were the same sorts of people as in the Gospels: the two sons of Zebedee were fishermen, Matthew was a tax collector, and so on. Sertan explained to Nikon that when the Calendar of the Saints gave no information about this or that person, he would use the apocrypha that he had obtained, with no little effort, from some Poles. Nikon approved this too once he heard that the words of the apostles in the apocrypha matched their image and fate no less than the words and images of the other apostles whose lives had entered the canon; it was like a test of the apostles, and of the apocrypha at the same time.

Nikon had several old icons representing all twelve apostles and two showing the faces of Christ's seventy disciples. Sertan had not seen them before, and – he told Nikon – he was struck by the resemblance to the faces of those he had chosen, as if the artist had used his own actors as the models. This was a good sign, and Nikon was troubled only by the fact that the apostles chosen by Sertan were younger, but there was an easy explanation for this: their time had not yet come and they were not yet ready. Their conversation, in other words, went very well; all of these newly revealed resemblances were a fillip to Sertan's confidence, and that was before Nikon let slip that he had prepared a present for him: three genuine Magi had been brought to the monastery from the Northern Urals. Sertan, who was minded to leave the scene with the Wise Men until virtually the last rehearsal, because he could not find anyone to play them and did not know what to do with these roles anyway, was overjoyed and went with Nikon to have a look at them. He was surprised at how different they were from the ones he had seen in paintings; even before this he had doubted the truthfulness of those pictures, and that must have been why the scene that included the Wise Men refused to come together in his mind. Now he decided – and said as much to Nikon – that he would finish the 'Adoration of the Magi' within a month at most, after which he would follow the sequence of events as given in the Gospels. Nikon was glad to have pleased Sertan and glad he was starting the next day, and merely reminded him to send over the actors he would be needing three hours before the rehearsal. And to continue doing so until further notice.

After seeing the Wise Men, Sertan found himself thinking, to his own surprise, that perhaps there really was somebody helping Nikon and him, and he decided to begin the rehearsal with the very hardest scenes – the ones where a great multitude of people followed and surrounded the Christ who was not there.

Sertan wanted to rehearse the events related in Matthew 8 where a large crowd follows Christ and He heals first a leper, then a centurion's servant, then others, speaks with a scribe, gets into a boat, His disciples get in too, and together they cast off from the shore.

In the evening he got his assistant to inform everyone taking part in this scene that at dawn they should present themselves, according to Nikon's instructions, at the Church of the Holy Sepulchre. The next day the peasants stood through matins, after which Nikon prayed with them for another two hours or so in one of the side chapels. Sertan was not present, nor would he be in the future when, before every rehearsal, Nikon prayed with all those due to take part. With time Sertan would gain a fairly clear idea of what these sessions were like; Nikon's frenzied passion and vision of Christ, he later learned, were such that those who were with him also began to see Christ, would continue to see Him afterwards and, therefore, could follow Him.

Right before the first rehearsal Sertan's old fears returned and, instead of making a start, he tediously, long-windedly, hopelessly – so much had already been done, yet it was as if he hadn't even begun, as if everything was still ahead of him, and he felt sure that nothing would work, that nothing could ever work – explained to them where and how they should stand, which direction they should walk in, where and how they should turn, where and to whom Christ would be speaking, what He would say and how they should reply, then he arranged them once more in their original positions and ordered them to begin with a wave of his hand. What followed is hard to understand as anything other than a miracle, for it turned out that all he had to do was put them in their positions and show them the spot where Christ was standing for them all to start moving as if Christ were really with them. They really did follow Him, turned, stopped, listened, then walked on, then stopped again, surrounded Him, listened, walked on again, always stretching out behind Him in a line as if He were right there amongst them. With their movements, their eyes, the way they arranged themselves around him in a perfect semi-circle so that everyone could see Him, they were unmistakably delineating Christ, His space, His bulk.

To confirm this impression, Sertan himself drew several sketches on paper of how they were walking or standing, and although he could not begin to understand it, he felt certain each time that this was no delusion – Christ really was there, Christ really was present. He was outlined by them in precise strokes, in the true and full dimensions of His life. And they did it all with a level of detail unthinkable for any play, not to mention one filled with crowd scenes. Over and over again, forgetting what he was doing or why – it was the truth that he was after: was this a miracle or wasn't it? – he would force them to walk *en masse*, to stop, then walk on once more: yes, Christ was there.

Even while he was still in New Jerusalem, before he was exiled to Siberia, it would sometimes occur to Sertan that the end really was approaching, that it was already at hand, and this was hardly surprising; he was far too bound up in it all and playing a far too prominent role – constantly thinking, constantly acting out every little detail in his mind – for the sense of the end not to enter into him, eat into him. Although Sertan, like any Christian, believed in the Last Judgement and the Second Coming, this had always seemed so far off to him that he had imagined the life of the human race to be something endless, but now, when he, like the others, had begun to believe that the end was nigh, the first thing he found himself thinking was that for at least one minute there would be such-and-such a number of people living on the earth and not one person more, and you could probably count these people, and how interesting it would be to know who would be the last person born on earth and how many would still be in the womb and not born in time. Of course, as the most innocent of human beings, these last would go to heaven, but it was precisely with them in mind that Sertan grasped the meaning of the words of John the Evangelist: that before the end calamities will spread, sin will multiply, and almost everyone will follow the antichrist, and he suddenly asked himself in astonishment: what was it all for? Why had people lived on earth? Now, before the end, this question was more than warranted; the time had come to draw conclusions and one thing was clear: people had not reformed, they had not even improved. Why then all this suffering and woe? Surely not just to allow God to manifest His glory and defeat the antichrist? Or was it to separate the wheat from the chaff, the righteous from the sinners? But then why was the history of the righteous also coming to an end, and why did the Lord God need there to be an exact number of them as well – and not a single one more?

Sertan felt as if he were walking a tightrope and he knew that there was only one way for him to survive: to avoid thinking about such things at all, to exercise extreme caution with Nikon, with the monks, most of whom obviously disliked him, and with the peasants, many of whom were no doubt relaying his every word to Nikon, as was the custom here, and to remember at all times that in Russia he was a nobody, worse – a heretic, a follower of a different creed, and whatever he said had to be as neutral as he could make it and valid for all Christians. Above all, it had to be, or seem to be, absolutely essential in Nikon's eyes, easily comprehensible and explicable. Only his neutrality and loyalty to Nikon, his complete lack of any independent agenda, could save him. But life was moving in a different direction.

It was Sertan's relationship with the Jews that first gave rise to suspicions of heresy. The peasants who had been given their roles were playing a sly game: they were bending over backwards to be in the wrong, and Sertan could do nothing about it. So then, to make them understand why the Jews were in the right, he began telling the peasants about everything he had witnessed in Poland. He played on their feelings by describing Cossack atrocities, then moved on to the Jewish way of life, to how Jews prayed to God, how they sought to understand and interpret Holy Scripture. During rehearsals he told them that for many centuries Jews had drawn up 'chronicles of sorrow' in memory of the calamities and persecutions which they had endured in various countries, but the persecutions were so numerous that almost every day became a day of fasting, a day of mourning, so then their teacher Rabbi Shimon Ben Gamliel forbade them from doing this any longer and said: 'We cherish the memory of the woes we have suffered no less than our forefathers cherished them, but we lack the strength to describe them all.' The Jews would say of themselves that the curse of Moses had come to pass amongst them: 'Also every sickness and every plague, which is not written in this Book of the Law, will the Lord bring upon you until you are destroyed. You shall be left few in number, whereas you were as the stars of heaven in multitude... Then the Lord will scatter you among all peoples, from one end of the earth to the other' (Deuteronomy 28).

'What should we do?' they said. 'How can we justify ourselves? Can we really deny our guilt, when our sins testify against us? The Almighty has caught His slaves in their crimes, and His verdict is just! We can console ourselves only with the thought that: "Whom the Lord loves He punishes"' (Proverbs 3).

Sertan's encounter with Jews happened by chance. It was during the Khmelnytsky Uprising, when his theatre, fleeing looters, ended up in Tulchyn some three weeks before several bands of Cossacks surrounded the town.[8] While the Cossacks laid siege, Sertan's troupe performed every evening for a whole month. They had been ordered to do so by the garrison

---

8   The Ukrainian Cossack uprising of 1648 in the Polish-Lithuanian Commonwealth, led by Bohdan Khmelnytsky and resulting in the creation of a Cossack Hetmanate.

commander, Prince Czetwertyński, and Sertan recalled how glad he felt that the actors had work to do. Citing that same order, he made them rehearse all morning long.

Czetwertyński, to judge by Sertan's description of him in the diary, was a courteous man who was no longer young and extremely fat. He breathed heavily and unevenly, wheezing as he did so. In the evenings, when his heart got tired of pumping blood around his enormous body, his legs swelled up and he could barely walk. After the second performance he took Annette, Sertan's lead actress, home with him, and she only came back the next day.

Sertan had wanted to leave Poland from the very first days of the war, and he would have done so were it not for Annette. In Poland, everybody waited on her hand and foot; she reigned supreme on and off the stage, and she didn't want to hear anyone even mention France or Brittany. Sertan was prepared to go back to France without the troupe, but not without Annette, so he stayed too. She was his, by any measure; he loved her and he was ready to wait until she came to her senses and came back to him. He had bought her in Rouen from her father, an acrobat and tightrope walker, when she was only twelve, and had turned her into a proper actress. She owed not only her gait, but her every movement, her every gesture to his training; her body was intelligent and obedient, and much came easily to her. She was talented and intuitive, so he was able to explain to her not only what the protagonists were saying in the plays in which she performed but also things that could never have found their way into drama, because plays are only a part of life, albeit, perhaps, the most important one. More than that: he taught her how to think and speak and, for that matter, feel; he filled her with everything he had, loved her always and, needless to say, could never have left her behind.

Annette's name was all over Sertan's diary until the very moment of his capture. Often the entries devoted to her would run without interruption for many pages at a time. Misha and I would grow weary of her, weary of translating these monotonous outpourings. Day after day Sertan would declare his love to Annette, complain, weep, beg her to come back to him – and then suddenly start swearing, calling her a slut and a whore, cursing both her and himself for making an actress of her, before begging her once more to forgive him and come back. I doubt she read these diary entries, but she probably knew of them.

Annette became Sertan's wife when she was fourteen, but she loved the theatre more than she loved him, and felt closer to the actors than she did to him; in fact, her first infidelities were with them. She undermined his relationships with the actors, undermined his authority; the feverish mood within the company, which almost led to its disintegration, was down to her. But Sertan was unable to give her up. Three years after their wedding the entire repertoire stood or fell by her and, with no way out, he told her she was free to see whichever actors she wanted. She became like all the rest, and ceased to be his wife. This had happened six years before, when she had just turned nineteen. Since then, she had only come to him twice.

Annette told Sertan herself that she had spent the night with Czetwertyński and that she would probably stay with him. She'd been telling Sertan about her lovers for some time because she was aware that her movements were being followed and that he already knew everything there was to know about her. Sertan felt no jealousy towards Czetwertyński: he was ugly as sin – Annette could not love him. By now there were people starving in the town, and the troupe could see that but for this affair the company would be in a bad way. Not that he was grateful to her, of course, but over the six years that they had been apart he had learned to pity her.

Sertan was surprised that Czetwertyński made them perform every evening, and he asked Annette why. She said that the prince loved her and loved the theatre, and Sertan, precisely because he pitied Annette and knew Czetwertyński was ugly, began telling her that her lover was brave and wise: just two days earlier, accounts of Cossack atrocities had brought the town to a standstill and only on their stage did life continue as if no one had ever heard of war, only there did the righteous defeat the strong and good triumph over evil. If the Cossacks had come a little earlier, they would have taken Tulchyn in a flash, but now everyone was ready to fight, everyone was confident of success, and it was the theatre that had made this possible.

Soldiers in Tulchyn were thin on the ground: only six hundred-odd Polish nobles and two thousand Jews, many of whom, it must be said, knew a thing or two about war. The common enemy had made allies of the Poles and the Jews, who now swore mutual loyalty. The Poles gave the Jews weapons, and together they set about fortifying the town.

Czetwertyński was old and rarely took Annette home with him; soon she began another affair. When Annette came to Sertan to tell him that her new lover was Ruvim, son of the head of Tulchyn's Jews, the Gaon, Sertan was frightened.

Ruvim was almost a child, but more Christ-like in appearance than any mortal could be. Sertan had also noticed him in the street some three days earlier and, without knowing anything about him, had immediately thought that here was the person he needed for his troupe: Annette as Mary Magdalene and the boy as Christ. Then, back home, the realisation struck him that Christ had been a Jew and, however outlandish the thought, he would not have been surprised to find that this was Jesus Christ come to save them, and if the boy was just an ordinary Jew, well, Christ had also been an ordinary Jew.

He could see that Annette was also thinking that Ruvim was Christ, and she probably said as much to Sertan; she told him that for as long as this boy, her very own boy, was with them, the Lord would not abandon them and the Cossacks would not take the town.

Even so, Sertan could not just let her go. He grabbed Annette by the hand and started yelling that she would end up destroying all of them, Poles and Jews alike, and that if Czetwertyński found out who he was sharing her with, he would have all the Jews killed and there would be no one left at all. But Annette seemed unhinged; she wouldn't listen to anything and merely repeated through her tears that she loved Ruvim and that nobody could make her feel as happy as he did.

This had never happened before. She had always told Sertan that she felt nothing towards her lovers; it was only as an actress that she needed them, she and the whole troupe. But now, when she told him that she loved another man, he understood something that should have been obvious long before: she would never come back to him, there was no point waiting, and there had been no point waiting all these years. He realised that she had never loved him and had probably never loved anyone except Ruvim.

He let her go. Now it no longer mattered to him what would happen to them all, to her and to this Ruvim of hers, or to Czetwertyński, or to all the other Poles and Jews.

Some ten thousand Cossacks were laying siege to Tulchyn, and they were led by one of Khmelnytsky's lieutenants, Hetman Gunya. Several times they came up close to the city walls, looking for the best place to storm the town, but they immediately came under sustained fire from the Poles and Jews, and were driven back with heavy losses. In the evening, just as soon as the Cossacks started retreating, the Jews sallied out, chased them down and, after a brief skirmish, killed up to fifty of them. That was when the Cossacks realised that they would never be able to take Tulchyn with the forces at their disposal, so they began gathering reinforcements from all around, promising plenty of loot to every soldier. The next time they approached the town, they already numbered about thirty thousand.

In the forest, not far from the fortress, they secretly constructed a large iron battering ram, so as to demolish the wall at dawn and begin their assault. But one of the Jews spotted them and raised the alarm. Czetwertyński and the Gaon sent help over just in time, and the besieged town managed to repel the Cossacks once more and put them to flight. After this failure, Gunya realised that he was simply wasting both time and men. The Cossacks convened a 'circle', and decided to seek an agreement with the Poles. That same night they sent a trusted man to Czetwertyński with a cordial letter in which they promised him and his fellow Polish nobles peace, on condition that they handed over all the Jews' goods as compensation. After brief deliberation, the Poles agreed.

Annette was spending the night with the prince. At dawn she came running over to Sertan and begged him to go and warn the Jews. At first he tried to persuade her that the Poles would change their minds, that they were honest people, but he could see she did not believe him. So then he told her that if everything she was telling him was true and the Cossacks really had struck a bargain with the Poles, there was nothing anyone could do. If he, Sertan, were to warn the Jews, then who knows, they might manage to get the better of the Poles, just as the Poles might manage to get the better of them, but one way or the other neither would stand a chance against the Cossacks on their own. Then, with a laugh, he quipped that if Ruvim was Christ, the Lord would defend the Jews and would not permit their destruction. He thought he had convinced her with this and that she wouldn't go to Ruvim, before realising, a moment later, that he was mistaken. So then he grabbed her, started kissing her and threw her onto the bed. She understood he was about to take her and, when he entered her, began crying and stroking his head: he had been her first, and she had once loved him. Then he agreed to do whatever she wanted.

That night Sertan visited the Gaon, who heard him out but said nothing to his own men. At dawn the Poles started calling out the Jews one by one and disarming them. When the Jews realised that the Poles were in cahoots with the Cossacks and had betrayed them, they wanted to kill all the nobles before engaging the enemy.

There were more of them, and the Poles could see that if it came to a fight, they would lose. The Jews drew their sabres, only for the Gaon to raise his voice and stop them. He said: 'Listen, my brothers, my people! We are in exile, scattered amongst the tribes: if you raise your hand against the Polish nobles in Tulchyn, other rulers will hear of it and, God forbid, take their revenge against our other brothers in exile. I tell you, therefore, that if such a misfortune has been sent to us by Heaven, we should accept this punishment with humility – after all, we are no better than others who share our faith. May the Almighty instil mercy towards us in our foes!'

The Jews obeyed him and put up no further resistance; they surrendered their weapons to the Poles and brought all their money and valuables to the town square.

When the Cossacks entered the town, Czetwertyński told

them: 'Here is everything you asked for.' The Cossacks took the goods and divided them, then ordered the prince to gaol the Jews. Three days later they told the Polish nobles to hand over the Jews. The Poles were too scared to cross them and did as they were told. The Cossacks led the Jews out of the town, herded them into a large garden, stationed some guards there and left.

Among the Jews there were three Gaons: Lazarus, Solomon and Khaim. They prayed unceasingly and exhorted their people to hallow God's name and not betray the faith. The people answered with one voice: 'Hear, O Israel: The Lord our God is One Lord! Just as in your hearts there is no one except God alone, so too in our hearts there is only the One!'

The next morning a messenger arrived from the Cossacks. He thrust his standard into the ground and declared: 'Whoever wishes to change his faith will survive if they come and sit beneath this flag.' After issuing the invitation three times and seeing not a single Jew rise to his feet, he opened the gate; the Cossacks entered the garden on horseback and massacred everyone they found in it.

After killing the Jews, the Cossacks decided to take the town castle. So then the Poles said to them: 'But you gave us your word! You will be committing a sin if you break the agreement.'

To this the Cossacks replied: 'Serves you right! Just as you betrayed the Jews, so we will betray you.'

The Poles began firing from the walls, but the Cossacks managed to set the castle alight, storm it and massacre the Poles. They dealt with Czetwertyński last. Before killing the prince, they raped his wife and two daughters in his presence, then one of his serfs, a miller, came up to him, doffed his hat and said with an ironic bow: 'What, pray, are His Highness's orders?' before adding in the same breath: 'Go on, get out of your chair. I will sit in it now and order you about.'

But Czetwertyński, all swollen with dropsy, could not get up. So then the miller pulled him to the floor, dragged him over to the threshold and sawed off his head.

Bringing his description of the Tulchyn slaughter to a close, Sertan noted in his diary that God had paid the Poles back for their treachery; moreover, on learning what had happened in Tulchyn, other Poles considered the punishment to have been fully deserved, and from that moment they formed a common front with the Jews and never betrayed them to the Cossacks again. Even when the latter swore that they would not touch anyone except the Jews, the Poles no longer believed them. Had this not happened, the Jews would have all disappeared without trace.

Two days after the slaughter, Gunya sent one of the Cossacks to the garden. There, the Cossack shouted that any Jews who had survived had nothing to fear: they could get up and go wherever they wanted. Some three hundred Jews stood up; they had all saved their lives by lying among the dead. They were racked by hunger and heat; sick and injured, barefoot and naked, they made their way to the town, where the citizens gave them succour and set them free.

After the Cossacks had killed the Polish nobles, Sertan was sure that the theatre company would be next in line. And sure enough, the Cossacks seized them and fleeced them but then one of their number, possibly the same miller who dealt with Czetwertyński, shouted that, having massacred the Poles, they were themselves like noblemen and should enjoy themselves like noblemen. The others liked this idea, and they did not touch the actors.

That evening Gunya summoned Sertan and said that the

Cossack host was keen to watch his plays, on condition that they acted as well as they had for the Poles, otherwise the Cossacks would take offence, and then it would be hard to stop them.

Annette was involved in every play in the repertoire, and Sertan wondered whether she would be capable of acting now that Ruvim was dead. Annette went off while he was visiting Gunya, and only came back in the morning. Sertan later discovered that she had spent the night with a Cossack who helped her find Ruvim's body among the other bodies in the garden and bury it in the Jewish cemetery.

Annette carried off her roles under Gunya almost as well as she always had, and Sertan thought that if they left Tulchyn she would slowly recover. But she was not fated to leave the town.

When Gunya left, only a small garrison remained in the fortress, and the troupe was free to go; but dozens of gangs were on the loose and the actors had to stay put. They spent another three months in Tulchyn until eventually a Polish detachment bound for the north drove the Cossacks out of the town. They were led by the nephew of the great hetman Koniecpolski. Sertan knew the nephew well, and the latter agreed to take the troupe with him. This was a rare piece of good fortune, and it would have been a crime not to take advantage. But by this point Annette was no longer in any state to accompany them. She had fallen ill two weeks earlier and was in a very bad way. Sertan and the Poles took her to a small Orthodox convent, the only one to have survived in the surrounding area, and persuaded the nuns to take her in. Sertan left her a fair amount of money, and they decided that as soon as she felt better and the roads became safer, he would come to fetch her. A year later, he did indeed make his way back to the convent and learned, from the inscription on a tombstone, that Annette had died just two days after his departure.

Essentially, everything Sertan told the peasants about the Jews was a director's ploy of which he was rightly proud; it didn't even occur to him that he might be accused of heresy, but that is precisely what happened. He had no trouble defending himself to Nikon, and it was only after he had sworn his innocence and laughed off the suggestion that he, Sertan, might espouse the Jewish faith, and after Nikon had agreed with him and also laughed, that he found himself thinking almost compulsively about the faith of the Jews, about their devotion to God, about Ruvim, who looked so much like Christ, about why they had accepted their death rather than massacring the Poles who betrayed them. Everything he had told the actors had been crafted so cunningly and so skilfully that something began to change inside him as well, just as it had, perhaps, in Annette. This frightened him, and he stopped talking to the actors about Jews, telling himself that enough was enough, but he thought about them ever more often, ever more compulsively. He was haunted by the image of Ruvim wrapped in a shroud like Christ, and at night he would dream that he, Sertan, had been present when Christ was being killed, and when He was buried.

There was no lack of heretical material in Sertan's rehearsals with the other performers either, whatever his intentions to the contrary. As in a Protestant service, there was no intermediary; Christ spoke through Sertan directly to the peasants, and they spoke back to Him, one on one. This was some other, non-Orthodox faith, more like that of the Strigolniki, one of the heretical sects Nikon had told him about (in a blatant hint at the punishment that would await Sertan if he chose this path).[9] Sertan was fully aware of this, and more and more apprehensive each day, but there was no other path open to him.

Who, Sertan often wondered, would end up playing Christ in his play? For whom was Nikon keeping this part? For Christ, who would appear when His time came, or for some other person? Nikon himself could be one of those others. With his fame and his power, he might well think that he was Christ incarnate.

Sertan's suspicion that Nikon was reserving the role of Christ for himself and that, when the designated period of time elapsed, it was Nikon who would appear to take the place of Christ, was well-founded – of that there can be no doubt. It was clear from their conversations that Nikon shared the conviction of many Russians that, at the Second Coming, Christ would be embodied in one of their number, and this second incarnation, which would bring the life of man on earth to an end, would be even more important than the first, which only marked the beginning of salvation, and therefore this second Christ would be greater than the first, and His grace would also be greater.

Listening to Nikon, Sertan came to the conclusion more than once that Nikon was convinced that Christ was already present on earth, and had long been present: He just hadn't announced himself yet. In every respect – his behaviour, his status, his fate, not to mention the unmistakable evasiveness in his actions and words – Nikon was the likeliest candidate to play Christ and when, following the peasants' prayer sessions with Nikon, everything suddenly started moving, moving more smoothly than could ever have been imagined – it was a genuine miracle – Sertan caught himself thinking that he, too,

---

9 The Strigolniki broke with Orthodoxy as early as the fourteenth century, criticising the corruption of its clergy.

now believed in Nikon: if Nikon could do all this then this was surely his play, which reinforced the suspicion that Nikon was Christ. But there was something else here too: Sertan did not like Nikon, there was no kindness in him, and it was hard to understand why, if Nikon really was Christ, he should need Sertan at all. All this was so murky and so dangerous; here in Russia, Sertan was a nobody and Nikon was his sole protector: crossing him, or even attempting to cross him, was out of the question.

When Sertan began to believe that in New Jerusalem people really were expecting Jesus Christ, he did not want Nikon to be Christ. He was jealous of Nikon, he disliked him, and it pained him to think that he should be preparing the ground for this man. Moreover, he remembered Ruvim and understood, intellectually at least, that Nikon was not Christ, could not be Christ; after Ruvim, he knew what Christ should be like. Sertan believed that he would be the first to see and recognise Christ, if Christ really were to appear, and his hunch was that He would be none other than Ruvim. It was the actors who were responsible for instilling this belief in him. While the rehearsals were under way, he was constantly aware of how they saw him and who they took him for, who he was for them; his connection with the actors was a visceral one and for some time now they had all been living only for each other, inseparably, like a mother and the infant in her womb.

There came a time, a year or so later, when Nikon began to suspect him, to suspect that Sertan's role was not enough for him, that he was aspiring to the role of Messiah. Nikon even spoke about this with the cellarer: what if this really were the case? Surely a Frenchman could never be the Son of God, and the Lord could never choose a Catholic – but who can know His ways? Unable to decide on a course of action, he merely told the cellarer to keep a close eye on Sertan.

Nikon knew that it was precisely from him, from Sertan, that the peasants had first heard Holy Scripture, that he was the one who had given it to them, and even if Sertan always took a neutral tone, emphasising thousands upon thousands of times that he was a nobody who had nothing to do with Christ, and even if on the many occasions when he could have lightened and hastened their labour by taking upon himself the role of Christ, so that the peasants could have acted with a partner rather than empty space, he never once chose to do so, even then, it was from him that they had come to know Holy Scripture, him they were always acting before, him they saw when they spoke, him they talked to, him they wanted to please and to tell that they had understood everything... everything. Practising in their huts, they would see before them now Christ, now Sertan – the man who would judge their work – and in their minds the two of them, Christ and Sertan, often merged into one.

Everybody, not only those acting in the play, noticed something else as well: Sertan was a stranger who had come to them from elsewhere, just as Christ once had. The way he played himself down, the way he emphasised that whoever Christ was, it certainly wasn't him – that was just as it should be. All the other candidates were energetic, assertive, resolute, while he was gentle and weak and kept himself to himself; there were so many others and they were all the same, so they were false and only he was true. But Sertan wasn't always weak: they were used to obeying him. This, too, was important.

Sertan could see, to his horror, that more and more of them were taking him for Christ, and he knew that Nikon knew this, that people were openly calling him Christ, and Nikon – the antichrist. But Nikon needed Sertan just as much as before, and a strange relationship developed between them, a game to see who knew what about whom. Belief in Sertan continued to spread: only he was merciful, only he did not punish, did not oppress. It was his quiet demeanour and daily labour that attracted others to him, because, as I've already said, many had realised by now that the main thing was not to stick out, for there was no way of guessing who was Christ and who the antichrist, and it was better to go slow and steady, without trying to get ahead of anyone else, better to work and please God, just as Sertan did, so it was Sertan they should cling to.

In trying to establish whether Sertan was Christ, Nikon sent one of his monks to Ukraine and learned from his reports all about Ruvim, about Sertan's attitude to Ruvim and about how similar Ruvim was to Christ. Hating Sertan as he did, he readily believed that Ruvim was Christ, and he was delighted to learn that the Saviour was not a Catholic. After Ruvim, Nikon ceased to fear Sertan, and their relationship became calmer. The very fact that fate had already brought Sertan face to face with Christ explained why he understood the Saviour so well, an understanding that was hardly in doubt when you saw how skilfully he pulled everything off, and above all, when you saw how his actors performed, as if they were not actors at all and as if this were all happening not here and now in New Jerusalem, but in the real Jerusalem 1666 years before.

Sertan could see that Nikon was ready to punish him at the next available opportunity; the only thing stopping Nikon was the knowledge that he wouldn't be able to do the mystery play without him. Sertan was sure that just as soon as he had broken the back of the play, Nikon would kill him, kill him because there were people who believed that Christ would be incarnated in him, a Catholic. And in fact Nikon blamed only himself for this heresy and repented, during confession, of the way he had almost forced Sertan to become Christ; if Sertan really was Christ (he taunted himself before knowing of Ruvim) then the Holy Land that he, Nikon, had created here in Russia was right, while the Orthodox faith of which he was leader was wrong.

Sertan understood that to save himself he needed to slow everything down, but the work had already entered a rhythm that he could neither stop nor change. He was already so immersed in this work that it was the only thing he lived for, the only thing that interested him, and everything else – whether he survived or was killed, whether he saw his play or he didn't – was of little concern to him, and the fact that he knew what Nikon thought of him and what Nikon would do just as soon as the rehearsals came to an end made no difference to anything. The rehearsals were going so well and it was so very clear that this was the real thing that all those in New Jerusalem who thought that they knew when the end would come – whatever the precise date they had in mind – began to take the view that it would start with the last rehearsal.

The monk who was dispatched to Poland and Ukraine to investigate Sertan and who told Nikon about Ruvim did not merely supply detailed information about where Ruvim was from and who his family were, but even managed to dig up Ruvim's grave and discover that he had not risen from the dead. The knowledge that Ruvim had been killed and buried but not resurrected was exceptionally important to Nikon. One day, however, he was struck by the blasphemous thought that the world would never be saved, that Christ had already come and the antichrist had defeated Him. The Orthodox Cossacks had killed Him when He came to them. They killed Him because they did not acknowledge Him as one of their own, which indeed He was not, so they were right not to acknowledge

Him: there was something important in this, something that tallied with His first coming. Nikon tried long and hard to get to the bottom of it, without success, though he was relieved that Sertan was out of the picture, while later on he even became convinced that Sertan had been wrong about Ruvim. But sometimes all this would start over again and, to his own amazement, he would find himself thinking that it probably was Ruvim after all, that it was only right that it should be a Jew, that Christ should be incarnated in a Jew.

Nikon spent eight years in New Jerusalem and when he was taken off to Moscow and nobody knew if he would ever come back, Sertan, who thought he would not, wrote the following in his diary, as if summing up those eight years in the Patriarch's life: 'God allowed the Patriarch to see the fruits of his labours. He managed to build almost the entire church, albeit in unfinished form, right up to the vaults, and to consecrate three chapels within it: the Chapel of Holy Golgotha, the Chapel of the Dormition built in the north-eastern side of the church, where the dark chamber known as the Prison of Christ is located in the Jerusalem church, and, beneath Golgotha, the Chapel of St John the Baptist, "who suffered for the truth, rejoicing", where Nikon wishes to be buried.' That was all.

Neither in this entry nor in any of those that follow does Sertan mention the play even once. These entries are composed as if nothing had ever happened in New Jerusalem save the construction of the monastery, or if it had, then he, Sertan, had never heard about it. Nobody in Russia could have read his diary so he had nothing to fear, and while Misha and I were translating this section I could only assume that after Nikon was taken away to Moscow, Sertan, freed from his influence and control for the first time in all his years at the monastery, was quickly emerging from this six-year-long trance, from all this madness and delirium, and was beginning to see everything as he had in the first few months of his life in New Jerusalem. He was the first to drop out, the first to stop waiting for Christ. But Misha did not agree with me: in his view, the extraordinary, uncharacteristic detail which the diarist lavished on the day of Nikon's departure from New Jerusalem indicates that, at least at the beginning, Sertan considered this day and everything else that concerned Nikon to be virtually the crux of the confrontation between Christ and antichrist. He had begun, once again, to suspect Nikon and thought that now, for the first time, the roles had been allotted once and for all, that now, for the first time, the dividing line was clearly visible, right there, passing between the only two people it could not divide. The doom, horror and finality of the last days lay precisely in this, as did the truthfulness of all that was happening. The battle had already been joined and it was unfolding not in some distant place but right here, in the new Holy Land, in its very heart, and far from emerging out of nowhere, out of nothing, Christ and the antichrist had appeared in the figures of the Patriarch of the Holy Land and of its Tsar. And nothing was happening in the way that it was supposed to happen, and nobody knew whom to follow.

'I think that on the day they came for the Patriarch,' Misha said, 'Sertan believed, albeit briefly, that Christ really had been incarnated in Nikon and that the time was at hand. Everything would begin at any moment.'

The Synod which was meant to judge Nikon had been convened as early as February 1666, but no progress was made until two Eastern patriarchs – Paisius of Alexandria and Macarius of Antioch – arrived in Moscow. On November 29, accompanied by a detachment of Streltsy, the Archbishop of Pskov, Arseny, arrived in New Jerusalem with several archimandrites and hegumens, and presented the Patriarch with a summons to appear at once before the Synod. Nikon started squabbling with the envoys, and his show of pettiness suddenly confused Sertan, who doubted once again whether Nikon was Christ.

Nikon said to those who had come for him: 'How could Their Holinesses the Patriarchs and the Holy Synod permit themselves the liberty of sending archimandrites and hegumens for me when the regulations state that in such cases two or three bishops must be sent?'

To this Arseny replied: 'We have come to you not according to the regulations, but by sovereign decree. So tell us: are you coming or not?'

Nikon: 'I do not wish to speak to you. I shall speak to the bishops. The Patriarchs of Alexandria and Antioch do not hold venerable sees and are considered fugitives. I, on the other hand, am appointed on the sacred authority of the Patriarch of Constantinople. If they have come with the consent of the Patriarchs of Constantinople and Jerusalem, then I will go.' In the end, he said: 'I will attend the Synod. I have a few things to take care of, then I will go.'

After this conversation, the envoys immediately dispatched a messenger to Moscow with the news that Nikon was intending to attend the Synod but was not leaving yet, and went off to the hostelry. Nikon attended vespers in the church and then instructed Archimandrite Gerasim and all the hieromonks and hierodeacons to be ready to help him perform the Divine Liturgy in the morning. Before withdrawing to his cell, he asked for three hymns to be recited in his presence: the Akathist to our Sweetest Lord Jesus Christ, the Akathist to the Mother of God, and the Canon of the Guardian Angel.

Nikon, it seems, did not go to bed at all that night. In fact, he asked for Sertan to be brought to his cell and spent two hours talking to him, but the details of this last meeting are not known. There is nothing in the diary except one short phrase: 'He instructed me to continue just as when he was there.' Afterwards, Nikon ordered the bells to be rung for matins.

After the service he summoned his confessor, Hieromonk Leonid, made his confession, consecrated the oil and anointed himself and the entire clergy and brethren. Then he returned to his cell once more and asked Leonid to read the preparatory prayers for Holy Communion.

At this point the archbishop and archimandrites sent someone to tell the Patriarch that they wished to see him on the Tsar's business. Nikon refused this request, saying: 'I am preparing myself for the Tsar of Heaven,' and immediately ordered the bells to be rung for the liturgy. Accompanied by candle bearers and choristers, Nikon entered the Chapel of Holy Golgotha, arrayed himself as usual in full hierarchal garb and began to perform the liturgy. Also present were Archbishop Arseny and Archimandrite Sergy of Yaroslavl. On entering, Sergy began a loud and indecent argument about the singing being done in Greek rather than Russian. Hearing all the noise, the Patriarch summoned Hierodeacon German and ordered him to tell the archimandrite to leave the church immediately, after which those who were with Sergy also decided, after a brief discussion amongst themselves, to leave the church and stand outside.

The liturgy was conducted in Greek, with Kievan chants. Then the Patriarch took Holy Communion before administering the sacrament to every person in the chapel; after this, he opened St John Chrysostom's *Homilies on the Acts of the Apostles* and spoke to the brethren about patience and how they should embrace misfortunes, sorrows and calamities with joy. By the time he finished, everyone was in tears.

After the sermon, Nikon blessed the brethren and went back to his cell once more. Archbishop Arseny came to see him soon after. Nikon asked him:

'Why did you send someone to me this morning and what was the decree that you wanted to communicate to me?'

Arseny said: 'The Tsar has decreed that you should go to the Synod in Moscow. If you do not, we will return and inform our Great Sovereign.'

To this, Nikon replied with the words of St John Chrysostom: 'Glory be to God for all things; I am ready and I am coming,' after which he ordered the horses to be harnessed and promptly left his cell.

The brethren wept as they accompanied Nikon to the stone cross on the Mount of Olives. Here he stopped, donned his stole and omophorion, and instructed the hierodeacon to chant a litany for the Most Pious Sovereign and His Ruling House, for the brethren of the holy monastery and for Orthodox believers, then he gave his peace, blessing and forgiveness to all. Having done this, he gazed for a long time at the monastery and at the monks accompanying him, and wept with them. Still weeping, he got into his sledge and left.

In Moscow, while the Synod is in session, Nikon makes one last attempt to prevent his predetermined removal from the patriarchal throne and all that would follow from it – exile, incarceration or execution. He finds himself thinking once again about Ruvim, endlessly asking himself whether Ruvin might be Christ after all, then suddenly he starts leaning to another view, to what he is hearing at the Synod day after day, over and over, from both the Eastern patriarchs and the other archbishops, as well as from the Tsar and the boyars and many ordinary laypeople: what if the end is not coming now after all, and everything he has been doing is merely delusion, delirium, sacrilege? Sacrilege to try to build the Holy Land and the Holy City of Jerusalem here in Russia, to create this resemblance, this likeness, and to use it to entice Christ to earth, to catch Him, as though in a net, with a throng of His own disciples and persecutors, all waiting, praying, craving for Him. An even greater sacrilege to think that you or any other person born from a father and a mother, incorrigible sinners from so long ago, from the very beginning, might be Christ. He is almost sure now that the monastery cellarer, Feoktist, has been right all along, right to warn him (not that he ever listened) that everything that is happening with his consent in New Jerusalem is a secret conspiracy on the part of the Jews to crucify and abuse Christ all over again, before the very eyes of Christian believers. Or perhaps they, the Jews, are hoping that it is not Jesus Christ who will come but their very own Messiah, whose glorious arrival they have been awaiting since the day of the destruction of the Second Temple. Realising that he is done for, that the Jews have tricked him and that he, Patriarch of All Russia, has become their tool and accomplice, yet rejoicing that he has finally escaped their net and repented, he denounces Peter and Simon, who were among the first Jews he baptised and with whom he discussed the play many times, both in its general outline and in its details, Jews who were closer and more devoted to him than just about anyone else. Now, everything they have said and done strikes him merely as a malicious form of deceit and betrayal, and, remembering Feoktist's words and cursing himself for not having listened to him earlier when he was not yet ruined, he publicly accuses them of treasonable offences and denounces them for abandoning the true faith, for returning to Judaism and plotting to crucify Christ.

This accusation is investigated with great thoroughness and Nikon, aware that it is being investigated, hopes to clear his name through his denunciation and remorse, and thereby to regain God's favour; his still greater hope is that they really have abandoned the faith, that his denunciation is true and the cellarer is right. But whether because the Jews prove slyer than the investigators, or because they prove steadfast and honest in their new faith, not a sliver of evidence is found against them, and Nikon, a broken man no longer capable of understanding what is happening, who is who, or where the world is headed, abandons his role, steps out of it, and is never mentioned again in Sertan's diary.

Nikon was deposed the very next day and the decision was taken to exile him to the Monastery of St Ferapont; meanwhile, a detachment of Streltsy was sent to New Jerusalem. The following morning, right in the middle of a rehearsal, the participants in the play, among them Sertan, were arrested. Together with their wives and children, more than two hundred and ten people were taken away. In Moscow, after a very brief investigation – a surprising fact in itself given the scale and importance of the case – they were sentenced to death for heresy, although, as so often at that time, the sentence was subsequently commuted to exile in distant Siberia, which was being colonised with such difficulty.

Those arrested were divided up for the investigation, and the documents show that the judges were certainly not treating them as a single case, nor did they view them as part of a whole that had to be seen as a whole in order to be understood. The peasants playing the Jews were charged with Judaising tendencies and sentenced on those grounds, while those who played Christ's disciples were eventually assimilated, despite many glaring contradictions, to the Kapitonists. They were sentenced, let me repeat, for very different crimes, which a detached observer would never have been able to connect. No connection was mentioned in the investigation either, and yet, whether by carelessness or by someone's design – now, of course, there is no way of knowing – they were exiled to the same place and sent off in one group, one convoy. Somebody's hand was surely guiding them. The hand, perhaps, of somebody who was waiting, as they were, for the end. In any case, all of them understood both the trial and their sentence in the same way: they had simply been given one final test, and the days of the antichrist's reign on earth were already being counted down. His forty-two months, 1260 days, were under way.

At this point, our collaborative work on the translation of the diary was interrupted. Misha and his mother redoubled their efforts to return to France, and made a lengthy trip to Moscow for that purpose. This attempt, which only a short while before would have stood no chance at all (neither Misha nor his mother had ever held French citizenship), was given life by the leadership's dalliance with de Gaulle. In France, two of Misha's uncles and an aunt launched a campaign for their repatriation through the press, from the communist *Humanité* to the right-wing *Figaro*. A biography of Paul Berlin was published at the same time, as were the reminiscences of his friends and the stories of others who worked in the French section of the Comintern and, like Berlin, had died long ago.

'The French in Russia' became a fashionable topic, pressure was applied, and in the end the president's office agreed to raise the Berlin question during de Gaulle's forthcoming visit to the USSR. The news travelled rapidly to Moscow, and following five categorical refusals at every level, insults and threats of imprisonment for staying in the capital without a residence permit, the Berlins were summoned once more to the Visa and Registration Office and given to understand that if de Gaulle's visit went well they would be let out. On one condition: Misha and his mother should keep a very low profile and not give a single interview. A few days later they received an assurance – this time from France – that a decision on their case had been reached and that it was favourable; no more pressure was required on either side, and they could start preparing for their departure.

On March 3, Misha returned to Tomsk, while his mother stayed on in Moscow. He telephoned me that same day and called round in the evening, bringing with him a three-and-a-half litre bottle of red wine which he had been sent from France. We drank it without haste, and he described all the ups and downs of his campaign in Moscow, who said what to whom and how. He named dozens of people – journalists, French parliamentarians, top officials from our very own Supreme Soviet and Ministry of Foreign Affairs – and described the receptions at the French Embassy. To someone like me, living in Tomsk in 1969, this whole story was like a tale from *The Thousand and One Nights*.

In the morning, when we had finally drunk the last of Misha's endless bottle and he was just about to leave, I told him that I would do whatever I could to help him. Misha replied that no demonstrations of loyalty were needed – he was the one who was leaving, while I was the one who would have to carry on living in this country, and anyway, there wasn't much to pack and he could easily manage on his own. We hugged, and he left.

I knew the date of his departure and decided I'd drop in to say goodbye the day before; till then, I'd leave him in peace. I realised that Sertan would be about the last thing on his mind – that was all in the past now – but the translation was almost done: there were no more than forty pages to go. I knew that if I went round, I'd end up mentioning it one way or the other, and I didn't want to make a nuisance of myself. Needless to say, Sertan's diary would have been a publishing sensation in France, so there was something in it for Misha, too, but I thought better of mentioning this, in case he thought I was being too pushy.

During Misha's absence from Tomsk, I'd struck out on my own and my research no longer depended so much on the diary. Sertan had done the main thing: he'd led me into this story and now I was able to understand everything I read in the manuscripts and documents Kobylin was constantly bringing me about the sect Sertan had spawned. I also knew that even in Russia I'd be able to find a person who knew Breton, if I really needed to. Still, I was sorry that Misha and I hadn't finished the job. I'd grown used to us translating together, to the joint effort, and I didn't much like the way Misha had forgotten Sertan so quickly – it seemed almost wrong somehow, as if he'd abandoned us both, Sertan and me. A week later I even said something along these lines to my father, but he wasn't very sympathetic. He merely reminded me that Paris was farther away than Kuibyshev. Then, a day after this conversation, Misha suddenly turned up. That same evening and all through the night he read the entries for the remaining year and a half of Sertan's life and translated them on sight. The gap had been filled, the debt repaid. A year or two later, when he was long gone, my father repeated and confirmed what I myself thought about Misha. He told me that in Sertan's fate Misha was seeking the life and fate of his own father. He needed to find out, before leaving, how his father had spent the last months and days of his life in Russia, and that was why he had turned up. My father was probably right.

When the translation was finished, it was already morning, and over breakfast I started telling Misha about the manuscripts I'd been studying while he was in Moscow. It followed, from what I'd read, that Sertan's actors had spent more than five months awaiting their death in jail and it wasn't until the middle of April that they found out that their sentence had been commuted to exile to Siberia. This was an exceptionally long interval – on the whole such decisions (to execute or exile) were taken quickly, within a couple of months at most – and I said to Misha that there must have been a serious struggle going on behind the scenes, and it was this that had ultimately determined their fate. I was convinced that this struggle could even be reconstructed.

It seemed to me that those who wanted to allow Nikon's project to run its course had won the day; they had saved the actor's lives in order that there should be somebody for Jesus Christ to come to. Needless to say, there is no way of knowing now who those people were. Some of them, I expect, were simply waiting for the end to come and trying to hurry it along; others may have feared that, without Sertan's actors, God's new chosen people would not acknowledge the true Messiah when He appeared to them, just like the Jews of long ago; and a third group may have hoped to earn their own eternal salvation by saving the apostles' lives. It was clear to me that there was no conspiracy here, since they were all thinking about different things and they didn't know anything, or wish to know anything, about each other, but when the matter was discussed in the chancelleries and in the Duma, they all expressed the same point of view, and Tsar Alexei, after some hesitation, agreed with them.

I was equally confident about those who insisted on the actors' execution. There was no doubt, I told Misha, that this group included intelligent statesmen who were used to weighing things up and thinking about the future, who understood that Russia was only just setting out on her path, so there was no way that the end could be imminent. Just a few months before they had succeeded in deposing Nikon from the patriarchal throne and securing his exile, and now they were telling the Tsar that enough was enough with this blasphemous theatre, with this monstrous sect spawned by Nikon; a fish, they told Alexei, stinks from the head, and there was only one cure: to have done with it as soon as possible, to have done with these apostles who had appeared out of the blue, with Cephas (Peter), and Jacob, son of Alphaeus, and Matthew the tax collector, to have done with the Virgin Mary and Mary Magdalene, with all these people who believed and behaved as if the world really had turned back 1666 years and that Jesus Christ was just about to appear in it. Such things, they told the Tsar, spread far too quickly, and tomorrow the new apostles might have thousands upon thousands of followers; near the White Sea, for example, entire villages had been burning themselves alive in their log huts for years, while across the Volga peasants were abandoning their ploughs and scythes to flee to the woods. If this continued, turmoil was sure to follow.

My own speculations struck me as very convincing and I wanted Misha to agree with me too, but he just said: 'My father was also sentenced to death and spent every day just waiting to be shot. True, this only went on for two months, not five, at which point they decided to give him ten years in the camps instead. Strange that none of them went mad. Five years of waiting to die, day after day – that should be enough for anyone…'

'Perhaps it was because there were so many of them and they were together,' I suggested, 'or perhaps they were expecting the end to come in any case, the end of everything, including themselves. They may not have known what form their end would take, but they were ready for the death it would contain.'

'Perhaps that's true,' Misha conceded, 'but it's still strange, just like the story of Ruvim. It's all strange.'

Then Misha left, and my father explained the difference between us: I was interested in those who decide, who lead, in history's agents, while if Misha was interested in anyone except his father, then only the victims, and my father was inclined to agree with him.

On April 28, 1667, exactly a month after Easter, which fell late that year, the peasants involved in Sertan's play were informed that on the orders of the Tsar their lives had been spared and they would be exiled to the Siberian district of Yakutsk and would live by the Lena River. Everything began to move quickly. Preparations for the convoy were completed within five days, and on the evening of May 2, just as the peasants were beginning to think that they would have to spend one more night in jail, a detachment of Streltsy arrived, took them out into the yard, bound them with heavy wooden fetters, tied them together in pairs and, satisfied that there was no chance of them running away, gave the order to set out. The Streltsy hurried them through Moscow while it was still dark, an entirely unnecessary precaution given that nobody there had ever heard of them and that, five months on, the Nikon case, of which they were considered a part, was already fading from memory. After passing Rogozhskaya Gate, the entire convoy paused, and the Streltsy, who had been charged with guarding the party and leading it as far as Tobolsk, relaxed a little; they untied the exiles, removed their fetters and manacles, took them off the road into a meadow, and let them rest.

Half a year in jail had left them as weak as children and now, after walking six miles in their fetters, they were so tired that no sooner had the Streltsy called a halt than they collapsed onto the ground and immediately fell asleep. They were woken only at sunset, lined up again and urged onwards.

Four days later, once they had passed the town of Vladimir and grown more used to their conditions, they were walking eastwards at an even pace along the eternal route of exile (Nizhny-Novgorod-Kazan-Urals-Siberia) when they were overtaken and stopped by a covered wagon. A cavalryman wearing a brand new uniform leapt out and called the name of the Streltsy sergeant who was leading the convoy. When the sergeant rode up to him, the cavalryman physically handed over Sertan, who was immediately transferred onto a cart piled high with the convoy's chattels. Sertan was in a very bad state and unable to walk on his own, so he was carried in that cart all the way to Siberia. The fact that he was with them once more, just as he had been in New Jerusalem, was taken by the exiles to mean that the Lord had not forgotten them, that He had not abandoned them. He was guiding them and everything was going just as it should.

Back when the Streltsy had come to arrest them in New Jerusalem, after Nikon had been deposed, somebody – probably one of the actors – had managed to steal into Sertan's cell in the hostelry just before it was searched by two chancellery clerks and rescue papers, plans and notes, including the diary. Acting on the advice of some unknown party, he had numbered the pages then cut them into thousands of miniscule fragments, mixed them up so that nobody could ever understand what was

written on them, and during a night-time halt at Nakhabino –
halfway between New Jerusalem and Moscow – shared them
out between all those who had been arrested.

In jail, where they were tortured, interrogated and searched
for five whole months, they managed to preserve every single
one of these scraps, which can also be understood only as a
miracle. Then, on the second or third day of their journey,
the exiles carefully matched the scraps and glued them back
together. When Sertan was brought to them, they hid the papers
in his knapsack and, relishing the joy and surprise he would
feel at seeing that nothing had been lost, resolved to wait. He
would have found his manuscripts that same evening at the
latest, so there wasn't long to wait, but they really had become
like children and barely an hour passed before they told him.
They were not disappointed: Sertan was glad, touched and
surprised; he even wept. Now, he had the chance to resume his
diary, and resume it he did, although his 'exile' entries are, as
a rule, brief and disjointed.

Previously, whenever Sertan had neglected his diary for
an extended period of time, he would subsequently describe
everything he had omitted in great detail, as if he were joining
the different parts of his life and making it whole again,
unbroken. So it had been in Poland, and in the first months
of his captivity in Russia, and when he had found himself in
New Jerusalem. Now, however, he rescued nothing from his
period of confinement, as if it had never happened, or as if
it were something so insignificant that it was hardly worth
writing about. Only later, once they had crossed the Volga and
Moscow was far behind them, did he make a few cursory and
usually jarring mentions of his time in prison.

At one point, Sertan writes that he was accused of being a
Polish spy and that throughout the interrogations the official in

charge of his case never once mentioned New Jerusalem, as if Sertan had never even lived there. On another occasion, Sertan comments that he had been expecting to die and to be subjected to the torture that was customary and even mandatory in such cases, but it never came, and all of this – the fact that he was not tortured, or asked about New Jerusalem – was puzzling and strange.

Sertan was already a 'goner' by the time he left prison; every morning he would cough for an hour or more and spit blood, but later on, if the day was warm and still, his chest would cease to ache, the coughing would abate, and for a few hours at a time he might even feel well and calm. To aid his breathing, he would place a bag behind his back and another behind his head, and travel in a semi-recumbent position. The cart moved at the same slow pace at the convoy, the things he was lying on softened the jolts, and he would spend long hours gazing at the sky or at the people walking or riding towards the convoy, or at the plain extending into the distance either side of the road. He was glad that the plain would never end but merely change, and even then only slightly – Nikon had told him about this – and so perhaps his life, too, would not end soon, but drag on as peacefully and imperceptibly as the movement of his cart.

He knew that he was seriously ill, that he was dying and had no more than a year left to live, and that there wasn't much to look forward to – every day the pain got worse – so the fact that he had been spared execution and allowed to live out his days to the end did not strike him as an unqualified blessing; indeed, when he thought about this at all, it was with a sense of surprise rather than joy. But when he saw his actors, he was glad and saw that they were glad, too, that they needed and loved him, and now that they were together again he found himself thinking more and more often that, strange though it seemed, he was not sorry he had ended up in Russia, and that actually, these were not only Christ's disciples – they were his as well.

Among the papers I bought from Kobylin just before Misha left for Moscow was the decree with the complete list of exiles in the convoy; by all appearances, it was a copy dating from that very time, the reign of Tsar Alexei, which is why it has retained all the features of an original. We have no grounds to doubt its authenticity, and therefore we know the names of every person involved in Sertan's play and exiled with him to Siberia. The list contains some two hundred and eight souls. They had been punished, as I have already said, for very different crimes: the Christians for Kapitonism, the Jews for Judaising tendencies, and there was also a third, very small group that included the Wise Men (the first to have learned of Christ's death) who had been sent to Nikon from the Northern Urals, as well as Pontius Pilate, Prefect of Judea, and the Roman soldiers who put Jesus to death, and a few other foreigners mentioned in the New Testament. This latter group, as far as I can tell, was neither charged nor sentenced, and it was exiled in the same convoy as the other participants in the play for the simple reason that the person in whose hands their fate resided did not want Nikon's project to die. However great their role in the Gospels may have been, all these people – the Wise Men, Pilate, the soldiers – were outsiders in those events and even, if such a thing is possible, accidental participants. After all, the Wise Men, who were astrologers and stargazers, learned about Christ from the arrangement of the planets, and they came not because they had placed their faith in Him but because they wished, as conscientious scholars, to verify their calculations. It was the same with Pontius Pilate: talking to Jesus Christ and deciding His fate, he was observing the events unfolding in Jerusalem from the outside, from Rome, and thinking not about Christ but about whether this was good or bad for the empire. As for the Roman soldiers chosen to crucify Christ, King of the Jews, and to keep order on Golgotha, they couldn't believe their luck: life in the barracks was dreary, and here was a chance to have some fun. None of them – the soldiers, the Wise Men, Pilate – had faith, and it goes without saying that they were incomparably further from the Jews and Christians than the Jews and Christians were from each other.

Even while they were still in New Jerusalem, Sertan had been afraid of their lack of faith, afraid of bringing them together with the other actors, because it was all too easy for them to destroy everything he was building; theirs was a perspective that, according to the logic of what Sertan was doing, should not exist at all, and the fact that it did exist meant that Sertan was attempting the impossible. To the other participants in the play, the Romans were alien and incomprehensible from the very start, and Sertan exploited every opportunity to emphasise and strengthen this feeling, using all the means at his disposal to distance the Romans from the others. That was why he had chosen the Romans from among those who had washed up at the monastery from God knows where, who had no family there, no connections or roots. The Wise Men were Nenets people from the Far North who didn't seem to know any Russian, Pilate was a Cossack who had lived on the Don for many years before he was taken prisoner by the Turks and spent fifteen years near the Bulgarian town of Kazanlak, where he also more or less forgot his native tongue, while most of the Roman soldiers were either Polish captives or Cossacks, like Pilate, who had been taken prisoner by Turks or Tatars.

Four years earlier, when Sertan was just setting to work on

the play, he had persuaded Nikon to provide separate housing for all these Romans (that's how he calls them both in his diary and in his other papers), and a small brick barracks was built specially for them three miles outside the monastery; they weren't allowed to leave it without special permission. It was there, in the barracks, that they had their rehearsals with Sertan. Not once did they rehearse together with the Jews and with the Christians, so the parts of the whole were kept entirely separate and no attempt was made to link them. If they were to come together and merge when Jesus Christ appeared on earth, the scenes would need to be repeated hundreds of times, and the ones involving all these groups would inevitably prove the most difficult to direct.

The decree and the list of exiles in the party were deliberately composed in such a way that understanding who was playing who in the play – who was being accused of Judaising, who of Kapitonism, who was a Roman – is quite impossible; only first names and surnames are given. All the exiles are grouped strictly by family, and it was evidently assumed that just as they had lived in New Jerusalem – one family per home – so they would settle in the new place.

Their entire past was effaced, forgotten and concealed in this list, which rendered them indistinguishable from all the other exile convoys populating Siberia in their dozens at that time, and thereby protected and preserved them. The exiles understood very well that a façade of equality, whether with outsiders or amongst themselves, was their best chance of survival, and they took great care to maintain it. In particular, they made no mention in any of their papers of their allotted roles in the play, and I had to spend a considerable amount of time combing and comparing a wide range of Kobylin's documents in order to finally pin down who was who.

Here is my incomplete reconstruction of the list of exiles:

Ivashka Balushnik (Joseph, husband of Mary) and his wife Avdotitsa (the Virgin Mary);

Kondrashka Skosyryev (John, father of the apostles Andrew and Simon Peter), who rented out fishing boats on the Lake of Reeds, which belonged to the monastery, his wife Akulina (the woman who had a flow of blood), his sons Ivashka (Peter the Apostle, Cephas), Yanko (Andrew the Apostle), Senka (Caiaphas the high priest), Vaska (one of the Pharisees who argued with Christ) and Mikhail (one of the men who bore false witness against Christ), his daughter Nastasitsa (Mary Magdalene);

Mitroshka Bochkar (Zebedee, father of the apostles James the Greater and John, Christ's beloved disciple), who rented out fishing boats on the Istra Ponds, his wife Olenka (Salome), his sons Fedyushka (James the Greater, 'Boanerges'), Nazarka (John the Apostle) and Stepanko (one of the blind men healed by Christ), his daughters Maritsa (the Canaanite woman) and Ustinitsa (the Canaanite's daughter), his sons Ivashko (Annas the high priest) and Fedyushka (Herod the Tetrach), his daughters Daritsa (Herodias) and Annitsa (Herodias's daughter);

Klimko Rodionov (Alphaeus, father of the apostles James the Younger and Jude), his wife Orinka (Mary), his sons Lavrushka (James the Younger), Oleshka (Jude), Yanko (another false witness) and Stepanko (a member of the Sanhedrin), his daughter Avdotitsa (Jairus's daughter);

Ivashka Romanov (Philip the Apostle), his sons Fedyushka (Joseph of Arimathea), Zakharko (Archelaus, son of Herod) and Petrushka (one of the blind men healed by Christ), his daughters Nastasitsa (the woman who could not straighten herself), Ovfimitsa (one of the women who followed Christ) and Praskovitsa (another woman who followed Christ);

Fedyushka Moiseyev (Bartholomew the Apostle), his sons Klimko (a member of the Sanhedrin), Maksimko (a member of the Sanhedrin), Levonko (a Pharisee who argued with Christ) and Karpushka (Lazarus), his daughters Olenka (Anna the prophetess) and Annitsa (a woman who followed Christ);

Nazarka Oskutin (Levi the tax collector, Matthew the Apostle), his wife Maritsa (Peter's mother-in-law), his sons Petrushka (one of the men who shouted 'His blood be on us and on our children'), Oleshka (one of the guards who seized Christ) and Danilko (the servant whose ear was cut off by Peter), his daughters Raiska (daughter of the Syrophoenician woman) and Vasiliska (the Syrophoenician);

Danilko Grebenshchikov (Thomas the Apostle), his wife Agafitsa (a woman who followed Christ), his sons Vasko (King Herod), Ivanko (a blind man healed by Christ), Semeiko (the boy with an unclean spirit healed by Christ), Stenka (the man with a withered hand healed by Christ), Gavrilo (a Pharisee) and Fedorko (a member of the Sanhedrin), his daughter Stepanidka (a woman who followed Christ);

Lavrushka Sazonov (Simon the Apostle, who was called the Zealot), his wife Ovfimitsa (a woman who followed Christ), his sons Danilko (a man selling pigeons in the Temple), Mikhalko (the man with dropsy healed by Christ), Ivashka (a leper healed by Christ) and Gavrilko (a member of the Sanhedrin), his daughter Domnitsa (a woman who followed Christ);

Yakushko Poluektov (Judas Iscariot the Apostle), his wife Natashka (a woman who followed Christ), his sons Ivashka (a man who followed Christ), Mikiforko (the dumb demoniac healed by Christ) and Fedorka (a leper healed by Christ), his daughters Raiska (a woman who followed Christ) and Akulinka (a woman who followed Christ);

Maksimka Tvorogov (Matthew the Apostle, chosen to

replace Judas Iscariot), his wife Fedositsa (Martha, sister of Lazarus), his sons Levonko (John the Baptist), Ignashko (a moneychanger in the Temple), Oleshko (Malchus, the high priest's slave, healed by Christ) and Fedka (a member of the Sanhedrin), his daughter Maritsa (a woman who followed Christ);

Petrushko Podkamenny (a Wise Man);

Yakushka Popov (a Wise Man);

Oleshka Yeremeyev (a Wise Man);

Timoshka Ondreev (a man who followed Christ), his wife Ovfimitsa (a woman who followed Christ), his sons Yakushko (a moneychanger), Mikiforko (an elder in the Temple) and Ivashka (a blind man healed by Christ), his daughter Domnitsa (a woman who followed Christ);

Mitka Filatov (a Sadducee), his wife Arinka (a woman who followed Christ), his sons Kurbat (a demoniac healed by Christ) and Yakushko (one of the seventy disciples of Christ);

Lavrushka Mukhoplyov (Simon the Leper), his wife Praskovitsa (the woman who poured precious ointment on Christ's head), his sons Mishka (one of the seventy disciples of Christ) and Danilko (one of the men who came up and seized Christ), his daughter Nastasitsa (a maid who recognised Peter);

Ivashka Pasolov (one of the seventy disciples of Christ), his wife Raiska (the other maid who recognised Peter), his sons Frolka (one of the seventy disciples of Christ), Savka (a member of the Sanhedrin) and Yakushka (Barabbas), his daughter Daritsa (a woman who followed Christ);

Aleksashka Bludov (one of the seventy disciples of Christ), his wife Agafitsa (Mary, sister of Lazarus), his sons Yakushko (Simon of Cyrene) and Logvinko (one of the robbers crucified with Christ);

Timoshka Raspopa (one of the seventy disciples of Christ), his wife Akulinka (a woman who followed Christ), his sons Vaska (a moneychanger in the Temple), Levonka (the other robber crucified with Christ) and Fedka (the man who gave Christ the sponge soaked in vinegar);

Matveika Zharnoy (Pontius Pilate), his wife Lenka Zharnaya (wife of Pontius Pilate);

Matyushka Tatarin (a soldier serving under Pilate);

Oleshka Perezarov (a soldier serving under Pilate);

Danilka Pechelyukhin (a centurion).

After passing Vladimir, the convoy reached Nizhny Novogorod without incident in the customary three weeks; there, the exiles were loaded onto barges and sent downriver to Kazan – the easiest part of the journey. In Kazan everything ground to a halt, and it was only on June 12, after a month of preparations, fuss and dithering among police officers and escorts (the real reason for the delay, it seems, was that the order had not yet come from Moscow as to who should lead the party to Siberia), that they finally set forth towards the town of Verkhoturye in the Urals.

They walked slowly, but they were usually on the road from dawn till dusk, only stopping for a brief rest at noon. Their convoy stretched out over the better part of a mile: a police officer and several Streltsy went in front, then the exiles: the Jews, followed by the Christians, followed by carts laden with bags, bundles, baskets and other chattels, followed by several more carts for the sick, the maimed, the exhausted and, if any space remained, the women, who would take it in turns to sit. Only when the hamlet or village where they were due to spend the night came into view did everyone, exiles and guards alike, bunch together and close ranks, and only then could you see that this was still a single convoy, that there were some people leading and others being led, and that, for today at least, their walking was done.

They walked a good fifteen miles a day, but rarely for more than four days straight, and usually three; later, once they had crossed the Urals and villages were few and far between, they would stop by the road for a day or two at a time, resting until they were told to move on. At the beginning, they often received alms – sometimes money, usually food – but after they had reached the Volga this happened ever less often: not only were villages rarer, but the people weren't the same. Once in Siberia, they no longer received anything and went hungry; were it not for a police officer's advice to save a little money in advance, they might never have made it all the way to Tobolsk. As for charity, it was each man to himself: sharing was the exception, not the rule, and only when somebody was unable to eat all the food he had begged 'for the love of Christ' would he give his leftovers to the person next to him or to someone else; more often, if he saw that he had collected enough for the day, he would abandon his position by the side of the road or towards the head of the convoy and let someone who had gathered less take his place.

Unlike the food, the money collected by the exiles was managed by the Romans from the very first day; they were considered more practical in such matters, perhaps because by this point there really was something unworldly about the others. These outsiders looked after the money and spent it on the party's behalf, buying everything in bulk, whether clothes, food or, when someone fell sick, vodka; even the apostles barely interfered in their dealings.

No sooner had they crossed the Urals than the exiles, as I have already said, buried Sertan in the hamlet of Dry Ravine, where he died on June 16, 1667. Ever since they passed Kazan it had been obvious that Sertan did not have long to go, and by the time they found themselves digging his grave in a small village cemetery, weeping and conducting the burial service themselves – there wasn't a single church or priest in the vicinity – they were already prepared for life without their teacher.

The police officers accompanying the convoy were old hands; they knew that marching the exiles all the way to Siberia was a long and arduous task, that success or failure depended on their charges more than it did on them, and that picking pointless fights from day one would only create self-inflicted problems. That was why they generally left the exiles to look after themselves; not only did they not try to stop them organising their own affairs, they did all they could to facilitate this by immediately acknowledging their recognised leaders. These, naturally enough, were the apostles, and first among them, in accordance with Gospel tradition, was Peter, so for the entire march, until they reached their place of exile, almost all the actors' internal affairs were decided by the council of apostles, with Peter at its head.

One question that arose as early as the second day was whether Jews, Christians and outsiders could mingle and walk with whomever they wanted – in entire families, say, or with their former neighbours, just as they had lived and been registered in New Jerusalem – or whether they should walk in groups that were strictly divided according to how they had been tried and sentenced; and who should go in front – Christians or Jews? This issue led to considerable disagreement and in the end, even though some Christians were unhappy with their decision, the apostles decreed that Christians would walk with Christians, Jews with Jews, and only the Romans should be split up and distributed equally among the party, because no one knew what to expect from them. Ignoring the grumblings of the Christians, the apostles decided that the Jews would walk in front, firstly because the Old Testament had preceded the New Testament, and secondly because the Christians could not be sure whether the Jews were as committed to their roles as they were to theirs, so by walking behind the Jews it would be easier to spot anyone trying to run away. Thus, the guards relieved themselves from the very beginning of their most important and most taxing duty – the prevention of escape – by relying on the apostles and delegating it fully to the exiles themselves. The good order within the convoy and the absence of a single fugitive were immediately noted, and from this point on the leaders among the exiles enjoyed the absolute confidence of the police officers, who no longer intervened in their affairs at all.

When Sertan joined the convoy, the apostles transferred all their leadership duties to him; for as long as his health permitted, every matter concerning the convoy would have to go through him and be decided by him. He was against this, but the apostles, and especially Peter, were adamant, and all agreed that this was the fairest and only feasible arrangement. Later, when it became clear that there was no hope of Sertan recovering, they gradually began to reassert their authority; now, they took decisions on their own, merely asking Sertan for his formal approval. There was a further reason for this: during these last months of his life, Sertan barely had a free moment. At the apostles' insistence, he was translating and dictating the entire text of the diary entries that concerned the play so that, if he were to die (and they knew he would die soon, as he did too), they could continue the rehearsals without him and, when the time came, perform the play exactly as he had conceived it. Leaving no stone unturned, they asked him about everything they could think of, wrote down every scrap of advice, every recommendation, whatever he said, thought or remembered, copied all his maps and models, all the details of his *mises-en-scène*, and when he died they had everything they needed to carry out his plans and intentions. Dying, he knew that his work would not go to waste, and they knew it too. He died a happy man, surrounded by his disciples – a death that few would not envy.

The last days of his life, after they had crossed the Urals, were spent in great suffering, without a moment's respite from a rasping cough, but during a halt on June 16 his coughing ceased and he even thought that he might live, and at that very moment, when he was smiling and they were standing there beside him, and it was sunny, and it was bright, and he felt better than he had for months, he died.

On August 2, six weeks after Sertan's death, the exiles reached Verkhoturye, where convoys would usually rest for a week or more before starting out again to their next destination, Tobolsk. Russia was behind them now, the Urals were behind them, and the exiles had accepted that they would never return.

The lands beyond Verkhoturye were deserted, the roads barely less so, and the exiles often felt that they were being kept under escort, bound and shackled, not as punishment for their crimes, but because it was feared that otherwise they might lose their way, disappear and perish.

In those years Tobolsk was still Siberia's capital city and its main staging post. It was there that exiles would receive most of the things they needed to set themselves up in the new place, their 'ploughman's gear', as it was then called: coulters, axes and some iron to spare; they were also given a subsidy, seeds and, above all, enough grain to last them until they were settled and able to feed themselves.

From Tobolsk the exiles were bound for the stockaded town of Yeniseisk where, after being given further supplies, they were to be sent on without delay to Yakutsk, on the Lena, where the local governor, Golovin, and his secretary, Filatov, would receive the convoy and set the peasants to work in the fields. The instructions from the Siberian Chancellery were to group the exiles together in a single village at a suitable spot on the banks of the Anga, to buy them horses with the subsidy, and if, on arrival, they were short of seeds (rye, barley, oat), to top them up from reserve supplies.

The police officers leading the convoy were obliged, by sovereign decree, to live side by side with the exiles throughout the first year of their new life, to keep a close eye on them and report everything they said to the secretary in Yakutsk, who in turn would write to Moscow. The exiles also had orders of their own: upon arrival, without dithering or waiting for the snow to melt, they were to start making ploughs and harrows, and then, as soon as the earth thawed, they should begin weeding, tilling and planting. In total, each person was expected to cultivate one and a half acres of oats and barley for the Tsar, and three for himself, along with three acres of winter rye for the Tsar, and six for himself. The police officers were entrusted with making sure that the exiles tilled the land 'with great zeal' (in the words of the decree) both for themselves and for the Tsar, that they loosened the soil properly and, most importantly in Siberia, that they planted the grain at just the right time, 'without tardiness'. To stop cattle trampling the crops, they were instructed to fence in the fields and, again without tardiness, to harvest the ripened grain, bind it in sheaves and stack it in barns. They were also expected to count and record how much of each grain they collected, how much they harvested per hectare, and how much they threshed per sheaf, so that the chancellery could know what the soil was like in one place as opposed to another, and exactly what and how much it produced.

In conclusion, the officers were tasked with making sure that the exiles did not neglect the Tsar's crops at the expense of their own, and that nothing untoward ever took place amongst them, such as rows or fights. Anyone found guilty of such things was to be beaten mercilessly with sticks.

The last leg of the journey, towards Yakutsk, was ex-cruciatingly long and hard. It was only in September 1667, thirteen months after setting out, that they arrived in Yeniseisk. It would have been pointless to press on: the rivers were about to freeze over. So, ignoring the decree, they wintered in Yeniseisk. Another ten months passed before the town governor, Anichkov, found boats and oarsmen; he sent the exiles on to Yakutsk the following July. They were supposed to have received more grain and seeds in Yeniseisk, seeing as they had already eaten a good part of what they had brought from Tobolsk over the course of the winter. They were due two years' supplies in total, on a ration of fifty-five pounds a month, which came to about seventy tonnes of food and thirty-five tonnes of seeds, but grain was in short supply in Yeniseisk – there wasn't even enough for the locals – so they received nothing on top of what they had brought with them from Tobolsk other than three coulters and an axe per head, and ten scythes and sickles per household.

Yakutsk could only be reached by water, up the Yenisei, the Upper Tunguska and the Ilim. The exiles were given flat-bottomed boats and seventy oarsmen and helmsmen, most of them Streltsy, but once again they failed to make it to the Lena. It took the convoy four months – until the end of November

– to reach the carrying-place to the Lena, by which time many oarsmen had fled and those who remained (fewer than half) were exhausted, so the convoy would lie idle for days, sometimes weeks, at rapids and riffles. It was impossible to go any further, so on reaching the carrying-place it was decided, for the second time since leaving Moscow, to stay put for the winter.

In January the governor of Yakutsk, whose responsibility it was to settle them on the Anga, learned that the grain the exiles had brought with them from Tobolsk would not even last another six months, and that they had a mere eight hundred roubles left, enough to buy only a quarter of the required number of horses, which were very expensive on the Lena. Clearly, they would have nothing to live on once they got there, so he made arrangements for them to be returned down the Ilim in spring, when the ice broke. By summer the exiles were back within the stockade of Yeniseisk where, for almost a year, to judge by the governor's report, they went hungry, wandered 'from porch to porch', and kept themselves alive 'by Christ' – which is to say, by begging. They had reached a state of complete debilitation when finally, some sixty miles from the stronghold, suitable land was found for them by the Keti River and those who were still alive were set to work in the fields.

During the two and a half years they had spent traipsing between the Ob and the Yenisei, the Siberian Chancellery had sent several enquiries to the Tobolsk, Yeniseisk and Ilimsk governors about their fate, but the reply was always the same: either they had not yet arrived, or they had already moved on. It was only in the autumn of 1668 that news of the true state of affairs finally reached Moscow. The displeasure with the governors was such that the Chancellery for Secret Affairs was ordered to open an investigation without delay into their negligence and other failings. The governors, needless to say, faced imminent disgrace and punishment: aside from this episode with the convoy, many people in trade and manufacturing had been sending petitions to Moscow in recent years to complain about extortion and abuses of the law; even on this occasion, though, the inquiry was smothered with the help of bribes and intermediaries in Moscow, and the matter went no further. Still, the very fact that an investigation had been launched on account of an ordinary exile convoy – on paper, it was no different from the dozens of other convoys trudging out of Russia day after day, deeper and deeper into Siberia – was strange and, perhaps, unprecedented. Entire parties had died or escaped in the past, yet the chancellery had always turned a blind eye. Moscow understood how hard it was to settle Siberia, knew that it was using criminals and little else to do so, and had long come to terms with the fact that barely a third of the exiles ever reached the place to which they were assigned and that fewer still managed to make new lives for themselves once they got there.

In the spring of 1669, by which point the local governor knew that the matter had been closed, an urgent decree was received in Yeniseisk, where the exiles had been wintering. It gave the strictest instructions to find all survivors of the convoy, however many or few there might be; not a single person was to be added to their number, and they, in turn, were not to bring a single outsider into their group. The exiles were to be fed and treated, well-clothed and well-shod, and supplied with all essentials; then, when a suitable place was found, they were to be settled near a town, but not too near: just close enough for it to be easy to keep an eye on the exiles without their wishing to visit the town too often, if at all.

The governor entrusted the search to the Streltsy sergeant; he gave him the complete list of exiles, told him what was in the decree, put the fear of God in him and threatened him with the Tsar's disfavour if anything went wrong. The sergeant already knew from one of the clerks that the governor was not exaggerating: in autumn, the local governor, along with those of Tobolsk and Yakutsk, had almost fallen into disgrace on account of this convoy; nevertheless, he was completely unable to understand the crux of what the governor was telling him, as if the governor were holding something back. Taken separately, everything he said made sense: the Streltsy should not use any violence against the exiles, they should accompany them to their assigned location at a very gentle pace, lest anyone die or fall ill, and they should ensure that the exiles lacked for nothing both on the journey and when they arrived. All this was clear enough, but then the governor started talking about how there had been precisely 208 exiles in the party when it left Russia, but less than a hundred had survived, and Moscow was saying that the Streltsy should settle every one of these people – no more, no less – near Yeniseisk and let them get on with their lives as they saw fit, just so long as nobody else joined them, and that it was his job as sergeant to keep the group exactly as it was now. He was also instructed to ensure that the Streltsy did not talk too much to the exiles and, of course, to ensure that there were no fugitives (although, to judge from what the officers who had led the convoy from Moscow had told him, there was little chance of that).

Out of everything the governor told him, this last point was the only one that the sergeant grasped; as for the rest, he could see that the governor barely understood it himself and was merely repeating what he had read in the decree. What particularly troubled the sergeant was how he would find these people and how he would ever be sure that he had found all of them and that all of them were who they said they were, that no one had sneaked in from outside, and no one inside the group had gone missing. By the time you've walked the length and breadth of the country in a single party of convicts, you're unlikely to view your companions as blood brothers, and anyway, exiles weren't in the habit of talking about one another – where they were from, how they made a living – and usually they wouldn't even know. But here it turned out to be different: the very first exile he found knew everything about everyone else, and the others also knew everything about everyone, and most importantly, they treated each other almost as family.

We do not know exactly who and how many were still alive by this point, but the group that reached the banks of the Keti and settled there must have been quite sizeable: almost one hundred people (men and women), to judge by one of the official documents sent to Yeniseisk four years later – or a little less than half the party that left Moscow. The village they founded is called Birch Groves (*Bereznyaki*) in the documents that were held in the government office at Yeniseisk, but from the very start, Kobylin told me, the settlers called it New Jerusalem amongst themselves, or simply Jerusalem, and they did so not in honour of the place where they were born and raised, as usually happens, but because they were convinced that, ever since they had started living here, the village had actually become Jerusalem, and all that was sacred and universal in that ancient city, all that the Lord God had chosen it for, had moved here with them. During the second year of their life in Birch Groves, they even laid the foundations of a church modelled on the Church of the Resurrection in New Jerusalem; though wooden and immeasurably smaller, in outline it was a precise replica. For some unknown reason, however, they abandoned it, having completed the foundations and only just started the walls. There is no sign of anybody having tried to stop them; on the contrary, the governor of Yeniseisk, according to his own report, gave them money to paint the walls and purchase a bell, a cross and church utensils, just as he had been instructed to do by Moscow.

Birch Groves was situated very advantageously, with an abundance of arable land, floodplains and, as was true of almost all Siberia at the time, plentiful game in the forest and fish in the river. The landscape was hilly and may have reminded the exiles of the lands around the Istra. The Streltsy brought them here when summer was already under way (the exiles' infirmity had delayed the start of their slow journey) and when it was too late to plough up the virgin soil or start sowing, but in any case, having arrived by the Keti, the exiles did not seem intent on doing anything. It was August and precisely thirty-four months had now passed since the day they had set out on their journey to Siberia, which was exactly the same amount of time Christ had spent walking and preaching across Palestine; soon, He would have to climb Golgotha, and they were in no doubt that the end was nigh. The misery they had endured for these past two and a half years was so great, and their path, the path of Christ's disciples and persecutors, across the new Holy Land – Russia – was so similar to the path He had walked in Palestine that even without these prognostications and calculations it would have been hard not to see that the last days really were upon them. Among those who had survived and reached the Keti were all the apostles, and this also confirmed the exiles in their belief that they had not been abandoned, had not been forgotten, and that the time was at hand.

The police officer and the Streltsy who accompanied the exiles to Birch Groves tried all summer long to set them to work putting up log huts and clearing the ground for autumn tillage, but neither persuasion nor force had the slightest effect. Surveillance was weak – only eight or nine Streltsy – and at the first opportunity the settlers would run off into the forest where, preparing themselves to receive Christ, they would rehearse their lines and their roles over and over again. There was something guilty about the way they ran off and hid; they clearly understood that the things the Streltsy were fruitlessly trying to get them to do and had to do for them – building and tilling – were things they should have done themselves, or rather had always had to do and always thought they should do, but here and now, and only for them, these things had become superfluous and pointless, but they were unable to explain or even express any of this to the Streltsy. This meant that the Streltsy, who were doing all the work, were right, but they, the exiles, were also right, although, when it came to it, the Streltsy were probably more right, because if the exiles were right it was an exception, while if the Streltsy were right it was the rule. This guiltiness was also apparent to the sergeant and his men, and it was because of this that they viewed the people they had brought to the Keti as holy fools and simpletons; even so, they were still expecting the exiles to explain, or at least let slip, why it was that they were not building or tilling, and why they kept wandering off. Despite the governor's warning, they wanted them to speak, but none of them had any intention of doing so; the exiles stayed silent and, as before, skulked away to hide somewhere just as soon as it grew light.

When they disappeared into the forest on the first day, the sergeant thought they had fled for good and got a real fright. This convoy had already been the cause of so many punitive sanctions and falls from grace that he strongly suspected he would be next in line once the governor found out; but towards nightfall the exiles unexpectedly returned, lit large fires and fell asleep there and then, side by side. He counted the sleeping bodies twice, was delighted to see that they were all there and that no one had wandered off, and felt much calmer; the Moscow officials, it seems, had been right all along – in this convoy, nobody ever tried to escape. So then he decided that the best thing to do was to leave them in peace: if they didn't work, so be it – the important thing was that they should stay put. This was sensible enough, of course, but he was under the strictest instructions to ensure they had everything they needed for their future lives, which meant that the Streltsy, for all their obvious displeasure, would have to till the fields and build the houses themselves.

At the beginning of September, the exiles' behaviour changed: some of them had already realised Christ would not come to them now and they were waiting for Him in vain. Their error, in the opinion of the majority, was not that the date of His coming, known and foretold so long ago, was wrong for the very reason that it was known and foretold (after all, it was not for human beings to know what would happen or when); rather, it lay in the starting point for their calculation. Many of them had been of the opinion, even before this, that the amount of time Christ would spend on earth during His Second Coming would not be the thirty-four months He had spent walking and preaching across Palestine, but the thirty-three years He had lived during His first coming. He would fight the antichrist for thirty-three years, and the Last Judgement and the end of the world would follow only in 1699 or 1700. The certainty they had felt in August that Christ would appear any day was inspired by the fact that for all the months and years of their life in Siberia they had been trying to calculate the appointed date by taking their own lives, their own calamities and fate, as their measure, and since all their strength had run out, even the strength to live and wait, they thought that it was just about to start, that the cup was overflowing and the time had come. In their weariness, they had tried to hasten Christ's arrival by moving away from the scenario that Sertan had developed, that they had rehearsed and staged with him. They had forgotten that there were too few of them to receive Christ, that many had died and their places had not been filled. If Christ really had come in August, it would have meant that the roles of the deceased were not needed, that they were superfluous and, therefore, that Sertan had been wrong. Now the exiles realised that in trying to hurry Christ they, and not Christ, had splintered and split between those who were essential and had been chosen, and those they could get by without. They had ceased to be a single whole, and just as they had divided themselves, so they had divided Christ, as if to say that the first thirty years of His life on earth, back then in Palestine, had also been unnecessary, that they had meant nothing and given nothing to mankind.

During the autumn of 1669 the exiles gradually reverted to the view that the Lord wanted them to follow Sertan to the letter, without changing a jot. Interestingly, the few who had remained loyal to Sertan throughout this time were all among those chosen to be near Christ when He was born, to know Christ from the first day of His life on earth, those who should be the first to receive and recognise Him. In the events that followed, not many of them played a leading role, in stark contrast to the apostles, but this did not stop them being treated by the other actors as a class apart, a kind of aristocracy; after all, it was to them that Christ had appeared first.

Vladimir Sharov

The knowledge of when Christ would come, whether in the first version (1669) or the second (1699), derived from the pagans – the Wise Men – who were certain that the fate of all that exists in the world has already been determined for good, and that nobody has the power to change a single thing. The Lord is as powerless as any human being. Creating the world, He created it from beginning to end, and as He made it He also lived through it, so whatever we are now and whatever came before us and follows us is merely the delayed reflection and enactment of what has already occurred. All destinies have not only been lived through, they have already been written, and whoever knows how to read knows what they are.

It would seem easy enough for us to understand why the exiles had such a need for dates, and such faith in dates; to wait for Christ every day, every hour, every instant, and see again and again that He still had not come was too much to bear, and yet, the way they were waiting for Christ in the summer of 1669 owed nothing to Sertan, even though he also had a precise date in mind when preparing the play. Sertan had had a different understanding of when Christ would come and how He would come, an understanding based on the conviction that He would come no earlier and no later than it took for the actors to be ready not merely to repeat what Sertan had taught them – to repeat it to Christ, not Sertan – but also to receive Christ in some cases, and to reject Him in others.

Working and rehearsing with each of them individually, Sertan had tried to cultivate their own personal, individual preparedness to receive or reject Christ, but now that they were on their own and they had canonised everything Sertan had told them, all his explanations and instructions, and thus had preserved him, as it were, in his totality, they veered ever more frequently to a very different version of Christ's coming.

Although their hopes for 1669 had been dashed, many of them continued to believe that what mattered was not their individual, inner preparedness, but the collective preparedness of the world: the world was ready, it had done everything in order that Christ should come, it could wait no longer. And from this it followed that Christ's coming could and should be hastened.

The earliest source for this version seems to have been the division of the convoy into Christians and Jews. The burden of those on whom it fell to play the Jews was such that a Christian could not even imagine being able to lift it, which in turn gave rise to the Christians' certainty that the Jews would not manage to bear this load to the end, that they would fail to carry out the role they had been assigned, so it was essential to keep an eye on them and be prepared to take any measure necessary to prevent them from becoming traitors, abandoning everything and walking away. And that was the first time in the history of the play that the first, having taken on the most, became last.

In the years that followed, this interpretation of the world among the actors would fade at times and revive at others (even if Sertan's authority would, formally speaking, remain absolute) until finally the wait for Christ, the wait for the Messiah and Saviour came down to a battle between the two interpretations of His arrival.

But back to 1669. From early September onwards the exiles in Birch Groves, having ceased to wait for the Saviour's imminent arrival, begin working alongside the Streltsy and things begin moving much quicker. Before the real freeze sets in, they manage to plough the land for spring sowing and build several large log huts where, crammed in any old how, they spend the winter. When the sledge road opens, the Streltsy go back to Yeniseisk, leaving only the sergeant to watch over them.

Externally, their life becomes ever less distinguishable from that of other exile colonies in Siberia: building until spring, then ploughing, sowing, haymaking and reaping. If they can spare time away from the crops, they continue with their homemaking and building even in summer – they put up log huts, barns, granaries – but most of the carpentry is done in autumn and winter, when the grain has been harvested and there is no more work to be done in the fields. The sergeant has nothing much to report, but a year passes, two years pass, and still he is not summoned back to Yeniseisk, so the exiles gradually resign themselves to his presence.

Though their minds are constantly turned towards the end, the settlers, strangely enough, prove more than competent at managing their affairs, and the village soon prospers. Two circumstances enabled them to flourish: first, Birch Groves occupied a remote spot far from the well-trodden route between the Ob and the Yenisei, so outsiders, whether soldiers or prisoners headed further east, rarely came this way, which also meant that the exiles had few additional obligations; there was only the poll tax to worry about, which they paid in grain and which, given the fertility of the land, was no great burden. More important still was the fact that they were in league with the Yakut nomads roaming nearby, who helped them a great deal, especially with horses. They owed the strength and durability of their bonds with the Yakuts to the Wise Men, who practised shamanism for the Yakuts and enjoyed great influence among them. Subsequently both the Wise Men and the Romans (among whom there was not a single woman, except for the wife of Pontius Pilate) entered into relationships with the Yakut women ever more frequently, but this did not jeopardise their loyalty to the play.

As pagans and outcasts adrift from the rest of the exiles, the Romans had drawn close to the Wise Men even before this, during Sertan's lifetime; now, through marriage to the Yakut women, they become blood relatives and grow even closer. All communication between the village and the outside world, being virtually taboo for the Jews and the Christians, is conducted exclusively through the Romans. The village needs them at every step. They understand this and, as likely as not, are satisfied with their role.

In Birch Groves, the exiles, taking the hint offered by the way that the grain and seeds had been distributed on the journey, once again live family by family, as they had in New Jerusalem. The territorial separation between Jews and Christians, which first arose in the convoy, no longer exists, and from the outside it becomes impossible to tell which of them are Jews and which are Christians. Only they know who is who. Nor will there be any outward separation later, for as long as they live in one place; only after external causes or internal circumstances disrupt their settled existence and force them back onto the road does it reappear.

Subsequently their lives alternate between clearly distinguishable periods of calm, stable existence (externally, at least) and periods of discord and persecution. The former are protracted, lasting for thirty to thirty-five years; this is the time of ordinary peasant labour, intense rehearsal, dignified and resolute waiting for Christ's arrival, and the certainty that the wait is almost at an end, for soon He will come. During these periods, the community does not stray from Sertan's teaching in spirit or letter, as if he really were still alive, still with them. Then, a clean break. Sertan's play is discarded and for several months everything he did is destroyed and dies; the crisis usually peaks in late autumn, winter or the start of spring, but never lasts longer than half a year.

It would be wrong to think of these crises as some kind of mass cyclothymia; no, these are the times when the exiles' own notions hold sway, their own understanding of what they have to do for Christ to come. And just when it seems that their path, their interpretation has won out for good, that the play, as Sertan planned it, has been destroyed, never to return, that is when it begins to be restored. But there is nothing to restore it from, and no one to do it, so the process of getting back to what was there before can take a generation or even two.

The exiles' decision to live strictly by family – each in its own home – is a burden for Jews and Christians alike, who once again find themselves grouped together under one roof. Frequent conflicts are, needless to say, inevitable, after all it is no easy task to share your life with people of a different faith, to run a household with them day after day, year after year. Even such simple matters as cooking, sharing a meal and celebrating Saturdays or Sundays are all but insoluble, and anyway, what is the point of trying to resolve them? Why not separate and live in different homes? After all, they are only together for the sake of appearances. But the exiles continue to live together in the same way generation after generation, and my own explanation for how this was even possible is that they were so deeply absorbed in their own roles, in the rehearsals. There is another, related question that particularly fascinates me: did those chosen to play Jews ever become genuine Jews, at least in the sense that they began to think and feel like actual Jews (circumcision was not practised among them, that much I know), or not? In his quest for absolute authenticity of performance, Sertan, whether or not he meant to, had certainly pushed them in that direction with the stories he told them about the Torah and the Holy Temple in Jerusalem, about the Jews of Tulchyn, the Gaons and Ruvim, but did he succeed?

Later, after the three partitions of Poland at the end of the eighteenth century, when Russia acquired the largest chunk of that country together with hundreds of thousands of Jews (previously forbidden from living in Russia), and these Jews ended up more and more often in Siberia and even, fleetingly, in the village inhabited by the exiles, as if fate were bringing them together with Sertan's Jews – at this point, without question, the latter started entering into their roles and understanding Jewishness more fully and meaningfully than ever before. By the time Paul I dies in 1801, the exiles have their own synagogue, cemetery, rabbi and cantor; some even learn a little Hebrew and start praying in that language. They study the customs, conduct, character and gestures of the Jews who come to their village, and imitate them as best they can. They find out all they can about the Jewish rites, learn them by heart, and expend enormous effort acquiring the utensils, books and garments needed for their synagogue by bartering through the Romans; they feel proud that they now have everything they are supposed to have.

All the same, I don't think they ever became real Jews, with the possible exception of one group. This group appeared when the village was flourishing and was more populous than ever. At that time every part in the play was taken, so many exiles were left without a role and with no prospect of one, because their parents had also never had roles; in other words, they had no future. Such people existed among both the Jews and the Christians, and they were known as the 'spongers'; they were seen as superfluous, useless people, and that was also how they saw themselves. Nobody could see any point to their existence and treated them accordingly. In particular, any one of them could be killed with impunity by those who had roles; they could also kill one another, and the leaders of the community would merely turn a blind eye. This shows that, legally speaking, the spongers were not considered autonomous; they were the responsibility of the closest relatives they had with roles in the play (a distinctive system of vassalage and patronage) and worked for these relatives, on whom they were entirely dependent.

It was among these disenfranchised individuals, or rather among the Jewish ones, that a new faith began to spread at the start of the nineteenth century. No doubt, it would be easy enough to find comparable doctrines in one or other Christian sect as well. They called themselves 'Abelites', considered themselves spiritual descendants of the devout Abel and believed that God was pleased with Abel because he was a shepherd, while Cain and his offering were rejected because Cain tilled the soil. The work of the shepherd, they believed, was the work of the free, while agriculture was the work of slaves and engendered slavery.

I know from Suvorin that until the eighteenth century agriculture was forbidden among Cossacks on pain of death; they, too, feared slavery. The slavery of the husbandman bore violence as its fruit; he reduced the variety of God's world to what he planted and grew, he tried to subordinate the entire earth to his needs, to decide himself what was to remain upon it, and he was certain that, of everything the Lord had created, only that which he needed had a right to life. The Abelites accused husbandmen of the remorseless, pitiless destruction of thousands upon thousands of God's creatures, and of intending to kill thousands more in the future.

The Abelites did not live for all that long in the community; by the time Napoleon went to war with Russia, they had already converted one of the local Yakut tribes and wandered off with it to the south-west, in the direction of the true Jerusalem. They were soon forgotten. The village took their departure calmly: it had no bearing on the play or anything else. All the same, the Christians found themselves thinking once again that the Jews could not be counted on; after all, none of the spongers among the Christians had been affected by this heresy and none of them had wandered off with the Yakut nomads. If the Abelites could leave, then so could the Jews who did have roles and who were needed for the Second Coming of Christ; they had to be watched.

When I came across descriptions in Kobylin's documents of their doctrine, of their faith and their departure, the Abelites initially struck me as being more like real Jews than Sertan's Jews, but I was probably wrong, seeing as none of the exiles, then or later, ever thought of them as Jews at all. They were born Jewish, people would say, but they had left the path intended for the Jews, the only path where a Jew could be a Jew, and the very fact that they had understood that they could leave it and did leave it meant that there had never been anything Jewish about them. As for all those Bochkaryovs, Frolovs, Sidorovs, all those who had kept the faith and were still following the road of the Jews, Misha and I talked about them, too. Ever since we had translated Sertan's diaries, he had deemed them to be real Jews, while I was convinced that their Jewishness, for all that they imitated Jews and believed themselves to be Jews, was steeped in Christianity; it was not Jewish in origin and it was not directed towards an eternal, living dialogue with God, but merely towards the repetition of what had come before – and no more. Their Jewish faith, I told Misha, was born not from Abraham but from Christianity.

'You may be right,' he said, 'but it led them onto the road

walked only by Jews.'

The exiles spent five years in Birch Groves, feeling more and more oppressed each year by the presence of the police officer, by the fact that they were almost never allowed out of his sight, that they were constantly being followed, were exposed on every side and had to be on their guard at all times. Save for the periods when the officer had to report to Yeniseisk, they managed to rehearse the crowd scenes no more than three times during these years, and that was only because they managed to get the officer drunk. He drank very rarely, though: there was something wrong with his stomach and he would throw up and writhe in pain every time he had a drop too much. Waking the next morning, he would vow never to drink again and, however much they tried to tempt him, would hold firm for months on end. They could see that the crowd scenes were coming out worse each time, that their confidence was draining away and that their movements were losing the naturalness and collective coordination that had once so astounded Sertan. For more and more of them, the silhouette of the One who walked before them, the One behind whom they walked, was losing its sharpness, blurring, fading, which meant that they too were now becoming confused, kept bumping into each other and losing Him.

At first they thought that by virtue of being outwardly indistinguishable from other exiled settlers, from the lives all around them – with their births, deaths, sowing, haymaking, harvesting – the police officer would soon be recalled, and everyone would forget about them and what had brought them to Siberia. Life was one thing back there, quite another over here; the country itself was no longer the same. Whoever you may have been in Russia and whatever you may have done there no longer mattered all that much if you behaved yourself here. But whether the officer had simply been forgotten about, which was possible, although he continued to send reports several times a year to Yeniseisk, where they were sent on by courier to Moscow, or whether somebody who knew their story thought that this business had not yet run its course – one way or another, he carried on living with them, the same officer who had brought them here in the first place.

Essentially, they were one-role actors selected by Sertan to play that part and no other, but here in Siberia, if they were to survive long enough to see Christ, they had no choice but to learn a whole new role from scratch, and now they felt that they were becoming professionals, that they could perform anything and everything, that the skills they had acquired by playing ordinary peasants before the officer were seeping into the play itself, and the play was dying, their lines were dying, and everything that Sertan, Nikon and their own faith had given them was dying with it. Once, Christ's parents had fled with Him from Herod, from Israel, from a land where people knew who He was to a land, Egypt, where nobody had ever heard of Him, and they only returned when Herod died and Christ had been forgotten. Now they, too, should flee from the powers that be and hide themselves away in a remote, secret place where they would be alone, where once again they would live only in Christ, wait only for Him, and it was there that He would finally come to them.

They knew that they had to leave Birch Groves, but for a long time they did not know how, scared that wherever they went they would be found and captured, and it was not until the autumn of 1674 that they thought of asking the Wise Men to appeal to the Yakuts for help. That winter, on the far shore of the Keti, some forty miles to the north of the village, the Yakuts located a low mound overgrown with pines and meadow grass; it was ringed round with bogs, and the only way of reaching it was to wait until the bogs froze over or to build a causeway half a mile long from a tiny tributary of the Keti. The Wise Men went with the Yakuts to see this mound, as did Pontius Pilate, who knew from personal experience what this work would involve. The spot was just what they were looking for: nobody would ever be able to find them there, and there was good land in abundance. If they prepared the logs in advance – and the Yakuts were offering to do this within a month – it would be easy enough to lay the causeway and cross the bog with their livestock and chattels.

By May 1675, when the officer was due to make his regular trip to Yeniseisk to give an account of himself and receive his salary, all of them – Christians, Jews and Romans – had firmly resolved to leave Birch Groves, make themselves scarce and start a new life on the mound that the Yakuts had found for them. This was typical of the harmony that usually reigned among the exiles, and it came from Sertan; in fact, it lay at the very origin of their play, and was founded on the conviction that, however different their various roles might be, each of them was equally essential and indispensable. Only if they combined all these roles into one could the thing they were living for – the coming of Christ to earth – become possible.

As a rule, the officer would be away for two to three weeks at a time; during this period, they would have to gather everything they would need for life in the new place, cover their tracks so well that nobody would even suspect there were any tracks to look for, sail to the new place, make the causeway, and cross over it to the mound. They had little time to spare, especially after deciding to give themselves only ten days for both the preparations and the journey itself: the apostles were not minded to take any risks, conscious that the officer might come back early for one reason or another. To keep to this schedule, they drew up a detailed plan well in advance of who was going to do what, where and when, and barely an hour, if that, after the officer had left, Peter the Apostle, who was their leader not only by virtue of his role, dispatched eighteen peasants – Christians and Jews mixed together – to lay the causeway, and another dozen to make the rafts on which they and the livestock would float down the Keti, while all the other men and women helped him get everything ready.

The preparations took three days, and on the morning of the fourth the Yakuts who had been brought by the Wise Men staged a Tatar raid on Birch Groves (such events had once been common enough in these parts). On horseback one and all, they made an uncertain start, huddling together like foresters come to town; they did not dare separate themselves from the group and kept riding up and down the village, talking neither to the exiles nor to one another – in fact, the exiles were reminded of themselves during their first rehearsals – but then, slowly getting used to the idea of what they were supposed to be doing that day, and already thinking and picturing to themselves how they would go about it – the older men among them had taken part in more than one such raid in their youth, and now they found it pleasant to remember that time, to persuade themselves that, if it came to it, they could still carry out a real raid just as well as they had then – the Yakuts began to break out of their huddle. The horses were far more sprightly beneath them now, frequently changing gait. One moment the horsemen would bunch together as before and slow their steeds to a trot, the next one of them would suddenly gallop away from the group into the distance while the others, geeing themselves up with battle cries, would immediately give chase, catch up with him, touch him with their short Tatar sabres to let him know that in a real fight he would never escape alive, then loudly celebrate their victory and stream through the village.

They were moving faster and faster now, and at first this merely increased the madness and chaos, or so at least it seemed to the exiles, but later, when the horses were galloping so fast that the exiles no longer even tried to follow them with their gaze, they suddenly saw that every home was now surrounded by a whooping, neighing vortex of horses and horsemen. The horses were lathering, which merely emphasised the similarity; indeed identical vortexes had formed around every cluster of exiles and even around every individual exile, if he happened to be standing on his own. Strangely enough, these vortexes, which sucked in and paralysed both the exiles and their homes, were not remotely affected by the way in which the horsemen would rein their charges in at full gallop, make them rear, then set them off in a different direction with their whips.

An experienced predator usually knows when its victim is beaten and has accepted its fate, knows when it no longer needs to expend any more strength on the fight. So, too, the Yakuts: seeing that the village was ready to die and that those who lived in it were also ready for its death – it was essential to the exiles themselves that the Yakuts should prepare them for the village's end, that both they and it should accept and come to terms with its death – the Yakuts began to pull on the reins and brought their horses to a halt one by one. Then, looking utterly calm, almost pacified, they drew arrows from their quivers, lit them and began firing them in unison, one after the other, into the sky; it was a bright day, but the black arrows with their burning tips were clearly visible against the sun. Next, someone sent his arrow up and to the side; after tracing a short crescent, it pierced the thatched roof of the nearest hut. The straw was still moist from the spring weather and the flame sizzled and steamed; everyone – both exiles and Yakuts – stood and stared, anxious that the fire would go out. But the roof finally blazed up, so then the Yakuts, whooping away, kicked the horses into a gallop once more and, shooting arrows as they went, set fire to the whole village in a matter of moments. The log huts were just beginning to burn and smoke was hanging thick in the air, almost concealing the flames, when the Yakuts, urging on the laggards and even using their whips when they had to, arranged the exiles as if they really were about to take them off into captivity: ten horsemen went in front, followed by the exiles – in the same order in which they walked to Siberia: first Jews, then Christians – followed by another ten mounted men behind them, then the livestock, then a rearguard of experienced warriors. After checking that the captives were lined up correctly, the senior Yakut gave the signal to leave.

At first they walked in the direction of the Keti, with the wind at their backs; even when they were a good half a mile from the village, the air was still so thick with the smell of burning and soot it was as if they had never left. Just before they reached the ford, their column turned to the right and they saw the pillar of black smoke above the village for the last time; then, both Yakuts and exiles headed upstream through the virgin pine forests that stretched in a thin line along the terrace of the river. After three days of almost continuous walking – they only stopped at night for two or three hours, and even that was only to feed and rest the animals – their party, maintaining its shape and order, emerged at the spot where rafts were waiting for the exiles and where, according to the schedule, they should part with the Yakuts. Here the river was met from the south by a narrow, pebbly ridge, the Keti curved around it, and it was along this ridge, strewn with small, sharp stones, that the Yakuts planned to set off towards their normal herding territory. No one but they could tell who, when or how many had walked over these stones, or where they had been heading.

As for the exiles, they intended to cover their tracks by doubling back on themselves. They would sail down the Keti back towards Birch Groves, then downstream for another twenty-five miles or so before striking out towards the place where they would make their new homes. Before saying goodbye, the Yakuts helped them load their chattels and, most importantly, livestock: the horses and cows were scared of the water; they were shaking and needed to be calmed and carefully tied lest they capsized the rafts and ruined everything. The exiles left almost a third of the animals behind on the bank; they were exhausted and would probably have died en route, so Ivashka Skosyryev (Peter the Apostle) ordered them to be handed over to the Yakuts. The latter received many other gifts as well – fabrics, knives, beads – and were more than satisfied; then the Yakut chief and Peter embraced. All the rafts except Peter's had already been unmoored and were slowly drifting towards midstream; when his finally floated off to join them, the animals on the river began neighing and lowing, and those left behind with the Yakuts called back to them from the bank.

The rivers of western Siberia are slow-moving, and their waters can seem as still as a lake. The Keti is no exception, which is why it took five days for the sprawling line of rafts to pass the ford for Birch Groves. The smoke had gone, but the smell of burning remained; the river could not forget this smell, and it was the last thing that remained of their village. Two days later the exiles reached the tributary they were seeking. Here, without stepping onto the bank or letting the animals onto dry land, they disembarked; those who had made the rafts took them apart, while the rest, wasting no time, set off along the tributary's hard sandy floor to the place, a few miles further along, where the causeway was supposed to begin.

The very next day the exiles were already on the mound. There, they established their new village, Mosslands (*Mshanniki*), which can be found on any detailed map of western Siberia, whether pre-revolutionary or Soviet; in fact, it exists to this day. Mosslands, and its immediate vicinity, is where the exiles and their descendants would live uninterruptedly almost until our own times; nobody, with the exception of the quickly forgotten Abelites, appears to have ever left this place. It might well be called the last homeland of the actors Sertan had chosen; it was where everything he had inculcated in them was made whole and complete. Indeed, the play, which had never been performed as he had planned, continued its existence in Mosslands for many, many years. By introducing a condition, on Nikon's orders, that had not yet been fulfilled – I mean, of course, Christ's coming to earth – Sertan gave the play an almost limitless life, and certainly a much longer one than any other play I know. He made it all but immortal.

Sertan and all those around him in New Jerusalem had thought that his play would be performed only once, but in fact it was never performed. From this we might draw the conclusion that whatever has not been fulfilled can live for a long time, whereas whatever has been accomplished dies an almost instantaneous death; nature might be said to confirm this rule. But Sertan himself had not prepared the play for a long life and, needless to say, could not have imagined what would follow: neither what this life would be like, nor that it would have a life at all, and here, too, we might pose any number of questions about the relationship between art and

216

the artist. How great and how enduring is the artist's power and responsibility? How well do artists know what they have created? It seems to me that they exaggerate both their power and their knowledge, and consequently their responsibility, while they underestimate the freedom of will which, echoing God, they almost always give to the work of their own hands.

The play which Sertan had rehearsed was taken to its conclusion in Mosslands according to its own internal laws; we can confirm that in this respect nothing was distorted. Work on it proceeded without any influence from the outside world, unless we include the influence of the isolated location and of the bogs that surrounded the village on all sides, which may indeed have spurred the exiles to focus on themselves. But the villagers themselves desired this isolation – that was why they had left Birch Groves, a decision that, as far as I know, they never regretted. At first, the work of Sertan's hands grew without any external hindrance, and the one and only influence on the play was time, understood simply as duration. My comment that Mosslands became their homeland can be amply justified: most of the exiles – and I include in that category the exiles' descendants, since, by never returning to Russia, exiles is what they remained – were born, lived and died there. More importantly, it was in Mosslands that their life settled into its final shape; it was here that its limits and rules were worked out, its rhythm and patterns, all sufficiently robust to endure without compromise for a great many years, even once the village had, through various ties, become a part of the surrounding world. The latter was subject to radical, constant change, it turned out to be fragile and frail, but the chaos blowing in from outside had no more impact on the exiles than the order that had existed before. They lived and died by their own laws. The structure of their world, created for one aim only, proved far better equipped for life than what lay beyond its boundary.

The exiles themselves, however, did not see Mosslands as their homeland. In a homeland, life goes on and on. There, death is less final than anywhere else, for you are in no doubt that you will be continued by your own children; a homeland is always filled with nostalgia, with a consciousness of the value of both life in general and the life you have lived – but the exiles were living for the sake of something else. They were waiting for the end, hastening it as best they could. For them, the end was the only reality, and it would be odd, given all this, to imagine that they could think of life as a gift or a blessing; if anything, life for the exiles was sin and evil, a synonym for their own torments and the torments of others. And there was something else: their place of birth meant nothing to them. To them Mosslands, just like Birch Groves, was Jerusalem, and Jerusalem was what they called it amongst themselves. Mentally, having once been chosen by Sertan, they had never moved anywhere again; they were still living in Jerusalem, just as they always had, because Jerusalem was wherever they were, the place where Jesus Christ would come to them.

The exiles lived in Mosslands, undisturbed by anyone, for more than forty years before the authorities finally found out about them. By then several Tsars had come and gone – Alexei, Fyodor, Sofya, Ivan – and the reign of Peter the Great was reaching its end. Everything, needless to say, had long been forgotten: both the story of their exile and the burning of Birch Groves. A large, wealthy village of the same name now stood on its ashes, and nobody would ever imagine that any connection might exist between it and Mosslands. When talking about themselves, the exiles would say that they had arrived from Russia under Peter the Great, that is, a mere twenty or so years before, but even this ruse was unnecessary, because nobody showed any particular curiosity towards them. A great many people were fleeing to Siberia at this time, especially Old Believers, and there were many villages like Mosslands. Once they had become known to the authorities, they were not subjected to any kind of surveillance, only to the same taxes and duties as everyone else. The most burdensome of these was enlistment, but they merely handed over the spongers, which caused no damage to the play. So long as they met all their obligations on time, without falling into arrears, nobody expected anything else from them.

However frightened the exiles may have been to find themselves exposed to the light (initially, they even thought of repeating what they had done in Birch Groves by burning down Mosslands and heading further north), their emergence from the underground proved beneficial in many ways. The surrounding world did not make an exception of them and, therefore, did not prevent them from making whatever arrangements suited them; what was more, this world offered hundreds of useful things without which life in the village was becoming harder and harder each year. They had traded with the outside world before, throughout these forty years, but only out of necessity and with the Yakuts as their intermediaries, which meant that it generally took a year or even two for whatever they needed to reach them. Now, on the other hand, merchants and pedlars regularly visited the village, and they could barter fur with them for whatever they wanted: a good harness, iron, fabrics, salt.

By the beginning of the eighteenth century Mosslands had become almost crowded: some 236 males, according to Peter the Great's census of 1717. As a result, not only had all the secondary roles been filled but, as I have already said, there were plenty of people left without a part or even the hope of ever getting one – not for as long as the village prospered and there were at least two candidates for every role that became vacant. In fact, it often occurred to me that all the spongers had to do was send a letter to the authorities denouncing the villagers for the burning of Birch Groves, or heresy, or lese-majesty, or whatever, link that to what was going on in Mosslands, and repressions would have been sure to follow, thus clearing a path for a good number of people. I think this idea occurred to the spongers, too: denunciations were indeed sent, hence some of the persecutions to which Mosslands was subjected. The sheer injustice of being allowed so near the sacred mystery while being fated to make way time and again for those whose superiority lay not in their faith, righteousness or talent, but merely in their birth – some gained everything from their birth, others lost everything – was such that it is easier for me to understand them than to condemn them. Speaking as a historian, I can say that the play needed these persecutions from outside; it benefited from them. Their principal victims were those who had already held their roles – and all the advantages that came with them – for many years; justice, thereby, was restored. The new performers were no worse than the previous ones, while their dedication and passion were even greater.

The persecutions kept the quantity of exiles in check. As they decreased in number, they got on better, more straightforwardly: no more quarrels, no more crime. Life would become calmer, as if everything extraneous to the rehearsals had faded away, and only the rehearsals remained. Most importantly, whoever survived the persecutions gained from them: some, like the spongers, were given parts for the first time, while those who were already involved were given more important roles, leaving nobody to criticise the informants with a clear conscience, or to grieve for the departed. However, only a few of the upheavals experienced by the village in the two and a half centuries of its existence came from outside and began with a denunciation; the cause of most of them, insofar as I can judge from the documents, lay elsewhere.

When he set to work on the mystery play in New Jerusalem, Sertan could never have predicted that all the actors he had chosen would die before it was performed and, therefore, that it would fall to quite different people, none of whom he had ever known or seen, to act it out. This is obvious enough, and we should not be surprised that his diaries say nothing about what kind of people, in terms of appearance, character and talent, should qualify for this or that role. Sertan knew all this without needing to write it down. The only notes he made for himself during the first days of working on the play were some rather vague estimates about the desired age of the actors: for example, between twenty and fifty for the apostles. There was one other thing: on the march to exile, a week after Sertan died, the community itself had suddenly had to decide how to replace one of the demoniacs, who had drowned while crossing the Ob. After lengthy arguments, the exiles eventually agreed that the right and lawful choice would be the dead man's immediate heir, the oldest in the line.

The system established by the exiles, so self-evident and simple in appearance, could function well only for as long as they were few in number, something they quickly realised as soon as the community began to grow. Firstly, many people were aggrieved by the rule that if your father or mother (inheritance was matrilinear for female roles) did not have a part, or live long enough to receive one, then his or her descendants lost all their rights. Secondly, with time it became difficult to tell who was the eldest in line: in large families a twenty-year gap between the first and last child was not unusual, so the children of the older brothers and sisters were often born earlier than their youngest uncles and aunts. A woman might even end up breastfeeding her child and her brother at one and the same time, and disagreements followed about what should take precedence – seniority in age or generation – although on the whole the exiles leaned towards the latter.

There were also all sorts of restrictions: apostles, for example, could not be played by the crippled, the possessed, the deformed, anyone with a birthmark, skin disease, eye disease, and so on. Some of these things, of course, are extremely subjective: how do you define deformity? For some, a large mole is a birthmark, while others would call a birthmark a mole; and in Siberia you won't find many people past the age of forty with healthy eyes and skin. It's not even easy to agree on who is possessed and who isn't. And how could they be expected to agree? After all, if you got a role you got everything, but if you didn't you spent your whole life as a pariah, an untouchable. Those who could lay claim to a role in the future would count the days until their father's or brother's term came to an end, or one or other died, and the longed-for vacancy arose. When this moment came, their sense of entitlement was so strong that they would stop at nothing (beatings, killings, bribes, denunciations) to get their role. Violence was commonplace, and everyone agreed that something had to be done.

The proposal put forward by the apostles leading the community looked sensible enough, but it betrayed their own self-interest all too clearly and the others never accepted it. The apostles wanted to make the age restrictions introduced by Sertan merely optional. They were constantly being broken in any case: sometimes there was no family heir of a suitable age, or else he was sick or feeble-minded and incapable of understanding and learning the role, or else he was a gambler and simply a bad lot. The apostles saw nothing good about the severity of these restrictions; they said that roles were often inherited by performers who were only a few months younger than the ones stepping down and would themselves soon need to pass the role onto someone else, with violence accompanying every such change. Would it not be better simply to abandon short-term roles and thereby offer some reassurance?

But the majority maintained, as it always does, that it would be better to leave everything as it was; for all their infighting, the people of Mosslands had grown used to the system and it had taken root. Few people, after all, are prepared to change long-established social structures, whatever they might be. This conservative impulse, sanctified by tradition, was a powerful force, even if the very word tradition seems out of place among people who were waiting for the end to come each and every day, who were ready for the end and were living for that alone. In essence, they were living for a revolution – a break with the past – the like of which mankind had never seen before. Even so, there were many who would have preferred this process of universal ruin to be more orderly and less chaotic, for it to be reasonable and fair. But they were scared of correcting Sertan.

Those without roles always viewed the apostles' proposals as merely a ploy on the part of those who already had roles to extend their privileges until their deaths. Nevertheless, the apostles' power was such that they would have got their way sooner or later were it not for the majority's total confidence in Sertan's infallibility, their belief that, if they wanted Christ to come, they must not violate anything of what their teacher had bequeathed. They understood that straying from Sertan meant leaving unworthy people in the role of Christ's apostles and disciples, people whom He, Christ, had not chosen, while those who were His true disciples would be kept away from Him, because the term of their apostleship, in the community's view, would be too short. And then Christ might not come, which was the only thing that all of them – both those who had a role and those who did not – were living for.

What I have just written represents my first impression of the fate of Sertan's play. Strangely enough, it appears to have contained a good deal of truth. Back then, whenever Kobylin visited, I could barely wait for him to leave so that I could read his latest consignment. So great was my excitement that I reminded myself of Suvorin ransacking log huts in search of manuscripts. My hands were shaking and I could barely sit still as I hurriedly flipped through the pages, desperate to find out where it was all leading, to catch a glimpse of both the beginning and the end. Only then, perhaps, would I understand why Sertan's play lived on, why there was so much life in it, and why, even so, it had died.

Essentially, Sertan had created a new people and a new community, unlike any other. The people he had begotten were surrounded by another people for years on end, neither mixing with it nor even appearing to notice it, yet everything it did, it did for this other people, for its salvation. It lived a very complicated, very adult, and even, you could say, elderly life, a life which, like old age, was turned towards the end. The life that surrounded them seemed foolish and childish, but that life, for all its simplicity, contained so much grief that it could no longer be borne, and everyone was waiting for the Lord, begging to be saved. To stop those little children from hampering their attempts to save them, the exiles adapted as best they could to their way of life. Like chameleons, they changed colour and became indistinguishable from everything around them; they could be neither found nor caught, camouflaged as they were by their complete equality with others.

But there was one thing I got wrong as I read Kobylin's papers. In order to put emotions aside and set to work, I had to get used to what I found there as quickly as possible, I had to locate the resemblance between everything I was reading about and everything I already knew; unsurprisingly, the transfer of roles from one person to another, so that one man could rise from rags to riches in the space of a single day while another could lose all he had had just the day before, reminded me of revolutions, and since the only revolutions I knew were social ones I thought that here, too, the loss of rights and privileges was just about the most important thing – only much later did I understand how very little this mattered to the exiles themselves.

The last months before the changing of the apostles were terrifying. The old apostles (and not only they) believed, just as they had on their first day of service, that they, and only they, had been chosen by Christ, which meant that the world was living out its last days, that the time was at hand; these long years had been a test of their devotion, but they had passed it; now the wait was almost over and He would come. But those apostles were being pushed out by the new ones, who also believed unconditionally that they, and only they, were the last whom He, Christ, would make first; they had waited all this time for Him, and He had waited all this time for them, His disciples. It was not unusual for the two groups to disagree on the date of succession, and then a kind of anarchy would ensue.

A dead time would begin, a time that should have had no

place in the world created by God, a time when Christ could not come to earth because there was no one for Him to come to. The chain of violence and pitiless killing that followed, the horror unfolding among the chosen and the faithful, merely served to confirm the exiles in the thought that this was it; if they, the chosen of the chosen, faithful of the faithful, had come to this, then the end, for everything and everyone, really was at hand. We should not forget that for a long time the only past that the exiles had acknowledged was the history of their relationship with God. Having been chosen for the most important mission and set apart from the rest of humanity, they looked only to Christ, and everything else in their life – working in the fields, having children – was done only in order to serve this preordained purpose in the right way. They did not notice any other people, any other life; even to look at another life or pay it any attention would mean to look backwards; they should return to those people later, in a completely different way, from a different perspective and in a different capacity, return to them after Christ, when everything for which they had been chosen and for which they had prepared would have become a reality. They had left the old world behind them, their minds were concentrated wholly on Christ, and all they asked of the world was that it should not touch them, not hinder them, not pull them out of this state of concentration and distract their gaze from Christ; only then could they be sure that they would not miss Him or a single one of His words, that they would remember everything, understand everything, and be able to teach others, to pass it all on. The process of waiting, in other words, was stretched out over centuries and generations, and the only explanation that the outgoing apostles could find for why Christ had not yet come and their hopes had not been fulfilled was that they had never really managed to renounce everything that surrounded them, never really fenced themselves off. They repented that they had been too worldly, that they had loved both power and life and had been unable (often for purely external reasons: resettlement, exile, and so on) to turn solely towards Christ, to become His and only His, to forget and cast off everything else, and merely believe and wait, wait and believe.

They knew that life had given them a chance that no other mortal had received, but they had let it pass them by, and the crisis they experienced on stepping out of the play was sheer agony; they yearned for one thing only – to stop living; they were insane and inconsolable. After so many years of praying, so many years of faith and humility, so many years of hope and love towards their neighbours, all their frenzy and hatred gushed out of them with extraordinary force; they killed like beasts, thought that everything was permitted to them, and were unable to stop. What did a human life matter now when soon, so soon, everything would end anyway? If they killed an innocent man, all the better; they would be helping him save himself by removing him from sin. And so what if they were destroying themselves? Things were already as bad and as terrifying as they could ever be. Because of them, life on earth and all its torments had been prolonged for yet another entire generation, they were responsible for all the horrors and sufferings it would face, and now, multiplying them, adding new ones, they realised that the calamities and catastrophes that would precede the Last Judgment, the calamities that, as is well known, would multiply without measure, required their own atrocities, too, the atrocities of those who had been purest and, until recently, almost chosen, almost admitted, and who had stopped before the last step could be taken.

The very fact that the same people who, just yesterday, had

been expected to become Christ's apostles were now burning, massacring, raping only served to confirm that the last days were near, that they would begin any moment. This cruelty was not merely a counterweight to their previous life and previous service, disclosing and emptying everything they had suppressed within themselves, but became their new role; the former apostles created and brought closer that backdrop of universal ruin which, so they – and others – thought, would provide the necessary colour and contrast for the Second Coming of Christ. Nobody, they thought, should regret the passing of the world that they were leaving, that was now ending for all time and all people.

In September 1801, six months after the Russian throne was occupied by a man who consented to the murder of his own father, various circumstances combined in Mosslands to give birth to a heresy that was almost the ruin of Sertan's play. For the first time in the history of the community, all twelve apostles were nearing the end of their term at the same time. Each of them had held the role of one of Christ's closest disciples for at least ten years, more than enough time for them to get to know each other well, to learn to love each other and grow loyal. They were strong, intelligent people and – most importantly, in view of subsequent events – they all viewed Ivashka Skosyryev (Peter the Apostle) as their leader and all held him in the same esteem. His apostleship, moreover, had lasted the longest: twenty-seven years.

At the close of the eighteenth century, perhaps for internal reasons to do with the exiles themselves, perhaps because echoes of the rationalist vogue had reached Siberia and even Mosslands, some of the exiles began to think both that man was personally responsible before God and that the Lord had given him freedom of choice, freedom of will. Granted, the absolute predetermination of their theatrical performance was no less manifest than before, and many remained convinced of the equally absolute predetermination (known only to God) of human fates, but still, the remorse that had accumulated among several generations of apostles, of disciples without a teacher, and the knowledge that Christ had not come and human torments had continued because they had proved unworthy of Him, persisted and survived.

If in the past actors had felt certain that they had received their role because they had been chosen ahead of the others, because it had been decided that Christ would come specifically to them, now they began to understand that the role was just the beginning, that they must also prove themselves worthy of Christ. He was the measure, and He would come to them only if they would be worthy. And so, within the space of a few September days, this line of thinking – a line of which they themselves were barely conscious (at its heart was the belief that the final choice of actors was yet to be decided), but which was in harmony with what Sertan had done, though it was not his – subordinated them to its logic and almost led to the ruin of the entire play. The exiles tried to destroy the play and everyone involved in it, and they very nearly succeeded.

Ever since they had received their roles, the twelve outgoing apostles had followed the example of Ivashka Skosyryev and led the life of saints and ascetics, which, in essence, is what they were. They were pure in thought and deed, loved Christ, and believed that He would come; they prayed for His coming, not for their own sakes, but because they could no longer bear to see human grief, and implored Him to come and save people because they could see that people could not save themselves. When the last day of their apostleship was over, they realised that Christ would not come and that evil would not end with them, or in their time. Their successors had not yet been chosen, so there followed a period when nobody on earth was waiting for Christ, a period of days without God. It was a time when everything in the world was, as it were, turned upside down, but everything had been turned upside down inside them as well, so they did not notice the change. Now it was given to them to see their old life from the outside, and so pure was it, so full of faith, that all twelve of them realised that Sertan's path was false and did not lead to salvation – and that was when they struck out on their own.

Some five years before these events, an exiled Pole by the name of Kiślicki – a native of Grodno, or perhaps Lublin – washed up in Mosslands and stayed there for almost two months. Back home he had been a librarian and a home tutor with, it seems, the Potocki family, but when Poland rose up against Russia, he joined the uprising's leader, Kościuszko, and served as his orderly throughout the war. When Suvorov routed the rebels, Kiślicki was taken captive along with many others; he was tried and found guilty for taking part in the mutiny, but since he had not opened fire himself, he got off lightly. He was sentenced to exile in Siberia where, together with several hundred insurgents, he was put to work cultivating the Baraba steppe. He didn't know the first thing about farming and a year later, after arguing about something with his fellow Poles, he left them and wandered all over Siberia from town to town. He was old, or seemed old, his clothes were dirty and ragged, and he spoke beautiful but peculiar Russian: he had taught himself the language in prison from a book of Gavrila Derzhavin's poems; everyone took him for a holy fool and willingly offered him food and shelter.

When the Pole turned up in Mosslands, there was something about him that reminded Peter of Sertan, so Peter ordered that he be made welcome, although usually the village would send outsiders on their way as quickly as possible. That evening Peter invited Kiślicki over, and they talked for a long time about Scripture and about Christ. The Pole was a highly educated man; he knew both Testaments well, knew Hebrew, and most importantly, having lived in a country with many Jews, he knew their customs. He helped the exiles understand and restore many details of the play, details whose meaning they had forgotten, and Peter was so happy that he told Kiślicki he could stay for as long as he wanted; but in spring, just as soon as the snow melted and it became warm, he left.

After ceasing to be an apostle, Peter, like the other eleven, thought a great deal about the life he had lived. His apostleship had lasted the longest, and it took him longer than anyone else to understand that everything they had done in following Sertan had been either insufficient or incorrect, that Christ would not reveal Himself to them, nor to their descendants, and that they were waiting for Him in vain. This was a terrible conclusion to draw from their innocence, and to be able to accept it and tell Sertan's other disciples, he had to know why this was so and what they must do now. He felt duty-bound to teach them what to do, otherwise it was as if he was always taking from them and giving nothing in return. Needless to say, not a single one of them would believe him, they would say that he had never had enough faith, that he had only seemed to live like a saint, which was why it had not been given to him to become a disciple of Christ. Simply imagining all this made him scared – perhaps they were right, perhaps this was how it was. Once again he reviewed his entire life and once again he assured himself that he had had faith, that he was innocent. It was then he understood that the answer was not to be found in the life they had lived since Sertan's death – a life constructed solely by Sertan – but beyond its boundaries, if there was an answer at all. But Peter knew almost nothing about the outside world. During the years of his apostleship, he had met very few people unconnected with Sertan's play: a few peddlers, a merchant who occasionally visited the village, the Yakuts they had dealt with ever since their time at Birch Groves, a dozen or so tramps – the village was off the beaten track, so they rarely came there – and Kiślicki, who resembled none of the other outsiders and whom Peter left till last, realising that if there was anything that could help them, anything that could tell them what to do in order that Christ should come, then it was the words spoken by this Pole.

Peter summoned his memories of the Yakuts, the merchant and the tramps, but he did not linger on them for long; instead he began recalling and recording in exhaustive detail – this labour took him more than a week – everything Kiślicki had said, and when he finally got to the end and read it all through he saw that now he knew why everything was as it was and why people's lives were going on and on, even if no one had any strength left and there was more and more sin, sorrow and suffering in the world, and the Saviour had not heard the prayers of those who were waiting for Him.

Among the batches of papers I bought from Kobylin at our first meeting there were seventeen pages of notes that can be traced back to Kiślicki. All are written in Peter's hand, and circumstantial evidence leaves no doubt that this is not an original draft but the definitive version of the text widely known in Mosslands under the title *The Word of Peter the Apostle*; I received a further five copies from Kobylin on subsequent occasions. The *Word* consists of a very brief and disjointed summary of episodes from the Old and New Testaments and parables from the Talmud; moreover, the text is put together in such a way that each of the fragments is preceded by the conclusion drawn from it, while the fragment itself serves to affirm and illustrate the conclusion. The following chapters of the Bible entered the *Word*: the story of Noah and God's promise to Abraham – the subject of both being the eternal life of the people that will descend from Abraham; God's promise to Jacob and His other promises to the Jews; the destruction of Sodom and Gomorrah; Moses in the Desert of Sinai saving the Jews who had made themselves a golden calf from the wrath of the Lord and their own destruction; Christ and the Canaanite woman, and Christ's words that He had been sent to the lost sheep of the House of Israel; Peter's words in the Acts of the Apostles, understood to mean that the conversion of all Jews to Christ must precede the Second Coming of the Saviour and the victory of the righteous; as well as the Jewish tradition that the world rests on thirty-six saints, the *Lamedvavniks*: it is for their sake that the Lord does not destroy the world, and if they should lose even one of their number, the world will not stand.

From these sources, Peter the Apostle draws the following conclusion: the world is terrifying, it is evil, and this evil comes from people, who know what they do but are unable to stop, who can be neither helped nor reformed; more than once the Lord has wanted to annihilate them, but the righteous ones always got in the way – they would not let the Lord punish sin. Living with and among the Jews, they had defended and shielded murderers, rapists, adulterers, idolaters, thieves; it was the righteous who had to answer for the world's sufferings. In destroying this world and abandoning it to flames, earthquakes, floods, beasts of prey and poisonous reptiles, the Lord would have saved the righteous and welcomed them into His eternal life, but they had preferred to remain among the people and not allow the world to die. This conclusion was also Peter's reckoning with his own righteous life.

The Jews were even more culpable than the righteous. Nothing could compare with their thirst for life. Several times they had managed to catch the Lord unawares and extract a promise from Him to make them as plentiful as the stars in the sky, never to destroy them, whatever their sins. The Lord had formed a covenant with them, and throughout almost the entire history of mankind He had looked at the world through the Jews and through their eyes. The Jews were His sole concern, they had taken Him away from other nations, and these nations, abandoned and forgotten by God, did evil because they thought that nobody needed them. Even Christ, even He, came to earth precisely in order to save the Jews. Now the Jews themselves had to renounce their covenant with God and free Him from the promises they had so cunningly coaxed from Him, and if they did not do that of their own free will, they must be forced to do so, and only then, when all human beings had once again become equal before the Lord and seen once more that they were all God's children, all equally dear to Him, equally beloved, equally needed, and that there was no first and no last, only then could the righteous be separated from the sinful and every man be rewarded according to his deeds.

Judging by the chronicle of the rehearsals – the fullest and richest source of facts about the life of Sertan's actors in Siberia – Peter the Apostle did not need long to bring many of the exiles round to his way of thinking, and the first instances of forced conversion of Jews to Christianity occurred as early as October 6. Even before this, attempts had evidently been made to persuade rather than compel Jews to convert, but they had led nowhere. The turn to violence came easily to those who followed Peter, for it had been inherent in the course of action he had proposed from the very beginning, and from the very beginning it had been justified by the guilt of the Jews. Some of the neophytes were even of the view – which Peter himself would later espouse – that violence was necessary as retribution for their sins; it would be wrong for the Jews to make a bloodless conversion to Christianity and become like everyone else just like that. And there was something else: if the Jews were still the Lord's sole concern, then the crueller the persecutions and atrocities, and the more numerous the killings of Jews, the sooner the Lord would understand that human beings could bear it no longer; they were in despair, they were sick, they had become beasts and monsters – just a little more and they would be beyond saving.

Thanks to the chronicle, we also know the exact balance of forces. Peter was supported by all the apostles whose term had ended at the same time as his – they continued to govern the community until it was known who would replace them in the play – and by the spongers, who, as I have already said, never enjoyed any influence at all, but now, according to Peter's doctrine, enjoyed the same rights as everyone else. The majority of the exiles, however, remained loyal to Sertan and spoke out against Peter and the persecution of the Jews. Those disagreeing with Peter included, in the first place, almost all the Christians, both those who already had roles and those hoping to receive them. For them, Sertan's authority was unshakeable, and they viewed Peter as a heretic and schismatic. These people were considered very influential and, no doubt, they could have quickly brought calm and order to the community were it not for their habit of subordinating themselves in all matters to Christ's closest disciples, the apostles – a habit inseparable from their loyalty to Sertan. But the new apostles had not yet been chosen, and their election depended entirely on Peter; as a result, passive resistance became the only course left open to the Christians. The Romans were also ranged against Peter: as sticklers and legitimists, they believed that everything should continue along the same path, that neither Peter nor anyone else had the right to change anything, that what he wanted was an abomination, yielding anarchy and chaos, which was why he had managed to attract the rabble, the spongers. What Jesus Christ wanted from people was quite different. He came into the world to save them, to teach them to repay evil with good, to sacrifice Himself for their sins; He came so that in Him, in Christ, people could become righteous before God. If Peter got his way and lured the exiles away from Sertan, there would be no Second Coming, as there would be nobody left for Him to save.

But from time immemorial the Romans had stood and lived apart from the other participants in the play, and they never openly interfered in relations between Jews and Christians. This was just that kind of case, and I doubt that the other exiles were even aware of their attitude. The Jews, too, were ranged against Peter. Peter's statement that they had used all their cunning to coax a promise from God, that they had arranged things in such a way that the Lord thought only of them, as a result of which the other nations, the nations He had forgotten and abandoned, had taken the path of sin, seemed fair to them; they had long thought that their forcible death really might free the Lord's hand, might hasten His Judgement and bring the end closer, so they should not resist their own murder. But they also thought that a straightforward death would mean accepting a lighter, milder fate; after all, it would spare them the most terrible thing of all: they would no longer have to destroy and give up to death the One who came to save them. This would also be an evasion of their roles, a form of desertion, albeit, perhaps, a more forgivable one than the departure of the Abelites.

When the persecutions began, that is how they would divide: some would give themselves over to be killed, others, terrified by the brutality, would try to flee and cling to life for as long as they could, but if it was their destiny to survive, they would return to their original positions, start rehearsing once more, and, just like the Christians, wait for Christ to come into the world, so as to perform their roles.

Between the sixth and the eighth of October the apostles managed to convert several dozen Jews to Christianity, but on the ninth, a Friday, the backlash began. By evening, when the time came to light the Sabbath candles, the recently baptised had openly returned to the old faith, ignoring the threats of Peter and his henchmen to kill the apostates.

Next, the Jews were given a week's respite: no one was allowed to touch them, although many wanted to deal with them there and then. Several times a day, supporters of the old apostles gathered in the pastures beyond the village fence to listen to Peter, James the Greater, Andrew, John and Matthew; they took away from them the message that killing Jews was necessary and indispensable for the common task, that it was good and the only possible path. Then, primed by necessity and the sense of their own rightness, they began to hate the Jews with a personal hatred, because the Jews had taken God away from each and every one of them, and sold them into evil and sin.

When they were eventually ready for the task, they marched into the village in a crowd led by Peter. There, they walked down the one and only street, tapping their sticks on the walls of the log huts, like hunters driving out game, and the Jews understood that it was just about to happen, and the crowd understood it was just about to happen, yet it passed through the entire village without killing a single person, then quickly thinned out; everyone wandered off home and calm was restored.

The next Friday, after sunset, when the Jews started celebrating the Sabbath as normal, they wept as they prayed, and thanked God for showing them mercy and staying His hand; they told Him that He had acted wisely, that their persecutors had apparently thought better of it (only a minority added the word 'apparently') and the village had settled down. Over the previous seven days they had learned something about the people who wanted to kill them, more, perhaps, than those people knew about themselves, and now, when they had finished praying and sat down to eat and celebrate, they spoke knowledgeably about just how difficult it is to kill the first man; it's impossible to do it on your own, they said, though it's much easier in a crowd, but even in a crowd there needs to be someone who starts it all off and you could bet your life that the spongers, none of whom were free and all of whom depended on other people, would never risk going first, even if later they'd be nastier than most, and the apostles would also copy Peter's every move, so it was only Peter they needed to fear, and even he would find it harder and harder to take the plunge with every day that passed. They also said that they were grateful to have had that week in their lives, that it had given them a great deal as Jews, and that now they understood their role so much better. Soon it would be time to resume the rehearsals once more (the new apostles had nearly all been chosen and the community would approve them in the next three or four days) and everything they had experienced would help them a great deal. This was one of the best and most peaceful Sabbaths the Jews had ever had; they rejoiced in the knowledge that never in their lives had they been as Jewish as they were now and that they were ready, at long last, to play the roles they had been given, in the way that Sertan had once dreamed they would.

Peter had understood long before that the killing should start on the Sabbath, that this would be crucial both for the Jews and for the Lord; on the day when He, having created the world, was resting, pleased with the work of His hands, they would set about destroying His world, killing those whom He loved most out of all His children, killing them when they were talking to Him, praying to Him, thanking Him, and this would be too much for Him to tolerate, however merciful He might be, too much for Him to forgive, and the end would come.

The morning and afternoon of October 16 were unseasonably warm. It's a rare year on the Keti when winter has not set in by mid-October and the water has not yet frozen over, when the bogs and the river lie open, without ice. The warmth and the sun had lured everyone out of their homes early in the day, and when Peter and the apostles arrived at the usual place, it was already crowded. People were lying in the sun and smiling; they were calm and at peace.

The spongers were only turning half an ear to what the apostles were telling them; they had heard it all many times before and could even come out with it themselves. But this was no bad thing. Peter could see that they were ready, that they had already got used to the idea of what they would be doing that very day; in fact it was as if they had already done it, so all he had to do was hold them back until sunset, until the Sabbath was under way. He couldn't wait for the Sabbath to come, and he couldn't stop checking the sun and the horizon, trying to work out how long there was left. They noticed his agitation and, following his example, kept their own eyes fixed on the sun, but they were still surprised and could not understand his impatience. They were simple and they believed in the immutability of the heavenly body's movement across the sky, whereas he knew that in the days of Joshua the Lord had already stopped the sun once at the request of the Jews, and he feared that God would try to interfere this time, too.

Some two hours before sunset a north-easterly wind suddenly got up, sweeping in dark clouds; snow fell thickly, then sleet, and it immediately became cold, but even though they were dressed almost for summer, the people did not disperse. They arranged themselves in a circle around the old, the weak and the very young, pressed close to one another, took each other's hands and prepared to hold on until Peter told them that the Sabbath had arrived. They knew that today they must not give in to God, that they must do what they had decided to do. But the wind grew fiercer by the minute, sweeping the snow up into the air, darkness fell quickly, and now the gusts were constantly blowing them off balance, hurling one then another to the ground. The circle would break, and while they were busy looking for the fallen and picking them up the cold and snow would penetrate their 'fortress', where the weakest stood, and the weakest would also need to be picked up and warmed, while those who still had the strength to do so were too stretched to help everyone. Soon people began losing each other; those who did not wait to be found wandered off to find their own relatives, and however much they shouted the gloom was too thick for them to be seen, nor, with this wind, was there any point shouting back: if you heard their voice, then they couldn't hear yours, and vice versa.

Peter waited for as long as he possibly could for the snowstorm to cease, or at least abate, but then he, too, was blown backwards, out of the circle; he fell and was almost instantly buried in the snow, and when he finally got to his feet he saw that there was no one around: he was alone. Unsure of where everyone was and whether they could hear him, he shouted at them to disperse, but no one answered; he shouted again, and again, and then, groping his way to the wattle fence and holding onto it with both hands, set off home.

By the time he reached his log hut, the Sabbath had begun. As he climbed the stairs he could hear Jews making merry and thanking God. He wanted to go back downstairs, grab the knife he used to slaughter cattle and go to them, but he had no strength left and he was shivering all over. He just about dragged himself to his bench and fell asleep, still cold and still crying.

He woke in the middle of the night; the snowstorm had subsided and all was quiet. He lay and thought that the Jews must be sleeping peacefully; they had told God that He no longer had to worry about them, and He, too, was calm and asleep. But it was still the Sabbath, still not too late; he just had to get up and grab the knife.

Even so, Peter would probably never have resolved to start killing the Jews all on his own, had there not been a betrayal in his life for which he could not forgive them. For almost thirty years he had respected the Jews he rehearsed with because they were waiting, just as he was, for the coming of Jesus Christ, and were dreaming about the salvation of humankind. He even bowed down before them: after all, they had taken upon themselves the heaviest and most terrible burden and – for the sake of others, for the salvation of others – they were ready to crucify Christ, to become Christ's murderers. But two weeks earlier, on the day that his apostleship ended and he, Peter, became Ivashka Skosyryev once more, the same man he had been before he was chosen, when he was ready and willing to take his own life – in fact he had a duty to take his own life, because Christ had not come to him, because he had been chosen but had proved unworthy, because, thanks to him, suffering and evil had not ended on this earth – he witnessed the exultation of his brother, Maksimko.

His brother, who had received his role on the very same day that he had, and left it on the very same day that he did, with whom he had lived under one roof for his entire life, eaten, slept, rehearsed, was exulting, with no thought of the other man's grief; no longer Caiaphas, no longer the man who had to send Christ to his death, he was exulting and making merry. So then Peter understood that the Jews were not waiting for Christ, that they feared His coming and that their devotion to the cause was a lie and a pretence; everyone else's grief was a joy to them, and perhaps the reason Christ was not coming was that He knew that the Jews did not want to crucify Him.

When Peter the Apostle, knife in hand, entered the room where the Jews were sleeping, he suddenly realised that not once in his life had he ever slaughtered an animal, or even killed a bird. He had seen it done on many occasions, but had never taken part himself. As a child, he had once watched the Yakuts killing young reindeer for some Yakut feast day, and he had seen how the animals, though still full of strength and life, had offered no resistance at all. He was astonished by the Yakuts' skill, and thought that the assurance, naturalness and speed of their actions expressed their own sense of rightness; the reindeer recognised it and, for that reason, did not resist.

Only one Sabbath candle still flickered in the main room, and that, too, was burning out; its flame was feeble and it swayed in the draught. The light barely reached the far corners of the room, but Peter could still make out almost all the Jews. Caiaphas lay closest to him; in fact, Peter was standing right over him. It was Caiaphas Peter struck first. He worked hard with his arm and the knife, aiming for the same spot the Yakuts aimed for when slaughtering the reindeer, and he must have succeeded because Caiaphas neither croaked nor groaned; he merely straightened out and fell silent. At first, he did not even bleed, and Peter realised that his hands were as righteous as the hands of the Yakuts, that just as they had been right to kill the reindeer, so he was right to kill the Jews. Then he went and struck Platoshka Skosyryev, one of the Pharisees who argued with Christ in Capernaum, and he died without even making a sound, without even opening his eyes; as he pulled the knife from his body, it occurred to Peter that the Lord would no longer get in his way, that He had given up all the Jews to him, accepted their deaths and that He, too, had realised that Peter was in the right. The moment he thought this, a baby started crying in a cradle near the floor in a pitch-black corner. Without even waking, the mother began rocking it, but the baby yelled louder and louder until it was screaming its head off and she had to get up. Still sleepy and unable to find the baby with her hands, she kept poking around in the cradle until eventually, after a good deal of cursing and swearing, she picked it up and put it to her breast; the baby calmed down and began sucking away. All this time Peter stood in the middle of the room and waited for her to finish feeding her baby, put it down and go back to sleep herself. He knew she wouldn't get in his way, but the thought of killing others right in front of her was distasteful to him. When the baby had had its fill and was pushing away, she turned round with it towards Peter, and although he was standing in the one spot in the room which the candlelight more or less reached, she did not notice him. He looked straight at her for a long time, but she still did not see him. At first he thought she was standing with her eyes closed, but then he saw that they were open. She turned away from him and put the baby back in the cradle, and only then did she scream.

The Jews seemed to have been waiting for her to do just this. As if reveille had just sounded, they started jumping down from the stove and the planks beneath the roof, from chests, trunks and benches. One of them knocked over the candle end, and the flame went out. Bumping into each other in the dark, they thought every time that they had just bumped into their murderer, and they screamed in the same voice as the mother. A pool of blood had already formed in the hut from Caiaphas and the Pharisee, and the screaming became more terrible still. The commotion was such that Peter, fearing they might accidentally knock him over and trample him underfoot, grabbed his sheepskin coat and went outside. He saw Jews jumping out of the windows, but he didn't give chase.

Soon there were screams from the other houses, too; shadows started swirling and swarming ever more thickly around them, and he realised that his brothers – whom Christ had chosen along with him – were killing Jews there as well, and he rejoiced that they had not abandoned him and he was not alone. Some two hours later all eleven apostles came over to him, and he told them that they had made a good start, that everything was going as it ought to go, and that, God willing, they would finish the Jews off the next day. After all, there was no point tearing after them in the dark: it was time for a well-deserved rest and he would merely instruct the spongers to guard the causeway; by morning, all the Jews would be in their hands – there was nowhere else for them to go.

Initially, the Jews, seeing and understanding nothing, simply took to their heels and fled their own homes, the homes where they were being killed, but then, on reaching the bog, the very edge of the island on which Mosslands was situated, they came to their senses, and those among them who still had any strength and any desire to live started flocking to the causeway from every side, hoping to escape. By daybreak all of them had gathered there, only to discover that the causeway was guarded and there was no way out.

They had run from their homes still dressed for bed, many were half-naked, and now that hope had left them, horror and fear left them, too; a drowsy apathy set in. They no longer had the strength to move; they sat or laid down in the snow, drifted off, fell unconscious. In the frosty fog they heard tender voices and began to feel warm, as if summer were all around them; the grass was fragrant, there were birds somewhere over the forest, now perching, now flying off, and these voices would call them, come towards them and, on reaching them, die.

One of the Jewish elders – Annas, president of the Sanhedrin – had managed to survive the night slaughter and now, realising that the Jews who had escaped with him were freezing and dying one by one and needed to move if they were to survive, he was groping for them in the snow, tugging them, hitting them, beseeching them, weeping and shouting at them, trying to force them to get up and move, even though he himself did not know why he was doing this, why he couldn't just let them die in their sleep, instead of being stabbed to death. Whenever, after long efforts, he succeeded in getting one or other of them off the ground, he would think that perhaps Peter was right after all: there really was far too much life in the Jews, and they really did love life far too much.

Several dozen Jews died, but Annas eventually managed to rouse the rest of them and force them to their feet. To stop them lying down again and falling asleep, he kept repeating to them, again and again, that close by, a mere half a mile from the causeway, there was a shallow spot, an unbelievably shallow spot, and, though they could not see his hands, he showed them just how shallow – no more than a yard and a half deep with a hard floor, because beneath the water the ground was frozen. That was where they could cross the bog and escape from Mosslands. To those who were short in stature and scared that they would drown all the same, he said that they would be carried across, that they would be picked up like children and carried over, but now they had to move, walk and not fall asleep; sleep and you die. He told them that God was with them, God would save them; it was one more test, but God would not leave them, would not let them perish: they were His people, and their covenant with Him was eternal.

Annas really did manage to rouse almost all the Jews who were still alive – he must have had enormous reserves of strength – and brought them to the place he had told them about, and when they dithered, too scared to set foot in the water, he shoved his way through to the front (previously he had always kept to the back of the group, following and helping the others). He had long known that not one of them would manage to get across through the icy water; while rousing them, he had forgotten this, or else it had seemed to him, as it did to them, that summer was all around them and the water was warm. Now, standing by the edge of the bog, he thought that the main thing was for them not to end up in the hands of the Christians, to be saved that fate, and he also wanted what Peter the Apostle wanted: he wanted the Jews, his people, to disappear and drown, for not a trace of his people to remain on earth, and for even the place where it had met its end to be unknown.

At the place where they stopped, the shoreline was clearly visible even in the dark, so the Jews had a clear sight of Annas entering the bog. Stretched out in a single line and holding on to one another, they followed him in and it was only when they were halfway across that suddenly both he and they realised all at once that they were walking on dry ground. It was a miracle. The bog had frozen over during the night, and now the Lord was leading them out of Mosslands, out of Egypt, where people wanted to kill them, to the Promised Land, just as He had once led their ancestors across the Red Sea. Together with Annas, the Jews fell to their knees and began to pray. That night they believed that God had not broken His covenant with them. And the miracle that had saved them gave them the strength to endure all that would follow.

The next morning, when Peter, the other apostles and the spongers crossed and combed the island, looking for Jews, they found not a single one alive, whether in the forest, the fields or the meadows. The Jews, it seemed, had all frozen to death overnight. Peter asked all the Christians how many corpses they had seen during the search. It was easy to count them: the snow that had fallen the day before was not deep, and the bodies were clearly visible even from a distance. Then Peter added all the numbers up, combined them with the Jews who had been killed in their homes, and saw that, truly, not a single Jew had survived – all of them were dead.

Killing the Jews turned out to have been strangely, embarrassingly easy. The Christians had plenty of strength left in them, and they felt aggrieved that it was all over so quickly and with such little fuss. They had spent so long preparing for this moment, too scared to make a clean break with their past, with Sertan, and to begin their struggle with the God who had forgotten them, and they had imagined the death of the Jews quite differently. The Jews, in other words, had tricked them. Peter understood that he was to blame. He should not have stopped the Christians the previous night, when they were all worked up, excited by the successful start; he should have let them chase the Jews and slaughter them until morning, just as they had wanted to. Now, it was as if it were not they who had killed Jews, but the Lord God, who had gathered them to Himself, granted them sleep, taken them in their sleep, and saved them. Many Christians desired the same fate for themselves and envied the Jews. Peter knew that he must not let them go home still thinking these thoughts. They must see for themselves – and, above all, get used to the fact – that the Jews were no more, that they were dead and there was no bringing them back. It wasn't enough to observe the snow-dusted corpses from the side, when there was no way of telling what the snow was hiding; no, they had to see for themselves and feel with their own hands that every Jew was dead.

Telling them that the Jews had to be buried, that his sums didn't add up and he needed to double-check, Peter ordered everyone to go round the island once more, taking neither horses nor sledges, gather the bodies and heap them up on the left side of the cemetery, where Jews were normally buried. This proved a difficult task; some of the corpses were on the very edge of the bog, and to fetch them they had to walk a mile in each direction. At first the Christians stacked the bodies tidily, but as they tired they started simply throwing them on top of each other and soon saw that the heap grew more quickly like that and that it was easier to see how much they had already done. The afternoon was well advanced by the time they found the last Jews and brought them to the cemetery.

It was very cold, they had eaten nothing since morning if they had eaten at all, and, after a day spent lugging bodies turned to stone by the frost, they didn't want to have to stand or sit in the snow, so they sat directly on the corpses and set about waiting patiently for Peter to let them go. He saw how tired they were, but told them that he couldn't let anyone go until they had done one more thing: sorted out the heap and grouped the Jews into families, so that he would know who should be buried where. Each should look for his own kin, and when they had finished they could go. Whether from exhaustion or from the cold, this task went badly from the start. The faces of almost all the Jews were crusted with ice. For as long as they were still alive, the snow would melt, but afterwards the water froze to their skin and especially to their beards; removing the ice was extremely difficult, and there was no way of telling who was beneath it if you didn't. But nobody wanted to try; instead two or three Christians would grab legs or arms and pull a single corpse in different directions, each of them shouting that it was his brother, sister or some other relation. Still arguing, they would start shoving each other into the snow, and unless Peter managed to intervene in time, an unseemly fight would ensue.

At first the apostles would patiently pull the fighters apart, but it wasn't long before they despaired of trying to keep order. Fearing a general mêlée, they forced the Christians and spongers back, ordered them to stay there and started sorting out the heap themselves. After efficiently disentangling the Jews, they laid them out in a row face upwards and told the Christians that, without moving any of the corpses, they should carefully remove the ice from each of them and clean them, after which it would immediately become clear who was whose. This did indeed prove to be the right course of action. When the ice had been hacked off the Jews, the apostles drove the Christians back again, formed them into an orderly queue and let them come up one by one to take a relative. The distribution of bodies proceeded apace, but when the thirtieth person took his allotted Jew, those standing in line began to stir: they were the first to realise that there were nowhere near enough Jews lying in the snow to go round. When the Jews ran out completely, fighting erupted once more. Those left empty-handed instantly routed the apostles and were just about to deal with those who had been at the front of the queue when a soft voice suddenly said: 'So all the others must have escaped.'

Towards morning Peter realised where he had gone wrong. When they were combing the island, the corpse of almost every Jew was seen and remembered by several people, and he, adding them together, had assumed them all to be different. Aware that they could only have escaped Mosslands via the causeway, he decided that the Jews had either bribed the spongers who had been guarding it, or had found some other way of coming to an agreement with them. He ordered the spongers to be brought to him and began to interrogate them. At first he interrogated them individually, but since that was getting him nowhere, he tried interrogating them in groups. He needed something, anything, in order to set them against each other. But they gave exactly the same testimony, whether separately or together.

The spongers told him that, just as he had warned, the Jews had indeed come to the causeway the previous day, but only three hours after they had got there themselves. Finding it guarded, the Jews did not even try to get through, nor did they go back the way they had come; instead, they just sat motionless on the snow. The spongers said they could easily have killed them all there and then: the Jews would not even have thought of resisting. But they remembered his orders not to move an inch from the causeway and were aware that the Jews may just have been leading them on with their show of exhaustion, purposely encouraging the spongers to kill those of them who were going to die anyway, while the rest ran away. The Jews sat by the causeway for a long time, and several of the spongers thought they had already frozen to death, but then the Jews got to their feet and walked off along the shore.

Everything the spongers said sounded perfectly plausible; it would have been difficult to make it all up, and they hardly looked capable of such invention, so Peter realised that they were telling the truth. Later that day it occurred to him that they had done a bad job of searching the forest the previous day. There were several small gullies where the Jews could quite easily have dug a hole and hidden. He said as much to the Christians, but they refused to accompany him. Even the other apostles abandoned him. They were all convinced that once again, as in the days of Haman, God had saved the Jews. Once more, the Christians felt terror towards the Lord and thought He would not forgive them if they started looking for the Jews again in order to kill them. They knew that neither in the forest nor anywhere else on the island was there a single Jew still alive, nor could there be, but they did not stop Peter from going. As soon as he left, they took some spades and set off for the cemetery. Digging into the earth that was just beginning to freeze, they made evenly shaped graves too deep to be reached by animals, wrapped each body in linen cloth, according to custom, and buried it. Then, without haste, they drank to the memory of the dead right there in the cemetery.

Peter spent a long time searching on his own for the lost Jews, climbed up and down ravines, and used a stick to poke among the previous year's leaves in holes and beneath the roots of big trees before it became clear to him, too, that there was nowhere for them to hide in the forest. He was ready to believe that God really had saved the Jews, but he also knew that only the previous night Caiaphas and the Pharisee had died quietly at his hands, without even stirring, because the Lord had given them up to him. He returned from the forest to the bogs and began walking all the way round Mosslands along the water's edge. Here and there the water was already covered with a film of ice, but in most places steam was still rising, and in the movement of the mist through the windless air he kept seeing walking Jews. He wanted to shout out to them, and for them to shout back to him and tell him where they were and whether they really had survived and how. From the causeway he walked in the direction taken, according to the spongers, by the Jews. He thought he might find some footprints, but everything was covered in a blanket of snow, as if nobody had ever lived on this earth.

Having completed a lap of the island, he did a second before deciding that there was no hope left and he had better go back, yet still he carried on walking along the edge of the bog. The frozen water was of no interest to him, and whenever he walked beside a long stretch of ice he would occasionally be struck by the peculiar thought that this circling around Mosslands *was* his path, that he would never leave it, that he would walk it until the day he died. Then, when there was open water once more, he would start seeing Jews again and fancy that he was shouting to them, or perhaps he really was shouting, and then he would strain his ears to catch what they were shouting back at him. The spongers from the causeway had told him that in the dark Jews looked like snowy tussocks in the bog, or like mossy hummocks; he remembered this now and thought that the Jews might be hiding from him as well, by pretending to be hummocks, and that he ought to have paid more attention and checked the ones that were so easily in reach. The very next instant it occurred to him that not long ago he had seen, not far from the shore, a hummock that closely resembled a man squatting on his haunches, but the ice around it looked thin and he had been scared to go near it. Now he wanted to find that place again and started looking for it; after a long while, when it was already dusk, he found it.

He felt scared again, just like the first time: the wind had blown the snow off the ice, which was transparent and, for that very reason, looked especially fragile and flimsy. But Peter started crawling all the same: he lay down flat on the ice, so as to make himself lighter, and started crawling. He needn't have worried. The ice here was firm, it didn't even crackle or squeak beneath him, and on reaching the hummock and touching it with his hand he saw that it was a man on his knees; he must have frozen in prayer. Peter brushed the snow off him and instantly recognised the robber crucified with Christ. Now he understood how the Jews had managed to cross the bog, and realised that they had set off in the direction to which the praying man's face was turned.

Peter returned to the village and told the Christians that now he knew where the Jews were. He said that God had not saved them at all. It was just that He did not want them to be killed here, in Mosslands. He did not want this because the Jews thought that they had been sent to Mosslands by God, sent to play the most terrible part, and they were proud that they had accepted their fate and stayed true to it. Had all the Jews been killed in their beds the previous day, Peter said, they would have died in the conviction that they had perished through no fault of their own, but the Lord knew that this was not so. That was why He had allowed them to leave and arranged things so that they fled from Him and from the role He had allotted them.

Then Peter told the Christians something quite different: he said that everything Sertan had taught them, everything they had been doing year after year, generation after generation, had actually been invented by the Jews so that, as in Palestine 1800 years before, they might once again abuse Jesus Christ when He came into the world.

This was a new accusation on Peter's part; certainly, it was not one of the reasons he gave the Christians, after ceding the apostleship, for why they should finish off the Jews. I don't think he came up with it all on his own, although I can't rule that out; it seems more likely that he was echoing accusations made against the Jews by the cellarer Feoktist and, following his example, by Nikon in the final days before his exile. Somebody must have spread these accusations beyond New Jerusalem, after which they had travelled by word of mouth. Peter also talked about Caiaphas and the Pharisee, about how quietly and calmly they had died, as if they had been waiting for him to come and kill them, which was when he had understood that the Lord was giving them all up to him. As for everyone else, Peter continued reproachfully, they had not believed the Lord, even though they too had been given the chance to kill the Jews. They had decided that He wanted to save the Jews, and had taken fright and refused to go with him, Peter, to find them and kill them all off. Peter alone had shown true faith, and it was to him and no one else that the praying Jew, with his face turned towards God, had revealed where his fellow believers had gone.

But, insofar as one can tell from the documents, Peter did not manage to convince many. The split that had appeared the previous day would remain and never heal. Why, then, did the Christians submit to his will and set off from Mosslands the very next day in pursuit of the Jews, leaving not even the elderly behind? To my mind, there is only one answer: they wanted to witness the miracle that the Lord had performed.

In the morning the Christians rose well before dawn to make their assiduous preparations for the journey ahead. They checked and repaired the sledges and harnesses, fitted skis lined with deer fur, taking two pairs each, and loaded the sledges with plenty of food and things to keep them warm. It was not until midday that they were finally ready to leave.

Even now, the thoroughness of these preparations remains a mystery to me. I know that Peter tried to hurry the Christians up, telling them that the Jews could hardly have got very far; half-naked and hungry, they had all long since frozen to death, and there would be no need to kill anyone. He kept repeating that they would be home within three days, or four at most, so there was no need to take anything except food. He could have managed on his own, but he was taking them with him so that they could see for themselves that everything was as it should be, that there was no miracle and never had been – the Lord had never thought of saving the Jews. On the contrary, He had dealt with them Himself, and now only corpses were left of the nation that had crucified Christ.

Peter's words sounded reasonable, of course, but the Christians still continued with their preparations, as if they knew that the chase would last a long time, perhaps even a very long time, and that no matter how many supplies they took with them, they would never be enough. Does this not mean that the group of Christians, who were sure that the Lord had worked a miracle and had saved the Jews who survived the night slaughter, had kept all its influence, and that despite Peter it had managed to convince the rest that the Lord would not give up His people to them so easily? What exactly they were saying and thinking I do not know. Some must have deemed the whole venture hopeless: having allowed many Jews to perish, the Lord had decided to save the remainder come what may; those closer to Peter, meanwhile, may have continued to believe that sooner or later the Lord would understand why they wanted to kill the Jews, understand that they were right, and give them up to them, but there's something else here that matters to me even more now: everything points to the fact that at this very point a new source of authority emerges among the Christians, and Peter is forced to reckon with it. If that is true, then much of what follows becomes clearer.

The start of the chase was so slow that it didn't look like a chase at all; people and horses were barely moving, and Peter, who had been waiting for them to leave since daybreak and getting himself into more and more of a state, was simply unable to understand that there was no malicious intent behind this slowness – they just hadn't got going yet – and ran from one team of horses to another, using his lash on man and beast alike without caring where it fell, on the back or on the face. While they were travelling through the village, he had the impression that very few Christians had come out, that many had taken fright and hidden themselves away (he even searched several of the log huts on the edge of the village, without success), but when the caravan of sledges – which included those already inching along down below, towards the bog, and those that were still just leaving the homes – stretched itself out into a column measuring almost half a mile, he realised how wrong he had been and burst into tears, overjoyed that no one had stayed behind. Then there was another delay: the ice was thin, the horses were sinking, and Peter had to send several teams of horses back to the village to fetch some boards to lay over the ice. Once over the bog, they gathered speed. There was a covering of snow everywhere by now, but it was not deep and the horses did not tire. Peter thought that if the going continued like this, they would catch up with the Jews in no time; he was amazed, and said as much, that the Jews had managed to get even this far. But the second day brought more bogs and gullies which had not yet frozen; the boards they had brought with them were no use here, and they had to unharness the horses and carry the supplies on their own backs. Fortunately, they had two pairs of light Yakut sledges.

For all his assurances, they did not catch up with the Jews on the second day or on the third, and Peter, unable to understand where they could have got to, became more and more afraid that the Christians had lost their way. The sensible course would have been to turn back, but he could see how unhappy everyone looked; he would never have managed to rouse them for a second trip, and in any case the snow would have been too deep to find anyone. Of course, the Jews might have turned off the path just to confuse them. He was afraid of this, although previously he had been certain that fear, fatigue and the proximity of death would ensure that they fled in a straight line.

In this, he was right: terror was driving the Jews as far away from Mosslands as they could go and did not let them turn off their path. And yet, it took a fortnight of chasing before the Christians finally came across the first corpse of the Jews who had crossed the bog, and once again they believed Peter. Then, week after week, they would find one or two more corpses and, by adding them to those they had buried in Mosslands, they could tell how many Jews were left.

Once the Christians had seen that Peter was leading them along the right path, he got on better with them, felt calmer and cheered up. And there was something else: finding the first dead Jew awakened their hunter's instinct, which would guide them whenever Peter tired.

Now that they were used to following in the Jews' footprints and had adapted themselves to the task, not a day, or even an hour, would pass without them thinking that they were just about to catch them, and that would be that; nevertheless, for a very long time they were satisfied with counting the corpses and occasionally killing those who had fallen behind in exhaustion (this seems to have happened three times in total). Only once, in mid-December, when the Christians walked day and night without stopping for forty-eight hours, did they catch up with the rearguard and kill the two Jews walking last; they could see the whole lot of them and thought they would finish them all off, but the Jews put on a spurt, and the Christians had no strength left.

That day was a watershed, and they would never forget how, emerging from a stunted and twisted birch grove, barely taller than human height, they caught sight of black dots on the next knoll – Jews plodding along, one after the other. The air was pure, and although the Jews were still some way off, the Christians had a clear view of how the dots changed places; the Jews who were up to it, or whose turn it was, would come out to the front and walk through the virgin snow, while the rest saved their strength and took care to step in their tracks, and so, however much and wherever they walked, only a single trail remained, and their pursuers could never tell how many had walked there: one person or an entire nation. As they followed the Jews and, as it were, became one with them by walking at the same pace and in their footprints, the Christians kept drawing closer and closer – after all, the snow was well-trodden and the going was much easier for them – and they could see that with each hour that passed the dots grew bigger and, ceasing to be dots, became people, and the people were also growing bigger and it was clear that they could not escape. Not one of the Jews turned round to look back, but they must have sensed the Christians behind them and started walking a little faster, although perhaps it merely seemed to the Christians that the Jews had hurried up – it's hard to imagine them still having the strength to do so – while the truth was that the Christians were tired and slower in their pursuit. Nevertheless, as I've already said, they caught up with the last two Jews and killed them, but this took time: it wasn't enough to kill the Jews, they also had to drag them out of the way; after walking for such a long time on a smooth path, none of the Christians would have wanted to walk round corpses and get stuck in the deep snow. The dead Jews were awkward to manoeuvre and unexpectedly heavy; the Christians struggled for a long time to shift them off the path, and when they finally succeeded the Jews had become dots again, not people. And however much they walked that day, these dots became smaller and paler until, at dusk, they disappeared entirely.

That night a snowstorm began, and by the time the wind began to die down the next morning the Jews had vanished, as had their footprints, and the Christians had to start walking through virgin snow once more. From this point on the chase, externally at least, ceases to be a chase, the strength of pursuers and pursued evens out, and the distance between them remains stable, as if it has been agreed and fixed in advance. Just like in the convoy, just like back then, they walk one behind the other, week after week, month after month, Christians behind Jews – and there is no way of telling who is leading them, or where. The Christians also become feeble, they also lie down in the snow and freeze, and the only difference between them and the Jews is that there is nobody to count their dead, because there is nobody walking behind them; they are the last. The number of these weak and frozen stragglers among the Christians grows and grows; how many exactly is hard to say, but it can't be much less than among the Jews, if at all. When Christians and Jews run out of strength entirely, they stop very close to each other, in full view of each other, as if they really are a single convoy; they halt for a day or two, then walk on. To stop the Christians treading in their footprints, the Jews try to maintain the gap between them and set off first. The chase lasts all autumn and winter. In February Peter the Apostle dies, and by that point, it seems, not one of the apostles remains among the living: the rest had perished before him, on the cusp of old age.

In mid-March, while crossing another series of bogs, the Jews see that they have arrived back in Mosslands. As is always the case when you try to walk in a straight line through forest or tundra, they had ended up going round in a circle. Terror and the entrenched habit of fleeing as far as possible had kept the Jews going and given them strength; now, they are incapable of starting out all over again, and what would be the point – they have nowhere to go. They do not enter the village, so as not to see the place where their brethren were killed; instead, they sit down in the snow by the last house and pray. The Christians find them a few hours later. The Jews are at their mercy, but the Christians do not kill them. The old apostles are no longer alive, and the death of the Jews is of no interest to anyone. Those Christians who until recently would have remained spongers till the end of their days have now received leading parts in the play and there are many roles, especially in the first few years, that remain unoccupied – very few Christians and Jews have survived. Those who had felt unhappy and hard done by, and who had been the first to follow Peter the previous autumn, have got what they wanted and now, once again, everything begins to arrange itself as it did under Sertan.

The killings of the Jews are expunged from life, expunged

by Christians and Jews alike, as if they had never happened. In fact, that whole time is expunged. The Christians and the Jews revive their former relationships, and daily rehearsals are resumed in the usual manner, beginning with the scenes that were being practised in September. The exiles have returned to their past and believe once more that the coming of Jesus Christ is at hand, believe that they will be worthy of Him and that it is to them that He will come.

How it was that the Jews managed to survive that October, the most terrible month of their flight, remains a mystery. Although perhaps we do not need to look too far for an explanation. Clothes and supplies were brought to the Jews by the Yakuts, and all of it came from the Romans. Believing as they did that the exiles' lives should not deviate from the law given by Sertan, that whatever had been established under him should be strictly observed, the Romans would help the Jews later as well, while always remaining in the shadows; they were cautious and only intervened in dealings between Jews and Christians in exceptional circumstances, and only through the Yakuts. The Yakuts did not just bring the Jews supplies, they also gave them rides on their reindeer sledges on three occasions, when the Christians had almost caught up with them. The fugitives had their well-wishers among the Christians, too, and specifically, it would seem, among the future apostles. Many times, as they walked out in front and led the way for their fellow Christians, these men would slow down the chase whenever they could, and they even did this on the day when, despite their efforts, the Christians caught up with the Jews and killed the two walking last. It was the new apostles who killed these Jews, but they did so in a roundabout, clumsy way: first they wounded them several times, then it took them an even longer time, stumbling and falling, to drag the bodies off the path. While they were fussing with the corpses, the other Jews moved further and further into the distance.

Later, too, attempts were made to finish off the Jews in one go, usually every other generation. Once again, there would be killings, pursuits, the deaths of enfeebled people who fell into the snow and could not get up, and once again the Jews, choosing the same route, would fail to understand how it was that they were fleeing in a straight line yet ended up in the same place they had left. They thought it must be God bringing them back to Mosslands, leading them, as it were, by the hand, because this was their place, their path, the path they should not leave.

With time, stopping-places appear along this well-trodden circuit among both Christians and Jews; log huts are built, containing supplies of firewood and food so that they no longer need to carry their food round with them, and there are even small churches and synagogues, with cemeteries next to them, where funeral rites are performed and the dead are buried. The stopping-places give the Jews some respite: they are safe there, like a child in a treehouse. And strangely enough, where previously there was nothing but cruelty, bloodshed and abomination, now there appears a certain regularity and rhythm, a certain order, though the hatred and terror remain. Now, the pogroms enter the lives of the exiles on a legitimate, structured basis. Every successive wave of killings becomes a new rehearsal, a new attempt, justified by repetition, to urge the Lord to hasten His coming to earth, a choice, a way of asking Him what they must do to make Him come. This is their own contribution to Sertan's work, and it lasts.

Mosslands continues to live a life apart. Externally, as I have already said, it looks no different from other villages, which are still almost as rare in this part of Siberia as they were a century before; it pays its taxes, sells its surplus, and nobody pokes their nose into its business or shows the slightest interest. The villagers continue to wait for Christ, to rehearse the roles they have been given, and to believe that the fate of humankind will be decided within their own relationship with God, and that all other people on earth, however many of them there might be, will follow them just as they themselves have followed Christ.

Living only for their mission, they become more and more afraid each year that external life might distract or hinder them. These fears have no foundations in reality, except perhaps one. Although both the Christians and the Jews believe that Christ will come to their own generation and no other, that their generation is the chosen one and the last, while all those before it were merely stepping stones, existing purely for its sake, there is also a different memory at work here, a more impartial memory. For this type of memory, the years simply mount up, each year is equal to any other, and there are no generations. Such memory is continuous: it knows that the world is becoming worse and worse, that evil is multiplying, and that, although many of them have not proven themselves worthy of Christ's arrival, His coming is nigh. And because Christ is so close, because He is already on His way to them, they are terrified of the life that surrounds them, and in order to hide from it and save themselves, they copy it more and more closely. They copy not just its contours and general appearance, but its essence, its customs, its character. The village turns out to be capable of genuine mimicry, but it replicates the life around itself in a dispassionate, entirely superficial way, unconcerned and untouched by anything; it lives, as before, only to rehearse, to wait for Christ, to be ready to receive Him. That is why it believes itself to be free from sin, whatever it might do.

When the Christians and the Jews were arrested in New Jerusalem and then sentenced and exiled to Siberia, they thought
that human history had ended, in terms of both its calamities
and its duration, and that their roles were all that remained. For
a long time to come, for two whole centuries, they clung to
this belief. It was only the Revolution that changed everything.
The grief and calamities that preceded the Revolution and that
the Revolution brought in its wake – world war, civil war, and
then, after only a very brief interlude and before anyone had
the chance to recover their strength, collectivisation – took a
heavy toll on Mosslands as well, try as the villagers might to
buy or ward off the authorities. Among the actors who died
were two apostles, and the villagers realised that evil could
be far greater than they had thought, that the limits had not
yet been reached – far from it – and that only now was the appointed time coming to pass, only now should the count begin.
Before was too early, before was the time for rehearsals and
nothing more, and all who had preceded them had had no other
duty than that: to save and preserve. They had been justified.
The soldiers who had survived and returned from the world war
were the exiles' main informants; it was from them that they
learned what was happening in the world, where it was headed
and how they should conduct themselves so that the thing they
had been chosen for should remain intact and uninterrupted.

In spring 1918, the Christians of Mosslands begin supporting the Bolsheviks and are considered Reds. During the civil
war, when Admiral Kolchak takes power in Siberia, the village
is redivided, by mutual consent, and the Christians become
Whites. This is precisely the moment at which Mosslands,
having multiplied after the half-century of peace and quiet
which preceded the First World War in Russia, prepares for

the departure of the old apostles, whose term has elapsed. The scale of calamities is such that the outgoing apostles do not believe that the Lord can come to anyone other than them. The killing of the Jews begins. It is facilitated by the change of regime. The Jews, who have now become a Red partisan brigade, flee, and the Whites pursue them with the hatred seen all over Siberia at that time. The Jews flee along their usual circuit, and in spring 1919, a few days before Passover and Easter, which almost coincided that year, the Lord brings what is left of them back to Mosslands. Many Christians have also died during the five-month pursuit; among them is Peter the Apostle, who had become an ataman with the Whites. The recent exchange of flags and the mutual losses reinforce the truth of the words of one of the first actors to have played Caiaphas: consoling the Jews, he had told them that no firmer bond exists than that between victim and executioner, and that nobody could be closer.

On returning to Mosslands, the Jews and the Christians make peace, the spongers receive the roles of those who have died, and the rehearsals resume. By this point Kolchak has already been seized and the communists are firmly in control of Siberia once more. On hearing that the Whites on the Keti have recently destroyed an entire detachment of Red partisans, the Bolsheviks send Chekists to Mosslands to investigate.[10] The peasants are called out and interrogated one by one, but both the Jews and the Christians give exactly the same testimony: nobody there has ever seen any partisans; true, there was a small detachment of Cossacks and officers, but it headed east long ago. The poverty of Mosslands, and the equality that seems to reign there, win the Bolsheviks' trust

---

10   Cheka: the first secret police agency instituted by the Bolsheviks; successor agencies included the OGPU, the NKVD and the KGB.

and they leave the village alone.

Under NEP, life in Mosslands returns, as it were, to how it was before the Revolution.[11] The village flourishes for seven or eight years running, and rehearses with its usual zeal. It pays its taxes and fulfils its obligations, but in all other respects keeps itself to itself.

Then, in 1929, two years before Siberia is declared a region of total collectivisation, the Jews start trying to persuade the Christians to transfer all their lands and cattle to them. The source of this initiative was Annas, president of the Sanhedrin. He appears to have been the first in Mosslands to understand where things were headed. The Christians, he told the Jews, could not see how the times had changed; now, in order to survive, you had to give everything away and there could be nothing worse than having too much. He told the Jews that they themselves needed the Christians to survive, because the Lord could only come to Christians. If they, the Jews, survived while the Christians perished, the Lord would never come and nothing would ever end.

'As for us, the Lord will use us as He deems fit,' Annas would say. 'If we are needed, as we were needed two thousand years ago, to crucify Christ and mock Him, then the Lord will save us from the hands of the communists; if, on the other hand, those people are right who say that while one of our number is still alive the Lord will not send Christ into the world, because He thinks only of us and measures evil only by us, then we will perish. In both cases we shall not stand in His way.'

For half a year the Jews tried to persuade the Christians that they were doomed, but they got nowhere. Only five of the Christians were prepared to believe Annas, but even they

---

11 The New Economic Policy (NEP): a concession to market forces and private enterprise introduced by Lenin in 1922 and ended by Stalin in 1928.

would not agree to share their fields and remained 'rich' peasants – or *kulaks* – in terms of how much they produced. So then the Jews decided to act. That winter Annas created a Committee of Poor Peasants (CPP) in Mosslands and launched mass requisitions in the village of grain, cattle and tools. The main thing he wanted was land. If somebody refused to give it away voluntarily, he would take it all. Hunger set in among many of the Christian families, and without the help of the Romans and especially the Yakuts they would never have lasted until summer. The Christians put up almost no resistance. They were rendered powerless by Annas's words and by his conviction that the authorities always took the side of the Jews; moreover, they weren't used to Jews acting like this, and they were frightened.

Cruelty and hatred grew by the day. Annas could not understand why the Christians were clinging so stubbornly to their land. It seemed to him that they had betrayed their cause and ceased waiting for Christ. He could see that time was slipping away and decided that only terror could help. Through the CPP he created a special unit that would make night raids on the village. The Jews committed robbery, rape and arson. Several Christians, including Matthew the Apostle (Maksim Tvorogov), were killed.

In mid-May, Annas (Ivan Bochkar) was called to the district centre at Bely Yar for a conference at which the schedule and course of collectivisation in the region were to be confirmed. To get there, he sailed down the Keti by steamer. At one point the ship ran aground and it took twenty-four hours to set it afloat again, so he missed the beginning of the meeting. He was given the floor almost at the very end. It was already night, and the delegates were tired. The chairman asked him to keep it brief. But Annas did not obey him and launched into a detailed, exhaustive account of the CPP in Mosslands and the special unit he had created. When he finished, the secretary of the district committee, Comrade Uchkuev, and all those present gave him a standing ovation. After the session, a delegate from the regional Party centre came up to him and told him that the decision had been taken to carry out a model dekulakisation operation in Mosslands; it had been fixed for June 4, and the village should be ready by this date. He told Annas not to leave without first giving a list of the CPP members and all the village kulaks, who were to be eliminated together with their families.

When Annas and the other delegates emerged from the district committee building, it was already light. Directly opposite the building was a small square with a monument to Russian-Yakut friendship (two men embracing on a plinth), a flowerbed and a bench. Bidding each other goodbye, the CPP members shook hands or embraced. Eventually everyone dispersed, and Annas was left alone. He sat down on the bench and began thinking that Peter the Apostle may have been right all along: for as long as there were Jews on this earth, nothing would end. Then he decided that Sertan must have been a rather simple and kind-hearted person, and perhaps there was a time when Christ really had wanted to come into the world according to his rules. And he wondered why Christ failed to understand that they could wait no longer. Then he thought once again that everything Peter had said about the Jews was true and so, without further hesitation, he wrote his own name and surname at the top of the list of kulaks. Below them he entered, in alphabetical order, the names and surnames of the members of the CPP, and below those the names and surnames of the remaining Jews, their relatives…

Annas brought four rifles back with him to Mosslands and

armed his unit. The next day he nailed an announcement to the gates of the church stating that any Christian who did not give up his land to the Jews by June 3 would be sentenced to death by a tribunal and shot the next day. This time Annas succeeded in breaking their resistance, and two days before the deadline the Christians entered the commune with the status of impoverished, horseless peasants.

On June 4, a squadron of Chekists entered Mosslands on horseback, as scheduled, and the new CPP members were ordered to summon all poor peasants to a mass meeting devoted to the elimination of the kulaks as a class. The speaker at the meeting was a certain Abdulov, who had arrived with the squadron from the regional centre. After the meeting, the Chekists arrested all the Jews on Annas's list of kulaks and locked them up in two large cowsheds that had recently been built near the pastures for the collectivised cattle. They entrusted the CPP members with guarding the Jews and left the next morning, crossing the causeway to the river, where a barge was waiting for them. The village had been informed that a week later another barge was to be sent from Bely Yar to collect the kulaks.

Left to themselves, the Christians could not understand what had just happened. Some thought the Jews really had saved them, others believed that the Lord was already coming to earth and had sent before Him a herald, Abdulov, to punish the Jews. The second group was larger and began slaughtering the Jews. They slaughtered them both as vengeance for their recent cruelties and because, if the Jews were being taken away, it meant that Sertan's play was history and that the Christians only had one path left to reach Christ – their own, as shown to them by Peter.

But there were not many spongers in the village at this time and, after replacing the guards, the apostles soon stopped the killings. They told everyone to wait. Perhaps the barge would not come at all, or perhaps Christ would come to them before the barge arrived: either way there would always be plenty of time for them to finish off the Jews or, if they so wanted, to ask the Yakuts, via the Romans, to shelter the Jews until collectivisation had settled down. All the same, some of the Christians were unhappy with the actions of the apostles and did not hide their feelings. They feared the apostles would let the Jews go. Some of them even began to suspect the Chekists of being angels sent to Annas by the Lord (that was why Annas had travelled to the district centre) in order to take the Jews away from Mosslands and save them. These people plotted amongst themselves and sent a watchman to the Keti to look out for the barge carrying the Chekists; when it moored, they would be the first to know and would have time to set fire to the cowsheds holding the Jews.

One week passed, then another, but there was no sign of the promised barge, and life in the village gradually calmed down. Fortunately, the villagers had managed to plough and sow back in May, but they had left the haymaking and potato harvesting far too late, so now they were out in the fields from dawn till dusk. Sometimes they even left the Jews unguarded. After St John's Day the Jews, and occasionally even the Christians, resumed their rehearsals. In mid-October, not long before the river was due to freeze over, a large detachment of Chekists entered Mosslands entirely unnoticed, but it had not come for the Jews. The peasants were informed that their village was to be turned into a prison camp.

That Mosslands offered an ideal location for a prison camp was something the Chekists had grasped right away, on their first visit to the village. They liked the fact that the area was so remote, but equally that there was a river close by along which convicts and supplies could be easily transported, and that the village was surrounded on all sides by impassable bogs (they made special enquiries about this); it was a proper island, with no way out except along the causeway, so it would be easy to guard, moreover the territory was extensive and could easily be expanded – a very promising site. Nevertheless, things moved slowly. At first, there was no money, then they didn't know how many prisoners they needed to house, and it was not until the summer, when a torrent of kulaks, Trotskyists and other saboteurs poured into Siberia from Russia and everything got so filled up that, however many were crammed into transit camps, there were still prisoners left over, while trainloads of new ones kept streaming in from the west, that they received the go-ahead from the authorities and were able, that very year, just before the water froze, to bring two parties of convicts to Mosslands where, together with the local prisoners, they started building and populating the camp.

Even though not one of them had ever received a prison sentence, the Jews would remain inmates of this camp until the end of their days. In the spring, when almost every month brought a new barge of convicts sailing down the Keti, many Christians were recruited as guards, who were in very short supply. The Christians were only too happy to comply if it meant being closer to the Jews. Chekists from Tomsk, Kemerovo and Novosibirsk were in no rush to work in such a hole, and the Christians quickly rose up the ranks. By 1933 both the head of the camp Ivan Skosyryev (Peter the Apostle) and the head of the secret police section Nazar Bochkar (James the Apostle) were Christians. They settled near the camp, which, just like the old village, was officially known as Mosslands, and were employed there as hired workers.

Both Jews and Christians interpreted the authorities' decision to allow them to continue living side by side as a sign from God confirming that the path on which Sertan had placed them was right and that the end was at hand. Zeks were herded into the camp in particularly large quantities after 1932, when several small deposits of black coal, which was needed to fuel the steamers sailing the Ob, were found in and around Mosslands. Although the seams were rarely more than a metre thick, the coal was easy to extract, lying as it did right under the frozen ground.

The coal in these parts is of good quality, building small mines was easy enough, and extraction levels increased year on year. For Christians and Jews alike, the transformation of Mosslands into a prison camp was a blessing, a gift, a sign that the Lord had not forgotten them. The Christians no longer had to fear – and this fear had been haunting them since New Jerusalem – that the Jews would abandon their roles, their place in life, and run away, as they had already tried to do more than once, when only God had brought them back, like foolish children. And on one occasion, when the Abelites left, He hadn't managed to bring them back at all. Now, Christians and Jews alike knew that everything would be fulfilled, that the world could be arranged in no other way, and that whether you drew the long straw or the short straw, you could not refuse it, even if it fell to you to bring Christ to Golgotha, crucify Him, and then sink into oblivion.

The camp brought the Jews, as it did thousands of other convicts, to the very brink of death. Day after day several people crossed this border. The fact that the prisoners were innocent, and believed themselves to be such, only confirmed the Jews and the Christians in their expectation of Christ's coming, and the Jews would comfort the zeks by telling them that the time had come when this was how things had to be.

I should add that the Jews of Mosslands took all the zeks, without exception, to be Jews, and assumed that they were among those who were not named in the Gospels, which was why Sertan had not chosen them. The only thing that surprised the Mosslands Jews was that every convict believed only in his or her own innocence and thought that everyone else had been arrested with good reason; they discussed this amongst themselves and realised that it was probably only right that people should be divided like this before the end and that, preparing for it, they should break all ties. They took care to remember this, although on the whole they had neither the strength nor the desire to think about anything except the play, about surviving until Christ came and they could finally perform it. It was their roles that sustained them; without them they would have died in the first and hardest year, when the camp did not yet exist, when they were still building it and living all winter long in tarpaulin tents, having buried more than half their people, as well as half of those who had been brought by barge in the autumn. Their end was nigh, and they were ready for it, ready for death, which had become their day-to-day life, their routine, so close that it was already a liberation and reward. Retribution was underway, they were already being paid back for not following Christ two thousand years before, for betraying and crucifying Him, and there was even the hope, in the way that everything had combined and come together, that they would have their fill of suffering before they died, that they would atone for a great deal, and that even if they didn't they would still be forgiven.

In the summer of '32, the authorities eased off on the Jews, and the rehearsals resumed. Those who had large roles no longer had to go out to work with everyone else, and, forcing out the 'thieves',[12] became trusties themselves, with easy access to jobs in the kitchen, the camp hospital and on the service staff. The rehearsals were organised by the Cultural-Educational Department, which answered directly to the head of the entire camp; their cover was the anti-religious play *Christ the Counter-Revolutionary*, in which both zeks and guards were involved. Its plot went as follows: Spartacus, leader of a slave revolt, tries to crush Rome and put an end to hateful slavery once and for all, while Christ – presented here in the form of a voice coming from somewhere on high – does everything in His power to hinder him, while pretending to be on his side, and tries to persuade the slaves to accept their lot, put down their weapons and carry their cross, just as He did Himself. There then follows a story within the story: Christ's life on earth as told by Luke the Evangelist. The story ends with a monologue in which Christ promises the slaves that they will be recompensed after their death, repeats that one must not lay claim to earthly power, that there is no power but from God, and that whoever fights for heaven on earth forgets about the eternal kingdom of heaven. He tells the slaves that insults should be forgiven and that if anyone has struck you on the right cheek, be neither angry nor vengeful but turn the other cheek, and so on and so forth. This play had been running for many years, and the camp authorities maintained that the rehearsals in themselves were an effective and much-needed form of anti-religious propaganda: by learning their roles and making them their own, the convicts discovered for themselves the reactionary essence of Christianity.

12 The 'thieves' – or professional criminals – 'lived by a whole set of rules and customs which preceded the Gulag, and which outlasted it'. They represented 'a totally separate community, complete with a strict code of behaviour which forbade them to have anything to do with the Soviet state' (Anne Applebaum, *Gulag*, pp. 262-3).

Whether in the central camp itself or in its nearby sub-units, the play had been performed in its entirety no more than a handful of times, mainly, it seems, because of the deaths of the actors: a great deal of time would pass before a replacement was found and the old performers got used to their new partners. Nevertheless, everyone who saw the play said that despite its rather feeble plot and lifeless dialogue (written by the head of the Cultural-Educational Section, which answered to the secret police), the acting was superb.

In the Wedding at Cana, where Christ turned water into wine, the role of the bride was played between 1932 and 1938 by the Mosslands Jew Anna Yerofeyeva. Her barracks bunkmate was Ruth (which she pronounced Rut) Kaplan. Both the Mosslands Jews and the guards had no trouble identifying, among the convicts, the Jews who were Jews by birth, deeming them to be the Abelites whom the Lord had only now managed to return to them, and only in part (they knew that there were many Jews still at liberty). They also knew that the Abelites themselves had not wanted to return to Mosslands: the Lord had brought them back by force. They took a very dim view of them, as they would of any traitor. The only thing that surprised them about the Abelites was their appearance: despite the fact that many of them had married into Yakut families in Mosslands, there was nothing remotely Yakut about their features.

Their attitude towards the Abelites deteriorated even further when, after the terrible winter of 1931-32, there began to be a shortage of Mosslands Jews and somebody suggested turning to the Abelites in order to fill the vacant roles – after all, they had been chosen by Sertan. This idea struck almost everyone as both impossible and reprehensible: if that were to happen, then the Abelites would effectively be forgiven and equated with the faithful Jews; moreover, if Christ were to come to the Abelites and not to the Jews of Mosslands who, year after year, generation after generation, had, like the Christians, lived and hoped for one thing only – to receive Him – then the Abelites would be right and their path, the path of betrayal and faithlessness, would also be right. Nevertheless, the Mosslands Jews and Christians did end up taking on Abelites for the parts, though this only made them hate them more. Their hatred led, among other things, to the fact that not one of the Abelites engaged in the play was let off heavy labour, and they died very quickly. As a result, the usual period of rehearsing and waiting for Christ lived by every generation of Jews and Christians and ending in their natural deaths was reduced, among the Abelites, to twelve or eighteen months, and it was not long before the generations of Abelites became as numerous as those of the local Jews. But even then, they were not forgiven, and nobody said that they had atoned for their betrayal.

Anna Yerofeyeva was probably the only person, at least at the beginning, who was well-disposed towards the Abelites. She did not care how or why they had come back; she was just glad that they were there and that the Lord, albeit right before the end, had brought the Jews together once more. Even though Rut pretended not to understand her, Anna told her more than once that she knew that Rut was an Abelite, that she was glad she had returned, and that she wanted them to love each other as if they were sisters. Anna had no sisters, only brothers, and she had often cried about this as a child. She told Rut that it was only good and right that they should be together, that she shouldn't grieve, that everything was fine. Rut was already very ill with the tuberculosis that would kill her a year later, and Anna comforted her by saying that death was something joyous. Many things struck Anna as joyous: wearing her real wedding dress, she was the most beautiful woman in the play and the most innocent of all the Jews; there was more of Christ in her than in anyone else, a spirit of celebration, joy, miracle – hadn't He turned water into wine, just like that?

Rut was also very beautiful. At school she had been known as 'the Turgenev girl' and was made to wear her ashen hair in a thick, almost metre-long plait. In the camp, she no longer had to. When the Chekists came to their home in the Donbass and presented an order for her arrest, the first thought that crossed her mind was that her plait, thank God, would finally be cut off. She had wanted to be rid of it for years – she liked short hair – but her father would not let her and nor, after her father had been arrested, would her husband. Here in the camp, her lips were always dry from TB, her cheeks were strangely flushed, and a persistent fever made her eyes look glassy. Her features became sharper and her face changed, but one could still picture how she must have looked before. Her illness did not spoil her, but merely made her look older; no one would have said she was only twenty-two.

Rut's father, Isai Kaplan, had worked as a mining engineer in the Donbass and, along with many others, was charged with sabotage in the famous Shakhty Trial of 1928. He died in prison two years later. While still at school, Rut fell in love with Ilya Grinberg, her classmate and her future stepmother's son. In '23 she and Ilya introduced their widowed parents to one another, and it wasn't long before Isai and Ilya's mother, Tema, were married. After finishing school, Rut stayed on in Gorlovka and worked at the local newspaper as a proof reader, and then reporter, while Ilya went off to university in Leningrad. He read Arabic and was a favoured student of the great historian Vasily Bartold. During these years they saw each other rarely and fleetingly; only in summer, usually on his way back to Leningrad from fieldwork in Central Asia, did Ilya stop for a week or two in Gorlovka.

In '28 he was meant to travel with a group of archaeologists to excavate Kushan monuments in the Pamir foothills, but the trip was called off at the last moment and he had a free spring and early summer ahead of him; to his parents' surprise, he came home in April. This time Isai and Tema managed to convince Rut to marry him. She still loved Ilya, but the Ilya of before, not the Ilya of now. Ilya had proposed to her on all his previous visits and each time Rut had dodged the question, even though it was always taken for granted within the family that they would marry. At school there had been something sad and touching about Ilya, and she had liked looking after him and protecting him. Leningrad and the archaeological expeditions had changed him a great deal, and now she could no longer see why he would want her. The only thing that hadn't changed about Ilya was his height and so, to avoid looking taller, she would never wear heels when they were out together. He could also see that he had changed and he enjoyed making fun of his old self; hearing this always upset her and made her feel that she no longer knew him.

A month after they married, Rut's father was arrested. At first, the investigator in charge of his case – his surname was Grayevoi – would call Rut in for questioning almost every day. She could see that he liked her, and several times he told her that he had nothing much on Kaplan anyway and hinted that the whole business could be hushed up quite easily if she agreed to sleep with him. But Ilya did not leave her side for a moment, always accompanying her to the prosecutor's office and waiting for her on a bench by the entrance; twice she almost took the plunge, but in the end she couldn't go through with it. Then her father's lawyer told her that the accused were probably going to be shot, and she went to Grayevoi herself, but he wouldn't even see her.

When the postman brought Rut notification of her father's death on January 13, 1931 in Lefortovo Prison, she jabbed the piece of paper in Ilya's face and started yelling that but for him her father would still be alive and free. Ilya couldn't see why, so, grimacing and thrusting out her jaw, she hissed at him hysterically: 'Why? Why? Because I'd have slept with the investigator, that's why, because I wouldn't have minded sleeping with him, that's why, because he's tall and handsome, that's why...' Ilya left for Leningrad the next day and they never saw each other again.

Even before her father was sentenced, Rut was forced out of the old flat – Kaplan had received it just before the Revolution, as soon as he had started working in the mines – and given a room to be shared with her stepmother, in a small house on the very edge of town. It was from this room that, for as long as her father was still alive, Rut and her stepmother wrote every day to the Central Committee, the Central Executive Committee, the Workers' and Peasants' Inspectorate, the Public Prosecutor's Office, the court, the OGPU, the Comintern, and directly to Politburo members from Joseph Stalin to Stanisław Kosior, to appeal against the verdict and request that it be reviewed. The reality of his death only sank in when they suddenly realised that there was no longer any reason to carry on writing. The authorities must have been well and truly sick of Rut by this point, because in April 1931, three months after her father's death, she was also arrested. For some reason she wanted Grayevoi to be put in charge of her case, too, but it was given to a different investigator; she was upset and was even about to kick up a fuss, but this was the last such outburst – from then on, nothing mattered to her any more. She was charged, it seems, with Trotskyism and sentenced to seven years in the Gulag.

Rut had only been living in the Mosslands camp for a short while when a letter from Ilya arrived, forwarded from Gorlovka. He said he loved her and blamed himself for her imprisonment. If only he had taken her off to Leningrad back then or, better, on some archaeological expedition to the middle of nowhere, nothing would have happened. He got carried away with these different solutions, comparing their pluses and minuses, and wrote about them with such sincerity that it was as if he thought everything could still be changed, as if everything could be replayed from scratch. It was clear that he had already thought these possibilities through and developed them further in his mind; in his second letter, he even lamented the fact that they had not managed to have a child before the arrest. In short, there had only ever been one bad option, one out of so many, and this helped him come to terms with life. Since childhood he had been strangely convinced that nothing in the world was irreversible, that nothing was beyond repair. This had saved him more than once, but that wasn't why he believed it. Previously, Rut had sometimes gone along with this, but now it irked her that, even after her father's death and her own arrest, he still had not changed. He wrote to her as if nothing had happened over the twelve months since they had last seen each other. For him, the 'nothing' in question referred to their conversation about the investigator. It wasn't just that he forgave her; he even told her that her flirtation with Grayevoi had never actually happened or could have happened, that it was all just delusion and delirium, and castigated himself for being such an idiot and believing such rubbish.

When Rut got to the bit in the letter about the investigator, she put that page to one side and wondered whether it was really possible that her father might still be alive if only she had slept with Grayevoi. Then she called Anna over to her bunk and started telling her about Crimea and Yalta, where she had spent nearly a month with her father in '25. Rut was very attached to Anna; she loved her, knew that Anna loved her in return, and almost immediately began giving her Ilya's letters. Not in their entirety, at first, but only the contents of the second part, which Ilya called the 'literary supplement'. In Leningrad he had been signed up by the Academia publishing house to translate the medieval Arabic epic *Sirat Delhemma*, about the valiant Fatima, and sent large chunks of it with each letter. It was a gripping tale: reckless raids, battles, duels, feuds and alliances between recent enemies, the machinations of Byzantine emperors and Baghdad caliphs, the abduction of beautiful women, conspiracies, the exploits of fearless, noble warriors – everything in this romance was subordinated to love, to a passion that acknowledged no obstacles. Rut read about Fatima every evening in the barracks after lights out, and sometimes, when there had been no letters from Ilya for some time and she was as desperate as everyone else to know what happened next, she would start inventing and recounting subplots that were merely hinted at in the original and turn them into memorable stories within the story: she had known since childhood that she had a real talent for imitation. This tale extended her life by a year, if not more: Vera, who was both their brigade leader and the leader of the 'thieves' in the women's section, protected Rut, got her off heavy labour, and sometimes even gave her extra rations, as did Anna who, like the other Mosslands Jews, was helped by hired workers among the Romans.

In the play Anna had the part of a happy and beloved

bride on her most joyous day, a day of celebration, but she was just fifteen, nobody had loved her yet, and nothing of the sort had ever happened in her life. The first rehearsals went very badly, she felt inhibited, and every time the groom held her hand or, worse, was supposed to kiss her, she took fright and, seeing that she had spoiled the scene, began to cry. Later, after meeting Rut, Anna found acting much easier. Now she would go to great lengths to imitate Rut's voice, movements, gestures, and she got better and better with each rehearsal until soon it became difficult to imagine the play without her.

For Rut, less than three years had passed since her engagement, and she still remembered everything; her marriage to Ilya had been so brief that she hadn't had time to become a part of him – in fact they had barely begun their day-to-day life together. All her old ties and relationships were still intact, and the fate of her father meant more to her than that of Ilya, not only because her father had been arrested and died while Ilya prospered, no, she was still living that earlier life, a life her marriage had not obscured in the slightest, and this, too, was a great help to Anna. But Anna also borrowed Rut's later thoughts about how her father could have been saved, about whether or not she should have slept with Grayevoi, and her final conversation with Ilya; Anna understood that this should not be part of her performance, and yet it was, every single time, because she was unable to separate one thing from another, and did not see or notice where she should draw the line.

Anna played Rut for almost three months when suddenly, in the space of a single day, she became a different person. The previous evening Rut had given her several of Ilya's letters in their entirety for the first time. His love astounded her. She had never known or heard of anything similar. Ilya's words to Rut struck her as something incomparably lofty and fine: this was pure joy, just as she had always imagined miracles to be. After reading the letters she realised that she, too, was now in love with Ilya, and she found that she could easily think and believe that he was writing not only to Rut, but also to her, Anna, and that he was her bridegroom. She kept borrowing Ilya's letters from Rut, reading them over and over again, asking for more, begging Rut to lend or give her at least one letter to take with her to the rehearsals. For Anna, Christ was love, and in this respect there was no one else like her in the entire cast.

Rut did not stand in the way of Anna's love for Ilya; she even encouraged it. She found herself reading his letters through Anna's eyes; her attitude towards him changed profoundly, and she changed too. She was seriously ill, saw that she was dying, and knew that she would never be with Ilya again; it was Anna who would continue and prolong her love. She understood that Anna loved Ilya more than she did, and she was happy that she, Rut, was the one who had given Ilya Anna's love, that this love had come from her and through her. If she had been at fault for anything towards Ilya, then now she had made it up to him.

Ever since school there had been something strongly maternal about her love for Ilya; she couldn't help wanting to protect him, shield him, hide him, and then, when her father died and Ilya left for Leningrad, she found herself living for a long time with his mother and began to see him through his mother's eyes. Here in the camp, knowing that she had not long to live and that she would never have children, she often thought how good it would be to have a son like Ilya: weak and needy in his childhood, strong and confident as an adult. Yielding Ilya to Anna, she told her about the Ilya she had known in the past, and in her stories he became once more a maladjusted, kind, soft child.

In October 1932, several of Rut's letters from Ilya were stolen. She discovered this the next morning, told Vera about it, and Vera, together with her workmate, turned the barracks upside down looking for them, but nothing was found. Anna knew that the letters had been stolen by Vera herself – nobody else would have dared take them without her knowledge – but Rut did not believe her. After the theft Rut told Anna that since she, Rut, had not taken good care of Ilya's letters, she should not and could not keep the others; and so, despite Anna's tears, she began to sell them off. Winter had arrived and she needed medicine, food and, above all, warm clothes – she was always freezing cold. The letters, or even just a single page, fetched an extremely high price and soon became a form of currency in the camp; they were sold, gambled, exchanged, and even willingly accepted by hired workers in their dealings with the zeks.

Rut had one last burst of life in the spring of '33, when, as I have already said, coal deposits were found in and around Mosslands and all the labour brigades, both those felling trees and those building a road from Mosslands to the Keti, and even part of the service staff, were tasked with building mines. They had no experience of this kind of work, nobody knew the right way to timber adits and drifts, and at first a mine would fall in almost every day; dozens were buried under the earth and crushed to death. Twice, despite her only semi-conscious state (she was constantly running a high fever), even Rut was brought over to the work sites – she had only two months left to live. She walked among the zeks burrowing into the earth like moles, and told them, like some holy fool, that they were going about it all wrong and they should summon her father, Isai Kaplan: he was an expert mine surveyor and he would be only too glad to teach them. She was in fine spirits and it seemed to her that her father was still alive and that she had come home to the Donbass, to Gorlovka.

A week later Anna, who was working as a nurse, managed to convince the camp doctor to admit Rut to the infirmary, even though there were no free beds. She died a long and painful death, raving for several days at a time then regaining consciousness once more. On the day before she died she called for Anna, made her sit down beside her, and in a hoarse, breathless and barely comprehensible whisper told her that she had managed to preserve Ilya's letters, every single one; they were under her mattress, and she was bequeathing them to her. But Anna had to be careful: to prevent the letters being stolen again, she should take them as soon as Rut died, before she was carried off to the morgue.

A year and a half after Rut, Ilya was also arrested. There was no connection here: he had been sentenced along with three other pupils of the recently deceased Bartold on charges of espionage. He was seized in his student hostel in Leningrad immediately after returning from a lengthy exploratory trip to the Kopet Dag mountains in Turkmenistan. The other three had been arrested four months earlier. Ilya got lucky: by the time he entered Kresty Prison, interest in the group had waned, the investigation was almost over, the sentences had already been decided and he received a relatively lacklustre interrogation – he wasn't even beaten once, despite never giving any evidence. All four were charged with the crime traditionally pinned on orientalists: spying for England, plus, in Ilya's case, Iran (the proximity of the Kopet Dag to the Iranian border had clearly played its role here, as had Ilya's knowledge of Farsi). Despite this additional charge, he received the same sentence as everyone else: ten years in the labour camps.

He was held for less than two months in Kresty before

being put on a prisoner transport to Siberia, just a week after the case came to court. The speed with which this happened allowed him to save his strength and perhaps his life; he was one of the few in his party to survive the winter of '32-33. They were unloaded from the barge straight into the snow, in the middle of nowhere, and the first thing they had to do was mark out the territory of the sub-unit of the camp where they would be living, surround it with barbed wire and put up watchtowers and buildings for the guards; all the while, they slept higgledy-piggledy on the ground, spreading a thick layer of fir branches beneath themselves and, so as not to freeze, finding a spot between the fires that were tended, day and night, by the 'goners' – the zeks too feeble to work. Instead of bread (there was none) or skilly, they were given several handfuls of oats, which they boiled in tin cans.

By summer, when the first barracks had been built and the sub-unit had filled out with zeks from two new, large convoys, less than one in seven of the original party was still alive. In fact, it was not until the midsummer of '33 that their sub-unit finally began to look like part of a proper prison camp, with all the requisite features from high-security barracks to bathhouse; it was only then that the prisoners found out what camp their sub-unit was attached to and, most importantly, that they finally got their own postcode, so that for the first time since their arrest they could start receiving parcels and letters. Until then it was as if they did not even exist: there were neither villages nor roads for miles around, and no one about except Yakut and Nenets nomads with their herds of reindeer. Only once a month, when one and the same Chekist would arrive on his sledge – or, after the ice broke on the Keti, his motorbike – to deliver orders and letters to the guards, collect reports and letters and, if there was still light, set off back again the very same day, did they see that they had not been forgotten.

In October, Ilya realised that he had been assigned to the same camp as Rut, but by that time she had already been dead half a year. Since he had always sent letters to her in the camp via her mother, he had never known her postcode, and it was purely by chance that he ever found out that she had been there. His sub-unit, which had been chosen for the quality of its coal deposits, stood some thirty miles west of Mosslands, the camp's central unit, and although formally it came under Mosslands' aegis, it was largely independent: it got everything it needed directly from Bely Yar. Until autumn there was nobody from Mosslands among either the zeks or the guards, and it was only in October, when it became clear that there was far more coal at the sub-unit than anyone had thought and the decision was taken to intensify extraction, that a couple of hundred zeks were sent over from Mosslands. There was a serious shortage of manpower, and it was too late to bring over other convicts from the transit camp at Tomsk: the Keti was beginning to freeze over, and the shipping season had ended. One of these new arrivals – a 'thief', by all appearances – had brought one of Ilya's letters to Rut with him and, after placing bets on separate pages, lost all of them one by one, before Ilya's very eyes.

Ilya's mother had learned that he and Rut were in the same camp before he did. She wrote to him about this in a hypothetical and very calm way. At first she wasn't going to mention it at all, because nobody could tell her for certain whether there was any communication between the camp's male and female sections; she was inclined to think that there wasn't and that it would only be more painful for Rut and Ilya to know that, having miraculously ended up so close to each other, they were actually further apart than they had ever been.

And there was something else: given Rut's beauty, there was no telling how things might have worked out for her in the camp, not that she would blame her for anything, and this made her still more apprehensive about any possible meeting between them. By the time Ilya received this letter, he already knew.

Before starting university, Ilya had spent exactly one year working as a timberman at one of the mines in Gorlovka. At that time, the mood among the young was exceptionally romantic: they worshipped the working class and were ashamed of their intelligentsia origins. Ilya, needless to say, already had a general understanding of coalmining and later, when he joined archaeological digs for several years running while a student, he also became a decent draughtsman; as a result, he was almost the main specialist at his sub-unit. Following the brevity of his investigation, this was his second stroke of luck.

He rose incredibly quickly in the camp, especially when we consider that according to the regulations his sentence ought to have confined him to heavy labour. In spring he became a foreman, then a brigade leader, and by autumn he was essentially in sole charge of coal extraction at the site. He had been helped by his privileged access to the sub-unit authorities, to whom he would recount, day in day out, the exploits of the beautiful Fatima, and receive an extra ration of oats in return. This unusual remuneration saved his life: he was a hefty, thickset man – just the type who tended to die first in the camps.

Without telling anyone what Rut meant to him, he tried two or three times to find out through intermediaries what had become of her; he didn't learn anything definitive, but it seemed very likely, from what did reach him, that she was no longer alive. When Ilya realised, from the letter gambled away at cards, that Rut and he were being held in one and the same camp, he became almost deranged by the thought that she might be so close to him, by his ignorance about whether she was still alive, and by his fear of actually meeting her. It was as if he had been infected by his mother's terror. After several months of 'normal' Gulag life he had suddenly landed plumb in the middle of some idiotic phantasmagoria: everyone around him – whether the zeks from his own convoy or those who had been brought over from Mosslands – seemed to be vying to come up with new stories about Fatima; their popularity was phenomenal and there were already dozens of competing versions. In some, the action had been moved to Brazil or Japan, or the recent years of NEP, or else it had been mixed up with other stories, and each teller considered it his duty to refer back to Ilya, and to beg him for a continuation, or at least a clarification of some detail or other.

He was probably making far too much of it all; he even began to think that their sub-unit had nothing else to do but read his letters to Rut, sell them, bet on them, and that the zeks were using them as a model for their own letters, merely changing the names before sending them by the hundred to their own sweethearts, whether outside the Gulag or in some camp nearby. What was more, Ilya's letters came back to them from outside. The letters were everywhere, they were surrounding him, pursuing him, floating before his mind, as if they and Rut were closing in on him. As in some large empty room, everything he said immediately created an echo, the echo reverberated and multiplied, called him, tugged at him, spoke to him in different voices and never left him, remaining, as he did, in that same room. He tried to escape, but there was no way out either for him or the echo, so then he tried to reassure himself that the letters and Fatima were no more than a hallucination, a delusion, but he did not believe this himself and knew that it was all real enough. He could see that he was going mad and thought he was trapped for good.

Yet somehow, he eventually learned how to cope with all this absurdity. He decided to dissolve it in things that he had long been used to and knew very well. He decided in his own mind that Rut had died, and that her papers, as so often happened, had fallen into many different hands. He'd had more than enough experience sorting out the archives of various orientalists – most recently, a year before his arrest, the archive of his teacher Bartold. The same thing had happened there, too: no sooner had Bartold died than a great many papers vanished, ending up God knows where. The history of his letters to Rut was a perfect illustration of the curious fate that could befall an archive, a strange fate, for sure, but no less real for that. The story of Fatima, meanwhile, was a jewel, a model of the most intricate processes of folk creativity, showing how legends spread and mingle, how new ones are born and multiply, how they combine different voices and different strata of culture and time.

In autumn 1933, the first deep shaft was sunk at Mosslands, just like the one at their sub-unit. Coal was in ever greater demand, and the older, shallow pits were being quickly exhausted. Progress on the new mine was slow. No one had any experience of building mines, and there were two major collapses, one after the other, in which several zeks were crushed and died. Work came to a standstill and the authorities feared accusations of sabotage, but with no little effort they managed to stop anything getting out. By this time Ilya's reputation as an engineer was already very high, and in December, after they had managed to work round a vein of quicksand and shaft sinking resumed, he was brought to

Mosslands. One or two days after his arrival he tracked down Anna and learnt from her how and when Rut died. With the help of the Romans, Anna had managed to bury Rut in a separate grave in the camp's cemetery. It was easy to find her among the others: at the head of the grave, Pontius Pilate's wife had planted a small, neat fir tree to which had been nailed a little plaque made from a tin can, bearing Rut's name and the years of her birth and death. That winter, the camp was in ferment; the recent accidents in the mine had thrown the extraction schedule off course, and the convicts were forced to work an extra half-shift every day to make up for lost time. Even the service staff was herded underground every other day on a rota. It was during the night shift, at an abandoned coalface, that Anna and Ilya became lovers.

Anna adored Ilya, and she was happy. She tried to speak to him in the kind of language used in the play, calling him 'My husband' or 'My one and only'. She was sure that he, like Rut, was an Abelite, and it surprised her that he should want to hide this from her. Anna's former bridegroom was among those who had been buried alive in the mine, and she was keen for Ilya to be brought into the rehearsals and given that role, and did all she could to make this happen. The feverish activity in the mine meant that rehearsals were few and far between, and scenes with numerous actors were not being worked on at all, but in spring, when the new mine was fully operational and the pressure had abated, the rehearsals resumed on a regular basis. On several occasions Ilya really did play Anna's bridegroom, though afterwards he refused the role for good.

Sometimes Anna could see that being with her was making him unhappy; she understood that this was because of Rut and said, as if trying to persuade him, that Rut herself wanted her, and no one else, to be with him, that the Lord had done everything Rut had wanted Him to do; He had performed a miracle, and now she and Ilya were together. After all, she kept saying, this really was a miracle: theirs was hardly the only camp in the country – according to rumours, there were plenty of them – and just look where he had ended up. Anna had a peculiar faith in miracles, and as he listened to her he would think that now he understood why Christ had turned water into wine at Anna's wedding: there was so much faith in her that you could not think of deceiving her. Also: she took such joy in miracles that making them for her must have been a particular pleasure. He knew better than Anna how many camps there were in the country now, and he could see that she was right: his ending up in Mosslands really was a miracle, but still, he could not shake off the thought that the reason the Lord had brought him to this camp was Rut, not Anna. Rut was right here, as were the letters he had written her, as were the stories he had sent her about Fatima, as was her grave – he could not renounce this, and did not wish to do so. All the while, Anna was behaving as if everything was going well and just as it should, as if he could not but be happy with her.

According to Anna's logic, the arrests of Rut's father, of Rut and of Ilya himself had all been contrived by the Lord in order to bring him here, to Mosslands, in order for her to fall in love with him, be happy with him and thank God for him. And Ilya, like the other Abelites, should thank God for bringing him to Mosslands, and thank Him separately for her, Anna. It was amazing how neatly this all fitted together, and Ilya, as a scholar, was astonished by the sharpness with which she had traced the line of their shared fate, by how quickly she had found an explanation and purpose for every last thing in his life.

If at first he was thrilled by the fact that she was an ordinary country girl and yet capable of such constructions, later these constructions scared him: he was terrified that she might be right. Whenever she began telling him that he was an Abelite and that it was the Lord who had brought him to the camp and given him to her, and that this was how everything should be – she always explained this very patiently and affectionately, but firmly and distinctly, as if she were a primary-school teacher – he hated her and was ready to beat her.

At the very end of '34 a son was born to them, and they called him Isaiah, in memory of Rut's father. Anna had been staking a great deal on the child, wanted it to be a boy and thought that in Ilya's eyes it would make her Rut's legitimate successor, but this didn't happen. Although their relationship continued, Anna could see that she was becoming more and more of a burden to him.

A little before the birth, or perhaps immediately after it, she was transferred to a special barracks for mothers coming out of labour; it was known, among both the guards and the zeks, as the 'mummy house'. Talking to her baby, Anna blamed Rut, as if she were still alive, for not giving Ilya up to her and asked her why. Anna stayed there until the end of '35, when she went back to her old barracks. Children were not supposed to be kept in the camp, and the rules stated that when a child turned one he should be removed from the camp and placed in a special, small children's home: two log huts joined together. That was where children were meant to live until the end of their mothers' prison term. The home was located half a mile from the camp, on the way to the settlement for Mosslands' hired workers. Most of the staff were convicts who had been granted special permission to work outside the prison zone.

Because of her pregnancy Anna did not take part in rehearsals in the second half of 1934, but once she had recovered from the birth she started acting once more. Her role remained the same, but she no longer played it anywhere near as well. She could feel that she was performing badly, but blamed her partners for everything and changed them frequently, sometimes even twice a year (fortunately, there were plenty of Abelites in the camp). Her last bridegroom was Misha Kogan, who had been in charge of a special operations regiment with the Far Eastern Command before he was imprisoned. Kogan was in love with Anna and took his role very seriously, but he wasn't cut out for it and looked silly on stage. She was often on the verge of refusing to act with him, but Kogan had had a gruelling investigation and would have died very quickly were it not for the perks that came with acting. Anna knew he was in love with her, and felt sorry for him.

Anna's decline was not immediately obvious: other Jews were also performing in a feeble and somewhat mechanical way; they were tired, and when rehearsals became a rarity again in '37 – less than one a month – they were relieved. By the end of that year the camp boss, Peter the Apostle, was no longer involved in the play: it was transferred from the Cultural-Educational Department (CED), which came under his remit, to the Cultural-Educational Section (CES) of the secret police. By tradition, the latter was run by James, brother of Christ and the second of the apostles in seniority and authority. If the Jews still continued, every now and again, to act out and rehearse one or other scene of *Christ the Counter-Revolutionary*, the guards (the Christians) no longer participated at all after the theatre changed hands. Following the example of the apostles, all of whom, except James, were due to leave their roles at the beginning of 1939 because of their age, they no longer believed that the rehearsals served any purpose, or that Christ would ever come to them. The closer they came to the end of the apostles' term, the better they understood that Sertan had been wrong: while the Jews were alive, nothing would end.

James was a full twenty years' younger than the other apostles; a mere guard until 1937, he had become the camp 'godfather' well before his time and completely by chance.[13] His father, another James the Apostle, was an expert at making ingenious crossbows which, after enjoying them and showing them off to the guards and zeks, he would usually sell to the Yakuts, often in exchange for animal skins. It was one such crossbow, apparently intended for a bear, that killed him: while testing it, he fired an arrow straight into his own stomach.

No sooner had they returned home from the funeral and raised a glass to James's father than Peter told him:

'We have received you as the real brother of Christ, and you should stick with us, not your peers. Nobody will replace us: we are the last. That's clear as day, and it is high time for you to stop clinging to Sertan – he's not your mother.'

An instructor from the Party's regional committee had recently visited Mosslands, and Peter stood up and repeated his words, as if he were giving a toast:

'Enough dogmatism! If Lenin had followed Marx to the letter, we would still be waiting for the October Revolution. The camps are still being built,' Peter went on, 'and we are only just getting started. Give it three or four years and half the country will be in prison, and I don't mean camps like Mosslands or even Kolyma: our Strict Regime Barracks will be nothing compared to what's coming. And anyway, the camps aren't even half the story: by the time we're done building them, there'll probably be a war on – like none we've ever seen. And now for the Jews. Let me state this publicly: I have nothing against the Jews of Mosslands, but they must

---

13 The 'godfather' was the head of the informers' networks in Soviet prison camps.

be killed, and I don't think anybody doubts this. They have bound the Lord hand and foot with their covenant, and He can hardly go back on His word. So it's up to us to act: we can and must help Him. He has done all He can to make this possible: He has given us power, and arms, and above all, gathered us in one place. The elimination of Jews as a class – that is our role.'

Everyone's glasses were refilled. Peter got to his feet, and once again his words sounded like a toast:

'Now for the rehearsals. They are no longer my responsibility, but young James's, in the CES. True, we all know they're pointless now. Half the roles are played by the Abelites, and they're traitors; it's not just us Christians who hate them – the Jews hate them too, even more than we do. And they're right to hate them. Those Mosslands Jews who waited for Christ with us generation after generation are almost all dead, while this lot betrayed their own people and fled. Now they've taken other people's places in the play and next thing we know Christ will come to the Abelites. Though I still hope that won't happen. The Lord knows that there has to be at least some justice. So why aren't we banning the rehearsals? Why aren't we simply putting a stop to them once and for all? So as not to alarm the Jews, that's why: better that they think life's continuing as normal, as it always has done. Frighten them and they'll beg their lives back from God. So the rehearsals should continue, but no more pampering: from now on, the Jews will go out to work with everyone else. No more cushy jobs for any of them, whether sick, old or dying,' he concluded.

Peter was conscious of how young James was and of the fact that, being young, he saw the rehearsals and Sertan exactly as Peter himself had seen them in the first years of his apostleship. Sertan had once meant everything to Peter, too, and he couldn't have imagined that the Teacher would come to them in any other way than Sertan's. That was how it had always been, and many years had passed before the apostles, repeating day in day out the words with which they would greet the Messiah, had finally understood that this was not what Christ needed from them, that the rehearsals were a waste of breath: Christ would not come to them, however often they repeated their lines. So then they began to seek their own path, but they always began too late, and even if they found the path, they never had time to walk it to the end. Meanwhile, their children came along to replace them, and they came with that same faith in Sertan.

Nevertheless, Peter was sure that one day – and not too far into the future, either – he would manage to bring James on board. He had known James since he was a child and, through his friendship with his father, the previous James, had come to see this boy as almost his own son; James really was very fond of Uncle Peter and followed him to the barracks, to roll call, to the office, as if he was on a leash. The wife of old James died a year before collectivisation, there was no one to look after the child, and from then on the boy spent half the year living at Skosyryev's (Peter's) house, sleeping with his children.

As a child, James was honest and naïve in the extreme, and Peter felt happy that he and James junior, rather than he and James senior, would be Christ's closest, beloved disciples. Peter had long been infuriated by the father's idiotic passion for crossbows and his petty trade with the Yakuts, which involved shouting and swearing for the entire camp to hear and was always followed by a monumental drinking bout; even his death had been stupid. He had been a childhood friend and they had grown up together, but even so Peter did not want Christ to choose him. But he loved James junior, and he was envious that such an idiot could have a child like that.

Peter had only contempt for his own children: they were jokers and buffoons who had been drunkards ever since they were at school, often in the company of James senior. Peter only had himself to blame for their drinking: their adulthood coincided with the time when he no longer doubted that life would end with him and his generation; he regretted having them and thought them useless and pointless – which is exactly what they became.

It took Peter a very long time to see that James, having become an apostle, had changed all at once, in every way, just as all of them had and just as the apostles had changed back then, the first time: Christ called them and they abandoned their homes, wives, families, boats, fishing nets and tax coffers, and followed Him. Sertan himself had seen and marvelled at what the word of Christ did to the peasants he had taken on for the play. To my mind, Peter found it simply impossible to believe that his influence on James had come to an end and that the only influence on him now was Christ. He interpreted James's resistance to him as the usual rebelliousness of the young, the desire to claim equal status, and he barely reacted to it at all. In fact, he did not stand in James's way for a year or more after this, convinced as he was that James would see reason.

For the first six months of his apostleship, James dwelled at length on what Peter had said at his father's wake. He realised, of course, that Peter had been wrong: even by the latter's own calculations – those three or four years it would take for the camps to expand, then war – the last generation would be not Peter's but James's. James was also repelled by Peter's patronising attitude towards the Lord: for Peter, the Lord was like an infant or a helpless, feeble old man. James believed in a different God. There were no doubts in his mind that Christ would come to earth and save human beings just as Sertan had taught; Peter had not been wrong about this, although there was one thing that troubled James and perplexed him: like everyone else, he loathed the Abelites and could not accept that the path of even one of them could be right, yet there was no other conclusion to draw.

Having become the camp's godfather, James did everything in his power to support the Jews of Mosslands and to keep the rehearsals going: his position gave him considerable authority, and Peter made a show of respecting it. He did not get involved when James let one or other Jew off heavy labour for several days – everyone was constantly out working at this time – or when he put the 'goners' in hospital. Peter merely made the others work harder, forcing them, as it were, to make up for those who had been let off, and he would put anyone who failed to meet their quota on a penalty ration, or in the Strict Regime Barracks (SRB). James invented all sorts of clever ruses to save the Jews, but Peter was far more experienced in the workings of the prison camp and had no trouble getting whatever he wanted. The Mosslands Jews were dying one after the other, and were it not for the Romans who, as hired workers, could sometimes sneak food in to them (the Jews, needless to say, received no parcels from outside), they would all have been dead by the spring of 1939.

The apostle of Christ and the secret police boss were fused in the person of James as inseparably and strangely as, for the Jews, man and God had been merged in Christ. A steady honesty came easily to him, whatever he had to do. On this point, for all his kindness and naivety, he was adamant. One of his ruses for saving the Jews was to sign up each and every one of them as his agents; he was able to push this through in September '38 and now he was within his rights, according to established practice, to help them as much as he wanted –

essentially, they were now under his wing. While recruiting the Jews, he immediately communicated the surnames of his new informers to Skosyryev. He had no doubt that he was doing the right thing by acting openly and within the rules, and by telling Peter straightforwardly and honestly: these are my people. Perhaps this made a kind of sense. Urging the Jews to become informers, he would tell them that only this could save them; he would swear that their recruitment was a pure formality and that their denunciations were of no interest to anyone, and he would tell them that they had a duty to survive, or else Christ would not come again and Sertan's project, the thing they had lived for, would die. But just as soon as one of the Mosslands Jews agreed and signed the requisite document, James would immediately start demanding that they get to work right away, yelling that 'dead souls' were no use to him and telling them, with the same fervour and conviction as before, that he wouldn't stand for dishonest people who took without giving anything in return. He, James, had no moral right to make exceptions for them by letting them off heavy labour or anything else if they didn't do their job; they had been lying when they had agreed to collaborate – but look, here's the document and here's your signature.

James would make a clear, neat summary of all the information he managed to gather from his agents and leave a daily digest on Skosyryev's desk; it was important to him to show Peter that his professional activity was no fiction, that he really had established the kind of effective network that the prison camp needed. His people were working and trying hard, and he had every right to demand the perks that they were due. In particular, it was from James that Peter learned that Kogan, the former commander of the special operations regiment, was preparing an escape attempt with several 'thieves' in the spring, in the general direction, it seemed, of the Chinese border. James was sure that he had covered his back and that he no longer needed to fear Peter. He was sure that Peter would now leave the Jews alone.

But Skosyryev made excellent use of the information he received from James and he was able to hit back with rare and unexpected force. Working his own channels, he conveyed the names of the informers to the 'thieves' – nowadays this might be called a planned leak – and, after they murdered three of James's people in the space of one night, James was forced to disperse his corps. No longer meeting any resistance from James's side, Peter moved the Mosslands Jews back onto heavy labour twenty-four hours later, and everything returned to how it had been before. Peter joked that James had been routed and fled the scene of battle.

James really did disappear from the prison camp for a week and a half. Persistent rumours circulated among the Jews that he had shot himself, but this was not true. James had an aunt, his father's sister, one of the demoniacs healed by Christ; she had run the household even during old James's lifetime and she was the only one to see him during this period. It was from her that Peter learned what had happened to James and how he was doing. It was clear from her account that he felt utterly broken and understood all too well that he had run out of ways of defending the Jews. She told Peter that she was scared that James might very well take his own life. But Peter was convinced James would be all right; they just had to leave him alone and let him come round. Sooner or later he would understand that he, Peter, had the Lord on his side. There was no other road to Christ; whether good or bad, his was the only one. He loved James as his son just as much as before and wanted them to be together. It's possible that at this time some of the apostles, and perhaps even Peter himself, were still unsure whether or not they were right: bringing James into their camp was meant to put an end to their doubts.

Strange as it may sound, the false rumour of James's suicide was met with elation by the Mosslands Jews. This was not a question of ingratitude. The Jews had never believed that he really wanted to save them. If Peter would always remain an apostle for them, come what may, and his role as prison-camp chief was merely a cover, then James, who had become an apostle so recently and unexpectedly, before his time, was, in their eyes, much more a prison-camp godfather than a close disciple of Christ. While recruiting them as his informers, he had told them that this was all just a game, an act, a front that was essential to their survival, pure theatre; they smelled a rat but yielded all the same. He spoke well, and he still retained his childlike honesty and enthusiasm, and it was this that confused them. Then James began demanding information and they realised he had tricked them, but it was too late. When the 'thieves' killed three Jews, they accepted this as their due and blamed neither the murderers nor Peter, only James. Becoming informers had broken them: they could no longer act or rehearse.

Even before this, the urge to die had been strong among this generation: many of the Mosslands Jews, like the apostles, would come to the end of the term set by Sertan and have to pass on their roles to their children, but there were no children, and for a long time the only replacements for Jews had been Abelites. For as long as they held on to the main roles, the Jews were still prepared to tolerate this, but the day was fast approaching when even the roles of high priests would fall to the Abelites, and that could mean one thing only: that everything the Jews had lived for since the earliest days, since New Jerusalem, had also been a game, a front and an act. And there was something else: having lost three people, they realised that fate was giving them the choice, as it were, between two deaths, two paths to death – the path of Peter and the path of James. The road onto which Peter was calling them was the one they knew, and the one they chose.

In mid-October, 1938, James returned to his post; he had been absent for precisely ten days and now he resumed his usual prison-camp duties. The change that Peter had been expecting to find in him had not occurred. On the contrary, all the indications were that he had decided on a definitive break with Skosyryev. He was a different man now: his childishness was behind him and there was a strength about him that had not been seen in him before. But it was as if Peter did not even notice this. He continued, as before, to urge James to join him, explained to him that they were brothers in Christ and should love each other. For a long time he did not react to any of James's hostile actions, nor did he hinder his attempts to have him removed from his post as head of the prison camp, as if these attempts were no concern of his; instead, for as long as it was still possible, he went along with everything for the sake of reconciliation. He continued to believe that James was not lost, that he would not turn his back on them as Judas had.

James came back to the camp with a firm idea of what he had to do next. Precisely two months later, on December 16, 1938, Peter the Apostle would turn fifty-five; this was the absolute limit for any apostleship, which meant that he had to retire both from his role and from his position as camp boss. If previously, until the episode with the informers, James had always acknowledged the unconditional seniority of Peter among the apostles, as sanctified by the words of Christ Himself – he might have considered Peter's decision to finish off the Jews mistaken, but he had not doubted Peter's honesty and sincerity, his faith, his desire for the same thing that each of them was waiting for: Christ, the Saviour, His Second Coming – these latest events showed James how wrong he had been.

To James it was obvious that a man chosen by Christ to serve as an apostle should be honest in everything, whatever came his way; the duty of every man to bear his cross honestly lay at the very foundation of his understanding of the world, and the fact that Peter had maliciously breached his duty as head of the camp could mean only one thing: that he could no longer be trusted. For Skosyryev, nothing was sacred, and everything was a means to an end; there was no one he would not betray without a second thought if it meant remaining in post and extending his authority. And his faith that he could force Christ to come to him, Peter, was false.

James remembered that back then, when Christ had come into the world for the first time, Peter had renounced Christ three times on the eve of the crucifixion in order to save his own skin, and he realised that this had been preserved in the Gospels for a reason: it was a warning to him to treat Peter with caution.

Seeing Peter in this way freed James from ordinary constraints and placed him outside the law; indeed, he was convinced that whatever actions he took against Peter would be moral and justified. But initially, even if he wasn't sure there was much point, he fought Peter honestly; he simply enjoyed the feeling that here, too, he was not like Peter. And this, of course, was a mistake.

James's aim was to seize power in the Mosslands camp even before Peter stepped down, and he was prepared to tolerate Skosyryev for the rest of his term as a purely ceremonial figure. He did not lay claim to the role of head of the prison camp, which was traditionally taken by whoever was playing Peter the Apostle; James considered this only natural and, once everything had settled down, intended to give the position to Skosyryev's eldest son.

James made his first attempt to remove Peter from power as early as the eighteenth of October, by writing his first denunciation and sending it to the district centre. I cannot say for sure whether he himself came up with this method, which he would stick with right to the end, or whether he was capitalising on a hint given to him by the Romans (having resumed his duties as 'godfather', he now consulted with them almost every day); probably, the second. On the other hand, the report which James dispatched to Bely Yar bore little similarity to the one they advised him to write. The Romans told James that the denunciation must at all costs be sent to Moscow and in secret, and they were prepared to do this for him; here, in Siberia, both the district and regional administrations of the NKVD would do all they could to shield Peter – he had been their man for years – so by sending the report to the district office at Bely Yar, James would be exposing himself to danger while leaving Peter unharmed. He had to understand that any attack on Peter was an attack on Peter's immediate superiors, so trying to win their support was simply stupid. And above all, the denunciation had to be composed in such a way that not to react to it would be out of the question; only a fool would worry about exaggerating or stretching credibility: the more far-fetched it was, the quicker and more decisively Moscow would respond. The Romans even drafted a text to fit the case. In it, Peter was accused of creating a top-secret hub for terrorist and subversive activity in Mosslands, of plotting to place agents in the main cities of the country with the aim of trying to assassinate leading figures of the Party and government, and of preparing a massive kulak uprising in Siberia aimed at splitting it off from Soviet Russia. But James used none of this.

The Romans had a good understanding of how the state worked, and there is no doubt that they gave sound and accurate advice. Had James listened to them he would have been able to deal with Peter before 1938 was out. Unfortunately, he was too young, too sure of himself, and too stubborn. He picked and chose the occasional crumb from the Romans' suggestions and, needless to say, the result was a mess. Although all the trump cards were in James's hands, he got nowhere until the spring of '39. This cost both the Jews and the other zeks hundreds of lives. With his respect for the rules and the system of seniority (crucial to his understanding of the honest execution of professional duty), James accused Peter of the following: first, he was failing to take care of the undercover agents in the camp and undermining the effectiveness of the secret police (he did not blame Peter directly for the deaths of the three Jews, because he did not know for sure whether their names had been publicised by Peter intentionally or whether he'd blurted them out in his cups – he had been drinking almost daily since the day of his father's funeral); second, Peter was mistreating the prisoners, hence the inexcusable mortality rate in the camp and the failure, for three months running, to meet the quota for coal extraction set by the state.

These were derisory accusations, and although James wrote more than a hundred such epistles, not one of them led to any action being taken. By March '39, James had finally realised that he would get nowhere by being stubborn, and from this point onwards his denunciations, which he now sent to the regional centre, began to change. As before, they contained no untruths but, thanks to new materials procured by the Romans, they looked far more serious.

James accused the entire camp leadership and all the guards of being former kulaks who had hidden their origins from the Soviet authorities; even before that, during the Civil War, they had been active participants in a large unit of White bandits that had accounted for the lives of dozens of Red partisans. This picture was crowned by the information that under cover of cultural activity and the rehearsing of *Christ the Counter-Revolutionary*, the head of the prison camp, Skosyryev (Peter), had been waging a religious propaganda campaign for almost ten years, with repeated attempts to bring about the Second Coming of Christ in the quickest possible time, in order, among other things, to bring an end to Soviet power.

In the spring of 1939, the situation in the Mosslands camp began to change. When the top brass of the security services had been dismissed in Moscow the previous November, and Yezhov – whom Peter had heard about on numerous occasions from Sergei Yegorov, the regional NKVD chief in Tomsk – was replaced by an obscure Georgian, Peter was not very worried. Mosslands was far away from Moscow, and events in the centre had, until now, never touched them directly; the political line was fixed and it did not matter much whether the person who implemented it was called Yezhov, Beria or someone else. But in January '39 a persistent rumour started going around that Beria was releasing many of the zeks imprisoned by Yezhov, and that a decision had been taken, right at the top, to reduce sharply the total number of arrests. True, no one had been freed yet at Mosslands: the camp was cut off from the world until the Keti became navigable again, and whenever Peter heard any of the apostles or guards talking about the Party's new line on this matter – the main evidence for which came from the new tone of the radio broadcasts – he would confidently claim that it was all nonsense and old wives' tales. The Romans were the main source of these rumours, so in February, in order to put a stop to these stories once and for all, Peter confiscated both of the radio receivers in the settlement, threatening arrest.

On March 1 Skosyryev asked the regional administration, as per usual, how many new zeks he should expect that year and, correspondingly, how much the extraction target would rise by; the total number of zeks had grown sharply and continuously until that year, but now it was even less than the previous spring – only the target had gone up. When he wired Tomsk to say that he could never fulfil the plan with so few convicts, Yegorov himself tapped back to say Skosyryev was an idiot and didn't understand the needs of the current moment. So the repressions really were running out of steam and his calculation that half the country would pass through the camps in the next four to five years was very wide of the mark. Doing the maths again later that same day, he worked out that, unless Beria was stopped, this task would require not one Five Year Plan but three.

For all this, Peter still hoped, still believed, that none of this was irreversible, when suddenly, on March 8, he received an urgent order from the district committee to send two Mosslands Jews, a professor of medicine and a colonel, to Tomsk with the first available convoy – not to be interrogated or to have their sentences extended, but to be freed. This was obvious from the order. Meanwhile, Peter's instructions were to give them money for essential expenses and to find accommodation for them outside the prison zone in the hired workers' settlement.

So either the Jews had managed to bribe Beria, or they had once again begged their lives back from God and won a further delay. But it was not this that frightened Peter: he knew that the Jews were at his mercy – he could destroy them in a single day if he had to, and then whose lives would the Lord have left to extend? There was something else: he found out that the old Yezhov secret-police crowd was being purged, that Yegorov, too, was not safe in Tomsk, and that any investigation into Yegorov could, thanks to James's denunciations, very easily bring Mosslands into the picture. If that happened, they would all be done for: NKVD special forces would be sent and they would be dealt with even faster than they themselves had dealt with the Jews. Peter understood that if Yegorov had not destroyed the denunciations and Moscow got wind of the fact that they had fought for the Whites and been kulaks until collectivisation, they were doomed, and that would mean they were not the last and were not destined to see Christ; in that case, James would be right and everything was in vain.

On March 10, on Peter's orders, both the camp and the hired workers' settlement were cut off from the outside world and, to all intents and purposes, placed under martial law. A permanent checkpoint was put up at the causeway and an announcement was made that nobody could enter or leave the island without the written permission of the head of the camp. The same applied to the right to use the radio transmitter, as well as the telegraph line recently installed in the settlement. Peter denied James and the Romans all access to these, tying them hand and foot.

It was as if James and Peter had switched places: Peter seemed to have come to his senses and become the man he was before – intelligent, strong, calculating. He had always been first among the apostles by any measure, and now you could see why. Next to him, James looked like a child. Peter could see this and now he understood why he had let James have his way: James really was a child in his eyes, the son of the friend of his own childhood. Peter loved him just as much as before and he was glad that he hadn't let himself be persuaded otherwise by Yegorov (after James's first tip-off, the Tomsk NKVD chief had come to Mosslands for some bear-hunting – he and Skosyryev had been mates ever since the village had been turned into a prison zone, and Peter had been made head of the camp at his recommendation – and Yegorov advised Peter to get rid of James, after all James would give him nothing but trouble, but Peter didn't listen and said, 'Let the boy have his fun. While you're holding the fort in Tomsk, I've nothing to worry about'). In fact, Peter had never regretted this; he had always known that he had no right to spill James's blood. The other apostles thought James was just another Judas, to be treated like any other traitor – the black sheep must be killed, end of story – but Skosyryev thought that if James had betrayed someone, then it was them, the apostles, not Christ; it was Christ who had chosen him, and Christ who should decide. Then, in May, Peter came up with an idea of how to use the 'godfather' and was relieved that James was still alive and in his old post – he needed both these things.

Although by this point James had lost all influence on the running of the camp, there was no further worsening in the situation of the Mosslands Jews. They joined in with heavy labour as before and slowly worked themselves to death in the mine; it was enough for Peter to know that they were at his mercy, and he did not try to force things. He knew that James was still squealing. It was hard to seal off the settlement entirely, and in the course of the spring the Romans twice succeeded in passing onto the Yakuts James's denunciations to the regional committee, but this was a lengthy, roundabout route which could take months and it seems that not one of the reports ever reached its destination; certainly, they played no role in subsequent events. James hoped that in May, when the convict barges began arriving in Mosslands and going back loaded with coal, he would manage to open a more direct line to Tomsk via the captains, but Peter anticipated this all too easily and he simply held James under arrest while the boats were moored at the Mosslands jetty.

As predicted, Yegorov was arrested that spring. This happened at the very end of April, and Peter realised that he was no longer covered. His allotted term was running out and he had to hurry. The crux of the scheme that he was counting on and had been working on for some time was a major armed uprising by the convicts; it was to start at the end of the summer – in mid or late August – and spread not just through the prison zone, but also through the mines, the workers' settlement, and the entire island. The plan was as follows: on the first day the guards would retreat to the other side of the causeway, losing up to a third of their number in combat, and then, twenty-four hours later, they would counterattack and, with no help from outside, indeed before any such help could arrive, would restore order. Peter had James down as the leader of the uprising, while his staff and chief co-conspirators would be the Jews and Abelites engaged in the play. There could be no doubt that the successful suppression of the mutiny would make Peter and the guards heroes in the eyes of the NKVD and more than make up for their previous failings. Crucially, the uprising should discredit, in one fell swoop, everything that came from James, all his denunciations – the denunciations of a turncoat bent on betraying the security organs in favour of the zeks; who would believe them now? And another thing: it would be easy enough to destroy not only the Mosslands Jews during the fighting, but the free Romans, too, and indeed anyone who could testify against the Christians and say they had been Whites or kulaks. Then there would be nothing to stop Peter's generation from waiting until Christ finally came to them and receiving Him when He did. And who would He come to if not them? After all, there was no one else left, everything ended with them; truly, they were the last.

Peter's plan, like any plan hatched during training exercises rather than on the battlefield, was too good to work in practice. The very idea of fomenting a prisoner uprising was naive, not least because there wasn't a single zek prepared to run the risk of organising and leading it, while James, whom Peter was counting on so much, was not the man he had been just a few months before, in winter: he had wilted, accepting that there was nothing to be done. Relying on him had been a stupid mistake. And it wasn't just James that Peter had been wrong about; he had thought that the worse the guards treated the zeks, the sooner the zeks would rise; he had urged the guards to inflict ever more punishments, ever more cruelties, repeating twenty times a day that sparks were what was needed, and then the blaze would surely follow. But there were no sparks, the zeks were docile and growing weaker, and several of them died each day.

Still, the plan was so beautiful that Peter could not bear to give it up and he wasted a whole month waiting for James to do something, anything. Eventually he realised how stupid the whole thing was – James, the uprising – and it was then, when he had no idea what to do next, that he suddenly remembered that one of the first reports written by James's informers had mentioned a certain Mikhail Kogan, an army man and a professional spy and saboteur, who, it seems, had been planning an escape attempt even then. A mass escape was hardly the same as an uprising, of course, but it would do as a poor second best.

Peter made inquiries about Kogan and established that

he was alive and doing heavy labour. He considered calling in the agent who had grassed on Kogan for a more thorough interrogation, but it turned out that Peter himself had handed the agent over to the 'thieves' in the autumn – he was among the three informers eliminated by them half a year before. This had been a mistake, and Peter wished he hadn't been so hasty. But then, a stroke of luck: he learned from a guard that Kogan, together with other Abelites, had been taking part in the rehearsals for some time and that he was playing the bridegroom in the Wedding at Cana. This was a gift: it meant that there was no need to change the main part of the plan, merely to replace James with Kogan as leader of the escape.

To make sure that he wasn't making a similar misjudgement with Kogan as he had already made with James, Peter called him in for a couple of chats. He would start with the play, saying he wouldn't mind acting with a girl like Anna himself, then he would talk about how unfair the world was: he knew full well that the charges against Kogan (espionage, sabotage, treachery) were all cooked up, and he knew how that was done – after all this wasn't his first year working for the state – but still, he was astonished by Kogan and the other military types: they could carry on writing their monthly petitions to have the case reviewed until the Second Coming, hoping each time that the authorities would acknowledge that a mistake had been made, that they would free them and even apologise. They knew full well that the entire prison camp, save for the 'thieves', was here by error. Civilians were one thing – they'd never seen anything but paperwork all their lives and they died after three years of getting here, but was Kogan happy to end his life like that? The Chinese border wasn't far away, and he'd had more than enough training for it, to judge by his dossier.

Kogan realised that Skosyryev was mocking him, but he

couldn't understand what he wanted from him. Talk of escape attempts did not scare him: his gang had broken up four months ago, and no one had anything else on him. The next day he felt calmer and decided that Skosyryev was probably curious about his army career and the fact that he'd once been decorated with the Order of the Red Banner – hence all the questions.

These conversations convinced Peter that Kogan was a man of action, just as he'd thought; having started something, he wouldn't stop till he finished, meeting any obstacles head-on rather than waiting around. He was just the kind of man Peter needed, and the fact that he understood Kogan so well was another clear advantage. But time was running out for Peter; he was counting in days now, not weeks or months, and if he wanted to get a move on, he had to find a way of helping Kogan. He found one.

From the very first year of mining, extensive use had been made of explosives – whether dynamite or ammonal – both for shaft-sinking and for open-cast work, and Peter, after waiting a bit so as not to scare Kogan off, attached him to a group of hired workers in charge of everything to do with explosions. Although Kogan had not been freed from supervision, no one would be watching him underground. The blasters working there were not up to much, and Kogan had far more experience; he quickly took matters into his own hands, which suited the hired workers just fine, not to mention Peter. He was sure that Kogan would put the explosives to good use.

Just three weeks later, an informer who had got in on the escape plan told Peter that they had hidden more than fifty grenades at the coalface and that it was all coming together. By this point the escape team had also been assembled and it included almost all those people, a dozen in total, with whom

Kogan had been plotting back in the autumn: eight 'thieves' and four regular zeks. Unfortunately, there were no Mosslands Jews among them. Even the date had been set – July 2. That was when the barge bringing a new batch of convicts was meant to leave with a cargo of coal. There was always complete chaos in the camp at such times and nobody ever seemed to know what was going on, so Peter approved his choice: those were ideal conditions for an escape.

Peter also liked Kogan's plan. It was precise, simple and allowed for the unexpected. The final version went as follows. In the evening, when the zeks finished their shift in the mine and came up, the guards would divide them into brigades and lead them to the fence surrounding the mine. It was here, by the gates, that the convicts were frisked for the first time; the second, much more thorough search was done before they entered the prison zone. The guards didn't like the first search: they thought it was pointless and often didn't do a very good job of it. Skosyryev had introduced it himself four years before, precisely because he feared zeks filching explosives from the mine, and he always made sure it was carried out. The zeks would sail through it, as they wouldn't have the grenades on them yet. The fence surrounding the mine consisted of rows of barbed wire stretched from post to post, but the rows were quite far apart. Not far from the gates, still within the territory of the mine, there was a shack where the explosives were stored, its rear wall pressing right up against the fence. A good week before the escape – to give everyone a chance to get used to the change – Kogan would remove a thin plank from the back wall while painting the shack and shove it inside; the shack was double-boarded, the plank would get stuck, and a kind of shelf would be formed, invisible from both inside and outside the shack. Kogan planned to bring the grenades over from the mine only on the eve of the escape.

At first, the road to the camp ran close to the fence. After carrying out the search, the guards were usually tired out, calm and laid-back. Sticking a hand through the fence and taking the grenades off the shelf would be easy enough at this point, not least because there were no watchmen between the road and the fence: there was simply no space for them there, and anyway what would be the point – it wasn't as if the zeks would want to break through the wire to the mine. But here, too, Kogan wanted to avoid the slightest risk: the grenades were to be taken not by one man, in case he missed, but by all twelve, so it would be just as well to distract the guards and other zeks. There was a decent circus clown in their brigade, another of Kogan's men, who was doing time for some misjudged gag; the guards and the zeks were quite fond of him and had watched him in the camp's amateur theatricals. It would be his job to occupy the guards with various pranks and tricks. The first stage had been worked out very neatly, no doubt about that; nevertheless, Skosyryev decided that it wouldn't harm matters if he also contributed by ensuring that Kogan's brigade would be escorted by complete incompetents.

From here on the zeks would be armed, but they were to walk calmly to the camp with everyone else. At the halfway point between the camp and the mine – just over a mile from both – there was a stream with three logs thrown over the water. Peter had been meaning to broaden this bridge for a while and more logs had been brought over, but no one had got round to it. The zeks bunched together here and got in each other's way, and there would always be a bit of a hold-up and a fuss before they moved on. The stream was just three hundred metres from the causeway, where, after the barge had set sail, there would, as usual, be only two guards left on duty. The causeway was not visible from the stream; it was obscured by the forest, which jutted out here and also obscured the camp and the mine. Just before the bridge, the zeks would throw grenades at the guards, but without getting carried away or wasting too many on them. Kogan allotted five men to this task and, correspondingly, just five grenades. Then, whoever was closest to the guards would take their weapons off them and run with the others to the causeway. There, too, the sentry would be removed with grenades by the first three zeks, after which the road beyond the causeway would lie open before them and there would be no one left to stop them.

Kogan's plan suited Peter perfectly. Adapting his own plans to it could hardly have been easier. Another boon was knowing almost the exact time of the operation: the brigade would approach the log-bridge about an hour after the end of the shift – Peter had double-checked this, although it was easy enough to work out – which is to say, at about seven in the evening. Now for Peter's own contribution to Kogan's plan. First, he had to get as many zeks as possible over to the bridge by 7.00 pm. Peter was well aware that there would be more than Kogan's twelve trying to escape, although he didn't know how many more; he needed as many as possible, and in particular all the Mosslands Jews. The men among them presented no problem: they worked in the mine and they would either be in Kogan's brigade or the one directly after it. Things looked promising with the female Jews as well; like all the other women zeks, they were assigned to agricultural tasks in midsummer, and right now they were weeding the field which bordered the stream and the log-bridge. Agricultural work was practically unsupervised by the guards; the hired workers were in charge of vegetable farming and took a fairly relaxed approach, but there were no escape attempts so no changes were introduced. The guards merely brought the zeks to and from the fields. The free workers even let the mothers see their children out in the fields – those who wanted to, of course – and assuming the kids were at least four or five and not too lazy, they would help their mothers with the weeding. Older children would already be working separately in their own brigades in a neighbouring field, but here, too, you could come to an agreement. Then, when the shift was over, the kids rarely went straight back to the children's home; usually, they would be allowed to accompany their mothers as far as the stream, where the women zeks would be handed over by the hired workers to the guards, as if at a border. The children never went a step further. The female brigade would finish its shift at the same time as the brigade in the mine, but it was closer to the camp so the women would enter the zone forty minutes ahead of the men. For Peter, it was crucial that the women should be delayed by the escort guards on July 2 and arrive at the log-bridge immediately after Kogan's brigade, or at any rate not before. Arranging this with the guards was easy enough. Things were more complicated with the Romans and the other free workers. In order to kill them all in one go, together with the Jews, Peter had to gather them in one place, and do this in such a way that no suspicions were aroused. But they weren't zeks and for a long time he couldn't see how.

Initially Peter wanted to arrange some kind of political meeting by the log-bridge, but no suitable anniversary or other pretext could be found, and anyway, holding it there would have looked stupid – they had a designated area for such events opposite the village soviet, and nobody would want to come all the way down to the stream. Summoning the hired workers for agricultural tasks would also have been odd; haymaking had finished a few days earlier, and there was nothing urgent that needed doing – the zeks could cope with the vegetables on their own. Besides, Peter knew that many of the free workers would, as usual, do their best to get out of weeding. It was then that he had an idea: it would be far better if the Romans met not by the log-bridge, which was merely the starting point, where the zeks and hired workers might easily begin trampling each other amid the general panic, but further on, where the causeway came to an end at the river bank, by the Mosslands jetty.

This was the right idea and he immediately found a pretext that involved no coercion and seemed entirely natural; in fact, he could have staked his life on everyone turning up. On July 2, a few hours before the operation was due to begin, he'd start a rumour through a guard – it didn't matter which – that *The Eagle*, a popular floating shop serving the local villages, might be mooring at their jetty that evening. (*The Eagle* was run by Yefremov, a very savvy 'captain-manager', as he called himself, and his boat was usually filled with good fabrics, often in a much wider selection than could be found in town, which locals rarely visited in any case.) While the Romans waited for *The Eagle*, Kogan's people would also come out by the jetty, from the causeway – there'd be no other way for them to go. According to their calculations, the jetty should be empty after the barge's departure the previous day; instead, they find a crowd of hired workers. Six apostles, with Peter at their head, are the first to notice the zeks, they fire at them and try to stop them, the zeks respond with grenades, but each time the Christians take up positions that leave the Romans caught in the crossfire. In the end some of the zeks still manage to force their way through and disappear into the forest, while the guards stay behind at the jetty and finish off any surviving Romans.

After the Romans it's the turn of the zeks. Squadrons of hidden sentries have been standing guard on the winding paths between the bogs since noon, and Kogan can't avoid them, whichever way he goes. He tries to dodge the ambushes by veering left, then veering right, but he only succeeds in wasting precious time. Half an hour later, having dealt with the Romans, the apostles approach from the rear, and it's all over. By this time the other six apostles who have stayed on the island have also killed all the Mosslands Jews in the prison camp – that is, all those who did not join Kogan. So now the Jews have finally been accounted for, the witnesses have been removed, and the case against James is watertight. Not only did he entirely fail to spot the uprising, but even worse, it was the actors in his own Cultural-Educational Section who organised the escape, led it and, to a man, took part in it. He'd never be able to wriggle out of that one.

But Peter's second plan almost came to naught, just as his first plan did. On the evening of July 1, less than twenty-four hours before the start of the uprising, James heard from someone that Kogan was preparing an escape and that Peter wanted to take advantage of it in order to deal with the Jews. He did not know who was planning to flee, how many, or the exact date but, to judge by various hints, he had probably been briefed about what was going to happen by one of the Christian guards rather than one of Kogan's men, which was why he attributed Peter's plan to Kogan. He was clearly convinced that Kogan's group included all or almost all the Mosslands Jews (in fact, as I have already said, it did not include one) and that it was they who had organised the escape, thinking they had no other way of saving their skins. In other words, James swallowed whole the account of the uprising which Peter was intending to put before the security services at a later date.

But James did not doubt that, whatever anyone else thought, the escape had been prepared by Peter, or at the very least had been agreed with him in advance and sanctioned by him. The whole thing was a provocation that would allow Peter to finish off the Jews. He knew that he had to stop the Jews come what may, and he thanked God and saw that He was on his side. After all, Peter had ordered James to be set free earlier that same day, July 1, while later that evening the Jews were due to do a run-through of their section of *Christ the Counter-Revolutionary*. The Lord had gathered the Jews just for him, in order that he might warn them and tell them that the Lord did not want any of them to escape and they should continue to rehearse.

Why was it that Peter, who had always been so cautious, suddenly decided to let James out a day before the escape? It wasn't as if anybody forced him to. No, it was because he was convinced that the die had already been cast. The Lord was with him and everything had been decided. What was more, the zeks' rehearsal on the eve of the uprising and James's presence there reinforced the accusations he would be making against the godfather – what was this if not the 'last meeting of the conspirators'? Peter had a further rationale: for the Jews, the rehearsal at the Cultural-Educational Section was proof that all was calm in the camp, no different from usual, and stopping James from joining the rehearsal after the barge had left would only cause unnecessary talk and alarm.

James entered the acting room in the CES just before the end of the rehearsal. He motioned to the Jews to stop and then very abruptly started beseeching them not to do anything, to surrender the weapons they had got ready, and even to go with him to Skosyryev and make a clean breast of it; better to receive a new term, he told them, than rise up and, even worse, escape. Escape meant death. The Jews knew nothing of Kogan's plans and, needless to say, understood nothing, but it was clear to them that this was a provocation of the kind they had come to expect from James ever since he had recruited them as informers and then actually forced them to grass, as a result of which three of them had been killed.

But even if they had suddenly realised that he was telling the truth and wanted what was best for them, wanted to save them, even then they would not have followed him; in the previous few months, something seemed to have snapped in them, their life was ending, and they had no strength left to live and wait for Christ. The Jews were not frightened by what, according to James, Peter was preparing; on the contrary, they saw it as a deliverance, they wanted to die, and hoped to die soon. They all agreed now that it was not Sertan but Peter who was right, and that their role, their mission was not to crucify Christ for a second time, but to be killed themselves. Now that their roles in the play had been taken by the Abelites, the death which they had always thought of as a form of desertion and flight had become a liberation and a reward; they thought that Jesus Christ Himself had freed them and it was no longer they who would lead Him to Golgotha – that would have to be done by the Abelites, or nobody.

James could not understand them. He saw that they did not believe him, and he tried to ingratiate himself with them, flatter them, blame everything on Kogan, anything just to stop them. He told the Jews that Kogan was an Abelite, a traitor, one in a long line of traitors, that the Lord had forgiven the Abelites, brought them back to Mosslands, but now the Abelites wanted to turn their backs on God and flee. How could the Jews believe Kogan and follow them, they who had never once betrayed their duty, who had always been true to

Sertan? But flattery was no use, and he could see that they did not believe a word he said, so he began once again to beseech and implore them not to do it. He said that the old apostles had been former apostles for half a year already, for half a year they had been nobodies, or worse, and it was because of them, because they were not righteous, not worthy, that Christ had not saved mankind, but they would not accept this and wanted to force God's hand. Their provocations were aimed not only at the Jews, but also at the Lord. Had the Jews really forgotten that this had all happened before: the apostles' term would be at an end, Christ would not come, so then, in order to force Him to come to them rather than someone else, they would start killing the Jews. But they would do well to remember that the Lord had always saved the Jews; not all of them, perhaps, but He had saved them nonetheless.

James told the Jews that there was a reason why Yezhov had been dismissed: there were reliable reports that arrests were on the wane; not only that, many prisoners were being released, and this was only the beginning – eventually everyone would be let out. Beria was doing all he could to make this happen and he had Stalin behind him. Soon the camps would be closed and all the zeks would be freed, including them. They just had to hold out a bit longer.

James laid his cards on the table and told them that he had long been trying to inform the regional Party headquarters of what was happening in the camp, but he had been unable to get either the Romans or Yakuts to help him: Peter, as they already knew, had his eye on him, and wouldn't let him put a foot outside the prison zone. Once, he had still managed to make contact with the region, only to find that the man in charge in Tomsk was Skosyryev's patron, Yegorov, who was quick to cover Peter.

'And today,' James said, 'I learned that Yegorov was shot a week ago, so Skosyryev no longer has any protection in the centre. They'll go after him now – his number's up.'

There wasn't much longer to wait, he told them. That very night he, James, would leave the camp, catch up with the barge and four days later – just four days, that was all they had to hold out for – he would bring back a special NKVD unit. He implored them to be careful, not to give into provocations. If they found that the guards were trying to force them, and only them, to go somewhere, they should stay put. In fact they shouldn't leave the confines of the camp. They could do whatever they wanted – just so long as they held out.

He kept repeating the same thing over and over again, and it was then that Caiaphas realised that he was simply unable to stop and, in order to bring an end to it, the high priest told James that they were grateful to him: his warning had saved their lives. This was what James had been waiting for, it was what he had come for. After hearing Caiaphas out, he burst into tears and began making the sign of the cross over the Jews and blessing them.

That night, he really did run out of the camp and, taking a shortcut, reached the Keti before the barge; when it arrived, he swam out to it and was in Bely Yar two days later. When he learned the next day that James had run off, Peter was about to send several men in pursuit, but he called them back. James was no longer a problem. It made no difference who James brought back with him to the camp in four or five days' time – everything would be over and done with by then; in fact, it even suited Peter that James would see nothing and know nothing.

Like the others, Caiaphas considered James a provocateur, but at the same time he was struck by his strange, mystifying air of sincerity. It had been like that even when James had recruited them as informers. Caiaphas did not doubt that he genuinely wished to save their lives. Even when James had forced them to grass, Caiaphas had felt that James believed there was no other way. And there was something else: what most surprised Caiaphas about James's words was that he attacked only Kogan, even though in the play there was no one less significant than he, and no roles less significant than his. After letting the Jews go home, Caiaphas kept Kogan behind and said to him, one on one:

'Well, bridegroom, your turn to speak.'

James had interrupted the rehearsal right in the middle of his scene with Anna: the wedding is in full swing, but the wine has run out and Kogan feels desperately ashamed; he is furious with Anna and her family for being so tight-fisted – what a shitty celebration. He looks at Anna – the woman he's been dreaming about for so long, for whose father he has worked for so many years in the hope of gaining her hand – almost with hatred, when suddenly the steward of the feast, prompted by one of the guests, fills the six stone jars by the gates, brings them to him, then to the guests, and says that this is not water but wine. Kogan doesn't believe him, but he tastes it; still disbelieving, he takes another sip, and another, then he starts gulping it down, realising now that this is the real thing, truly excellent wine, and there's no end to it. He feels happy, feels like laughing out loud and kissing Anna.

Now, while the Jews were still drifting out of the Cultural-Educational Section, he played this scene out to its conclusion in his mind, delighted in it once more, and replied to Caiaphas with a cheerful smile:

'Well, maybe the godfather's right. I always thought Skosyryev was a bright spark, and this is certainly a clever ruse – enough to get anyone a promotion.'

'And what did he promise you?' Caiaphas asked.

'Nothing – why should he have? I didn't even ask.'

'Have you been to see him?'

'Yes,' said Kogan. 'He had me round twice, said there must have been some kind of misunderstanding with us military men, said he felt sorry for us, especially me. We're birds of a feather, he said, seeing as I'm not just a soldier: I've also done counter-espionage. He ended up saying he'd find me easier work to do, so he stuck me with the blasters.'

'So you knew you were dropping us in it?'

'Maybe I did. But if Skosyryev wants a rebellion and wants us armed, then let's wait and see who comes out on top. At least a third will get away, that's for sure.'

'And then what?' Caiaphas asked. 'Where will you go?'

'Far away – that's no trouble for the likes of us. And if they kill us, at least we'll die like human beings.'

'Fair enough,' Caiaphas agreed. 'Maybe you really will get away.'

On July 2, Kogan kept to his plan, neither postponing nor changing anything. It was clear from what James had told him that neither he nor Peter knew the exact date of the escape, and this suited him well. Kogan, like any spy, had a keen nose for danger, and he knew that if he spotted anything untoward in the camp, he could backtrack in time. But nothing had changed, the escort guards were just the same and behaving in just the same way, and Kogan decided to risk it.

In the afternoon he took the grenades from the mine as scheduled, carried them to the shack and tidily set them one by one on the shelf. Then he endured five hours of torture waiting for the working day to end, imagining that someone had discovered the grenades by chance and he would stick his hand through the gap only to find it empty, or that Peter had replaced the grenades with dolls, or removed the fuses, or that, when the men would collect the grenades, the escort guards would catch them. He needn't have worried: everything went off improbably smoothly, without a hitch – no small thanks to their clown, who was on such good form that the operation could have been repeated ten times without risk. The clown didn't stop at the shack: he carried on entertaining the guards and zeks, and they reached the stream in less than half an hour and in the highest spirits. Here, though, something occurred that had not been foreseen by either Kogan or Peter.

Kogan was convinced that by this point the female brigade would have passed through long before and the log-bridge would be empty. He didn't know that on Peter's orders the guards, having taken the women off the hired workers at the usual time and place, had not led them to the camp, but had made them sit on the ground to wait until the brigades arrived from the mine so that he could let those through first. The brigade that included Kogan and his men arrived at the bridge half an hour later, but its guards would not let them go ahead of the women's brigade. It was led by a lieutenant, unlike the female brigade, which was led by a sergeant. The lieutenant asked the sergeant why he was violating procedure: why was he running late and why had he still not crossed the stream? The sergeant started saying something about Skosyryev, but the lieutenant told him that Skosyryev would never dream of giving an order like that and the sergeant had better get a move on. But the sergeant dug his heels in. They were arguing right in front of the ordinary soldiers and zeks, and the lieutenant, angry that a junior officer was refusing to obey him in public, grabbed his pistol and ordered the female brigade to its feet. The women immediately did as they were told – they had no idea why they had been kept there for almost an hour – got up, set off, and the guards, surrounding the brigade almost by habit, slowly and with obvious reluctance started leading it across the stream.

Needless to say, neither Kogan nor anyone else could have foreseen the squabble between the officers that would lead to them having to wait their turn for so long, or the fact that the women's brigade would block their path and leave them nowhere to run, and while the women were walking unhurriedly over the log-bridge, one of Kogan's men cracked: he accidently pulled the pin from his grenade and it exploded. This was a signal: the others nominated by Kogan chucked their grenades and the guards – their own and those of the second brigade right behind them – were killed on the spot, while Kogan and the man standing next to him used their knives to finish off two guards walking behind the women: the guards did not have time to turn round. They had done an excellent job of eliminating their convoy, losing only one man, who was killed by his own grenade, but none of this got them very far: they still wouldn't be able to get to the causeway. Three of the guards leading the female brigade opened fire on them from the other bank, and the zeks had to drop to the ground.

At first the two male brigades and most of the female one buried themselves in the grass and lay prone where they had been walking just a moment before, but then, noticing that the bullets were flying high above them (the ground on their side was very uneven and higher than on the opposing bank) and that they were safe, they plucked up courage and started crawling about.

The zeks found one another surprisingly quickly and after just a few minutes of swarming around in this peculiar way they had already divided up into their chosen groups.

Kogan's people fanned around him in a semi-circle, while the Mosslands Jews surrounded Caiaphas; Anna, who was lying in the most dangerous spot, right next to the log-bridge and half-covering her son with her body – he had been weeding with her, and they were just saying goodbye when the shooting began – was eventually found by Ilya. The 'thieves' also came together, as did the ordinary zeks, and the sectarians, and the communists.

Happy that they had been able to choose who to be with, they all lay there for a long time without moving; then Kogan, after exchanging a few words with his men, left them, pushed his way through the zeks, and crawled up to Caiaphas. At first, no one tried to stop him. But then the Jews suddenly understood that Kogan was the person the 'godfather' had been telling them about the previous day and they decided to try to spoil his plans: they cursed him, grabbed his jacket, wept, and one of the women even scratched his face, but he was stronger than them, elbowed them aside, and lay down next to Caiaphas.

'Looking for another miracle, bridegroom?' Caiaphas said.

'No need for that,' Kogan laughed back. He was carrying an assault rifle and was as cheerful as when the wine had arrived. 'There's still plenty in the bottle.'

'Afraid not,' said Caiaphas. 'There's an entire platoon arriving in half an hour.'

'If the godfather was telling the truth yesterday,' Kogan said, 'nobody will be arriving. Skosyryev was just throwing us a bone with this lot – he's waiting for us somewhere else. Listen,' Kogan went on, 'I've only got a few men, and yours are doing nothing, so here are some matches and have them set fire to the hay. It won't take much – the hay's dry, and I need smoke. When it catches fire, we'll go ahead and you can follow.'

'No,' said Caiaphas, 'we won't.'

'Suit yourself. But get them to throw the matches anyway.'

All around them, on both sides of the road, the meadow was dotted with haystacks, and there was plenty more hay spread out to dry; they'd scattered it a week before and just left it there – it had been a hot summer, not a drop of rain all June. The hay should have been stacked long ago, but there was no one to do it, and even now half the meadow had still not been cut; the grass was getting old and going to seed. The haystacks blazed up like gunpowder with the very first match, the stubble caught fire almost immediately, and the flames spread in all directions. Finding a pile of hay, they would leap and crackle like firewood, then carry onto the next, licking the ground. Where the grass was uncut, the flames would race up the stems in a thin ribbon then go out, but there were always more of these ribbons, and they touched and intertwined until, with the wind at its back, the fire eventually took hold of the entire meadow.

The wind was very strong: it chased the smoke right along the ground and refused to let it rise, blowing it to the side where the guards were lying low and, luckily for Kogan, were shielded from its gusts. Everything was on fire when Kogan crawled over to Caiaphas once more and said:

'Any second thoughts?'

'No, we'll stay.'

'But they'll shoot you all,' said Kogan.

'Maybe they will,' Caiaphas agreed.

'Well,' Kogan said, 'thanks for the smoke. One last thing: if I know anything about Skosyryev, don't go back to the camp – they're waiting for you there – and don't go down the mines either: they're waiting for you there, too.'

'And don't stay here,' said Caiaphas.

'And don't stay here,' Kogan repeated.

He gave his men the signal to advance. Standing up straight – there was no seeing them through the thick smoke in any case – they began their unhurried descent towards the gully; twenty-odd 'thieves' trailed after them. Then, just as slowly, they crossed the stream; everything was still calm, and it was only when the zeks had already grown tired and fed up of waiting that Kogan's men finally came up against the guards. Bursts of gunfire could be heard, and grenades exploding, then everything went quiet again. Another ten or fifteen minutes passed before the people left in the meadow heard exactly the same noises, but dulled by distance and the forest; they were coming from the causeway now, and Caiaphas realised that Kogan was already there.

The hay was burning fast, the haystacks nearest to them were smoking as much as before, or even more, but flames rose from them less often now and, leaving behind an ever-widening circle of dark brown earth, the fire was moving away – towards the bog, the mines, the camp, the forest. The earth was hot, dry and smoking as much as the haystacks. The Jews were still lying right next to the road, and only now did Caiaphas realise that they were all alone – the zeks had dispersed. Some had gone with Kogan, the 'thieves' and much of the women's brigade had made for the hired workers' settlement, where there was a shop selling vodka and food, and a few had realised that this wasn't the end of the story and had hidden themselves away in the forest.

Seeing that there was no one else in the meadow and that they were the last, Caiaphas realised that it was time for them, too, to go. He got up and set off just as slowly as Kogan's men had done before. He walked towards where the fire, reaching the edge of the bogs, had already gone out and the brown circle had expanded. The Jews also got to their feet and trailed after him unhurriedly. At first they huddled together, but they soon arranged themselves into a tidy line and walked as if they wanted only Caiaphas' footprints to remain on this earth. He entered the bog; after hesitating for a moment and huddling together once more, they went in after him. They must have been afraid, though, because now they held each other's hands and wouldn't let go. To them it seemed as if they were walking across the bog, but from the side it must have looked as if they were drowning. Their feet sank deeper with every step, and they barely had any strength left to pull them out of the mire; the shoulders of the shorter Jews were already underwater. Caiaphas continued to lead them, and they continued to follow. They were so tired, so ready to accept whatever came their way that they didn't even feel or notice that they had suddenly stopped drowning and their feet had stopped sinking; the bottom had become hard and cold: they'd reached frozen ground.

The precise fate of Kogan's unit and Kogan himself is not known to me. The shooting on the other side of the causeway continued into the night then stopped for a couple of hours before resuming at first light, then dying down again towards midday. Some zeks seem to have escaped, but I've no idea how far they got. As for the runaways on the island – though they weren't really runaways – they were dealt with much quicker by the guards; it was all over that same morning. The guards combed the island twice over with dogs, and either caught or killed the zeks. They were mad at having lost fifteen of their own men, and fired on meeting the slightest resistance.

On July 3, Peter gave the guards the afternoon off, and on the following day he ordered them to fetch the corpses and put them in a separate part of the cemetery. The zeks and hired workers who had been killed by the guards were to be counted then buried, and the zeks were to go in a communal grave. At this point, Peter did not yet know that the Mosslands Jews had fled, and he was sure that they were among the dead. The surviving zeks were gathered for a roll-call and checked against the lists, then those who had been outside the camp during Kogan's escape were called in for individual questioning: who had they been with, where had they gone, what had they done. When the roll-call confirmed that there were no Jews left alive in the camp, he felt glad and reassured: now everything was in order.

On July 4, the corpses began to decompose in the heat; Peter was scared of new escapes and wouldn't allow the convicts to leave the zone, so the guards had to drag the dead themselves. They found many of the bodies two or three miles from the camp, in the forest, the bog, the field, the meadow, in houses in the settlement or in abandoned mines; by nightfall the guards were so worn out that they could barely stand, and Peter had to give them some of the zeks from the service staff to help them bring back the last bodies. Worst of all was the smell: nearly all of the guards brought up whatever was still in their stomachs, and nobody ate a thing for the entire duration of the task.

A whole day of witness confrontation and interrogation – Peter questioned those of Kogan's men who had been taken captive, those who had tagged along with him for the escape, as well as the zeks who had remained on the island – proved productive, and by the evening Peter already had a clear idea of what had happened on the meadow, at the jetty and in the forest, of who had been where and when. The fact that they had divided up into their own groups by the log-bridge and then gone off in those groups simplified things greatly. The zeks had no trouble remembering and naming who they had been with and, after checking and double-checking their evidence, he satisfied himself that it was accurate and that he'd made no mistakes with his calculations. He did wonder at one stage during the interrogations why it was that nobody ever said anything about the Mosslands Jews – true, they'd all seen them and they could all describe exactly where they had been lying in the meadow during the shooting, but after that they vanished from their accounts; however, Peter was so delighted that the Jews had not gone off with Kogan, meaning that even if some of Kogan's men had managed to hide, then at least they weren't Jews, that he immediately forgot all about it.

All those killed during Kogan's uprising were buried – if that is the right word for it – on the night of July 4. This was despite the fact that Peter had told Matthew (who was in charge of the unit tasked with searching for corpses and bringing them to the cemetery) not to do anything without him and, above all, to postpone the burial till the next morning. They knew that he was planning to make a speech by the graves of each of the guards who had been killed and bury them with military honours, like a soldier killed in battle. In fact, he thought he should also say something by the graves of the Romans and by the communal grave of the zeks – to explain himself in some way and say goodbye.

While conducting the interrogations, it had occurred to him more than once that the right thing to do would be to divide the zeks and the Mosslands Jews, and bury them separately. But then Peter decided against this; in the end, the zeks had repeated the fate of the Jews, perished because of the Jews, and therefore, were not so very different from them. Naturally, Peter also thought that the soldiers and Romans would be buried in coffins, as one would normally expect, not just buried in the earth, and on the afternoon of July 4 he visited the carpenter's workshop himself to demand that the requisite coffins – all seventy or seventy-two of them – be ready by the next morning. But nobody needed them, and nobody waited for them. Matthew didn't even collect the ones that had already been made. All he did was dig a grave for each Roman and each guard, though at the beginning he had actually been planning to put them in with the zeks to save time. These individual graves were no better than the communal one; the deceased were buried at night and in such haste that Matthew didn't even try to identify the dead – in many cases this would have been impossible anyway. The corpses were tipped into the nearest available grave, and there was no telling who was who. The plaques with names, ranks and dates that were added later are entirely arbitrary: if any of them bear any relation to the truth, then it is only by sheer chance.

All this was rather gruesome, of course, but late that night, after the last corpses of those who had been killed were finally brought to the cemetery, Matthew had realised that there could be no question of waiting till the morning to bury them, as Peter had instructed. The bodies were deteriorating so quickly that the guards wouldn't dare go near them any longer, and it was getting harder and harder to force the zeks to drag the dead. Matthew should probably just have sprinkled the corpses with earth, but the idea did not occur to him. At about one o'clock that night, leaving the guards and zeks to dig the graves, he went off to the camp to ask Peter what he should do and tell him that they could not wait until the morning, but Peter was fast asleep at his desk in the office where he had been conducting interrogations all day. Matthew couldn't bring himself to wake him. He left a sheet of paper on his desk, just as they had agreed, with the exact number of the guards,

Romans and convicts who had been killed – thankfully, their different clothes made it easy to tell them apart – then he roused thirty men in the next barracks and took them back with him to the cemetery, grabbing a portable generator and two searchlights from a workshop on the way.

With fresh manpower and some light, things started moving quicker, but no sooner had they really got going than there was an almighty downpour. Guards and zeks alike thought that Matthew would call a halt and let them go back to the camp, but he gave orders to continue.

The cemetery was in a hollow, the soil was clayey, and even after a month's drought the moisture had nowhere to escape. In the space of just a few minutes the graves that they had dug filled up like swimming pools, and the bodies that had been placed in them, but not yet covered with earth, floated up to the top. All attempts to bury them got nowhere: the earth sank to the bottom, while the bodies, bloated by gas, remained on the surface. One of the zeks thought that some of them should keep the bodies pressed to the bottom with spades while others shovelled in stones and earth to keep them there. This probably wasn't the worst idea, and it certainly seemed to help during the night, but the graves were so shallow that plenty of corpses still floated up by the morning and almost every third grave – not to mention the ditch where the zeks were buried – had arms and legs sticking out of it, as from under a blanket.

When Peter woke up, Matthew and the guards working with him were still asleep. Peter took the piece of paper with Matthew's calculations of the dead on it, and failing to realise at first that the total – 108 men – was the total of all those killed the previous day, not just the zeks, he combined it with the number of people who had disappeared from the camp, and his sums added up. He had expected the total to be out by a few – it would have been a miracle if it hadn't: some must have got away, some must have drowned in the bog, others would still be lying beyond the causeway or in places on the island where the dogs had not found them – but now he saw that this wasn't the case, and he thought once more that that was that: there were no more Jews on earth, not a single one. They had all been dealt with.

He picked up the piece of paper again so as to circle the number of Mosslands Jews for the benefit of the apostles, and it was then that he noticed that Matthew had given him the total of all the dead: not just the zeks but also the Romans and the guards. It wasn't 108 zeks who had been killed, but exactly half that number; so it wasn't just two or three people who were missing, but fifty. This number tallied strangely with the number of Mosslands Jews in the camp. Distrusting his own calculations, he spent more than an hour adding and subtracting, getting himself confused and sometimes even ending up with the number he wanted again, but then he would see that he'd made a mistake and recount once more, unable to accept that the Jews had survived yet again and got away. Eventually he decided that enough was enough and he was simply driving himself mad, but the next minute he began to think that the Jews had not gone anywhere (and where could they have gone?), that Matthew must have got his sums wrong, and that they must have walked past plenty of corpses in the dark without noticing them.

Having reached this conclusion, Peter sounded the alarm and woke the guards, including Matthew and his men, who had been asleep for less than three hours, and when the soldiers presented themselves before him, he set about very calmly, even gently ticking off those tasked with gathering the corpses and taking them to the cemetery: they'd been careless.

Matthew objected that they had searched the relevant area very thoroughly, and moreover they had done it twice and with dogs, to which Peter replied, with the same calmness as before, that he was not blaming anyone and that he understood perfectly well that it was hard to spot anything at all in the dark and in the forest; they'd done very well for the first day. But they had not found them all – far from it. He had just checked and it turned out that there were more than fifty men missing, so where had they got to? If they were on the run, then they needed to be chased, if they were hiding on the island somewhere, then they needed to be found, and if they were dead, then their bodies needed to be retrieved. After keeping back fewer than ten men to guard the camp, he divided the rest into two groups so that they could do one more search – this time, with him in tow – of all the places where the zeks could be hiding. He was only really interested in the Jews, and he went with the group that was meant to be combing the island. Taking the dogs with them, they covered every nook, every grove and hollow, every house, cellar, pit and adit, but all they had to show for it at the end of the day was one single corpse, which, as if to mock them, had been lying a mere thirty metres or so from the gates of the prison zone.

Finding nothing on the island, Peter remembered that Matthew had buried the dead the previous night, contrary to his instructions, and now he brought the guards to the cemetery to dig up the graves and check whether there were any Jews among them. He was hoping to find out whether only Jews had run away or whether the fifty included other zeks as well. He also wanted to verify Matthew's account, to check who was buried where, so he ordered them to excavate not only the ditch with the zeks but also the graves of the soldiers and Romans.

Because Peter was constantly hurrying and chivvying the guards as they worked, the graves were dug up in terrible haste and some of the bodies were badly damaged and even mutilated: arms had been chopped off with spades and heads had been sliced through. But he wasn't the only one to blame for this. The corpses, as I've already said, had been lying there without coffins, and with earth thrown over them any old how.

To Peter's displeasure, it proved impossible to identify any of the deceased by their faces. They were thickly smeared with clay and watery mud, beneath which the faces, whether or not they could be cleaned, were so worn and distorted by decay that few could be recognised. In the end, they managed to identify about twenty bodies, but there wasn't a single Jew among them.

Now Peter no longer doubted that it wasn't corpses they had to find but living Jews. He understood that the Jews had deceived him, that they had used Kogan's uprising as a cover to flee Mosslands. He said as much both to the apostles and to the rank and file, told them that he had been wrong to blame Matthew and his co-workers, and asked their forgiveness – if anyone was at fault here, then it was only he, Peter.

'Don't think that it was the Lord who saved the Jews,' he told the Christians. 'It was cunning that saved them. The Lord is on the side of the Christians. The Jews have simply been granted a respite – a few more days and they will all have been dealt with.'

The Christians listened coolly and gloomily to what Peter had to say; unlike him, they were haunted once more by the fear that everything they had done and were continuing to do was not pleasing to the Lord, that the Lord did not want them to catch and slaughter the Jews. But they were soldiers as well as Christians, and when Peter dispatched two of the guards to the barracks to gather the Jews' things – he was planning to hunt them down with dogs – they didn't think of refusing.

But Peter's new idea also got off to a bad start: the other convicts had long since divided up anything of value, and nobody could have said for sure that the rags that they eventually handed over at the guards' insistence were specifically Jewish. There was, however, some clothing in the camp that still preserved the smell of the Jews: one of the apostles remembered about the theatre costumes kept in the Cultural-Educational Section; these were fetched and given to the dogs, who soon picked up the scent not far from the log-bridge.

This success was short-lived. A minute later the dogs lost the Jews, span about on the spot, began whimpering and refused to go any further, for all their guides' efforts. Following a trail on a burnt-out meadow, where there had been a downpour just the day before, proved impossible.

But Peter's decision to try to find the Jews first and foremost, to try to understand them, to understand how they had escaped and where they would have gone, was the correct one, and it quickly occurred to him that previously they had escaped from Mosslands by the only route possible – across the bog, somewhere or other. Now all he had to do was discover where exactly, to find the place where the bottom of the bog was hard from the frozen earth and where the bog became passable. To this end Peter ordered the guards to take fifty of the tallest and healthiest zeks from the camp – the same as the number of the guards he had with him – and grab several balls of strong, thick rope. Then, when the zeks were brought over, he arranged them along the edge of the bog – one every ten metres – and told the guards to wind the rope firmly round each of them and tie it, after which he ordered them into the water. If the water came up to the zek's neck and he started drowning and spluttering, the soldier holding the other end of the rope would pull him out to shore. Then the zek would be led to a different spot, but always ten metres away from the last in the line. If they carried on like this, Peter estimated, they would have covered the entire bog by evening, but in fact it took only two hours before the fortieth zek touched frozen ground and was able to cross the bog at the precise point where the Jews had crossed before him.

Following this early success, many Christians began to think once more that Peter was right and that the Lord really had renounced the Jews and handed them over to them. Peter saw that the soldiers' mood had changed and demanded that they go after the Jews right away, taking nothing with them except the dogs and a small supply of food. He told them that almost all the fugitives were 'goners', or women, or old men; they couldn't have got far, and the Christians would catch up with them in a day, maybe two. But the soldiers hadn't slept for three nights, they were exhausted, and the apostles, after a quick discussion amongst themselves, decided to wait until the next day before leaving.

Peter was right to hurry; three and a half days passed before he and his men set out after the Jews, and twelve hours later a special unit of the NKVD entered Mosslands, commanded by Major Sukhorkov and guided by James. The unit took control of the prison camp without a shot being fired and the guards were arrested, but when James asked Sukhorkov to give him some men to seize Peter, the major refused outright, saying he had received no such order.

Peter already knew about this unit and knew that it might go after them, but he almost managed to ruin everything himself. Convinced that the Jews were somewhere close by, he decided to travel light, with no stopping or overnighting. He had no doubt that they would catch up with the Jews in two or three days, but wearing out and weakening his men by denying them even an hour's rest was a mistake. Yes, the guards were healthy and well-fed, while the zeks were debilitated by hunger, scurvy and several awful months of heavy labour when they had been falling like flies, yet in the end pursuers and pursued proved almost evenly matched: for much of the way the guards, in fear of their lives, walked very cautiously, checking the path several times over with sticks and poles. During the first few days, when the Jews were walking in single file and their trail was clear and well-marked, the soldiers did indeed almost reach them, just as Peter had expected. But then the Jews began to die, the line broke and the Jews fanned out, barely looking under their feet and avoiding only those places where one or other of them had already been sucked in. Those whose strength had run out simply wandered off a few metres so as not to get in anyone's way or make anyone stop to help them, and there they would normally sink and drown.

The way in which the Jews fanned out and, above all, wandered off to die threw the dogs and soldiers off the scent, and when two of the guards also died and a third was pulled out just in time, the Christians slowed down and even tried not to walk in the convicts' footsteps – which they now thought of almost as a trap – but parallel to them, as a result of which they kept losing the trail and were forced to retrace their steps and look for it again. Hours were often wasted like this, allowing the Jews to pull away. Those who had drowned in the bog became, as it were, expiatory sacrifices that allowed the Jews, on finding higher ground, to rest, gather berries and, if there happened to be a lake nearby, catch fish.

For the first three days of the chase the Christians continued to believe Peter, continued to believe that the Lord had abandoned the Jews and wanted them to die, but then they grew tired. They were tired of walking, tired of not having anything to eat, of always being scared that they would sink and then the mire would suck them in – the soil swayed and quivered beneath them at every step – tired of the heat, the mosquitoes and horseflies, of Peter not letting them sleep, and now, however much he swore at them and however much he threatened to shoot them, they walked at a snail's pace and heard nothing. Now, they felt sure once again that their time really had passed, and that the Lord was stopping them from catching the Jews, those 'goners'. They would never catch them; they themselves would merely sink into the bog and die.

They no longer cared whether they drowned in the bogs or were shot dead by the NKVD men, who, Peter said, James was just about to bring, or had already brought, to the camp. They walked and thought that they had done the best they could, that they had played their role, and if it had not fallen to them to meet Christ and become His disciples, then they were no more to blame for this than those who had come before them – it was just that the time had not come; but if, nevertheless, it was their fault and Christ had not come because they had proved unworthy of Him, well, so had many others before them. They were tired and wanted only to stop and lie down; they didn't want to walk, they didn't want to keep sinking in these bogs, as flat and as bare as the desert, where there was so little of anything, so that even a distant flower was visible, or a scrawny pine tree with a dry, barkless peak, and where, if you lay down on the moss, every tussock was a hill crowned by a garden with whortleberries beginning to turn blue, with red bilberries like apples, and unripe cranberries just starting to redden.

When it became impossible to force them to go any further and they had already reached for their rifles – Peter, who was urging them on, was on his own against three, and they had him at gunpoint – and when the others, on Peter's side, were also standing still with rifles in hand, and all of them were losing their minds from the heat, the mosquito clouds, the fatigue, the motionless lakes up by the shore, oval or circular, on each of which swam a small flock of ducks – drake, hen, ducklings: they kept firing long volleys of bullets at them but never hit anything – now, with their assault rifles aimed at each other, they were glad that they were no longer shooting ducks and that they could no longer miss. Paradise was all around them: the earth was soft and alive, as warm and soft as a stomach, and it made the same sounds as a stomach and purred just as contentedly, and the moss which covered it was as soft and warm as wool, and winding over the wool, like embroidery, were cranberry bushes with their fretted, firm dark-green leaves, and berries shone through these dark-green leaves, and every tussock was a garden, and the lakes were very still, not a wave or a ripple, and a flock of ducks was advancing like a big ship, and insects were plastering their eyes, ears, mouths, noses, never giving them a moment's rest, stopping them from sleeping and eating away at them; and stupefied by these insects and this paradise, because it really was paradise, they understood that everything was coming to an end, that they would never catch anyone up, that if they returned they would be shot, and what did it matter whether they lived or died – they had lost, they had missed their chance: Christ would not come to them, and there was nothing left for them.

Over these long years of service and rehearsal, when everything had revolved around them and they had been sure that Christ would come, they had accumulated a great deal of dissatisfaction and jealousy, especially in these last few months and days, when they had begun to feel and to fear that they would not be God's chosen ones, and they had begun to ask who was to blame, begun to accuse and to hate. Back in the camp they had all had the same task – to hold out a bit longer – and the same belief that they were God's elect; they had been bound together by Christ, and when they had killed, they killed together and were bound by the same blood, the same excitement, the same rush to kill everyone quickly enough and the same plan of how to go about it, but now they had lost all this and they needed to know who was guilty, to punish that person, to resolve and simplify everything that had gone on between them over the past fifteen years.

Their rifles were raised and they were not supposed to lower them again; they understood this and wanted to shoot, only nobody could bring themselves to fire the first shot, and it was then that some attentive little soldier, utterly unmemorable in every way, with a sweet, obliging face and the least important role – one of the hundred-odd demoniacs healed by Christ – suddenly realised that they were on the path that the Jews always took, that they, the Jews, were walking their usual path and would never turn off it. He – and, it seems, only he – knew this path, knew that not one of the previous Jews had ever turned off it, so nor would these, and he shouted himself hoarse trying to tell everyone, fearing he wouldn't manage in time and they would start shooting. He grabbed them by the hand, stared into their eyes, wept, and slowly but surely they understood that they would no longer need to wander around blindly, that now they would catch the Jews. But they kept their rifles raised for some time longer, because they were scared that someone else might shoot; they had come far too close to that, and now they were scared that someone might not have understood the 'demoniac' or not have believed him.

But everyone had understood, and everyone had understood

that they were together again and that nothing was lost; the Jews would not get away, nobody would help them, and this time nobody would save them. The Lord had given them up, given them up to their deaths, and when they were killed, everything would begin. The demoniac knew the path well, knew all the dangerous places, and now they were walking quickly once more.

Previously, the route by which the Jews had escaped from Mosslands and by which the Lord had brought them back had taken several months, broken by long halts whenever they and their pursuers could walk no further; now, the Jews and the Christians walked it in less than three weeks. When the surviving Jews came out on the road that led to the causeway and onto the camp, where they hoped to find refuge, they already knew they would not make it. The guards emerged from the forest at almost the same time and they also knew that the Jews would not make it. The Jews were stretched out along the road in a long straggly line, dusk was only just beginning to fall, there was still plenty of light, and the only people it could help were the guards. The guards would catch up with some of them, shoot them, and move onto the next group and shoot them too. At the head of this line were the three Jews the guards would reach last – Anna, Ilya and their son Isaiah. About eight hundred metres before the causeway Anna and Ilya realised that they, too, would not make it. So then they lay down on the ground, pressed up close to one another and shielded their child.

Both Ilya and Anna still had more than a minute left to live. Anna lay next to Ilya, held his hand and pressed her hip against him, knowing that he was her husband and the father of her child, knowing that for the whole of these long three weeks he had walked beside her and carried her child, that he had worried only about her and her child, loved only her and her child, and forgotten all about Rut. And she was grateful to Rut that he had forgotten her.

Then the guards shot them dead; they were happy that they had succeeded where everyone before them had failed – not one Jew had got away, and therefore the mission of this nation had been fulfilled, everything was at an end, the cup was overflowing – and they set off towards the causeway, where other soldiers were already waiting for them.

Isaiah spent the night under the dead Ilya and Anna, and in the morning, when they had grown quite cold, he crawled out from beneath them and spent a long time trying to shake his mother awake and then his father, although he had long known what dead people look like; both of them were cold and alien, bound only to one another, hand in hand. In the end he realised that he would never manage to raise them or wake them, and he set off along the same road that they had been walking but had not completed. He was walking along the path that he had always carried inside him, walking to the camp, to his home. There were only a few hundred metres left to the causeway, those metres that his mother and father had not managed to walk the day before, and he almost walked them, but right before the causeway he turned off to the side. From that moment on, he was no longer a Jew.

A day later he entered a village on the bank of the Keti, where Maria Trifonovna Kobylina took him in and adopted him as her son.

November 1986 – June 1988

Author's Afterword (2015)

The History of a Novel

I am not going to elaborate here on Anna Akhmatova's endlessly quoted lines, 'If only you knew what rubbish / Poetry grows from, knowing no shame'. Instead I wish to take this opportunity, rare in literary life, to thank the people without whom this novel would never have been written, or else would have been a different thing entirely. In the academic world, such acknowledgements are only to be expected. Almost every monograph begins or ends with a long list of all those who have helped you in one way or another. But when it comes to literature, this practice is unusual, certainly in Russia, and may even look rather strange.

The Rehearsals, like any other work, was preceded by a series of events that were all important to me, though largely unconnected in themselves. But gradually, page by page, they cleared a path for the novel from beginning to end.

It all began as early as 1982, when my father, who disliked private property in any shape or form, yielded to my pressure and signed up for one of the plots of land, each measuring 600 square metres, that the Literary Fund was giving to writers near the Istra Reservoir outside Moscow, close to the village of Alyokhnovo. The Fund had been allocated two hundred hectares of poorly drained peatland. In low-lying areas there were a great many underground springs where concrete was the only solution. Anyone who tried to ignore this in the hope of saving money soon learned that a house built on sand is heaven compared to a house built on water. In no time at all, the springs would wash away the ground, mainly clay, beneath the foundations, after which our writers' ambitious, but flimsy constructions would immediately begin to look like the illegitimate offspring of the Leaning Tower of Pisa. A dozen of them collapsed onto their sides; two even sank.

After receiving our plot, we did nothing with it for three years. We had neither the money nor the enthusiasm. When we finally set to work, things went badly from the start. Although we didn't find a spring directly beneath us, progress was slow. The labourers we had hired were layabouts to a man.

In central Russia, the ground freezes in winter and thaws in summer, so you have to dig to a depth that the frost cannot reach. But our foundations were dug to only a third of that depth. To make matters worse, our crew had shamelessly cut corners on the breadth as well. Whether it was for this or for some other reason, we had an almighty row, and after tipping some panelling into a pool of water, just to punish us, the workmen headed south for a holiday.

It's with some horror that I and my family recall the unpleasant, gloomy mood in which I constantly found myself at that time, my strange, unstable state of nervous agitation. I couldn't understand where this mood came from, let alone whether there was any way out of it. Winter was approaching, and our country estate – or rather, my private hermitage – was shaping up to be a complete disaster. I was sick and tired of standing and waiting on the turn-off from the main road to the village of Buzharovo (with the Monastery of New Jerusalem, built entirely of white stone, looking straight down at me from the hilltop). That was where I spent almost every day from morning till dusk, sometimes in the rain, sometimes in the wet snow. It was there that I tried to flag down dumptrucks carrying sand and gravel: the plot needed to be raised, otherwise it would be completely flooded by spring. I'd had enough of waiting for the three cubic metres' worth of prepaid floorboards that should have been delivered more than a month ago; they were never going to arrive and I now realised that I, like so many others, had simply been conned.

Still, there was something else happening inside me that had little if anything to do with these difficulties. Now, looking back more than three decades later, I'm inclined to think that I was, as it were, heavy with child, though I was far from convinced that I could actually find the stamina to go through with the birth.

Evidently, any novel by any author, however sad its contents, is a way out, and proof that a way out is actually possible. Your life seems aimless and meaningless, then all of a sudden you are shown the way and even nudged in that direction, lest any doubts arise.

A brief digression: I am a historian by education and wrote my dissertation on the second half of the sixteenth century and the beginning of the seventeenth – in other words, on the reign of Ivan the Terrible, the political system he instituted, and the Time of Troubles that followed the death of his son, the last Rurik. Patriarch Nikon came later and had never been the object of my sustained attention. Those twelve years of the Troubles, when any and everyone sold and betrayed each other time and again, left the old Russia in pieces, and I understood that the country which emerged from the Troubles was very different from the country that entered it. So if I was going to choose a new direction, it was never going to be the new Tsars, the Romanovs. Which is not to say I had never heard of Nikon.

One of the employees and tour guides at the monastery's museum was an acquaintance of mine from the Historical-

Archival Institute in Moscow. During the summer, we spent several days strolling around the monastery, and I learned that during the war both sides had adjusted artillery fire through openings in the dome of the church. As a result, the monastery had been almost entirely destroyed by 1945. Later, reconstruction began and it still hadn't ended, forty years on. The task was approached in a completely random fashion. They couldn't even decide what form the restored monastery should take: the one originally chosen by Nikon or the one it took from the mid-eighteenth century onwards, when it was redesigned by Rastrelli.[1] One way or another, they always took the cheapest option, but even then the work would not be completed. Either the funding was too stingy, or else everything was simply stolen as usual. The holes in the dome would be boarded up, and New Jerusalem would be forgotten again for several years.

I also knew, of course, that the monastery was a very serious attempt to replicate the Church of the Holy Sepulchre in Jerusalem in every possible detail. In fact, even now I can recall my acquaintance telling me – and I hope I'm not muddling too much after all these years – that the hieromonk Arseny Sukhanov, who travelled to Jerusalem on Nikon's orders to sketch a copy of the Church of the Holy Sepulchre, even included graffiti with Arabic expletives in his drawings, while knowing neither their meaning nor the time in which they had been written. All this became much more than a matter of architectural pretension: both Nikon and the people around him were convinced that Christ would come again and save His chosen people only if even the tiniest features of the authentic Church of the Holy Sepulchre were successfully

---

1 The architect Francesco Bartolomeo Rastrelli (1700-71), best known for his many projects in the late-Baroque style in St Petersburg.

preserved and if the Saviour acknowledged it as true.

So there I was flagging down these wretched gravel trucks right under the hill, on whose north-facing side thousands of peasants, month after month, had once tipped innumerable cartfuls of sand, turning this land into the Promised Land and everyone who lived there into God's chosen people. And right there, down below, thousands of others had dug a canal, correcting the course of the river. Moreover, they actually knew why they were doing it: here, on this earth, with their own hands (subsequently, our history would endlessly replay both these themes: the Promised Land, God's chosen people) they were building the Holy City – the New Jerusalem. So as you built your puny little dacha, you knew that you were doing it on sacred land, in the place where someone else, three hundred years before, had built the City of God – the salvific city-temple – and, unlike you, had done rather well.

I remembered being told that in his own mind Nikon was Christ, Adam, and the new ruler of the Kingdom of Jerusalem. I remembered being taken round the back of the monastery to the Garden of Gethsemane, where the Patriarch erected his own private hermitage: a tiny church built on an artificial island. It contains one single cell, in which there is room for just one stone seat. Evidently, this was where Nikon repaired to pray and think about all of the above, and in particular about what awaits us in the near future. All this came back to me as I tried to wave down the trucks, and it became harder and harder for me to rid myself of things that I was not yet ready to absorb.

Even so, I was quite prepared to refer to the Istra, curving round behind my back, as the Jordan, and the waterway flowing right beside me as the Hebron stream. I was even prepared to call the hill that divided them Mount Zion, and the smaller one, a little to the east, the Mount of Olives. Further off to the north, beyond the river, was Mount Tabor. I recalled that a monumental cross had been erected on the Mount of Olives to commemorate Christ's Ascension.

The village of Chernevo, not far from today's Krasnogorsk, was called Nazareth in Nikon's time, while in the village of Safatovo, renamed Resurrection, the Bethany Convent was meant to have been built, along with the Church of the Lord's Triumphal Entry into Jerusalem. The so-called Zinovyevskaya Wasteland was renamed Capernaum. Not every name was changed, though: to the south of the monastery, the oldest village in these parts – Ilyinsk – kept its name because of the monastery of the Prophet Elijah (in Russian, Ilya) located south of Jerusalem.

I knew that at the beginning of the project Tsar Alexei had come to see the monastery being built and seemed to approve of it. An inscription was even made on the back of the cross on the Mount of Olives, in memory of one of these visits. But later the Tsar and the Patriarch fell out, and in 1666, when all Orthodox Rus was preparing for the end of the world, Nikon was deposed from the patriarchal throne. Meanwhile, his beloved child, New Jerusalem – where the resurrection of the righteous was meant to begin – became the main evidence against him.

The document signed by the participants of the Great Moscow Synod in 1666 and by the hierarchs of the Greek Orthodox Church declared Nikon guilty of building new monasteries in which he had used 'improper' names such as New Jerusalem, Golgotha and Jordan, thus 'cursing by means of the divine and mocking by means of the sacred'.

One more significant fact: Nikon asked to be buried in the Church of the Resurrection, and specifically, in the Chapel of St John the Baptist, which is located directly beneath Golgotha. According to tradition, it was beneath Golgotha in Jerusalem that the skull of the first man, Adam, was placed. In the actual Church of the Holy Sepulchre, this is the place where Melchizedek and the Kings of Jerusalem are buried.

To return to my own story: the state of mind in which I found myself, this sense of not knowing how to cope with it all, persisted for some time until two events, occurring almost simultaneously, as if by design, put their seal on the path that I would eventually take.

On a rainy, freezing day towards the end of October, after hanging around Alyokhnovo to no purpose almost until nightfall, I returned to Moscow and, without going home, went straight over to my friend Sasha Gorelik, who lived nearby. Sasha's doors were always open. Here, people drank, exchanged books, flirted, played bridge and chess, and above all talked incessantly about everything from politics to quantum physics. On Saturdays, football and bathhouse were added into the mix.

So in I went, all soaked and filthy, took off my coat and shoes, and sat down at the table, ready to launch into a long moan about the ever-increasing hopelessness of my dacha project – winter was on its way, the panelling would start to rot in a week or two, and why had I ever got involved in the first place? The kitchen in which we were sitting was small and cramped; to make space for me, everyone had to spend a lot of time shuffling around. But before I could even start whingeing, someone said: 'You can whinge later. First have a drink.' I had a drink. We started chatting about this and that, but it wasn't long before I was feeling sorry for myself again. Once again they stopped me in my tracks: 'Complain all you like. But first have another one.' And so it continued: have a drink, play a couple of rubbers and then we'll see. In the end they only gave me the chance to vent my frustrations when it was already morning and I was no longer in the mood; nothing seemed quite so terrible anymore. Then we all went home.

It was a pretty mixed crowd, although most were physicists and mathematicians, people who were good with their hands and had done their share of low-grade moonlighting. Yes, we had helped each other before, but in fairly small ways – moving flats or laying concrete. But now, two days later, seven of them suddenly turned up in Alyokhnovo on the Monday, having taken a few days' leave, and put up this wretched house in three days, from top to bottom. I didn't hammer in a single nail. My one responsibility was alcohol – there was a shop nearby well stocked with Cuban rum, if memory serves – while my wife made the sandwiches.

So the dacha got built, and I could forget all about it. Suddenly, I had time on my hands. I should mention that by this point I'd been living the life of a sponger, to use the language of the time, for almost a year – a dangerous occupation in the Soviet Union of the mid-80s. And it had happened for the following reasons. Until 1985 I had studied and worked in a very peculiar institution, the All-Union Research Institute for Documentation and Archival Work. It was never very clear what was being done there, or who was doing it. But the department for the study of early texts, to which I was lucky enough to be assigned, stood out for the unusual decency of its staff.

The department was headed by Oleg Fyodorovich Kozlov, who singled me out for privileged treatment. I didn't know much about the actual discipline of 'archaeography', so I would usually be given the kind of work that most humanities students bend over backwards to avoid. Namely: everything related to mathematics. But the maths was fairly straightforward, and there was plenty of it.

We ended up with a kind of unwritten contract. I would take on a job, come up with the necessary formulas and make the necessary calculations, in return for which, and in accordance with the importance, complexity and above all urgency of the task (criteria decided by Kozlov alone), I would be given a set number of days or weeks off during which I was free to do as I pleased. Wherever I went, the department would cover for me. This system remained in place for several years and suited everyone. But then a new Institute director was appointed, and he made no effort to conceal how much he disliked me. It was clear that something nasty lay in store for me. Not that this bothered me all that much: I'd been wanting to leave for some time.

Here I must also mention that Oleg Fyodorovich, an intelligent man with a very subtle mind, was on the shy side when dealing with his superiors. There was an obvious reason for this. If I was ready to pack up and leave at the first opportunity, he had nowhere to go. He was used to coming in to work every day and told me that his life would fall apart without that routine. Moreover, though a well-known scholar in his field, he was terrified that if he was forced out of the Institute he would struggle to find a position anywhere else.

After receiving another chunk of additional leave, I went off to see my family, then living on Lake Pühajärv in Otepää (the same town, incidentally, where the Tartu School held its first seminars on structural linguistics), and only when I got back from Estonia did I learn that a great deal had happened while I was away, and that I was out on my ear for unauthorised absence. Oleg Fyodorovich washed his hands of the whole business and made no attempt to defend me. It was not a pretty story, and in the end Kozlov and I did not even manage a proper goodbye.

A year later, when the epic story of my dacha-building finally reached its unexpected conclusion, Kozlov called me to say, 'Vladimir Alexandrovich, I very much wish to see you.' With the events at the Institute still fresh in my memory, I said, 'Oleg Fyodorovich, are you quite sure this is necessary?' 'Yes,' he replied. 'Please do me this favour.' The metro station Okhotny Ryad, on the red line, suited us both and we agreed a time. What followed was more like the plot of a spy novel.

As I descended the escalator, I saw that he was already waiting for me between the platforms. I felt glad that we had made things up and wanted to tell him as much, but he didn't give me the chance. Without even saying hello, he thrust a folder under my arm, rushed to a train that was already leaving, forced open the closing doors and disappeared into the carriage. In some astonishment, I went back up the escalator and took the green line back to my station, Aeroport. Only at home, after untying the ribbons, did I realise what had happened: I had been chosen by Kozlov as his heir and successor in his study of the Schism.

Oleg Fyodorovich had long been dreaming of writing his Habilitation thesis on the topic of the Schism, but one day he realised that he lacked the energy for it and decided to give me the folder containing his entire bibliography. There were hundreds of index cards, sometimes with brief annotations. Some items had clearly been consulted and read, others not. Freed from the hassles of the dacha, I had resumed my habit of making almost daily visits to the Historical-Archival Institute, and found myself calling up books from Kozlov's folder. I devoured one after the other.

Until then I had been simply unable to take in anything

connected with New Jerusalem and the Holy Land, and I tried to push it all away from me at the first opportunity. I told myself that the Church of the Resurrection was just a mockup, just an imitation of the real thing, something like the VDNKh exhibition space in northern Moscow, with its dozens of pavilions dedicated to Soviet achievements, or like Disneyland, or, at best, like a crib in a Catholic church. Sometimes my idle blasphemy would go even further and I'd think of New Jerusalem as the set for a Soviet production of a foreign opera with the mandatory Florentine villa in the background.

I went on telling myself these things and reassuring myself until one fine day I realised that I was resisting in vain: all this was already inside me.

First published in Russian in the almanac *Tekst i traditsiya* (vol. 3, 2015). Translated by Oliver Ready.

verve

1439 p. 60, 139, 146, 163,

Abelites